Death is My Ride or Die

THE DEATH CHRONICLES

Death is My BFF
Death is My Ride or Die

KATARINA E. TONKS

DEATH
IS MY
RIDE
OR
DIE

BOOK 2 — THE DEATH CHRONICLES

wattpad books **w**

wattpad books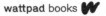

An imprint of Wattpad WEBTOON Book Group

Content warning: blood, violence, mention of death, swearing, mentions of sexual assault and rape

Published in Canada by Wattpad WEBTOON Book Group, a division of Wattpad WEBTOON Studios, Inc.

36 Wellington Street E., Suite 200, Toronto, ON M5E 1C7 Canada

www.wattpad.com

First Wattpad Books edition: September 2024

ISBN 978-1-99077-800-1(Trade Paper original)
ISBN 978-1-99077-882-7 (eBook edition)

Library and Archives Canada Cataloguing in Publication information is available upon request.

Printed and bound in Canada

1 3 5 7 9 10 8 6 4 2

Cover design by Hillary Wilson
Typesetting by Delaney Anderson

"Dedicated to the one I love: me."
—Death

I

FAITH

Tick. Tick. When I opened my eyes, the illusion that I was safe evaporated.

Across the way, Malphas, dressed in silk, lounged on a Victorian-style red velvet couch. His raven-black hair was woven together in warrior braids and neatly tied back. Bathed in soft lighting, the room was bare except for a large Persian rug, a rather ornate coffee table, and the couches where we sat opposite each other.

Moments before, I had been in the corn maze in Pleasant Valley fighting for my life against hell hounds and demons. Malphas had grabbed me, and now we were . . . here.

Death's motionless corpse looped through my mind. The painful howls of a man I'd believed to be unstoppable. My aching heart was anchored to the image of him dying. I wanted to believe he'd survived. That he was a force of nature and nothing could take him away from this world, but deep inside, I knew not even Death was indestructible.

I'd wanted nothing more to do with him. He'd played me from the beginning. He'd spared my special soul as a girl, only to return once my power had matured to collect it for his own cryptic, selfish reasons. He'd used his alter ego, David Star, to gain my trust and make me fall for him. And yet, time and time again, he'd saved my life, showed me glimpses of a man who maybe had the capacity to feel. He'd given me hope. Hope that it wasn't all a lie.

No matter how hard I tried to rationalize calling on Malphas as a good thing, a necessary thing, I felt guilty. The coldhearted creature who'd claimed I was only a possession but kissed me like I was his saving grace was gone. I'd killed Death.

"Let's not get dramatic," Malphas said. "He's alive. I sent his soul to a different realm temporarily."

I sat up straight. "You just read my mind."

"Indeed."

Death had said it was difficult to read my thoughts, whereas Malphas seemed to pick apart my brain with ease. It was frightening, to say the least.

"What do you mean, you sent Death's soul to a different realm? What realm?"

"He's in Limbo. You may know it as Purgatory." Malphas smoothed a wrinkle in the fabric covering his forearm. "There are other worlds besides the human one. They're mostly abandoned and filled with darkness and other things . . . things that wander into the mortal realm and go bump in the night. Limbo is a complex realm that parallels Earth. A place for wandering and forgotten souls. That is where Death's soul lies."

"How long will you keep him there?"

A shrug. "Can't hold him there for all eternity, unfortunately."

And the Father of the Year award goes to . . .

"If Death's soul is in Purgatory, then where's his body?"

Malphas grinned. "Inaccessible at the moment."

My fingers curled against the cushion beneath me, drawing my attention to a tear in the velvet material. A layer of dust blanketed the old-fashioned furniture, and the walls were sparsely decorated with peeling wallpaper. Cobwebs curtained every nook and cranny.

"They have makeover shows for this, you know," I said.

"Hmm?"

"Your evil lair. It sucks. Looks like a haunted mansion for cockroaches."

"Faith, Faith, Faith . . ." Malphas leaned his forearm on the cushion beside him and dragged a sharp black fingernail across the velvet. "Still mouthing off after everything that happened?"

As I homed in on that deadly finger, I felt a scraping sensation inside my mind, like a claw digging into my brain. I had no idea what Malphas was capable of. I had to tread carefully.

"Your aunt is rumored to have possession of an object," Malphas continued, "an object that Ahrimad requires to fully walk this realm."

Ahrimad was the death god who'd cursed Alexandru Cruscellio, aka Death, more than two thousand years ago. When Death was a child, he had been tricked into releasing Ahrimad into the human world. In return, Ahrimad had promised to give Death the opportunity to kill the person he hated the most in the gladiator arena. Which, ultimately, had led to Death killing his own father, Malphas. That was why Malphas hated his son and was seeking vengeance in the present. Even though Alexandru had ultimately destroyed Ahrimad (which had led to him becoming the next death creature), both of Death's enemies from the past had found a way to rise again. Now they were working together.

"Torturing your aunt over this . . . special object . . . would be a waste of energy," Malphas continued. "Hunters like her wear jewelry and engrave tattoos into their bodies that limit my power. So, I waited.

I waited for the right moment." He reached out to touch the small wooden metronome on the coffee table between us. Bobbing left to right in an irritating rhythm, it began to tick faster. "Your essence is so peculiar; I knew right away you were the one. The one my son *spared* with the Kiss of Death. You, my dear girl, are a treasure."

"You can save the 'join me' evil villain speech. I'm not helping you with whatever twisted plan you have up your sleeve."

Tick. Tick. This time, the metronome reverberated in my ears and vibrated my vision with an intense pressure. Malphas's image blurred. I craned my neck to the side and winced. The sensations left me at once as the ticking faded to background noise again.

"Either you are with me or you are against me," Malphas said calmly. "No matter which option you choose, our paths will inevitably cross again. I always get what I want, one way or another."

"You're a sick, heartless creature, and you don't scare me," I said, my voice trembling so hard I had to tighten my muscles to speak.

"You called for me in your hour of need, and I answered. I was the weapon, but you pulled the trigger."

"It was a mistake," I hissed between clenched teeth. "A moment of weakness, not need. I was scared, and I should never have relied on you. Only a monster does what you did to your son."

"Alexandru is hardly my son. He never appreciated the sacrifices I made for him."

"You *abused* him."

"He was never meant for a delicate mortal hand."

"You act like being human is some disease."

A thin, icy smile crossed his face. "Because it *is* a disease, Faith. I was mortal, once. I've lived it."

Tick. Tick. Tick.

Malphas watched me intently as the metronome droned on, my eyelids drooping closed.

"The binding spell attaching Alexandru's soul to Limbo will wear off eventually. If he manages to get back sooner, which I suspect he will, then he'll be weak. You're the only one who can get close enough to him to complete this final task."

Malphas snapped his fingers. The metronome stopped.

One moment, he sat across the way; the next, he sat beside me. He clamped his hand down on my shoulder, and our surroundings strobed in and out of darkness. I stared deep into the void of his unfeeling eyes, sinking, sinking. Claws scraped the inside of my skull, and panic spiked as I felt paralyzed beneath his touch.

Instinct snapped into place. I shoved against the sensation of his power with all my might, all my will, and the scraping subsided. My heart skipped a beat. I'd mentally shoved Malphas away without him noticing.

"We can help one another, Faith." Malphas reached into his pocket with his free hand and pulled out a blade between his fingertips. "You want to escape the consequences of the Kiss of Death, and I—I want Death out of my way."

Malphas released my shoulder. The lethal gleam in his dead obsidian eyes made my stomach knot.

"If Death escapes Limbo, he will go to the D&S Tower ball to warn Lucifer," he continued. "I have arranged for you to be escorted to this event. Should you encounter Death there, you will stab him with this blade. It's laced with poison. A poison that will paralyze him for an hour and keep him out of our way. Long enough for us to deliver our message."

"What message?" I whispered.

Malphas grinned, black venom seeping from the tips of his incisors. "That we will get what we want, no matter what it takes, and what we want is the *Book of the Dead*."

The world spun as I processed this.

"You foolish girl," Malphas chided in a soft voice. "You feel so deeply for Death, but he'll never love you. He's incapable of it." He paused and handed me the dagger. "A little advice, Faith. The trick to life is not to let the imitation of what was once there fool you into believing it lives on in the present. Beyond the shallow depths of any façade, there's always the truth." As he leaned back, his features shimmered into a dreadful creature with translucent skin and bluish-black fangs. "You need only peel away the mask."

He vanished. The room plunged into darkness, and I sprang upward. Malphas's room was gone. I was in my bedroom.

Glancing down at my lap, my breath caught in my throat when I saw the dagger still clenched in my hand. It hadn't been a dream.

II

DEATH

Time moved faster in Limbo.

According to the digital clock on my temporary communication portal between Limbo and Earth, which I'd created with an incantation, an hour had passed since my soul had been banished and sent to the realm of lost souls and memories. I had tried to contact Lucifer, but the dusty old coot was worse with technology than I was and hadn't picked up. Glenn could have helped, but the little crap had hung up on me. He'd get what was coming to him after I escaped.

When my soul had shot through Limbo, it'd landed in a mirrored version of Times Square. The rowdiest, flashiest area of New York. Limbo sucked the life out of the bustling heart of the city. Here, it was a dead land. Cold, gray, depressing as hell, and void of any life except for the distant moans and wails of lost mortal souls.

An ideal vacation spot, if not for my current circumstances.

"Call Ace," I commanded the incantation.

I'd placed the communication portal in the front window of a tourist store. The reflective glass rippled like silvery water as the warlock, my last resort, appeared in the reflection.

"*Bonsoir*, my old friend." Ace greeted me with a broad smile. He stood before a mirror as though he'd anticipated the call, and I ground my fangs. "You have gotten yourself in quite the dilemma on this mystical night. Another ghost from your past has perhaps awakened, and you are there. In Limbo. Imprisoned. Unable to feed, deteriorating, and poor Faith, *votre amour* . . ."

My already foul mood flared. *He's getting a real kick out of this.* I hadn't seen this clown in more than three hundred years. Not since Ace had declared himself neutral like the delicate flower that he was and severed all communication with Hell.

"I want out, Ace. What do you want in return?"

"The *Book of the Dead*."

I boomed with laughter. "You're joking."

"When I caught word that *you* spared a mortal ten years ago, I'll admit I got curious." Ace steepled his fingers together, tapping his various rings against one another. "Curious enough to shift my store to Pleasant Valley. Now I believe I know the truth. Faith's family has a connection to the Guild, yes? Her mother's sister, Sarah Pierce, protects the *Book of the Dead*. But, like many before her, she cannot read it. Then I did a little more digging . . ."

"Did you dig your grave too?" I growled.

"Lucifer believes that Faith can read the grimoire—"

"*Silence.*" Casting a sharp look at the dull wandering souls around me, I leaned my hand on the glass and lowered my voice. "If that gets out, I'll tear off your good leg and feed it to my hounds."

Ace smiled. In my blind rage, I'd just confirmed for him why the girl had been spared in the first place. I believed she was the prophesized soul that could read the *Book of the Dead*.

"All I need is one spell," Ace said. "One spell to reverse the black magic that has affected my leg. I have tried everything, believe me. I feel confident I will find the answer in the book. Ensure that I have a look at the grimoire with Faith, and I'll release your soul from Limbo and get you back into your body."

"Your price is steep," I hissed. "Even if I wanted to, I cannot make that promise. The book isn't mine to bargain."

"Then it appears you are out of luck."

It shouldn't have come as a surprise. I'd *betrayed* him in more ways than one. Nevertheless, the realization that Ace would leave me stranded set me off-balance. My mind teetered between righteous anger and something else, something far too pathetic to admit out loud. I truly had nobody.

"We were friends once," I said in a low, almost imperceptible murmur. "Some might even say brothers."

Emotion flickered over the warlock's face, vanishing like smoke. "That was a time when I could trust you. Trust that you wouldn't stab me in the back, and what did that get me?"

Ace's voice had grown rough and thick with emotion, the quick, jerky movements of his hands communicating hurt. All the weak, mortal emotion surfaced in him like gold in a river of opportunity, and an idea came to me. If Ace left me here, I was screwed. Which meant I needed to get creative and take what I wanted by force.

"If not for me, you'd be dead," I said, lifting my chin. "You would have remained fragments of burnt bones and ash. Don't forget how all of Rome turned on you, how they *burned* you at the stake, and I brought you back. *I brought you back—*"

"How *dare* you hang that over my head!" Ace shouted, and his violet eyes electrified to white, vibrating the portal. "I paid my debt to you. For *centuries*, you used me for my magic, and I let you, because I thought you were my friend. But the evil that has plagued your soul is incurably foul. You're manipulative, draining—a parasite in every sense of the word. Your mother, Gods rest her soul, would roll over in her grave if she knew what you've become."

I pounded my fist into the frame of the incantation. "Fuck you."

"No, fuck you, Alex." Ace smoothed his hair back with a heaving breath and collected himself. "It's been fun catching up. Real fun, but I have a ball to attend tonight, and I won't be late."

He started to pull back, and I knew exactly where to strike.

"Kalace, wait."

The warlock froze at his true name and evaded my eyes. I gripped the incantation on either side of me, shadow darkening the frame as I leaned toward the portal.

"You gave Faith my mortal name," I began in an imploring manner, "so you must care about her safety. If she doesn't die by my father's hand, then maybe it will be at Ahrimad's. Could you bear it? Letting an innocent die because of an old vendetta with me? I can save her, but not if I'm trapped here."

His silence told me he was not convinced.

"At least tell me if you've seen anything unfolding tonight," I said, hoping I wasn't laying on the pleading too thick.

Ace scrubbed a hand over his face. "Ahrimad will indeed be amongst the guests at D&S Tower this evening. If he senses the power of her soul, she will be in deep trouble. If you somehow weasel your way out of Limbo, this information may help her."

"I knew you cared about her," I said with a nod of appreciation. "The unfortunate part about caring, though, is it leaves the soul awfully vulnerable."

Ace's brows drew together in confusion. Then he realized.

I punched through the air faster than he could shut the incantation, my power gushing through my side of the portal and into his like water. Ace staggered back with a curse, darkness clinging to his body like chains. I had one shot at this, and I manifested forward, my soul disintegrating into mist as I traveled between worlds. I fired into Ace like a bullet, entering straight through the warlock's mouth.

I sank my claws into his soul and squeezed, gaining enough control over Ace's body that I could feel the pain in his arm as he collapsed to the ground. Through his eyes, I saw we were in his séance room. Now I had him.

Ace clutched at his throat and writhed across the ground. I didn't have full control over his limbs yet. He rolled onto his stomach and crawled to the middle of the room toward his fallen cane. His fingertips brushed the crystal at the head before he curled into a tight, convulsive ball.

"You won't . . . last," Ace wheezed out between tight breaths. "I'll . . . fight. You bastard . . . "

He shoved at my soul one last time to expel my essence, but I held on with a stranglehold that promised to take him down with me. I could feel Ace's fury as he finally surrendered, and I slowly surfaced above his consciousness.

An old pendulum clock ticked, breaking the silence.

Lifting my legs to my chest, I leapt up onto the balls of my feet like a cat.

I looked down at Ace's hands, turned them over, and tucked his fingers tightly into his palms. When I turned toward the mirror behind me, the warlock's features stared back. A grin spread over my new mouth.

I stretched out a hand toward Ace's magical staff on the floor and gestured toward myself. "Come here, sweetheart."

The cane flew across the room, landing in my iron grip.

"*Very* fine," I said, turning my new weapon over in my hand. "Snooze, you lose, warlock."

Prowling across the room, I snatched a cell phone off the reading table and unlocked it with face recognition. Then I dialed reaper Leo, the Sin of Envy.

The call connected.

"Malphas expelled my soul from my corpse and probably abducted Faith. I'm possessing a body temporarily. Ace, the warlock. I'm going to see if I can recover my corpse, and I need you to check Faith's home and see if she's there. Rally the boys too. Have them run surveillance at the D&S ball. Once I find Faith, I'm bringing her there."

"Is Lucifer aware of this situation?" Leo asked.

"No, and we're keeping it that way for as long as possible. Wait for further commands and contact this number only."

"Yes, my lord."

I hung up.

Being in a mortal-like body was a pain in the ass. I couldn't fly back to the corn maze to see if my body was still there, and I had to conserve Ace's magic, or else his body would get fatigued. Storming from the building, I searched the parking lot for a vehicle and narrowed in on a black Harley Davidson.

After hot-wiring the hog, I peeled out at full throttle toward Pleasant Valley Farm. When I got there, I dumped the bike and made my way down the dirt path of the haunted hayride. Now within reasonable manifesting distance, I shut my eyes and focused. Ace's power to manifest felt akin to mine, feelers of magic stretching out across the land. Wind swirled as I disappeared and reappeared in a clearing in the corn maze. The sigil's lines had burned marks into the barren ground.

I cursed.

It'd barely been two hours, but my corpse was gone.

Movement fluttered above me. Tilting my head up at the bright floodlights, my nostrils flared as I noticed a single raven circling above. I raised Ace's staff to smite it into a bucket of fried chicken. It landed on one of the lights, low enough that I could see its vibrant blue eyes, and I hesitated. The creature cocked its head at me. A raven with blue eyes?

The raven flew away as I set the staff down. Ace's phone chimed in my pocket. Leo's number lit up the screen, and I answered.

"Faith is at home," he said. "Unconscious on her bed."

I couldn't help but feel a *sliver* of relief, despite the rage I felt toward her. Had she somehow gotten home on her own, or had Malphas taken here there?

"Guard her," I ordered. "I'm on my way."

Manifesting back to the motorcycle, I cursed as I wasted more of Ace's energy. The weaker his body became, the harder it would be to possess it.

I skidded to a stop in front of Faith's house and then jogged up the lawn.

"She just appeared there." Leo manifested beside me, cloaked in darkness. "I placed an enchantment on her parents so they won't wake up."

I approached her bedroom window and hovered my hand over the glass. The protective magical ward I'd placed around her home remained.

"Malphas must have materialized her inside," Leo said, aligned with my thoughts. "One moment, the room was empty; the next, she was there. Think it's a trap?"

Peering through the glass, I saw Faith's petite figure sprawled across her bed. I couldn't tell if her chest was moving, and Ace's stomach felt like lead. She couldn't be . . . dead?

Uttering rapid Latin under my breath, I dismantled the ward. Then I gripped her bedroom window and raised the pane.

"What are you doing? You'll incapacitate yourself."

Creatures of the night couldn't enter a mortal's house without permission.

"Ace is a neutral entity," I said. "Might be a loophole."

Thankfully, I was right.

I hurried to the bed and pressed two fingers to Faith's neck. Her pulse was very slow at first but quickened as I whispered her name. I suspected this was my father's doing. His mind control had exhausted her consciousness. She would come to soon.

I cast a glance at Leo. "Go to the ball. Say nothing to Lucifer yet. I'm handling this."

"Yes, my lord." Leo melted into the night.

I turned back toward Faith, my mood darkening.

She looked peaceful, porcelain . . . angelic.

And I wanted to make her fall.

Fall into my never-ending hell.

Time to get this show on the road.

Bracing my hand beside her head on the pillow, I leaned into the shell of her ear. "Awaken, my traitor."

III

FAITH

A blustery blast of air swirled through my bedroom window, startling me into an awareness that I was no longer alone. I stuffed the dagger quickly beneath my leg.

"Bonjour, mon ange!"

I whipped my head from the window and met the bright violet eyes of the man now standing in my room. Everything still felt dreamlike, detached, and in my brief dissociation, I didn't think he was real. The warlock from the Crossroads bookshop wore a purple satin suit jacket with an ornate Victorian tapestry vest beneath. Luxurious black velvet lapels and metal buttons down the center decorated the vest. His pants matched the obsidian fabric lining the jacket.

"Ace?"

He bowed theatrically and twisted his hand in a fast gesture, producing a red rose from thin air. *"Ton sourire est un don.* Your smile is a gift."

"What—what are you doing here? In my bedroom?" I inhaled the fragrance of the flower's petals, which blossomed to life in my hand.

Ace checked his watch.

"*Oh là là.* We are going to be late! We should leave as soon as possible. *Dès que possible.*" Those colorful eyes drifted over my clothes, which still showed signs of the attack in the corn maze. "First, I will need to cook you up something creative to wear"—he tapped my knee playfully with the large octagon-shaped crystal at the head of his golden cane—"since I'm your dashing date for tonight!"

I swung my legs over the bed, tucking the blade discreetly into the back of my jeans. "Now hold on, Frenchy. *You're* the escort Malphas mentioned? The one who's supposed to make sure I get the *job* done tonight?"

Ace removed his top hat, running his hand through his colorful hair, and studied my clothes again. "Perhaps this color for you, *oui*?" He smoothed out the lapels of his extravagant purple jacket. "Although, I do fear that Death would prefer a depressing obsidian with skulls and gore adorning your gown . . . "

Ace pointed at me with his cane as though to do something to my clothes, but I swatted his hand away.

"I asked you a question, Ace. Since when are you working for Malphas?"

"Do not worry about my role, *ma chérie*. Why don't you remind me what yours is tonight instead? Malphas did explain the plan, didn't he?"

The cold dagger pressed against my hip, reminding me what I'd been asked to do.

"I was told to attend the D&S Tower ball," I said. "If I come into close contact with Death, I'm supposed to incapacitate him with a poisonous blade so that Malphas can crash Lucifer's party."

Ace stared down at me, his expression impenetrable.

"Why aren't you saying anything? Aren't you in on this? What happened back there with Malphas? With that—ticking thing?" I pulled the dagger out of my jeans and held it up. "And seriously? A dagger? What is this, *Macbeth*? It's the twenty-first century, and I'm up against the Angel of Death. You could have at least given me a military tank or a wrecking ball. Or one of those fancy drones, so I could attack him from very, very far away."

When Ace didn't respond again, I raised my eyebrows.

"Did you really think you could get me to poison Death? First of all, I can barely endure the pain of plucking my own chin hairs, let alone killing someone, and second, the guy can bench-press me with his pinky. Now, don't get me wrong, I've done some stupid things these past couple weeks, but I'm pretty sure Death would *literally* eat me, flesh and bone, if I tried to stab him. He calls me 'cupcake,' for crying out loud. I'm already walking on thin ice. And last but not least, I don't want to find out how deep Death's fetish for sharp objects and violence goes, so no thank you. I'm out."

"You weren't susceptible to Malphas's hypnosis," Ace said. "He tried to charm you . . . "

A droplet of sweat fell down my forehead. The rant had taken the wind out of me. "Yep, he tried to manipulate me to finish the job for him. Figured it was best to play along with his creepy mind games to avoid getting eaten by that psycho too."

Wrath ignited his violet eyes. "How did you break the charm?" he demanded.

"I pushed back."

"What do you mean, you pushed back?"

I threw my arms into the air. "I don't know the terminology for what I did! I felt Malphas in my head, it hurt—a lot—and then I evicted him."

Ace went quiet again, thinking this over.

"Is Death alive?" I asked.

"Yes."

I slumped against my bedroom wall in relief but kept the knife clenched in my palm. "Malphas persuaded you to help carry out this plan, didn't he?"

Ace had shifted his attention to one of my paintings on the wall, so I could no longer see his face. "And what if he did, Faith?"

"Then neutral force, my ass. I thought you were trying to help me with your little clairvoyant show, but all you're concerned about is yourself and your profit."

"It's not like you've been honest about yourself either, *mon ange*." Ace turned his glare on me, and the temperature in the room plummeted a few degrees. "Whose side are *you* on?"

"I'm on *my* side! I can't trust any of you. Look at you. You'll do anything for anyone if there's a valuable trade involved. Have some self-respect. What did Malphas offer you, anyway? A *World of Warcraft* expansion pack? A bag of birdseed?"

"If Death is deprived of souls for small amounts of time, cut off from his reapers and the earthly realm, he will begin to deteriorate and gradually mummify. Tonight may be your only chance to escape him and Lucifer."

"Like you care what happens to me. If I go after Death with this toothpick dagger, he'll rip my head off!"

Ace's hands hovered around the blade in my palm with a pensive expression. He pivoted away from me and slowly walked the perimeter of the room, analyzing every inch of my personal space. Bending down to pick up something on the opposite side of my bed, he rose with my childhood teddy bear, Mr. Wiggles, clutched in his hand. The old, mangled bear was falling apart, his left arm hanging on by a literal thread. He set it down on my bed.

"That dagger is bewitched," Ace said. "It will give your arm unnatural strength and speed when you use it. If he hasn't killed you by now, I have to think he wouldn't tonight. You could still carry out the plan."

"What you're asking me to do is horrible. He hurt me. A lot. But I'd rather find another way out of this mess than make him suffer out of revenge."

Ace walked over to my bedroom window and peered outside. "Yet you assisted Malphas and Ahrimad in their scheme to rip his soul from his body . . . "

"Don't talk to me like you know me, Ace. You don't know anything about me. You have no idea what I've been through these past couple weeks."

"Perhaps you forget your position in this matter." Ace turned his head over his shoulder, lips tight, rigid cords bulging in his tense neck. The lamp on my nightstand hummed, the lightbulb flickering briefly and threatening to burn out. He glided closer. "You owe me a favor, Faith. And you will follow through on your word or you will deal with the repercussions of denying me. Starting with your family."

I pushed off the wall, a bull charging at a red flag. "I swear to God, if you lay one finger on them—"

"You'll what?"

"I'll kill you," I swore.

Ace exploded in strident laughter. "Corner a dog in a dead-end street and it will turn and bite. If you would do as you're told, all of this could have been avoided."

"Sure, blame me for everything!"

"I am so *sick* of that mouth of yours."

Coldness washed down the back of my neck. I stared into his glaring eyes, and my breath hitched. *It couldn't be.*

In a leap of faith, I reached up, gripped Ace by both sides of his skull, and crushed his mouth to mine. He froze, and then his hands gripped my waist. A low moan escaped me as he yanked me into him like claiming a feast. Our mouths slanted again, his tongue licking mine—

Suddenly, I was slammed against my bedroom wall with Ace's hand wrapped tightly around my throat, and I was three feet off the ground.

A wicked grin framed Ace's mouth.

"*Bonjour*, cupcake."

IV

Fury ripped apart Ace's carefully even features, revealing the beast within.

"Now *this* is satisfying. Having your fragile little virgin neck clutched in my hand." The French accent had departed, exchanged for an all-too-familiar mysterious lilt that stressed and rolled over certain letters with an erotic purr. He cracked his head sharply to the side. "Well," Death growled, "in *Ace's* hand."

Death.

It was him.

"*How?*" I bit out.

"Malphas sent my soul to another realm. I had to possess a body to get back here." His fingers tightened, holding me in place with a viselike grip. "Watching you squirm, plead for oxygen with your eyes, it would normally be a turn-on. But not right now. Right now, I'd much rather kill you."

A shadow crept over the whites of his eyes. Through the blotches in my vision, he grinned, and I was sure he would choke me to death.

Instead, he released me.

I crumbled to the wooden floor, clutching my neck as my breath rasped out in rapid pants. Husky laughter tumbled from his throat. "Killing you would be a blessing; it would free you from me. Your punishments are piling up. Don't think for a second I'm not keeping track."

"Never doubted you," I wheezed.

"You wait until I have my body back." A snarl lifted his lips. "I'm putting that feisty mouth of yours to work."

I flashed him a seething look. "In your dreams, death breath."

"Do you have any idea," Ace grated between clenched teeth, crouching down to my level, "what it feels like to get your soul ripped from your body?" His finger hovered over my chest, drawing a shape. "Imagine a dull knife slicing around your heart, slowly cutting you open while you are wide awake, imprisoned in the torment. It is the worst pain conceivable, the most violating act."

"I had no idea what Malphas would do to you—"

He fisted my shirt, pure madness consuming his eyes. "You betrayed me. You knew damn well what you were doing—"

"You betrayed me too!" I tore his fingers away.

We rose to our feet simultaneously, our faces inches apart.

"Calling on Malphas was a mistake," I continued breathlessly, "but I didn't *help* him do anything to you. Let's get one thing crystal clear. All I want is my life back. It was never my intention to hurt you. You *deliberately* hurt me! Once I saw you were in pain in that sigil, I tried to save you, and not because you're my most prized possession. I did it because I'm stupid enough to care about you. When I was hurting, when I was really hurting and vulnerable and defenseless, you didn't give a *shit*! You walked away and had a good laugh about a job well done! How am I more in the wrong here? Tell me!"

He wet his lower lip with his tongue. "Aw, are you going to cry? Do you want your precious sheltered life back, angel? Your life is never going to be the same. In fact, I fully intend to make it worse."

My hand cracked across his face.

He clutched at his jaw and worked it, freeing a frightening laugh. The bedroom darkened, shadow consuming the ceiling until it looked like a black void.

Death came at me at full force, and I backpedaled, slamming into the wall as he ripped through my personal space and planted his hands on either side of my head. "The things I would do to you if I didn't need you—*argh*!"

Suddenly, Death staggered, grimacing as his whole body locked up. He released a low growl, and my fingers gripped the dagger. I contemplated stabbing him now. Stabbing him while I had the chance to save myself.

"Ace is kicking you out, isn't he?" I asked instead.

"He's . . . trying." He took three hard inhales through his nose and exhales out his mouth. The fight seemed to pass as his shoulders relaxed again. Hissing a foreign sentence to himself, Death stalked the width of my small bedroom back and forth.

"You said you need me," I said, tucking the dagger back into my jeans. "I'm assuming you need my help getting your corpse back."

"Not just my corpse, my *scythe*," Death snarled, his fury at full force again. "Ahrimad is free. I suspect he's feeding off my scythe's power to remain corporeal. Once he finds a way to stay corporeal in the mortal realm without the blade, we're all screwed."

A realization struck me. "This is what Malphas meant when he told me he was the least of our worries now. He was talking about Ahrimad. It was never about you; it was about bringing Ahrimad back." I maneuvered away from the wall to stand closer to him at the center of the room. "Why are you trying to bring me to the ball? To use me as bait?"

"No. I wanted to keep you by my side so I can protect you. Then you started babbling about Malphas and an escort, so I played along to get more information." His gaze held mine for an intense beat. "But don't get it twisted. I plan on keeping you safe tonight so that I can punish you myself after I get my corpse back."

I sifted through my mental bucket list: *Make the Grim Reaper fantasize about torturing me a trillion different ways. Check!* "I guess chivalry is dead after all."

"I could go on, and in great detail, believe me." He stopped pacing back and forth and settled for circling me. My chest heaved. If I stabbed him to get away, it was game over. I stealthily gripped the blade at my hip again. "Would you like to hear what I plan to do to you, Faith?"

"Ignorance is bliss."

He bared his teeth in a nasty smirk. "Shame. You're not the only one who's creative."

Death struck like a viper; his hand positioned over mine on the hilt of the dagger. I jerked, but his fingers were strong as steel around mine. Our eyes connected, ice to fire.

"Naughty, naughty girl." With a sly smile, he guided my hand up, pulling the weapon free from the waistband of my jeans, and then he released me. The dagger remained in my grasp.

"Why don't do you just do it?" he taunted. "Put me down, Faith. Execute Malphas's plan. I'm weak in this body. Unable to feed. All you'd have to do is slice me with that butter knife, and Ace's body will be paralyzed within a minute. There's your way out of tonight. It's right in your grasp."

My fingers tightened around the handle.

"I'll make it easier for you." He dropped to his knees with his arms spread out.

"You've lost your mind," I gasped.

"Haven't you heard, princess? You're famous now." Ace's crazed violet eyes and sinister grin perfectly mirrored the delirious parasite possessing his body. "You need me tonight, just as much as I need you. Since you kept refusing my complete protection to shield you from my kind, rumors have spread. Now every wicked creature in this realm knows that I marked a mortal's soul with the Kiss of Death and brought her back to life. Bet they'll be curious as to *why* too. Can't say I didn't warn you. Let's hope none of them track your delicious scent *here* to Mommy and Daddy first—"

I lunged forward with the dagger raised and clutched Death by the throat. Instinct kicked in, and his hand snapped out to grip my forearm as he bared his teeth like an animal.

Breathing me in, his mouth spread wider into a taunting smirk. He loosened his grip so that I stayed in his clutches, but not hard enough to break any bones. Then he did the unthinkable and dropped his arms completely and complacently to his sides.

"That's right, baby," Death purred, freeing a deep, sinister laugh. "Choke me."

Heat splayed over me, and I propelled my arm to shake him, hard. "Shut up. Shut up, or I'll fry you like I did the other night. I swear to God, I'll do it!"

His jaw clenched shut at the mention of *that* night, and his eyes narrowed to slits. He examined me that way, motionless, and made no move to fight me. Beneath my fingers, Ace's pulse thrummed steadily, and I was reminded that if I hurt Death, I'd hurt the warlock too. Ridding myself of the Angel of Death wasn't the answer. Not now, at least. He was the only thing standing between my family and the rest of his monstrous world. And he knew it.

"Question," Death purred. "If you're going to execute me—since I don't get a last meal and all—could you take your top off first?"

"What is your problem?" I exploded, and his forehead puckered in surprise. "You're over two thousand years old and you still don't know how to treat women?"

"I—"

"It was *rhetorical*," I snapped. Ace's skin paled a little as he tracked the now ignited-with-my-power dagger in my hand. I waved it about like a deadly conductor while I spoke. "I've given you plenty of opportunities to apologize, Death. You haven't, not once, and now you're demanding my help. Do you understand that if you had been nice to me from the beginning, or—I don't know—toned down the 'I'm the predator, you're the prey' vibe you expel from every deadly pore of your body, I probably would have trusted you from the get-go? Hint: women *love* kind, honest men."

"Since when?"

"You're a hopeless cause! And I'm kicking you *out*!" Releasing his throat, I turned, intending to storm toward my bedroom window and haul it open to shove him *through* it, but Death grabbed the hem of my shirt and drew me back.

"What if I say I'll compromise?"

I crossed my arms over my chest. "This oughta be good."

Glancing around in contemplation, Death scrubbed a hand across his jaw. "I swear to you, on my soul and my throne, that if you help me tonight, we will sit down and discuss our deal with your soul. I'll leave room for renegotiations in the contract you'll be given. Your family *and* your friend Marcy will remain under my protection. You have my word."

"Why should I believe your word?"

"Because I'm still on my knees," Death replied. "Because you and I need each other."

As if predicting I'd walk away again, he captured the backs of my thighs with his fingertips and held me in place. The fact that I let him destroyed me.

"Whether you believe it or not, whether you trust me or not, and whether you hate me or not, I've kept you alive when nobody else could. I must recover my corpse, and I need your assistance. Please."

We kept eye contact as I considered the idea that he was only acting this way to get his corpse back. I mean, honestly, the bastard was laying it on as thick as London fog. He'd even gone so far as to say his own forbidden word: *please*.

I was so sick and tired of this supernatural crap.

I didn't have much of a choice here, though. If Death didn't get his body back in time, there would be hell to pay. And the consequences wouldn't affect just me. They would affect my family and many, many other innocent lives.

"I'm with you." I stepped out of his grasp and tucked the dagger back into my jeans. "Only for tonight. And only if you accept another demand."

He scrutinized me, silent. It was empowering as hell to have an immortal being on his knees before me. All he needed to do was dangle a bunch of grapes over my mouth while fanning me in a tropical location to complete the fantasy.

"I want answers, Death. You give me answers, and I'll help you get your corpse back."

"I'll allow one answer."

"One? You're kidding, right?"

"One question, one night." He climbed to one knee before rising to Ace's tall, but not so intimidating, height. "I could always force you to help me."

"Could you?" I countered with a sly smile. It drove him mad

that I didn't kiss his feet every time he barked out a command. He was used to being worshiped, but I needed to be his equal for this to work. "A part of you wants me to help you willingly."

Death widened his stance, a muscle in his jaw twitching. "Another part of me wants you to be obedient."

"Forcing me to do anything for you tonight would be counterproductive."

"Hmm." Death strode around me to get to my dresser. He tugged open the top drawer to investigate inside. "Three questions," he clipped. "That's it."

"Twenty."

Death twirled a light-blue thong around his finger. "Twenty. *If* you slip these on."

I took an angry swipe at the thong, but he slingshot it across the room, where it vanished into smoke. "Hey! Those were my favorite!"

"Key word: were."

My face felt hot. "Twenty answered questions, you bastard. Tonight."

"Zero."

"Bye-bye!" I gave him a sarcastic wave as I jumped onto my bed. "Best of luck tonight!"

Death bared Ace's teeth and growled. *"Fine,"* he snarled. "Twenty questions. Tonight. After I get my corpse back, we'll revisit the rest of your spoken demands."

We shook on it. That familiar coldness washed down my neck as our hands firmly but briefly connected.

"Now for your outfit." All business, he yanked me up off the bed and gave my figure a critical once-over. "I want her in black," he commanded to nobody, or so I thought.

Hidden shadows peeled off my bedroom walls and brushed my skin like feathered kisses. My clothes evaporated as the shadows transformed and a dress unfurled down the length of my body, rippling darker than an obsidian sea. A sleeveless A-line ball gown with a provocative V-neck that cut past the swell of my full cleavage and complemented the communion cross around my neck. The skirt of the gown fanned out at my waist in enticing layers of tulle that pooled at my feet. I stepped forward, and my Converse sneakers dissolved.

"I'll admit that was impressive, bearing in mind you aren't even in your own body. But next time, warn me before you go all fairy godmother."

"Warning." The hard line of his mouth twitched.

Shadows clung to me again. Heels slipped onto my feet, and my hair was pulled back from my neck, piling in curls over my head. The hem of the gown was now the perfect length, lightly kissing the floor.

"Wow," I marveled. I never wore dresses and found them uncomfortable, but this gown was an exception. It was made for a princess. "This dress . . . it's breathtaking."

"For what it's worth, it's not the dress." Death's eyes met mine, and the soul peering out from behind Ace's face was predatory. Any trace of that look washed away as he turned his head and ripped his gaze away from mine. "We should go. The event is commencing soon, and my soul needs to return to my corpse."

He swirled the warlock's cane, and shimmering smoke gathered around us.

The world blurred and narrowed in at hyperspeed, like getting shot through a tunnel. Our surroundings had changed, but I could hardly process where we'd landed. Disoriented and deprived of oxygen, I shoved away from Death and braced my hands on my knees as I dry heaved.

"Seriously?" I coughed out. "No warning or anything?"

I looked up from the wet pavement and froze. Death had managed to use the warlock's magic to teleport us all the way from Pleasant Valley to New York City. We were standing in an alleyway, and not just any alleyway—the one where Malphas had attacked me outside the D&S Tower.

"Come on." Death gripped my elbow and steered me to a line of guests snaking across the side of the building. This whole situation was so awkward. Maybe because I'd told Death that I cared about him, and he hadn't acknowledged it in the slightest. Talk about a pathetic declaration better left unsaid.

"Doesn't the warlock have a limp?" I asked. He'd been walking perfectly fine, whereas Ace usually leaned on his cane.

"It's a psychosomatic pain," Death said. "A consequence of conjuring black magic."

"Why isn't it bothering you then?"

"Because I'm not a pussy. I'll saw off his bum leg before I use a cane."

Oh.

"I changed our identities with illusions," he explained as we stepped into the line. "Our voices are altered too. The last thing I want to do is keep up the image of the warlock and speak croissant the whole night. You won't be able to see the illusion or hear the change in your voice. The dagger Malphas gave you will be invisible as well; it's hidden in a strap under the layers of your dress."

"Is there a reason I still have it?"

"Just in case."

He didn't elaborate. I didn't expect him to.

"This line goes on forever," I grumbled. "We should rent a tent."

"It'll move once the doors open. I'd manifest, but I have to conserve Ace's energy. His human body is hungry, and I already wasted energy traveling from your home." He brought his head back, as if he was tired of waiting too. "My soul gets depleted faster on Earth than in Purgatory."

"What happens when you get completely depleted? At midnight will you turn back into your true form, a talking skeleton?"

"Let me clarify a few things for your waning intelligence, cupcake." Evidently, he was triggered by my joke, and I couldn't stop smiling. "I am not, nor have I ever been, a skeleton. I have never owned an hourglass, I am not a headless horseman, I don't drive a rickety old wagon, I do not hold a mortal's hand like a friend while we walk into the heavenly light of the afterlife, and—"

"You do not, under any circumstances, moan in the middle of the night, wandering aimlessly through a graveyard?"

He scowled. "You're asking for it."

I dug my teeth into my lip.

The woman ahead of us glanced over her shoulder, frowning at us.

"We roleplay," Death explained smoothly. The woman turned back around. "Ugly, nosey-ass mortals."

"Why is Devin launching your art program for underprivileged children at the D&S Halloween ball? What is this event, really? An actual monster bash? A front for a satanic sacrificial party?"

"All you have to know is Devin thrives on attention." He leaned into me and kept his eyes on the entrance ahead. "I'd tell you more about what's beyond those doors, but I'd have to sacrifice you."

"This whole 'don't tell Faith anything' habit of yours is absurd at this point. I get it, you're a control freak who doesn't want to give me answers. But right now, I'm scared shitless, and you're the only person I can talk to. If you expect me to sit quietly on your lap the whole night, like an obedient little dog, you've got another thing coming."

"That's the second time we've discussed the idea of you sitting on my lap."

I tried to play it off coolly, except that my face was suddenly hot from that obvious innuendo. "Did you just man-filter everything I said?"

"Yes. That would be question nine."

The line moved forward as a pixelated screen at the building's entrance exploded with a short video of Devin and David Star. They looked impeccably beautiful, back to back, their eyes piercing the camera with a sizzling intensity. I found it eerie and unsettling to know that these two men, these celebrities the entire world fawned over, were the Devil and Death in disguise. I wanted to ask Death more about their alliance, but I knew he'd find a way to dodge a major question like that right now. Besides, he was counting the questions I asked, and I didn't want to waste my chances.

We reached the front of the line. Death produced a crumpled piece of paper from his suit jacket. Glancing at it, I saw messy cursive that said *milk*, *eggs*, *bread*, and *ground meat*.

The ticket taker's face spread into a big plastic grin. "Welcome to the D&S Tower Halloween ball!" He took out an ink pad and a stamp. "Would you like to make any additional donations—?"

"Stamp us," Death demanded and held out a wrist. The chirpy man stamped him with the D&S Tower logo, and right before my eyes, it disintegrated into his skin. I was next. Sure enough, the stamp disappeared into my skin too.

Death had totally just snuck us into the event with Ace's grocery list.

The tower lobby was a madhouse, like Grand Central Station during peak hours. A hive of activity and sound, bustling with guests—all of whom appeared to be human—conversing and making their way toward the back of the building.

"Now we wait and see if Ahrimad shows up," Death said, guiding us through the crowd "My father can't hold my scythe, so he won't have it."

"But Malphas held it in the corn maze."

"He must have held it briefly, then. My scythe is a blade of death. Ahrimad is the only other creature capable of holding the weapon indefinitely without bursting into flames. He is the only other creature who can wield it, and the power of the blade will allow him to temporarily stay corporeal."

"What do you think Ahrimad plans to do with your scythe? What kind of power does it have?"

"I've wielded it for over twenty centuries, and even I don't know all its power. The possibilities are endless."

Awesome. "Could he destroy the world tonight? World domination seems to be a hot trend among the evil type. I'd like to give my parents a quick call if our planet is going to self-destruct or something."

"Highly unlikely. No villain can take over the entire human realm in a single evening. World domination is a marathon, not a sprint."

In other words: *Yes, he can destroy your world, but don't worry, obliteration takes time. I would know!*

"It's not going to happen," Death reiterated, although his rigid posture spoke volumes to the contrary. "Don't worry your pretty little head."

"What if he kills you in Ace's body?"

"He won't have the chance to."

"So your soul *can* be destroyed."

"Was that not just implied?"

I crossed my arms and turned my back on him. "Friendly reminder that I'm helping you tonight."

Surprisingly, I stepped through security without any questions. Once the guards were finished scanning us, any pleasantness in Ace's features vanished, shifting to the menacing demeanor of the monster hiding underneath. Death's illusions had worked. We were in.

Death stalked over to my side.

"Walk," he said, grasping me by the elbow again.

I tore from his hold once we were a fair distance away. "Relax, alpha male. We'll get to Devin and all will be well. Grind your teeth any harder and Ace will have to wear dentures."

"Don't comfort me, Faith. I'm fine."

"Sounds like it!"

"I'm piggybacking another man's fucking body. It's well within reason to be furious."

"As long as you don't take it out on me, buddy."

As we entered the ballroom, Death pulled me sharply to the side behind a large bouquet of Halloween-themed orange and black dyed flowers. I was just about to tell him off for dragging me around like a dog on a leash when he cupped a hand over my mouth and flattened me against the wall with his body. The pure homicide in his expression sent fear, and maybe a dash of something *else*, down my spine.

Devin Star strode past us, paused to scan the room, and then continued through the ballroom. On his arm was my aunt Sarah, or at least I assumed it was her since her face wasn't turned toward me. Her blond hair was piled elegantly on top of her head, and she wore a beautiful, sparkling silver dress. Her toned body and pale skin bore no lacerations or damage caused by the wraiths and the hell hounds in the corn maze.

I started to move toward her, but Death placed a hand on my shoulder and secured me to his side.

"What the hell is *Lucifer* doing with my aunt?" I whispered.

"Looks like the hell hounds dragged her here to be his date." Death raked his hand aggravatedly through Ace's hair. "Damn it, that was my chance. I should have approached him."

"Now who's the chicken, *buddy*?"

He turned on me. "How about you shut your mouth, or I'll shut it for you, buddy?" I should have been frightened, but I felt a lick of something unwelcomely close to desire at the tension between us.

Get a grip.

I examined the patterns on his tapestry vest to distract myself from the inconvenient fantasies I was having about him. "What are we going to do now?"

"Sit down and locate Devin after his presentation." He peered out from behind the flowers and checked if the coast was clear. "Heading to the stage right now will draw unwanted attention to us."

Unexpectedly, his fingers weaved with mine, and he drew me into the ballroom.

Curtains were draped across the spacious ceiling, and amber lights shimmered behind them. The rest of the room was decorated with elegant Halloween accents, splashes of orange and black, and bouquets with little pumpkins on each table. An enormous chandelier made of countless arms branching out with dazzling crystals and golden lights spread a warm glow along the ceiling and the hardwood floors.

Death selected an empty table and dragged out a chair for me. In front of the seat lay a card written in calligraphy and a black masquerade mask. I pulled the skirt of my gown under me and took my seat as Death sat down next to me.

"Put on the mask," he ordered, lifting his plain white mask off the table and pressing it to his face. Instantly, the party favor transformed into a unique decoration that matched his suit. Fascinated, I lifted mine to my eyes. As if by magic, the mask clung to my face without any string or ribbon.

Death unfastened his purple suit jacket while his gaze swept the room like an assassin, landing on one table.

Seven men in identical obsidian tuxedos sat there. They had athletic physiques and wore red masquerade masks. Laughing loudly, three of the seven were taking turns tossing hors d'oeuvres into each other's mouths, baseball-style.

"Friends of yours?"

"I don't have friends," Death said. "They're my subordinates. My seven reapers."

As they continued to fling food at each other like drunken fraternity brothers, one with a pink Mohawk missed a clump of food and chaotically flipped over his chair in the process. He rolled to his feet in a smooth somersault and played it cool, suavely fixing his hair. Death gripped the back of my chair with a white-knuckled fist and visibly strained to remain in his seat.

"Damn it, Romeo," he hissed.

"One of your reapers is called *Romeo*? With an alias as scary as Death, I would have expected hardcore names for your subordinates. Like Shovelhead, or Cobra. Do you have a reaper named Bubbles?"

Death fiddled with his butter knife on the table. "This is a prestigious event. They're behaving like a bunch of imbeciles."

"Deep breaths. Everything is going to be okay."

"If you feed me one more clichéd motivational line, I'm going to rip out the nearest person's teeth and fasten them around your neck like a choker."

"Chill. It's not like you can discipline any of your reapers in your current situation."

"*Chill?* You think this is funny, don't you?"

"I think this is hilarious. The Grim Reaper is having a panic attack in another person's body. You should try diaphragmatic breathing." I inhaled a much-needed breath from my own belly and sighed dramatically. Death's cold stare flicked down to the thin strips of fabric over my breasts as I did so and lingered for several beats. When our eyes met again, his were an intoxicating blend of brooding, sinister, and carnal. His tongue tucked inside of his cheek, as if he were barely restraining himself.

I smiled sugar-sweet. "Chill."

He lunged at me.

"Welcome to the D&S Tower," proclaimed a voice behind us. Death slammed his ass back into his seat and composed himself as civilly as a rabid animal. The waiter's eyes were a disturbing shade of red, and I dropped my attention quickly to his sharp nose. "Can I offer you two something to drink? Have you looked at our Halloween-themed drink menu?"

I didn't drink alcohol, plus I was eighteen, but I wasn't about to blow our cover. "Oh—um, hold on." I reached for the fancy menu by my plate and read.

To Die For Drink Menu
The Black Cauldron
Poisoned Passion Fruit Kiss (Vegan-friendly)
Gin & Terror
RIP Lemonade (Vegan-friendly)
The Grave
Witch's Brew (Eye garnish optional)
Bloody Mary
Zombie's Goblet (Contains meat)

The waiter cleared his throat.

"Riiight," I said, skeptical about ordering any of these. "The Grave sounds promising."

"I bet it does," Death muttered as he inspected his own drink menu. "You've already got one foot in it."

The waiter switched his attention to Death. "And for you, sir?"

Right before my eyes, the waiter's face shimmered away. His skin paled until it became nearly translucent. Two sharp canines poked out from his lips. *Vampire*. No flipping way. Chairs shifted around us, drawing my attention to the rest of our table as other guests were seated. The assembly of people—if I could even call them people— consisted of frighteningly ugly creatures in fancy clothes. They talked amongst themselves in various foreign tongues. I gaped at them, feeling like a lone rabbit trapped in a forest overpopulated by wolves.

Death was speaking in a rich foreign language to the waiter. He indicated certain items on the menu and made a cutting gesture with his hand. *What the hell is he saying?*

"Pardon me," one of the guests at our table said with a croaky voice. The creature spun its head one hundred eighty degrees, like an owl, to face a different waiter walking past our table. My stomach churned at the visual. "When you get the chance, kindly fetch me another Witch's Brew. Two eyeballs, this time. I do enjoy those cute garnishes."

"Of course, ma'am," the waiter replied. She disappeared and reappeared at another table with a tray of appetizers in an instant.

"First time at a D&S Tower ball, eh?" asked a hoarse, accented voice to my left. "Oh, how I love watching the brainwashed mortals mingle with us every Halloween. You look a little pale, dove. Are you not from the Netherworld?"

I gaped at the *thing* in the chair beside me. Its gray, hairless, dog-like face contorted as it sipped noisily from a massive goblet, although it wasn't slurping with its mouth but instead through its straw-like fingers, which were dipped into the thick, crimson liquid of the drink. Blood. As it continued to devour its beverage, the beast offered me a thin smile, and I glimpsed its huge incisors.

"Well?" the stranger prompted. "Do you not understand the mortals' English?"

"I don't live in the Netherworld," I squeaked. "I live . . . further north. I think."

"I see." It scrunched up its nose, which could only be described as a more terrifying cousin of a muzzle. "You're approaching your cyclic bleed. What species are you?"

Fingers pinched my arm. Death dragged my chair closer to him. "Thank God," I breathed. "That thing just asked about my—"

Death cupped my jaw and slanted his mouth possessively over mine. The caress deepened as his tongue parted my lips, edging inside. Blind pleasure shuddered through me, and a soft moan escaped from my throat. When his hand glided over my bare back, reality crashed into me, and I shoved him away.

"What was that for?" I exclaimed.

A flicker of amusement rippled over the warlock's features. "Keep your voice down," he cautioned as our waiter appeared out of thin air to place our requested drinks in front of us. In my peripheral vision, the creature I'd been speaking to turned its attention elsewhere. "You were speaking to a species of chupacabra, and he scented your next period. I laid my claim before he tried to sample a taste."

Ew. Thank God Death had intervened, but if he expected a thank you, he wasn't getting one. I adjusted the silky straps of my dress instead. My lips were swollen and claimed all right, but not to the extent they had been the night he'd kissed me in my bedroom. *I need to stop thinking about that kiss.*

The lights dimmed.

At the head of the ballroom, past paparazzi and guests I now knew weren't all human, Devin Star stood on a sleek stage. He looked like a god amongst golden spotlights, sporting a bloodred tuxedo.

"Good evening," Devin said in a booming voice. Any noise in the room halted immediately. "And thank you all for joining me on this monumental night."

V

"I am Devin Star, president of D&S Enterprises," Devin began, as if everyone on the whole planet didn't already know who he was. "Every year, we host events at the tower to raise money for various charitable organizations and give back to my beautiful city and its citizens . . . "

"Why aren't we trying to find Ahrimad or Malphas?" I asked Death, tuning out Devin's speech. "Shouldn't they be here?"

"Again, I'm trying to avoid any unwanted attention," Death replied through tight lips, his attention focused on the stage. He wore an impenetrable expression. "Before we do anything, we need to wait until people start walking around, or for the entertainment to begin. I can remain in this body for about three more hours."

I played nervously with the layers of my dress. Three hours. That seemed like a decent amount of time. "When will the entertainment begin?"

"Once the guests are done eating. When the show ends, I'm

going to try to draw Devin out of the room to tell him what's going on. I don't want to spark a commotion in the ballroom."

I tuned back in to Devin Star's speech.

"This year, our annual Halloween ball is going to be slightly different," Devin was saying, "as the organization you have graciously donated to tonight is my own. I am thrilled to celebrate the launch of our new youth art program, Painting Pioneers. For the past year, I have been working rigorously on this project with my son, David, to give underprivileged children in New York City a creative outlet to cope with various mental health concerns. Unfortunately, my son is under the weather and could not make it tonight, but we are both *eternally* grateful for your support for our cause . . . "

Then Devin grinned, a beautiful display of straight white teeth and sparkling sapphire eyes. At that moment, half of the audience erupted into thunderous laughter. The other half, the human half, seemed to have missed the hidden punchline.

"Devil's horns!" exclaimed one of the neatly dressed "men" at our table. He was one of the creatures I'd seen earlier, except now he wore an illusion of a handsome human man. Nausea built up in my belly at the memory of the vile thing beneath. "This is funnier than last year's event. Look at all these brainwashed air-breathers around us. Do they honestly think the Stars care about the mortal youth?"

"Do you think Devin's doing a satanic sacrifice this year?" the woman who had requested the witch's brew with two eye garnishes asked. When I concentrated on her, I saw the creature beneath again. "That was delightful last year!"

"For legal reasons, I don't believe they can this year," the first man answered. "Damn Heaven and their new rules for public displays of sacrifice. Good thing I still have a juicy video on my phone from last year of Death ripping out that mortal man's heart and hurling it into the crowd. I was so close to catching it. *Hi-larious!*"

I glared over at Death, who wore the smuggest expression.

"What the hell is wrong with you?" I hissed. "*Mortal sacrifices? And now you're manipulating children in this bogus art program—?*"

I stilled as Death gripped my leg under the table in a firm grasp. "Keep it down," he warned in a low voice. "It's a real program. There needs to be an element of trust for us to manipulate mortals, and children aren't our main target audience. As for the sacrifices . . . let's just say the mortals who get an invite to these events *deserve* to be my playthings."

"Wow, you're a real hero," I said sarcastically. "More like you and Lucifer find any loophole you can to go about your psychotic ways unpunished."

He arched a mischievous brow like I'd hit the nail on the head. "I don't give a fuck if I'm punished, cupcake. It doesn't get worse for me than it already is."

I was rendered speechless. *I can't believe I keep making out with this guy.*

Devin Star stepped off the stage to chat with a few guests. To the world, he was dazzling, beautiful, angelic. To me, he was just another monster with a gorgeous veneer over the truth. The longer I stared at Devin, the more my vision narrowed, until it was just me and him in the room, and that's when his façade wavered.

Devin's features sharpened as he turned his head to the side, his charming mouth working with words I could no longer hear. The spotlights reflected off patterns beneath his skin, which resembled reptilian scales. His skin shimmered, changing from a golden bronze to a ghoulish reddish gray. His fingers lengthened, sharpening into talons as massive horns gradually sprouted from his skull. The captivating sapphire eyes the entire world was in love with now held the ruthless, wicked intentions of a sinister creature. The rest of his illusion broke free at once, revealing the venomous Fallen angel

Lucifer. When Devin glanced to his left and smiled at the woman in a business suit beside him, his countenance was no longer charming. His smile was an evil, chilling display of razor-sharp teeth that dared anyone to challenge him.

Death gripped the back of my chair. "You see him, don't you?" He'd been watching me the entire time. "You see past his illusion of Devin Star."

"Yes," I whispered in horror.

A loud slurping noise drew my attention to the chupacabra. His illusion of a human man had slipped again as he dipped his bony fingers into his fresh goblet of blood. My mouth felt dry. I gulped down the Grave concoction, quickly realizing it was delicious and rat-poison-free but highly alcoholic.

"Why?" I asked Death, coughing as the drink burned my throat a little. "Why am I beginning to . . . ?"

"See into my world?" Death offered, grinning like a piranha.

"What's happening to me?"

Silence.

My whole body pulsed to the pounding rhythm of my heart. "You know what all of this means, don't you?" I lowered my voice until it was barely audible. "You know what I am."

"I told you: I know everything about you, Faith."

"Have I mentioned how much I love when you're vague and enigmatic?" I asked sarcastically.

"Get used to it, princess. I lost track of those questions of yours: that one can be fourteen."

We stared at each other. Me, furious, and him, amused.

The waiter returned and placed a plate of food in front of me, squashing all my anger.

A meat dish and a salad. Not trusting the meat, I pushed the plate toward the center of the table, sloshing Death's drink a little before he plucked it up. The salad had questionable red slices of some sort of vegetable, peaches, sweet potato, and crumbled cheese with greens and a vinaigrette.

This sure wasn't my usual food of choice.

I poked my fork into the dish and cautiously brought a red slice to my mouth to chew. "Phew," I said and pretended to wipe sweat off my forehead, "they're just beets." I scooped a larger forkful. "And they're not bad."

Death dropped his napkin into his lap but made no move to eat. "Beets are an aphrodisiac."

I stabbed at the salad, avoiding a beet this time. "I would need twelve truckloads of beets to ever come on to you."

He didn't laugh. Instead, he angled his body in my direction and watched me with a painful intensity. I busied myself with my food. One of his hands gripped the table, and the other gripped the back of my chair. From the corner of my eye, I saw him leaning into me.

"Your first kiss," he said, mischief coating his voice. "Stolen. Just like that. Tell me, was the big, grand kiss wasted on me?"

"I don't know," I answered calmly. "Is it grand for your first kiss to tell you it shouldn't have happened? Is it grand for them to screw with you just to get in your pants?"

"Virgins and screwing don't mix well with me. I'm not a gentle giant."

I sipped my drink again to relieve the sudden dryness in my throat.

He leaned closer. "I want to hear you say it," he whispered huskily. "How hot and bothered I get you. How you crave me. A nice, good human boy won't do it for you anymore, will he? Say I'm wrong."

I'd never focused so hard on beets in my life. "Have you always deflected with anger, humor, and perverseness? Your defense mechanisms are showing."

"So spiteful," he murmured. "Must be all that pent-up estrogen."

"Never to be released by you."

"I'm curious, does the nun have an elaborate fantasy for losing her V-badge too?"

The second Death had his corpse back, I was going to penalty kick him soccer-style in the dick. Why was I not at all surprised that *David Star* had never had a serious girlfriend? Death was a total hound.

"I can visualize the first-time attachment syndrome already," Death continued. "When you finally lose it, you're going to koala hug the poor lad's leg all the way out the door. I'm cringing already."

"What'd you lose your *clumsy* virginity to, Roman man?" I interrogated. "A toga? A hole in a tree? When I give it up, it'll be to someone special. Someone who's kind, thoughtful, hardworking, and honest. A simple, easy love."

He reclined in his seat again and let out a hearty laugh. "Now that's a riot, cupcake."

I feigned interest in his opinion. "How so?"

"There is no simple, easy . . . " He shook his head like he couldn't finish the rest of the ridiculous statement. "You're romantically delusional."

"You made sure of that, now, didn't you?"

This time, he had no response. He wore a surprisingly calm, patient expression, as if anticipating I had more to say.

"I just want to know if you honestly . . . " I laid my palms flat on the table. "You know what? Never mind. It's not worth it."

His head tilted. "If I what?"

"Pretended all that time," I blurted. I tried to hold my emotion in, but my rigid control crumbled as my throat tightened. "Pretended to care about me. Pretended you liked me after the interview and at the carnival. Pretended that you wanted to get to know me. It all seems ridiculous now, doesn't it? One big laugh at my expense. You didn't have to kiss me. You didn't have to save me again in the corn maze."

His stare bored into mine. "I don't know what you want me tell you, Faith."

"Tell me the truth," I whispered. "Tell me it wasn't all a lie."

"You two should get married," the chupacabra chimed in. He was the only other guest still at our table; the rest of the frightening creatures had left to converse with others. "Or star in a soap opera."

Death whipped his attention to the chupacabra so quickly that I thought Ace's head would snap off his neck. "Why don't you suck me, leech? Go find a goat in the lobby to stick your filthy fingers in."

Appalled, the chupacabra threw down his napkin, shoved his chair back, and stormed off.

"Here's the thing, cupcake," Death said, lowering his voice back to a huskier level again. "You're getting yourself worked up about you and me, and you're making a scene. If you make a scene, I'm going to blow a fuse." He picked up his butter knife, twirling it once around his fingers. "And if I blow a fuse, I'll lose my chance of getting my corpse back tonight. If you are the reason I don't get my corpse back . . . " He released a harsh laugh. "You better believe your body will be next in line for my taking."

We sat in silence. It felt like I was at prom with a terrible date, and I desperately wanted to go home and watch Netflix.

Out of nowhere, the lights shut off, blanketing the room with shadows. Death reached for me in an instant, his hand encircling my wrist. A slow piece of instrumental music broke the silence. A spotlight aimed at the ceiling outlined a man dressed in black and a woman dressed in white. They both wore beautiful lace masks and dangled from a web of silk ribbons, their bodies partially intertwined as they rotated slowly.

The music picked up, and the man threw himself away from the woman and dove backward, falling headfirst toward the ground like a diver as he untangled himself from the silk. My heart caught in my throat. The spotlight went off, and some of the audience screamed, thinking his fall was accidental.

Another spotlight went on, this time at the center of the ballroom. The man now stood there, motionless, with his hand outstretched toward the woman, who'd somehow dropped from the ceiling and stood beside him. The audience exploded in applause over the trick. Elegantly posed around them were men and women in dark clothes with exotic masks, gelled-back hair, and makeup that contoured their facial structures, adding an eerie, skeleton-like appearance to the actors.

The man in black and the woman in white performed a pas de deux, their feet gliding across the floor as if it were ice. They slid expertly around the ballroom, wowing the audience with various flips and twists. They moved closer and closer together but never touched. Whenever the man was about to embrace her, she'd slip away. To me, this performance expressed a story of two people who passionately desired each other but could never be together.

The music altered, and the lights came up. The dancers broke away from the floor in elegant pirouettes and flips. They paired up with members of the audience, urging them onto the floor to dance. The dancers would then go back and pull another person onto the floor, pairing them with their previous partner, and so on.

"Dance with me." Death rose beside my chair with his hand outstretched toward me. "We'll get closer to the stage this way, where Devin is seated."

I glanced at his hand. "No."

There was a flicker of emotion in his eyes, which evaporated like smoke. "Why not? Scared?"

Besides the fact that it felt so weird to be dancing with a possessed man, it was also weird to wrap my head around the fact that Death himself was asking me to dance.

"Not at all," I replied. "I'd rather gouge my eyes out with a melon scooper than dance with you."

"You forget our deal," he threatened.

I turned my attention back to the man in black and the woman in white along with the background dancers.

"I can't dance, not like that," I admitted.

"The music is hexed," Death informed me. "Everyone knows the moves without dancing it before. The enactment you just watched is the prelude to Eternal Ballet of the Seraph. It's presented every few years on the eve of Halloween for Lucifer's entertainment. Last couple standing is the most receptive to the magic of the hex." He motioned impatiently for me to take his hand. "Where's that competitive side of yours? Last time I checked, you were a *Disco Rebel* pro."

My mind betrayed me as it jumped back to the carnival when David Star and I had competed against one another. That was the first night in a while I'd let my hair down.

I reached for his hand.

VI

In one swift motion, Death drew me to him. The air fizzled, currents of rippling energy crackling against my bare skin like static electricity. A popular, mellow electronic R&B song blared around us. It was as if we'd entered another world, burst through an invisible fishbowl in the ballroom, and were now at a club instead of at a fancy party. Couples around us were pressed against one another, grinding sensually.

"Not what you expected?" Death asked as a feral grin spread across Ace's face.

"I thought this would be a ballroom dance."

"It is. The hex has to settle in, become acquainted with you." Death closed the space between us with one smooth stride and seized my waist. I froze. Heat splayed through me as his fingers spread down the small of my back. "Relax," he whispered at my ear, guiding my hips into a sway. "Play with me. Let go."

"I shouldn't be doing this with you."

"That's what makes it fun." His breath was a hot caress against my ear as his fingers smoothed over the exposed skin of my back. Where I was quivering and unsure, he was steady, confident. The air around us vibrated, and the sensual beat of the music pulsed through my body, leaving a heavy lust in its wake.

With lowered eyelids, I moved rhythmically in place. Death pulled back slightly and watched with the warlock's violet eyes.

"And now, feel free to gather around for the Eternal Ballet of the Seraph," Devin Star announced. Death watched Devin like a hawk as he descended the stairs and headed to the dance floor.

"He's joining the performance," Death said.

Which would make it much more difficult for us to speak to him.

The music shifted to classical, and we shifted with it. My movements gradually slowed, as did my rampant hormones, but the hex remained, pulsing in my veins like liquid fire. Everyone in the middle of the floor maneuvered into a formation.

While Death was distracted, trying to spot Devin again on the floor, I homed in on a man who wore a silver mask that covered most of his face. He stood like a statue at the far end of the ballroom, hidden amongst other guests who were trying to get a better view of the spectacle. When he caught my gaze, he stared back for a prolonged length of time, then turned, melting into the crowd.

What the hell?

Applause drew my attention elsewhere. There was an upheaval of praise from the seated guests as couples twirled around the dance floor with elegance and grace. Women were occasionally flung into the air and hung there by tendrils of colored light, as if abandoned by gravity. My jaw went slack.

"Don't tell me you're afraid of being tossed two feet into the air?" Death taunted, his fingers grazing the back of my tulle skirt as he guided us into formation.

"If my feet lift so much as one inch off the ground . . . "

His smile was slight and close-lipped. "It wouldn't be so bad with me. I've had wings for hundreds of years."

I snorted. "Why make dramatic exits into black mist if you have wings? Trying to one-up Dracula?"

"I manifest when I'm not traveling long distances. Like I've said, an angel's wings are considered an intimate part of their body. I choose to conceal mine."

"How come? Because they're the size of buffalo wings?"

He grunted something vile under his breath.

"My wings are scaled to fit the rest of me," he hissed.

"You seem defensive. You know what they say about the size of a guy's wings."

Like a taunted animal unleashed from its cage, Death snatched my left hand with his right and yanked me closer by the small of my back with his left. Captured.

"Careful, cupcake," he rasped at my ear. "Once I have my corpse back, I can make you eat your words."

For a second, I was rendered speechless by the sinful thrill his threat brought me. My knees jiggled as I placed a stiff hand on his shoulder. In heels, I was nearly level with Ace's six-foot height. Staring into the warlock's violet eyes, I imagined what this moment would have been like if Death were in his own body. His broad shoulders, the strength of his hands, the loom of his menacing height. This was a bad idea. A very, very bad idea. Now I had a lot more nerves and a lot more uncertainty about putting myself through this night.

"Devin," Death said, indicating he'd found him in the crowd with a nod of his chin. "He's right ahead of us." As we neared the back of Devin's flawless tuxedo, I investigated his blond partner. Her body type and facial structure were nearly identical to my aunt's. However, it wasn't her.

"We have to briefly break out of the hex to get to them," Death said. "Hold on tight." I held on to him for dear life as he yanked us against the force of the hex. The air whipped painfully against my skin, as if we were going against the ocean tide. We flowed back into the dance beside Devin and his partner.

Devin's sapphire gaze slid to us in puzzlement.

"Hey, Grandpa," Death greeted with phony cheerfulness. "It's your favorite"—we spun—"Fallen angel," he finished. "Thanks for answering your damn phone." We spun again. "I lost my body in a corn maze two hours from here. I had to possess Ace to get to you."

Devin's eyes widened. They clung to Death, even as he twirled with his date. *"Death?"* The muscles in his face constricted with anger. "How?"

"Malphas used black magic to trap my soul in Limbo. All the Light Angels that he's killed? They were sacrifices. To bring back Ahrimad. It worked, and now Ahrimad has my *scythe*. He could very well show up tonight to crash the party."

"You're joking," Devin snarled. "He has your scythe? Your *scythe*—?"

"Where the hell is my aunt?" I demanded, seizing the moment.

"This is Faith, by the way," Death said, nodding to me. "She's under an illusion and knows about the whole Lucifer thing."

Devin Star kept his icy stare drilled into Death's. "You're weak. How long can you stay in this body?"

"Not long."

Devin's expression darkened to a calm fury. "Stay in the hex until I return, or you'll screw up the dance and draw attention to yourselves. I'll send Fallen to find your corpse and begin evacuating guests immediately."

"Nothing can go wrong now," quipped Death dryly.

Famous last words.

We shifted away from Lucifer, sliding across the dance floor in rhythm with the music, and that's when the nausea hit me. It scaled up my throat in a foreboding purge as powerful emotions hit me full force. *Rage. Revenge. Kill them all.* My knees gave out, and I scarcely avoided vomiting. Had Death not held me up, I would have collapsed.

"What's wrong?" Death demanded, our bodies still forcibly moving to the hex. "What's happening?"

"I don't know," I panted out, gaining back strength. "We have to stop. We have to stop right now."

Death's face scrunched up in a fleeting wave of pain. "*Can't*," he growled. "I don't have enough energy left to remove us from the hex. We have to wait until the end of the song." He winced again, nostrils flaring.

"Is Ace kicking you out?"

"That's the main issue, yes." He twirled me roughly around and pulled our bodies closer as the dance continued. "We might have another problem on our hands." His breathing was labored now. "Ever since I left my body in Limbo, I've been able to feel my corpse. A weak but distant connection. That connection just got a *lot* stronger. My corpse is closer."

"Devin's Fallen recovered it already?"

He shook his head once, eyes unfocused. "No, no, this feels strange. You're right. Something is wrong."

A chill shot down my spine. "Are you telling me that your corpse has moved? By *itself*?"

"Not by itself. Someone else would have to control it." He dipped me, mimicking the remaining couples around us. Frustration tightened his features as he picked me back up. "I'm essentially a brain-dead corpse without my soul. Theoretically, for a brief amount of time, while my soul is traveling between Earth and Limbo, someone could summon my corpse and take control of it. Like a puppet."

"What?" I half-screamed. "You knew this could happen, and you're just telling me now?"

"It was the worst-case scenario."

Horror struck me at a sudden realization. Maybe Malphas or Ahrimad had control over Death's corpse. In this room full of people.

"Our illusions," Death panted. "I can't . . . hold them much longer." All at once, his eyes rolled back into his head, and the hex rippled around us, forcing us to continue moving. My hands shot out. I grabbed the warlock's frame and held on with all my strength, fighting against the current of magic spiraling around us as Death fought to hold on to his host. He was losing this battle. Blood trickled from Ace's nose as he suffered a wild seizure.

"Death! Death, you have to hold on! Don't leave me, you idiot!" I grabbed him and shook him hard. "Ace, if you can hear me, let Death stay a little longer! Ace, please! *Please!*"

Ace's violet eyes flipped down, and Death's soul remained.

"Get Devin," he gasped out. "*Now.* He'll protect you."

He was leaning heavily on me. We were forced to keep moving in the dance, and I felt a prickling sensation on my neck. I rapidly scanned our surroundings, the hex digging into my back like sharp knives as I fought against it.

The room blurred, spinning, like I was briefly viewing the world from a carousel, until I locked onto two glowing amber eyes rimmed by black charcoal. Black markings scored his neck, and he wore a draped cloak. Death's cloak. My blood ran cold.

Ahrimad.

Watching us. Watching this disaster from the outer ring of the dance floor. And smiling. *He can see through our illusions.*

The chandelier flickered above us.

A blast of energy tore us apart, and I was swept away in the disorienting energy of this vicious, evil dance.

A pair of large, powerful hands caught me from behind and steadied me. Something sharp on the pointer finger prodded at my skin.

With my back to my new partner, we rocked to the beat. Practically hyperventilating at this point, I tried to find Ace's body, but once more, he was nowhere to be seen. I was possessed by the music again. Trapped.

With all my might, I hurled myself out of the rhythm, but my partner seized my body from behind again and pulled me back into the sway. The music shifted in intensity, and so did we. The song decelerated as my partner spun me into a dip.

The music had stopped. A woman released a shrill, hair-raising scream.

The dance floor was upside down as I remained arched back, held in an elegant pose. I felt the heat of my partner's lips brush the exposed skin of my cleavage, and reality slammed into focus.

"What the fu—!" Jerking into awareness that I'd been held under a trance, I lifted my head to my chest to view my partner and froze. The man with the silver mask. His eyes were down, fixed on my collarbone, and he inhaled. Faded lines of intricate tattoos snaked up his neck and curved up the sides of his face, just like Ahrimad's. Stubble carved his sharp jaw. Two lip rings pierced his bottom lip.

It can't be . . .

The hair lifted on the nape of my neck. Slowly, as if frozen in time, I turned my head to the side. Past guests exiting the ballroom in a frenzied panic, I saw Devin Star. He was spread out inelegantly on a wrecked table, as if his entire body had been hurled into it. He released a frightening growl and rolled onto his side, clutching at the torn fabric of his shirt, his red tuxedo stained with black liquid. His blood. Three deep lacerations disfigured the side of his face. Bronze skin stitched itself together and transformed to unnatural reddish gray serpent scales, revealing the devilish creature beneath.

Nearby stood Ace, bracing his hands on another table to keep himself upright. Beads of crimson fell from his nose, while his left arm, violently marred by claw marks as well, dripped blood onto the floor. His expression was vicious and Death-like as his wild gaze tore across the ballroom and locked onto mine. Pure dread ripped across his pale features.

My heart jackhammered. The creature that had me in its clutches released a deep, throaty growl.

I knew that growl all too well.

Death's corpse.

"Oh, great."

VII

Being held by the corpse of the Grim Reaper, which was currently controlled by an external force, was certainly not the most relaxing experience of my life.

But hey, at least he wasn't trying to eat me.

As I struggled to stay still, the corpse's tongue flicked out to trace my lips. Warmth spread through my body. Christ on a cracker, I was getting turned on by a corpse. But how could I not? What I could see around the silver mask was utter perfection. Michelangelo himself might have carved that angular jaw, shadowed with dark, delicious stubble. His lips were full and kissable. *This is not him. This is wrong and sick on* so *many levels.*

I tore my gaze away, trembling as the corpse straightened to his full height with me tucked in his arms. Around us was utter chaos as guests scrambled to leave the ballroom.

"Stun the humans and dump them in the lobby!" Devin Star ordered seven men in tuxedos. Death's reapers. Their eyes glowed with power as they were given the command. "*Nobody* leaves this building!"

Devin stormed toward me, halting when Death's corpse grabbed me firmly by the nape of my neck with his taloned hand. The humanlike appearance of the corpse's face wavered like a hologram as his jaw unhinged, revealing a mouthful of fangs that extended like daggers. Terror paralyzed me, and the corpse unleashed a bestial howl of warning. The monstrous sound echoed around the ballroom like thunder and rattled the massive chandelier overhead.

I was so screwed.

Up close, the corpse's eyes were too alien and terrifying to be real. The eyes that had haunted my dreams and stained all those canvases I'd painted rapidly dilated as the corpse turned his head down to look at me.

"Hey," I whispered, my voice trembling. "It's cupcake. Remember me?" His pupils swelled as I spoke. He inclined his head. "Of course you don't. It's not *you* you. But you gotta have some instinct in there that we know each other, right? You don't want to hurt me. We're friends. Kinda. Let's not get into the nitty-gritty . . . "

The corpse released a low, menacing growl that made me audibly gulp like a cartoon.

"Faith!" Ace's voice snapped my attention to the violet-eyed warlock, who was still presumably possessed by Death. He stood beside Devin in a wide stance like he was prepared to attack. "I'm going to distract . . . well, *myself*. Soon as you get the chance, you run like hell."

The corpse leaned in to inhale my throat. When I leaned away, I felt those claws dig unhappily into my spine. "Are you *sure* this is a good idea?" I squeaked.

"You're going to get her head ripped off!" Devin exclaimed.

"You got a better idea, old man?" Death snarled.

Judging by the sickly color of Ace's skin and the gleam of sweat over his brow, Death didn't have much time until he was expelled from the warlock's body. He had to get back in his corpse. Fast.

Fate had other plans, as a ring of blue fire sprang from the ground. It startled Death's corpse into releasing me. The fiery blaze circled around Death, his corpse, and me until we were imprisoned, leaving Lucifer and the chaos around us muffled by the crackling flames.

Two dark figures emerged from the fire like gods summoned from the depths of the Underworld. I rushed backward into Death and grasped the warlock's arm.

One of the figures was Malphas. The other was less corporeal, waning in the light like a mirage against the fiendish flames . . .

"Ahrimad," Death said.

Ahrimad narrowed in on the warlock and lingered. "Alexandru." An unnerving smile revealed the sharp ends of his teeth. "You look so . . . unlike yourself."

"Same to you, Casper," Death sneered.

A vein in Ahrimad's forehead bulged. He shifted his face slightly to Malphas, and the raven demigod's complexion changed. Suddenly, Malphas snatched Death's corpse by the back of the head, bringing it to stand by his side. Despite the corpse's imposing size and monstrous strength, Malphas controlled it with ease, like a giant puppet.

Ahrimad's amber eyes fixed on mine, sharp and intense, predatorial. "Is this fragile little thing the mortal he spared, Malphas?"

"Yes," Malphas replied.

"What do you want?" Death ground out.

"What do I *want*?" Ahrimad turned away from me to Death, laughing under his breath. "I want *that which belongs to me*. I want to reign once more as the mortals' greatest fear and turn them into the hogs they are meant to be. I want to be corporeal, and I want a body.

I shall never again have the one you took from me, only this illusion of the vessel you destroyed. Nevertheless, this will all be rectified once you hand over the *Book of the Dead*."

Death curled his hands into fists. "Looks like you're barking up the wrong tree. Lucifer doesn't have the book either."

Ahrimad's amber eyes flared to life, frightening and intense. He turned his head to Malphas. "*Malphas*. Find me the truth in his mind."

The raven demigod's complexion shifted to an otherworldly monster. He took a step away from Death's empty corpse, dark veins spreading outward from his soulless eyes like a disease as he focused on his son. Death kept his head forward; his jaw set as he stared down his father in what appeared to be a silent battle. A small, vicious smirk lifted the corner of Malphas's mouth, and suddenly, Death dropped to his knees with a scream, clutching at his skull as though to keep it together. It didn't stop there. Malphas continued to unleash his power on Death's host in the most casual, unrelenting manner, all while Ahrimad cackled like a madman in the background. It was too much to bear, too much to watch. I clutched at my chest, frozen in a helpless panic, knowing that if I didn't intervene, Death's soul would leave Ace's body.

I fumbled for the hidden dagger in the skirts of my dress and curled my fingers around the hilt.

"*Leave him alone!*" The words tore out of me, and I lurched into action. I lifted my arm and threw the dagger with all my might. The knife released from my palm toward Malphas with a burst of light. At the last second, he veered out of the way, and my eyes widened as the knife hit Ahrimad instead. The light and the blade slashed into his semi-transparent face. Bile rose in my throat at the missing portion of Ahrimad's jaw. He glared at me as the blue fire surrounding us transformed to black, consumed by hissing shadow.

"What *was* that?" he demanded. Death's scythe suddenly appeared at Ahrimad's side, imprisoned in his white-knuckled grasp. The second Ahrimad touched the blade, his wound healed and he solidified, a dark halo outlining his silhouette. "You *dare* attack me?"

Scythe in hand, Ahrimad started toward me, and I imagined that massive blade could cut me in half with ease. Having no idea what I was doing and little time to react, I curled my fingers in tight and punched toward Ahrimad. Energy vibrated down my arm and exploded outward like a lightning bolt, nearly knocking me off my feet. Missing by a mile, the light carried into the dark shadow wall behind Ahrimad and burned a hole straight through.

"You missed," Ahrimad mocked.

But it wasn't over. The hole I'd formed in the wall broadened, outlined by a vibrant ring of my strange light, which burned like an eternal blaze even as the darkness tried to consume it.

Dark and light, like oil and water.

Ahrimad slowly turned away from the strange phenomenon to look at me, and an eerie feeling of being exposed crawled over my skin. I felt him seek something deeper—seek *my soul*—as he peered into me.

A small, serpentine grin lifted his lips. "Interesting."

A force slammed into the wall of shadows from the other side, exploding like a bomb.

Malphas, who now had Death and his corpse kneeling submissively on the ground before him, barked out, "Forget about the girl! The portal is closing!"

The portal? What portal?

"This is not the end," Ahrimad said to Death. "May tonight serve as a reminder: the Devil cannot hide in his tower any longer. This is just a taste of the chaos that is to come. The grimoire will be mine."

Ahrimad lifted the scythe, and the staff blazed a brilliant blue, electricity firing from the top of the blade. The energy rocketed into the mirrored ceiling of the ballroom, causing one of the mirrors to ripple like silvery water. Ahrimad dematerialized into black smoke and shot up into the ceiling. He was gone. But Malphas lingered behind.

Death's father remained at the center of the ballroom floor, using his son's empty corpse as a shield. The corpse foamed at the mouth like a rabid animal, its mismatched eyes rolling back into its head.

"*Fight me*, you coward!" Death exclaimed, his voice raw as he staggered to his feet. He moved with jerky, mechanical strides, as if Ace's legs were no longer fully cooperating with him.

Over the corpse's shoulder, Malphas's features visibly strained, his lips twitching. I had the strangest thought that he'd stayed behind because he'd wanted to say something to Death, but he *couldn't*.

Malphas shoved the corpse forward and exploded into a thousand ravens. They spiraled high and vanished through the mirror still rippling in the ceiling above us.

And that's when it all went down the crap chute.

The corpse stumbled between me and Devin and Death. It unleashed a bloodcurdling howl as it *grew*, joints popping, bones snapping. Clothes tore, its height and width expanding just like it had in the alleyway when Death had fought off Malphas's demons. Except now I could see the transformation, the man becoming the monster, well over seven feet of muscle and rage. Ink blotched the corpse's tan skin in patches, spreading across the body like wildfire until it was night itself. Features sharpened, too sinister to be human. Shadows fired from his broad back, unfurling in wicked tendrils and briefly outlining the exoskeleton of two enormous, invisible wings.

Then the corpse roared, the deafening sound unlike any apex predator in my wildest imagination.

All I could do was gape in disbelief.

Another creature suddenly crashed into the corpse, tackling it to the ground. The red, scaly being rippled with lean muscle, a barbed tail with an arrow point slashing the air behind him. Lucifer. He crawled onto all fours before standing, a forked tongue flicking out of his mouth.

"Get her out of here!" Lucifer thundered, his voice monstrous and otherworldly. "We need the girl alive!"

"I'm not leaving until I'm back in my corpse!" Death snarled, gripping his wound as Ace's body bled.

Fire exploded from Lucifer's hands as he charged to attack Death's corpse first, and I managed to snap out of it enough to get out of the way. Death's corpse launched into the air to avoid him, plumes of smoke momentarily outlining his phantom wings again as they swept forward. One flap and they cut through the ground like it was made of papier-mâché, the sheer force hurling wind through the ballroom like a hurricane. I held on to one of the guest tables for dear life, but when the corpse lowered to the ground, I imagined those lethal wings sliced back like a pendulum of doom.

I felt a sharp pain in my side and screamed. My hands released the table, and I was tossed back, only to land in waiting arms.

"Cue girlish swooning," Death said dryly.

I fought to catch my breath. "Nice catch. Now get your hand off my ass."

"Get your ass off my hand." Death set me down—and not very gently, might I add—as I nearly toppled over. But I realized it wasn't him that had affected my balance as a wet warmth drew my attention down to my torso, where a massive gash tore into my side. Shock had numbed the sensation until now, and blood poured from the wound.

"*Shit*," Death hissed.

I could see *bone* and bit down on my lip not to scream. The raw pain of the injury was like a branding iron. I must have almost fainted, because time seemed to skip forward a few seconds, and now Death was holding me upright. My eyes were glued to the deep gash as the most miraculous thing happened: my skin began to heal. The gash was closing inch by inch, and the pain was dissipating . . .

I looked up at Death with wide eyes. "Was that you?"

"No."

"Oh, okay. Cool. Awesome. Because that would have made me feel *better*." The room spun. "Welp, good luck getting your body back. I'm going to go pass out now—"

"I don't think so." Death hauled me up into a standing position again. "Go out there and distract my corpse so I can sneak up on it and get back inside."

"*What?* Have you *seen* your corpse right now?" I said frantically. "The fangs? The talons? That famished, unrelenting need in its freaky eyes to tear my flesh apart?"

"That's just my resting face, cupcake."

"You need me? Then we're at an impasse. I want a guarantee that when you're back in your body, Aunt Sarah and I get to go home safe."

"The only impasse between us," Death said as we watched his corpse slam Lucifer into the marble floor, "was me five seconds ago considering tossing you in front of my corpse and forcing a distraction." Then he pinned me hard to the pillar and loomed over me, Ace's once kind features transforming into Death's fearsome wrath. "Be a good girl and do as I say," he said, "or the first thing I'm going to snack on when I'm back in my body is your mommy and daddy. Got it?"

It wasn't like I had any choice other than to help the jerk.

"Now here's what you're going to—" Death started, but I was already shoving past him and heading into the war zone. "Or you can just go out there and wing it!" he growled after me.

I stood in the centre of the ballroom floor and planted my feet.

Ahead, Lucifer was taking a beating from the corpse, but every laceration the beast tore into his scaly red skin appeared to be healing rapidly. Things quickly took a turn to for the worse as Lucifer noticed me. His eyes widened. "What are you doing, Faith? Get back!"

The corpse bit down on Lucifer's shoulder and tore, tendons ripping from muscle, and he howled in pain. The corpse tossed Hell's king away like a discarded Frisbee and then its attention twisted to me. And it *charged*.

As the monstrous creature closed the gap between us, something built inside of me. Growing, raging, about to burst at the seams. My fingers tingled with warmth. All my emotions, everything I felt in that moment, flooded to the surface and threatened to overflow.

In my peripheral vision, Death snapped into action and began to run at me to push me out of the way. He wouldn't get to me fast enough as his corpse lunged toward me with talons outstretched.

"Stop!" A burst of blinding white energy shot from my hands and smashed into the corpse. When I opened my eyes, the seven-foot monster hovered over me. His claws hung in the air like frozen knives at my throat, and he was stuck in a bent position.

When I glanced over at Death, his eyes were so wide they might've popped out of the warlock's head. "Whatever the hell you're doing, keep it up!"

I kept my glowing hands raised, somehow maintaining the blinding white light.

Death tossed Ace's walking staff to the side and inhaled deeply, chanting in a foreign language as he exhaled. The massive chandelier in the ballroom flickered, and my vision started to blotch around the sides.

Exhaustion crept into my bones, and my biceps shook. The light radiating from my fingertips dimmed as I struggled to hold on.

The warlock collapsed to his knees, gasping for air and writhing on the floor. Blood poured from his nose and the corners of his mouth. His arms, fingers, and legs bent as his body seized until a dark substance began to ooze from his nose and mouth.

The black matter tore across the air and smashed right into Death's paralyzed corpse. The corpse animated again and fell back, hitting the ground as a dead weight. Death's body shifted with harsh crunches, shrinking down until he resembled a human man. He lay motionless on his back, naked, drenched in sweat, skin as pale as snow. Lacerations marred his chest and his leg, black, oily blood seeping from the wounds. I thought the worst.

Death shot upward, and I screamed. He hadn't done it with sharp inhale like I'd seen in movies. No, he wasn't breathing at all. His pupils were expanded over his irises, and his fangs poked out from his parted lips. He was back.

A hand landed on my shoulder, and the hair at the back of my neck prickled.

"You're coming with me," Lucifer said.

VIII

If being trapped in the clutches of Death's unpredictable corpse was the most terrifying moment of my life, then riding in an elevator with Lucifer, even in his Devin Star form, was a close second.

The burly personnel on either side of me, paired with Devin's unnerving silence, shrunk the already claustrophobic box from hell. As we scaled higher and higher, the temperature climbed with us, until sweat poured down my spine.

The elevator doors opened, and I all but threw myself out into a pristine marble entryway. We walked a short distance through a set of glass doors into a waiting room.

"Where's my aunt?" I demanded in a burst of bravery.

"Here, safe, at the tower," Devin responded.

"And I'm just supposed to believe that?"

"You may see her shortly and confirm it yourself. First, you and I need to have a chat."

One of Devin's men shoved open a door into a private waiting room, crossed the room, and held open another door for us. Glancing back at the second bodyguard blocking my way out, I didn't have much of a choice but to walk into the Devil's office.

The room was luxuriously decorated with red walls and sleek, modern furniture. Lucifer had expensive, sophisticated taste, and he made a point of showing it off. Ambiguous, extravagant art, displayed like trophies along the walls, depicted dark themes that unnerved rather than welcomed.

Devin stepped up onto the raised platform holding his desk and filled a glass with amber liquor.

"I need to know what happened to Death," I said, feeling so small looking up at him like this. Maybe that was the point. "We left him at the ball, and he—"

"I'll handle it." Devin downed his drink and poured another. "Grant me a short while to deal with the mess downstairs." He flicked away a charred piece of his shirt from his shoulder with an aggravated grumble and stepped down from the raised platform. "Do you need medical care?"

I absently touched my side, where Death's wing had cut through me. *Well, I did.* "Um, no. I'm good . . . "

Devin's glacier-blue eyes flicked to the blood staining the satin of my dress, but he didn't press further. He strode to a wall and touched a panel, opening a door that led to a walk-in closet, then disappeared inside.

"Here." Devin returned wearing a fresh dress shirt and handed me a stack of clothes. "Some leftover sample apparel. A medium should fit you, and you can use my shower in the bathroom."

"Can you at least tell me if Death's going to be all right?" I asked.

"He'll recover," Devin said, buttoning his cuffs. "I'll be right back." Pinning me with a firm, terrifying look that read "don't try anything stupid," Devin turned and vanished in a surge of flames.

That's one heck of an exit. One of Devin's bodyguards stood by the door, and I imagined the second was still in the waiting room. Sighing, I headed for the bathroom.

This was the last place in the world I felt safe taking a shower, but I had to get out of this gown. Reaching back, I felt for the dress's zipper, but I couldn't find one. I thought I'd be imprisoned in the damn thing forever when the fabric magically disintegrated, melting off my skin into a fine mist. The mist thickened into the shadow it had been fashioned from, and the darkness launched itself across the tiled floor and slithered into an AC vent.

"Okay, then," I said, looking down at my bra and panties. At least Death's shadow dress had decided to self-destruct while I was in the privacy of a bathroom.

I checked my body for any sustained injuries. Inspecting the bare skin on my side confirmed that the wound had in fact completely healed on its own.

Awesome. And scary.

Using a damp towel, I quickly scrubbed the blood from my not-wound and changed into a set of navy-blue D&S Tower sweats. The entire concept of the Devil and Death selling merchandise to their brainwashed mortal fanbase was beyond screwed up.

When I exited the bathroom, Devin's office was empty, except for a security guard watching a scene from *Yellowstone* on his phone.

A headache throbbed around my eyes, and I rubbed at my temples with my fingers. Crossing the office, I did some light snooping to find some water. A sleek, dark wooden wraparound bar displayed various bottles of liquor against the windowless side of the office. Maneuvering behind it, I popped open a red mini fridge and squatted down, my mouth dropping open when I discovered six ice-cold bottles of root beer. My favorite.

I have something in common with the Devil.

"Grab me one too?"

I nearly leapt out of my skin. Devin was leaning against the opposite side of the bar.

"Um, sure," I muttered, gathering two bottles.

Rising to my feet, I set the root beer on the bar and slid it toward him. He gripped the bottle and cracked it open with his teeth in one fast, slightly disturbing motion, and then walked away.

I followed Lucifer the Almighty to a long glass meeting table.

"Please, have a seat, Faith."

He indicated the spot across from him.

I slid into the cold, cold chair, my teeth chattering from adrenaline. Unscrewing my root beer, I took a large gulp and paused. Devin had brought his own root beer to his mouth at the same time, and our eyes connected. He set his bottle down with a clink and flipped the cap like a coin.

"I won't beat around the bush," he began. "Your life was spared when you were a child because of a deal. A deal that guaranteed us possession of your soul once it fully matured."

"The deal between *me* and *Death*."

"I'm sorry?"

"That 'deal' was between me and Death," I said firmly. "How is he? Did you see him downstairs?"

"No, I'm afraid I didn't. I'm sure he's collecting now. In the small window of time that Death lost his scythe and was unable to consume mortal souls from Limbo, he surely paid for it dearly. Now he's weaker. It wouldn't be safe for you to be around him right now."

"But I'm safe with you?"

"I'll admit, I made a mistake," Devin replied, which was the last thing I'd expected him to say. "I should never have passed the baton to Death. Things would have gone much more smoothly if I hadn't. You see, Faith, some men take more than two thousand years to mature. I apologize deeply for the pain he has caused you. It is clear to me now that he was never up to the task of . . . "

"Winning my favor by taking advantage of my innocence?" I offered.

Devin sat back in his chair, mystified and a little amused. "I was going to say *befriending* you."

I steepled my hands together on the table. "I know what you're trying to do here, Dev. Get on my good side. Butter me up. Here's the thing, though. I see what you are now. Under all your pretty lies is a monster who's only out for himself. Everything Death did to me, you let happen. Heck, you *orchestrated* it and made him do your dirty work. You're no better than him, so don't act like I'm better off with you. You tricked me, lied to me, kidnapped my aunt. At least Death had the restraint not to bang one of my family members against her will."

Devin's amusement vanished. He stood up abruptly, knocking back his chair with a clatter. "*I beg your pardon*, young lady?" His face seared red, scales leaking through his human illusion as heat leapt across the table. I leaned back almost out of instinct to avoid getting caught in the blaze.

"Is that what Sarah told you?" Devin asked in a deadly whisper. "That I *raped* her?"

"She didn't have to." I could hear the unevenness in my voice. "Death insinuated you two had something going on, and I know her. She'd never sleep with the Devil. Not willingly. Which means you manipulated her emotions."

Just like Death manipulated mine.

"For your information, young lady," he snarled, "you couldn't be more wrong about me. I've had every opportunity to ruin Sarah's life and her reputation in the Guild, and I haven't once acted on it. We were never supposed to—"

Devin's lips snapped shut, like he'd revealed too much. He lifted a hand and wiped it down his face, erasing any trace of his real identity in a frightening instant.

"Your aunt is here due to her own decisions," he said with finality.

"She's here because you want the *Book of the Dead* and you think she'll get it for you." I pushed on with my own assumption. "But why now? If you knew that my aunt had it all along, why not just take it from her? What's stopping you?"

"This is neither the time nor the place to discuss the grimoire, or your aunt. This is about your soul, and that's all."

Dang. I could see where Death got his refusal to give me answers from.

Devin lowered back into his seat and calmly adjusted his cuff links. "I cannot force this contract on you," he said. "You were not of legal age when you struck that deal with Death, and technically, according to recent amendments to Seraph law in the United States, you have to be a willing, legal adult to give your soul to Hell. All I ask is that you consider your options before you leave this tower. *All* your options."

"Why do you want my soul so badly?"

"I won't lie to you, Faith, I believe your power to be of great use to me." Devin motioned his hand toward the table between us, where a thick stack of papers appeared on top of it. The parchment was oddly thick and off-white; upon a closer, disturbing inspection, I wasn't so sure it was even made of paper. "If you sign with me, no harm shall ever come to you or your family from Ahrimad or Malphas. You have my word. It was never my intention to let this spiral out of control."

"Yeah, because all of Death's deception and scheming is *so* beneath you," I said sarcastically.

"Despite the unfortunate events of tonight, only I have the

resources to truly protect your loved ones from danger," Devin replied, all business. "The second you walk out of D&S Tower, you, your family, and your friends will all be left unprotected. Think of your power too. Running away from your destiny will not change who you are. Who you're meant to be."

I felt so vulnerable, so alone in this, and so scared out of my mind. And yeah, a part of me wanted to give in to end all this. But I couldn't trust these *fiends*—these damnable monsters and their evil façades of Devin and David Star. I had almost been the perfect prey. Death had used David Star to toy with my inexperience with men, and when I fell for him, he'd used my emotions against me. All the things that *really* mattered to me—my family, Marcy, art, and school—had all faded into the background, until it was only him. Him, circling around me like a lion that had separated a gazelle from the pack.

He'd almost finished me off too.

Death had tried to weaken me. He'd tried to tear me from my ordinary life, and he'd *failed*. He'd failed, and now I had the upper hand. I had all the power. Power that I would lose if I gave my life to them.

When I looked up, Devin's glacier eyes fell to the table between us. He already knew my answer.

"Who I'm meant to be won't be decided by anyone but me. My answer is no."

"I'm disappointed, but I of course respect your decision." The Devil stood, the contract vanishing in a plume of smoke. "Good luck to you, Faith Williams. Should you change your mind, you know where to reach me. Leo will escort you to an armored vehicle outside and drive you home."

"Leo?"

"That would be me."

I jumped and clutched at my chest with a shriek, looking at the man now standing directly to my right. Burnt gold eyes, slightly slanted in shape, flashed briefly with silent amusement, the only indication of emotion in his steely face. I recognized him as one of the reapers that Death had pointed out earlier.

When I looked back at Lucifer, he was already gone.

Leo placed a hand on my forearm. "Inhale, please."

I hadn't processed what he'd asked before my world spun. I stumbled forward with a sharp, wheezing breath, vertigo still overcoming my sense of balance as I took in the chaotic lobby of D&S Tower. A group of humans, some of whom I recognized as guests from the ball, were huddled on the sidewalk. Their eyes were glazed over, focused on a man with a pink Mohawk. He had the mortals enraptured, his arms outstretched like a conductor. What was he doing to them? Feeling my gaze, the man turned his head, and I recognized him as another of Death's reapers.

Leo guided me down the sidewalk and opened the door of a black SUV. I peered inside and saw a familiar face.

"Aunt Sarah!"

"Hey, kiddo."

IX

Aunt Sarah sat beside me in the car, her blond hair piled into a messy bun and her bright blue eyes, nearly identical to my mother's, hollow from lack of sleep. Between running from demons, monsters, and demigods and having sleepless nights the past few weeks, I imagined I looked the worse for wear too.

When the SUV rolled forward, we didn't talk at first.

"You lied to me," I said. "My whole life, you lied to me."

"I know." She took a deep breath. "I've been lying to my sister too, but it's what I've had to do."

"That's not a good enough answer."

"It's the only answer I've got, Faith," she said. "I wish it wasn't, but it is, and I hate myself for it more than you know. But the Guild has rules. Rules that I swore to follow. One of them is that no outsiders are allowed in. The fewer people who know, the better. The safer."

"Yeah, because I've been kept real safe. Great job."

"That is *not* fair," Aunt Sarah said, emotion thickening her voice. "I wanted to tell you, give you a chance to join the Guild, but I also wanted you to live a normal life. When I found out David Star had taken an interest in you, I informed the Guild, and they told me to stay out of it until they had more answers. Like I said, rules. But I was so worried about you that I had to get involved to find out why Death was pursuing you. Then the hayride and the corn maze happened. Everything just went to shit. I had no idea what had happened to you, Faith. That Death—that he'd *spared* your soul."

"What about Devin Star? How am I supposed to trust you when you had a relationship with *the Devil* himself?"

"It wasn't a relationship, it was—" She cast a look at Leo in the driver's seat and lowered her voice. "It was a mistake, and we can't talk about it here."

"Oh my God," I groaned, pushing my hair away from my face. "I'm going to have the spawn of Satan as my little cousin."

"*Faith,*" she warned.

"What does Devin even want from you?"

"All you can know is he's keeping me at D&S Tower. Indefinitely."

As my mind raced with dark assumptions as to what that could entail, Aunt Sarah patted my hand to bring me back to the present. "I'm proud of you, you know that? I don't know another eighteen-year-old who could go through what you have and then reject Lucifer on top of it."

I forced a sheepish smile. "You're the one who taught me to stick to my guns."

And I couldn't tell if Lucifer had respected that or if it had pissed him off. Honestly, I was surprised that he had let me go, and I couldn't shake the disturbing feeling that he had only let me go because he felt confident I'd come crawling back.

"On your mother's side," Aunt Sarah began, "your

great-great-great-*exponentially great*-grandfather was an original member of the Guild. Your mother has no idea that I'm a hunter, or anything about our family history in *that* sense, and she never will. The Guild runs by a code. We recruit only descendants of Guild members. One child per family. Once that child is eighteen, they're educated in our ways and the ways of the supernatural. Our family has yet to skip a generation."

"Are you planning on having a child?"

"I was. With Michael."

My heart sank. Michael was Aunt Sarah's ex-husband, whom she'd married in her mid-twenties. Aunt Sarah swallowed hard and looked down at her lap. "Michael and I tried for four years with no luck, and then he got sick . . . Then I was confirmed infertile, and everything fell apart. The Guild has never pressured me to have a child, but it is considered an honor to pass down the knowledge of the Guild from one member to another."

"This whole Guild thing sounds like a twisted cult."

"It's not," Aunt Sarah said with a shake of her head. "We keep things within the family of hunters to protect our own."

I followed her gaze out the window and watched the world race by us in a blur. Keeping secrets to protect her own. That was something I could definitely relate to. "It must be hard. Keeping this secret life from my mom."

"You have no idea. Lisa and I have always been so close."

I pointed toward Leo in the driver's seat in front of me. So far, he hadn't said a single word. "You know this guy?"

Aunt Sarah shifted in her seat. "He's a reaper."

"I know that, but is he like Death?"

"No, not like Death. Not exactly." Aunt Sarah seemed uneasy. "He's one of the Seven, basically the embodiments of the Seven Deadly Sins. Their origin is unclear, but the Guild believes they were damned souls that were created by Death and Lucifer centuries ago to alleviate Death's Seven Deadly Sins curse."

"The Seven Deadly Sins curse. That's the one Heaven gave him that forces him to distribute souls to Heaven and Hell, right?"

"That's part of it," Aunt Sarah said. "The other part is that Death experiences the actual Seven Deadly Sins. Pride, avarice, envy, gluttony, sloth, wrath . . . "

"And lust," I added quietly, the memory of Death pressing me up against my bedroom wall replaying in my brain.

"From what I've gathered, the Seven Deadly Sins is an incapacitating curse, meant to hinder his free will and make him more compliant. In case he decided to go off the rails and kill everything in sight."

I only eat the parts of a mortal's soul I'm supposed to have, Death had told me. *Unless, of course, a poor soul meets me on a bad day . . .*

I shivered in my seat, wrapping my sweatshirt tightly around me.

"We don't know exactly what Death did to deserve such a harsh penalty," Aunt Sarah continued. "All we know is he aided in Lucifer's rebellion by freeing him from Heaven's realm. Both of those evil fucks were cast down together and turned into Fallen. Death suffers from the sins, and Lucifer can't walk the mortal realm for long lengths of time."

"That explains why Death does all of Lucifer's dirty work," I said.

"The Seven all have a connection to Death, a shared power for collecting souls in the mortal realm. They determine whether the soul goes to Heaven or Hell. But they don't eat parts of the soul like he does. They don't need mortal energy to survive and motivate them to get the job done. They just follow Death's orders, I think."

Leo caught my eye in the rearview mirror and then made a left turn.

"Do you feel like you made the right choice today?" Aunt Sarah asked.

It was the last thing I'd expected her to ask. "Why would you say that? Of course, I do."

"I want you to have a normal life, and I never, ever wanted you to enter this world." She took a deep breath. "I feel like I've led you astray."

Emotion tightened my throat. "At the end of the day, I made my own decision."

If that screws with fate, then so be it. If I risk losing who I'm supposed to be, then so be it.

By the time we entered Pleasant Valley, I was unbelievably tired. As soon as we arrived at my house, I popped open my door and got out.

Aunt Sarah had stayed in her seat, and an awful sensation churned my stomach.

"You're staying with him," I said.

"I could only come with you if I promised to come back."

I felt like I would be sick.

"You have one minute to say your goodbyes," Leo interjected.

"*Goodbye?* What do you mean, goodbye?" I leaned back into the car, clutching my aunt's hand. "I'll see you again, won't I?"

"I called your mom earlier," Aunt Sarah said softly, "and she thinks you went to D&S Tower for the Halloween ball and are staying the night at my place, since I'm closer to the city. I'm supposed to drive you to school, so you're going to have to come up with something clever if she wakes up before you do."

"You didn't answer my question!" I was on the verge of tears now, my throat closing. "When will I see you again—?"

Aunt Sarah just gripped my hand tighter, her eyes glistening. "I need to follow Lucifer's orders and stay at the tower. Be strong,

Faith. I love you." Quickly, she added, "Whatever happens, don't you dare—"

A gust of wind picked up, and I jumped back before the car door slammed shut. Icy tendrils prickled my arms as I turned, glaring accusingly into Leo's otherworldly gold eyes.

"Seriously?"

"Have a good night, Ms. Williams," Leo said.

My chest felt heavy as I watched the car drive away.

Walking on autopilot to my front door, I found the spare house key under a rock in its usual hiding place and quietly unlocked the door. Creeping down the hallway to my room, my legs ached with every careful, tiptoed step.

All I wanted to do was dive onto my bed and fall asleep forever, but if my parents knew I'd gotten home this late, they'd think Aunt Sarah had lied to them and ground me for an eternity. Which meant I had to be a little ridiculous and hide until they left for work.

Taking one of my smaller decorative pillows and the blanket off my ottoman, I went into my walk-in closet and made the worst excuse for a bed with a heavy quilt and a pillow on my wooden floor.

Life could have been worse.

I could have sold my soul to Satan.

X

DEATH

I lifted my cheek from the cold marble floor and took in the lifeless mortals strewn all around me.

The last thing I remembered was my soul returning to my corpse at the Halloween event. I'd woken just in time to catch Lucifer whisking Faith away. Hunger had torn at my insides like talons, and what happened next was . . . a blur.

Now satiated, I was covered in human blood. I'd obviously blacked out and had a feast.

Oops.

I staggered to my feet, four of Lucifer's Fallen coming into focus as they surrounded me. Their expressions showed various degrees of fear. Judging by their torn uniforms and wounded bodies, they must have tried to restrain me during my frenzy.

I felt humiliated. I'd lost control again, and so quickly after returning to my body. In my position, showing any weakness at all was unacceptable.

"What the hell are you all looking at? Show's over," I snarled at them. My gaze sliced across the disheveled ballroom, past overturned tables and a mess of food on the floor, to where a small group of mortals from the ball were huddled against a wall, glassy-eyed and brainwashed. "Get back to work wiping their memories. We can't risk exposure. And clean this shit up."

The soldiers bowed their heads dutifully.

Bending down to lift the limp wrist of one of the dead humans, I checked the time. Only about fifteen minutes had passed since I'd returned to my corpse and Lucifer had taken the girl. He was probably talking to her about the contract right now, and the fact that I wasn't involved infuriated me.

My unexpected snack gave me the clarity to focus on another urgent issue: I was naked.

Storming from the ballroom and into the lobby of the tower, I headed toward our D&S merchandise store. Glass shattered and alarms blared as I crashed through the front door to steal an XL pair of "I <3 David Star" sweatpants. *Ugh.*

I thought about where Lucifer might have taken Faith. The logical answer was Devin's office, but there was a ripple of magic blocking off the elevators to get there. Wards had been triggered to protect the core of Hell. I shouldered open an emergency exit to get outside and concealed myself with my shadows. Sprinting down the middle of the street between cars, I leapt off the ground, wings unfurling from my back as I took flight and scaled the immense height of the tower with hard downward strokes.

I let the wind carry me down to the roof and landed on bare feet.

Pacing back and forth, I counted each minute that passed in my head. Lucifer and Faith would be done with their meeting soon. Him taking control of the matter of Faith's soul was his way of punishing me, and if I showed any annoyance about it, or barged in on them, it would suggest that I actually liked the girl. It pissed me off that he'd undermined me. I was the one who'd spared Faith's life. *I'd* drafted the contract for her soul. Those big fat tears that would slide down her precious face as she gave away her soul belonged to *me*.

Heat whipped at my back as Lucifer manifested on the roof behind me.

I waited for him to gloat.

Instead, he was silent, and I cocked my head to one side.

"She said no?"

"She said no," Lucifer confirmed in a grim tone. "She refused to sign."

There was a sharp pain in my chest that shocked me to my core. I stared out into the city. "Then she's dead. It's over."

"Oh, she's very much alive," Lucifer said, and tension released from my shoulders. "She refused to sign . . . *anything*."

A smirk curved my lips. He hadn't given her the form to legally deny us. I turned to face him. "Then you still have time. Heaven isn't aware yet that we're behind on expiry dates of mortal souls. Hers may be overlooked for at least a few days."

"I won't be doing anything," Lucifer said. "*You* will finish this."

"What?"

Lucifer trod closer. "You got us into this mess, so you will get us out. Faith isn't just scared of us; she's scared of your father. Good thing your strongest illusions are of people you've killed. It's why you're so damn good at being David Star."

Asshole. Pressure built in my jaw from clenching it. "You want me to stage an attack as Malphas to traumatize her."

He nodded once. "Break her. Completely."

"I don't have my scythe, and I'm underfed. I'll need at least a week."

"Four days. No longer."

Goddamn it. Weakened and without my scythe, four days was impossible.

"Consider it done," I said.

"Excellent," Lucifer said with a slice of his grin. "While you're at it, you really should focus on recovering your scythe. You're looking frail. That just won't do for my second-in-command, now, will it?" He strode past me, clapping me hard on the arm as he went, and my fangs gnashed together.

He'd dislocated my shoulder.

"Four days, Alex," Lucifer repeated. Then he vanished into a surge of flames.

More than anything, I needed my scythe back. That conversation had been Lucifer's vindictive way of telling me he had no intention of helping me get it.

I grasped my injured arm and maneuvered it, popping my shoulder back into place. "Motherfu—" My vision momentarily went black, and I wheezed in a breath that my corpse didn't require. The pain subsided eventually, leaving me with an irrepressible rage and the urge to reap more blood.

My palms lifted and beckoned the night. Darkness consumed the roof in an instant, clinging to my torso and forming a new cloak. Dragging on a new pair of leather gloves, I sent a message to my reapers to meet me at the warehouse in thirty minutes.

Meanwhile, I had time to kill.

Shadows poured over my shoulders and launched at my target, clinging to his mortal frame and burrowing in like parasites. They rapidly ate away at his skin as he screamed and writhed against my hold in terror.

The beast inside me purred at the gruesome sight. *Delicious.*

More shadow wrapped around my gloved hand as I punched forward and plunged my fist inside his chest. I latched on to his life's essence and tore, ripping his soul and scream out clean. The body sagged lifeless against the brick wall, and I inspected the cerulean orb of his spirit hovering in my palm.

The mortal had lived his life practically a saint.

"What a loser."

I crushed his soul to smithereens in my fist and sent him to Hell anyway.

Perhaps that was a little too harsh . . . I laughed darkly at the thought. *Nah. Let them straighten it out down there. I don't have time for this.*

Pain radiated up the sides of my temple, promising another vicious surge of hunger.

Without my scythe as my guide, I had to collect souls the old-fashioned way, something I hadn't done since Lucifer had summoned a wizard to set up my scythe to organize the souls I need to hunt via Wi-Fi. We'd had Wi-Fi decades before the mortal world.

Growling under my breath, I held out my hand, summoning an absurdly outdated scroll. My to-kill list unfurled past my boots and almost flew into a rancid puddle on the sidewalk before I hastily reeled it back in with a curse.

"Ridiculous," I grumbled, uncapping a ballpoint pen with my teeth to manually cross off the mortal's name. "I feel like fucking Santa Claus."

But the dead had to be collected somehow. The time I'd been in Limbo had set me and my reapers back on soul collecting. The only thing keeping the shell of my human body from decomposing was my soul. My corpse had suffered significant malnourishment without me inside it.

I would have plumped back up in a week on my own, but I didn't have time for that. Brooding, I shoved my to-kill list into my cloak and stalked down an apartment alleyway alongside an orange cat. My legs bent as I jumped, propelling myself off a fire escape and scaling the building to the roof with ease.

Soon I was back in the air, rocketing past Manhattan. Hurling winds and rain carried me down onto an old industrial warehouse, where I landed with perfect balance on the peak of the iron structure. The old glass windows had been refurbished in places from ongoing renovations, but there was a gaping hole in one of them. I tucked my wings in and dropped through it, landing on an iron beam ten feet below that speared the center of the warehouse in two. I leapt off and flipped as I dove backward, plummeting from the forty-foot drop.

My boots smacked against hard concrete. I shook off the water from my cloak with a sharp tug. "Evening, boys."

Ahead, the Seven Deadly Sins stood in formation like lethal soldiers. They'd formed an aisle so that three stood on one side and three stood on the other. Clad in all-black armored uniforms, their faces concealed by cowls.

"Where's Leo?" I demanded.

"Driving your little girlfriend home." It was Blade, the Sin of Wrath, who delivered the snide remark. Lucifer had told Leo to drive Faith without informing me. He'd undermined my power again, and the message was clear: *Your people are mine to command, and so are you.*

I reined in my anger and composed myself. "We will continue without him."

Striding forward, I prowled down the path the reapers had created. My arms stretched out as I moved, my power lapping out like wisps of dark smoke toward their chests. The pendants they wore around their necks glowed as the mortal essences stored inside absorbed into me.

When I reached the end of the aisle, the euphoria of feeding heightened my senses, and desire flooded my body with a rousing warmth that made me shiver with pleasure. Wildly erotic thoughts suddenly surfaced, involving Faith wearing a sexy angel costume and straddling my lap.

I slammed the fantasy to the grave and whirled around with a growl. Sure enough, the other reapers were feeling this too as they all shifted anxiously on their feet.

"*Romeo,*" I snarled.

Romeo, the Deadly Sin of Lust, grinned from ear to ear. "Apologies, my lord. Seems I overshared." He sliced his tattooed hands through the air, the dark-pink swirls of his power retreating into the gem around his neck.

I shrugged back my shoulders to reset *once again*. "It will come as no surprise to you that my strength has declined after tonight's events," I said, slipping back into my authoritarian role. "I commend you all on your efforts to gather these souls for me. You are all loyal soldiers indeed. Now, someone brave tell me how behind we are on the dead."

"We are currently fifty-four thousand, six hundred souls behind, my lord. According to the new Souls app, at least," Wolf, the Sin of Avarice, replied and held up his phone. "But Glenn noted there was a glitch in the system."

"I bet he did," I grated.

Speaking of those who'd betrayed me. I had a plan for Glenn's guillotine-style execution, but it would have to wait. I had more pressing matters to tend to.

"Our numbers should be the least of your concerns," Blade drawled, his Irish accent thick and his irises glowing a furious red. "Your scythe is gone. What's the plan to retrieve it?"

My own wrath fed off his like a leech, and I could feel the balance of our shared anger shifting more onto me. Damn it, the effects of my curse were already intensifying.

"The scythe will be recovered soon," I said, circling around the reapers as I spoke. "Ahrimad has relocated into one of the Otherworlds. He's in a weaker form, but we anticipate he's building an army."

"With your father?" asked Wolf.

"Yes," I replied tightly. "It appears Malphas is allied with Ahrimad."

"Will you send Lucifer's soldiers after them?" This time it was Gunner, the Sin of Gluttony, who chimed in.

I clasped my hands behind my back. "I will not be sending our own aimlessly into the Otherworlds. We will wait, keep collecting, and fully prepare ourselves for battle. Ahrimad will ultimately return to the mortal realm, and when he does, we will be ready."

"Since when do we take the bitch way out of things?" Blade lashed out. "I'm sure as hell not waiting around while your general father trains an undefeatable army for Ahrimad."

I shut my eyes, desperately trying to keep it together.

But Blade was relentless.

"The longer he doesn't have his scythe, the longer we all suffer," Blade reminded the group. "We *all* should have a say in what happens next." He turned to me. "You working alone got us into this mess in the first place. You let your guard down while trying to screw that little mortal slu—"

His statement never got to its end.

Shadow expelled from my body, firing into his mouth and choking him to his knees with rasping gasps. Prowling forward, I slammed my foot into his torso, shattering his sternum with a sickening crack. He collapsed to the floor and cried out in agony.

"I will remind you all that I am your superior, your *master*." My voice thundered through the cavernous space, and I cut my seething gaze to each reaper. "I will not be disrespected. When I give you an order, you do it. The end. If anyone else has a problem with that, speak the fuck up now."

The reapers all bowed their heads, lowering their gazes. As Lucifer's second-in-command, it was my duty to maintain order and obedience in all subordinates. Especially the Seven, as their success at collecting was imperative to balancing my curse. The reapers were driven by their own individual impulses in connection to my Seven Deadly Sins curse, and failure to control them affected their duty.

Blade was slow to rise to his feet, clutching his chest. His ruby-red eyes were still ignited with power. He lunged to fight me when Denim, the Sin of Pride, simply placed a massive hand on the Irishman's shoulder and kept him back with a firm shove. Towering over the other reapers, Denim was built like a bulldozer. His deep ebony skin was tattooed with markings similar to mine, just like the rest of the reapers. His stoic gray eyes had an orange glint around the pupil.

"It's the curse, my lord," Denim said in an appeasing manner. "We're all starting to feel it. Some worse than others."

Behind him, Blade licked his curled lips. He slowly sheathed his knife and bowed his head in obedience.

His best attempt at an apology yet. I let it go.

Coming forward, I clasped Blade hard on the shoulder. "The Seven are stronger when they're unified," I said, "when they are *balanced*. And when you are all balanced, so am I. Keep your rage under control." I turned to speak to the rest of the Sins. "There are trials and uncertainties ahead, but I promise you this: I will retrieve my scythe and kill everyone who tried to stand in my way."

After the reapers left the warehouse, I lingered behind and walked the premises, my mind sifting through memories as I approached the metal table. Not too long ago, Faith had been strapped there by my shadows while I'd sucked demon venom from her veins to save her life.

I'd tasted her light on my tongue and let her keep it.

In four days' time, it would be mine again.

XI

FAITH

"Argh."

I woke up with a crick in my neck and Skittles mewing outside the door. Easing into a standing position vertebra by vertebra like an old lady, I pried the door open to pick my diva cat up like a baby. Across the room, the digital alarm on my nightstand read: Wednesday, November 1, 10:00 a.m. *Oh my God*. I'd managed to knock out for five hours on the floor without waking up. It crossed my mind that the mysterious power had drained my energy, or maybe I'd just been exhausted from all the stress.

I rubbed out the knot in my neck as I moved across the room. Being the sleep-deprived, messy-haired, puffy-eyed-from-crying zombie that I was, I wanted to face-plant into the bed and sleep for all eternity. As I leaned my knee onto my mattress, something crinkled in my pocket. I slid my hand inside and pulled out a folded piece of paper.

Faith,

There are things I couldn't tell you on the way home.

Before Michael, I met Devin Star. He was beautiful, charming, and I was so naïve that I fell for him, until I found out he had a secret agenda. The Guild protects the balance between good and evil in the mortal realm. Therefore, we are in possession of the Book of the Dead. *Devin crossed paths with me right before my father passed the grimoire to me.*

Faith, I am the protector of the Book of the Dead.

When I started training for this responsibility, I had a moment of clarity. I realized how stupid I was being. I cut ties with Devin and warded him off from my apartment. He never came looking for me again.

There are rules with the Book of the Dead. *Heaven made sure a long time ago that no creature of the night can touch it. Only the protector of the book can pass it down to another, and they don't need to be a blood relative or a Guild member. If you can believe it, the grimoire has been in our family for over a century. When I die, since I don't have a child in the Guild, another member will take on the role of protector.*

This all being said, it is well-known that nobody has been able to read the script in over three hundred years. Until now. I think that Lucifer and Death believe you *can read the grimoire, and we must never let them test this theory.*

Whatever happens, you made the right choice. Above all else, Lucifer cannot get his hands on the spells inside the book. You are everything good, and I am so proud of how strong you are. Now burn this note, kiddo.

Love you,
Aunt Sarah

Hurrying into the kitchen, I found a lighter in the junk drawer and lit the note on fire before dropping it into the sink.

Aunt Sarah knew where the *Book of the Dead* was, and she could hand it off to anyone she wanted to, but Devin Star couldn't touch it or read it because he was Lucifer and a creature of the night. If I really was this chosen person who could read the book, Devin's opportunity to use me had passed, since I'd denied him my soul.

So Devin had to let my aunt go at some point, right?

No, because there was more to the relationship between her and Lucifer. There had to be.

Yeah, no way was I going to school today.

After anxiously cleaning up my room to declutter my space, I unplugged my cell phone from the charging cable and checked my missed messages. Marcy had texted me a bunch of times the night before.

Are you still at the farm???

Hellooooo?

BITCH, HELLO???? R U ALIVE?

I sent off a quick reply.

Me: Sorry, got home safe!! My phone died.

Marcy: Dude, you need to charge your phone! I was so worried about you and Thomas, and everything is just so weird right now. What the hell happened last night at the corn maze?

Me: No clue. I hope Thomas is okay.

Marcy: Me too. His eyes looked so strange. I swear they were like black . . .

Marcy: Do you think it's drugs like his big bro?

Me: IDK. All I know is Thomas is not our problem anymore. We can care without getting involved.

> **Marcy:** Harsh. True tho. Thomas messed with me, and I shouldn't get involved. But I hate how he dumped all that on you about telling his mom he loved her?? WTF was that???

I felt wracked by guilt at the thought of not delivering that message to Thomas's mom yet. Malphas's underling had infected Thomas with his venom, and his body had accepted it. Now he was one of the raven demons. His life was ruined, and it was all my fault.

> **Me:** I just hope he gets the help he needs.
>
> **Marcy:** Me too. Also, WHY AREN'T YOU AT SCHOOL RN?
>
> **Me:** Woke up with a bad stomachache. That time of the month. ☹
>
> **Marcy:** Awww. I feel u. Need me to drop off anything later to help?
>
> **Me:** Nope.
>
> **Marcy:** Ok, love u cutie, get some zzz's & feel better!!!!
>
> **Me:** Love u!

Aching everywhere from the stress of last night, I forced myself to take a hot shower to loosen my muscles and changed into clean pajamas. Face-planting into my bed, I slept another four hours, which left me surprisingly well-rested, but I still felt a little shaky. Despite my lack of appetite lately, I worked down two pieces of toast with butter and strawberry preserves and a big, cold glass of oat milk. Slowly, I started to feel like myself again.

My parents wouldn't get home from work until around six. With only a handful of hours to myself, and with all the reasons to distract my thoughts, I went back to my roots. Pulling out my paint-splattered stool, I sat in front of my canvas and started to paint.

And for the first time in a long time, I found peace.

It was finally Friday, and I'd survived three days since walking out of Hell.

Word of Thomas Gregory's disappearance had spread like wildfire throughout Pleasant Valley High School, the story shifting from person to person like a bad game of telephone.

Thomas had overdosed on drugs, just like his older brother. Thomas had run away. Thomas was dead.

I felt devastated, wracked by anxiety and guilt.

Thank God Marcy was coming over that night for a much-needed sleepover.

The smell of freshly baked muffins wafted into our living room from the kitchen. Mom slaved away in the kitchen baking blondies, Marcy's favorite dessert. Before we had guests over, she always made baked goods like muffins, cookies, or cupcakes. According to her, the scent of baked goods made everyone feel right at home. I couldn't help but think about when David Star had come to my house, and she had just made cupcakes. How David had stopped my softball bat from connecting with his skull. The bat with strawberry icing on it, which he'd licked off with unflinching eye contact. Warmth flooded my body as I replayed the kiss at the end of the night, and how he—

No, no, *no*. Why was I thinking about that maniac?

I pushed all thoughts of *him* aside and tried to focus on the baseball game. One of the Yankees hit a hard line drive. The outfielder on the other team dove for it and missed, and we leapt up from the sofa and cheered.

"What happened?" Mom asked as she walked into the room with a plate of banana-nut muffins. We all took one, and Mom sat on the other side of me with her legs curled in.

"Bases are loaded now. I smell a grand slam!" My dad hurried into the hallway and returned with his jersey inside out.

Mom rolled her eyes. "Here we go again with the game superstitions . . ."

Laughing, I bit into my muffin. "Mmm, wow!"

"Aren't they delish?" She bit into hers. "I used a different recipe this time. Super moist."

"Please, never say that word again."

The Yankees didn't hit that grand slam, but they won the game. Mom and I made two pizzas with pepperoni, mushrooms, peppers, onions, and (gasp) sliced pineapple for Marcy. Skittles jumped on the stool beside me as I washed my hands in the kitchen sink, her tail swishing back and forth. She looked up at me with her big doe eyes, and I discreetly snuck her a piece of pepperoni before Mom saw. She ran away with it like a bandit.

Things felt so normal. For the first time in a long time, I was happy.

"'Sup," I said, taking Marcy's bag as she entered our home a little while later.

"Nuttin'." She bumped my fist with hers. Skittles pranced over to greet her, weaving between her legs.

"Well, howdy, little baby!" Marcy bent down to pick my cat up and held her like an infant. "Oh, that's a little baby . . . "

"She is, in fact, just a little baby," I agreed.

"Hey, Marcy!" Dad called from the living room.

"Hi, Mr. Henry!" Marcy shouted back. She insisted on calling both of my parents by their first names that way. They thought it was hysterical. "Heard the Yankees had an awesome game!"

"That they did, that they did." Dad kissed Marcy on the cheek before plopping back down on the couch. "Did your dad catch it? Or is he out fighting crime as usual?"

"Dad's out fighting crime as usual, but I'm sure he caught snippets of it on the radio. He never misses a game."

"My man," Dad said approvingly.

"Something smells yummy," Marcy said, still holding Skittles as we meandered into the kitchen. "What are you guys cooking in there?"

"Pizza." I beamed. "With added pineapple, since you're a literal sadist."

Marcy adjusted Skittles to one arm to hold out her hand toward me. "Hater energy, begone."

"Hello, my other beautiful girl!" Mom took off her oven mitts and shuffled over to give Marcy a hug. "Hungry? I made pizza, blondies, and banana muffins."

"Oh my gosh, that sounds like so much work!"

"You know I love baking for my girls. How's life? How's your father doing?"

"Same old, same old. We have a big volleyball tournament next weekend, so I'm excited about that."

"That's amazing! Your father must be so proud. Will he be going?"

Marcy's upbeat expression saddened ever so slightly. "Um, I think so, yeah. It doesn't matter, it's an away game. Those can be harder for him with his job. I'm sure he'll show up to a few this season, though."

Skittles wiggled in her arms, breaking the brief tension as Marcy set her down and returned to her bubbly self. "Anyway, how was your trip to Hawaii, Mrs. Lisa? You got tan, lady!"

"The food, the scenery, everything was so beautiful," Mom gushed with a sigh. "I wish we could have stayed there forever." She looped an arm around my shoulders. "We missed our baby girl way too much, though!" She proceeded to theatrically kiss my head until I wiggled away from her with a laugh.

Mom, Marcy, and I talked for a while longer while we all nibbled on pizza. Dad chimed in with his usual funny jokes to try to distract from the fact that he'd snuck into the kitchen to make his ice cream sundae with a blondie *before* dinner. The failed heist ended in my mom smacking him jokingly with her oven mitt as he ran out of the room with the whipped cream. Looked like Skittles wasn't the only bandit in the house.

Mom and Dad always went out of their way to make Marcy feel like part of the family, and I could tell she appreciated it, especially with her mom being gone. Even though we were best friends, Marcy had been busier with her volleyball friends the last two years. It felt like old times again.

"So, I got some more info," Marcy said later once we'd relocated to my bedroom. "About the whole Thomas sitch . . . "

I was eating my third piece of pizza at my vanity and froze. I chewed slower, hoping my face in the reflection in the mirror in front of me didn't give away my inner panic. The last thing I wanted to talk about was Thomas and the corn maze, because then I thought about Malphas, and Death, and his missing scythe, and the *Book of the Dead*, and no—no more!

"Do you remember Tommy's uncle Ben?" Marcy continued, mixing face masks in the little tie-dye ceramic bowl I'd made in art class. "The one we met at his house a *loooong* time ago?

"The guy who collected old-fashioned yo-yos and smelled like cooked mushrooms?"

"Yep."

"Of course, I remember him. He was funny."

"Funny in an odd sort of way. Like you!" Marcy dodged the rubber band that I quickly flung at her like an assassin.

"Apparently, Ben and Thomas's father had a big falling-out. Ben moved out to Colorado, and the Gregorys think Tommy might have been influenced by him or something. Like, to run away. The cops found sketchy messages on his computer between Ben and him. Dad said Thomas was feeling a lot of pressure from his dad about swimming. You know how Mr. Gregory is."

Like I could forget. Mr. Gregory had been an Olympic swimmer before a rotator cuff injury forced him into retirement. Now he was the head swimming coach for Pleasant Valley. It was no secret that Thomas's father berated and pushed his son harder than any of the other kids on the team.

"Did they confirm Thomas is with his uncle Ben?" I asked.

"Not yet." Marcy used a plush blue headband to push her hair back. Then she sat crisscross applesauce on the blow-up mattress and took little squirrel bites of her pizza and her banana muffin like she was savoring it all. "At least there's a lead, though, and it might not be drugs . . . "

"He'll be okay, Mar." I twisted my pizza crust between my fingers, urgently getting away from this topic. "So, how's Nathan?" *Great transition, genius.* "You two an item yet?"

Marcy coughed a little on her pizza. "Oh, Faith, Faith, Faith . . . "

"What?"

"Nathan and I are just hooking up. It's totally not serious."

"Oh?"

"There's nothing wrong with that, you know." She seemed hurt, like she wanted validation from me about it.

"I just think Nathan is good for you. He seems nice."

"And he is. He's nice. But *yawn*, you know?"

"Oh my God. Marcy . . . "

"What? Am I wrong? Plus, I've been thinking about it a lot, and I don't know. Is now the time to be looking for a boyfriend? 'Cause it feels like now's the time to be dating an older drummer in a band. I'm going to be in the city for fashion school next year. Long distance is not the mood or the vibe."

"True, long distance is not the mood-vibe," I agreed.

"See, you get it." Swiping on her phone, she changed the song playing on my Bluetooth speaker through Spotify. "How about you? Apply anywhere else other than SVA?"

Blood rushed to my ears at the mention of one of my top college choices. It was my absolute dream to attend the School of Visual Arts. With all the madness of the past few weeks, I'd completely tabled applying for colleges.

"Did you know pineapple is a zombie fruit?" I blurted.

Marcy swiped a bit of mask on her cheek and paused. "Huh?"

"There's an enzyme in it called bromalin, and it tries to break down the proteins in your mouth. That's why pineapple can burn when you eat it. Zombie fruit."

Marcy narrowed her eyes, raw honey, nutmeg, and milk dripping off the brush in her hand and into the bowl. "Don't tell me you didn't *apply* yet, Ms. A Student?"

"B student."

"*Excusez-moi?*"

"*Vous êtes excusé.* I'm failing chemistry."

"*What?*" Marcy exclaimed. "You, Faith Williams, failing chemistry?"

"I missed the deadline on a big lab assignment." *While I was being chased by venomous demons created by a raven demigod.* "I'm talking to my teacher next week to hand it in late and get some credit. It's fine."

"Holy shit, Faith." Marcy set down the untouched face mask and sat down on the vanity beside my chair. "This is bad, isn't it?"

"I mean, I can get my grade back up . . . "

"No, I mean the *reason* you're failing. We both know I've had my fair share of flunks, but this is *you* we're talking about here. What's going on?"

I chewed on my thumbnail. "Can't a girl just miss an assignment—?"

"Did something else happen with David Star?"

I spun my chair away from her, pretending to look for a hair tie in my drawer. "I said it's fine, Marcy. Drop it."

"Clearly not," she said, crossing her arms. "You haven't failed anything since the third grade."

That result had been a mistake, since the teacher had accidentally graded one number ahead for half of my pop quiz, and she ended up correcting it.

"What's this?" Marcy asked, holding up a folded piece of paper that she'd plucked off the floor. "'Tick-tock'?"

My heart fell into my stomach.

Death's note.

"Oh, that?" I snatched it out of her hand, shredding the paper into little pieces of confetti before dumping it into the trash. "That's just a note to humble myself. Tick-tock, life is short! Ha ha!"

Marcy stared at me like I'd just sprouted Medusa snakes as hair.

"Okayyy, let's look at the facts," Marcy began, flicking out a manicured nail as she counted off. "You, an *A student*, are failing chemistry. You're skipping school, like, all the time now—very unlike you. When you do show up to school, you're tired, day-dreaming, and, frankly, a bit of a sour bitch. More than the usual loveable amount."

"Kiss my ass."

Marcy gave me a pointed look. "You've been doodling those freaky green cat eyes all over the place again," she continued, "and you've just been acting weird. And if none of that is enough proof, you literally just said 'ha ha' out loud like a total weirdo. So, can you be honest with me? What's going on? Is it David?"

I felt frozen in place, emotion tightening my chest.

"Why don't we talk about it, Faith? You'll feel better."

I wasn't one to dump my problems on other people. I tended to keep everything to myself until it all surfaced, until it all exploded. However, all the paranormal happenings in my life were much harder to keep to myself.

I rubbed my hands down my face. "David is part of the problem." *The other part being the ancient villain half of his split personality.* I didn't mention that part. "We, uh, had a big fight . . . recently."

"You never did tell me what happened after he showed up at Manuel's."

"He came to apologize." *And manipulate my gullible butt.*

"Apologize for what? For letting the MF girl of his dreams go? You're funny, smart—nix that current chem grade—and you have the biggest heart of anyone I know. But it's not bigger than that ass."

"Marcy."

"Not to mention, you're gorgeous. Capital G for emphasis. Not in a 'I know I'm hot' or attention-craving way like everyone else who's hot either. In a humble, girl-next-door kind of way. Which makes you even hotter."

I laughed despite the surge of tears blurring my vision. "I'm such an idiot, Marcy. There were so many warnings that we were wrong for each other, but I ignored every one of them. I think I loved him."

"Oh, Faith . . . " Teary-eyed, my best friend pulled me into a bear hug, and all the emotion I'd suppressed the past few days came pouring out. I broke down in tears.

We stayed up late playing card games and doing each other's nails while binging *Buffy* on my TV. Between laughing until we wheezed and talking about all our stressors (minus anything supernatural, obviously), hanging out with my bestie had been the medicine the doctor ordered.

Marcy passed out before I did. I made sure the blanket was fully on her before I crawled into bed and hugged Mr. Wiggles to my chest. The lamp beside my bed was still on. I reached toward it but paused, my fingertips haloed by the light. A small, uneasy sensation shimmied down my spine at the thought of plunging the room into darkness. I slowly pulled my hand away and curled into a tight ball underneath my comforter to sleep.

I was in an abandoned mausoleum.

At least, I was pretty certain I was, based on the gray, crumbling marble and the crypt plates on one wall. My body felt light, numb, detached. Slowly, I looked down at my fingertips, which were haloed by a soft, white light.

A bad feeling prickled the back of my neck.

I was not alone.

When I turned, I faced a floor-to-ceiling mirror. I had no reflection. The glass surface rippled like water, and suddenly, from its depths, a bulge appeared on the surface. I moved backward. A face and body came forth, stretching across the mirror's surface like someone was shoving against a barrier between worlds. The barrier broke as a man emerged.

Ahrimad.

He stepped through the mirror like a door, just like he had in my vision of the willow tree with Alexandru. I remembered how he'd vanished into the mirrored ceiling at the D&S ball too. His amber eyes burned with wrath, but their spite was not directed at me.

He couldn't see me.

I assumed this was in the future, that some time must have passed, because Ahrimad appeared weaker, nearly unrecognizable. He was too pale, too thin, too sickly, like a parasite had drained him from the inside out. His cloak—Death's old cloak—hung off his wiry body, and in a bony hand he clutched Death's enormous scythe.

Another figure emerged from the mirror. *Malphas.* His eyes were like sharp onyx stones as he stalked the perimeter of the room, critically analyzing every inch of it. He sneered at a crack pipe on the floor and kicked it to the side.

"This place is foul," Malphas said, his rough voice grating like sandpaper. "It reeks of mold, and it's filthy. I strongly advise we assemble elsewhere."

Ahrimad strode past Malphas, a disturbingly evil grin stretching across his serrated teeth as he looked around the cold, dead space. "It is perfect. This is where we will house our army."

I gasped awake, jolting upward from the bed. My alarm clock read 7:30 a.m.

It had just been a dream.

Or maybe not.

Deep breathing did very little to calm me. With each exhale, my breath clung to the air like tiny clouds. The room was as frigid as a meat locker. Raking back a strand of damp, sweaty hair from my face, I crawled to the end of my bed and froze.

Marcy's spot on the blow-up mattress was empty.

Jumping off my bed, I jogged into my bathroom. Empty.

Hurrying back into my room, my attention snapped to my bedroom window. It was open, the curtains blowing in an icy breeze. A sliver of sunlight dawned on the horizon and seeped through the evergreen trees in the distance, creating a strange blue tint along our entire front yard. In the middle of the lawn, facing the street, stood Marcy.

My heart slammed into my ribs.

"Marcy?" I leaned out of the window. "Marcy!"

She stayed motionless, unresponsive. A cloud cast a shadow over the yard, darkening our surroundings to a dull gray. When I looked toward the horizon, I realized it wasn't a cloud at all.

Rawk! Rawk! Rawk!

Hurling myself through the window, my bare feet hit wet, dewy grass, and I tried to run. My body didn't seem to get the message. My limbs were heavy, lethargic, like moving through a dream. I stumbled to my knees. The air rippled in the sides of my vision like a mirage, and from behind the old oak tree emerged a dark figure with onyx eyes.

Malphas Cruscellio.

"Get away from her!" The scream tore from my throat like a roar, and heat rushed down my arm. Acting on instinct, I hurled out my hand, light unleashing over my surroundings, but my arm never made the full arc toward Malphas. One of the ravens had darted down from the sky toward my face, and the trajectory of my power sliced into the creature instead. It disintegrated into nothing. Another raven speared toward me, and I stumbled out of the way at the last second.

When I frantically looked up, Malphas was gone.

Marcy was gone too.

Gone.

In the blink of an eye.

XII

Malphas had taken Marcy.

I climbed back through my bedroom window and lunged for my phone in a panicked mess. I started to dial the police, but then I pictured how it would all play out. Who would believe me?

My parents. My parents would believe me.

Every breath came out as a harsh wheeze. I sprinted to my parents' bedroom, only to find their bed empty. Sobbing at this point, I forced myself to keep moving to the kitchen. The breakfast counter had a note on it: *Going to gym and running errands with Dad. We'll get groceries & sandwiches at the deli. Be back by lunch. XOXO.*

They were out. They were safe. But Marcy wasn't. Dizziness shifted my surroundings, dark splotches filling my line of vision like splattered paint. Forcing in a few deep, slow breaths, I hurried back to my room and lunged for my phone again.

"Shit!" I'd deleted David Star's number.

I threw open drawers and nearly toppled my dresser, wildly tossing out clothes. Until I found it. Devin Star's business card.

I dialed the number on the little white card. My hand shook so hard that I almost dropped the phone.

"D&S Enterprises, how can we help you?"

"Devin Star," I rushed out between sobs. "Devin Star, I need Devin now—"

"I'm sorry, Mr. Star is unavailable at the moment—"

"Listen to me, she's going to die!" I shouted. "My friend was taken by Malphas, and he'll—he'll kill her!" Oh God, what had I done? What had I done? "Tell him it's Faith Williams. It's Faith Williams, and this is an emergency!"

The line went dead quiet on the other end, until I heard a muffled conversation.

Then the voice returned.

"It will be handled, Ms. Williams. We'll send someone to escort you to the tower."

"I don't want an escort, I want help! You can't just—"

The line went dead.

I stumbled back, catching myself on my bedpost.

I hastily yanked on a pair of black leggings and an oversized sweatshirt. The worst-case scenario kept replaying over and over in my brain as I sat in the small foyer by our front door. Waiting, rocking in place, clutching my communion cross around my neck and my phone against my stomach as I watched the clock in the living room, counting the minutes ticking by.

Ten minutes. Twenty. Thirty.

The doorbell rang. I scrambled to get up. I gripped the steak knife I'd taken from Mom's chef's block, peered through the sidelight window, and threw open the front door.

A familiar man stood on my porch.

"You're the guy from the car ride," I said. "Leo."

Death's reaper.

He gave my puffy, tear-stained face a passive once-over. "I have orders to take you directly to D&S Tower. Do you need to take anything with you?"

At that point, I was so defeated and broken that I didn't care enough to answer him. Moving forward, I stepped out of the safety of my home and onto the porch, closing my front door behind me. The reaper's golden eyes flicked to the knife in my grasp before he held out his palm.

"You're safe with me, Faith."

I handed over the weapon.

Getting into the passenger seat of his SUV, I wiped my clammy hands on my pants and glanced at the reaper in the driver's spot. "You got a last name, Leo?"

He said nothing. Leo the reaper it was.

Adrenaline caught up with me, and my limbs trembled so hard that my teeth chattered together. Leo pressed down on the gas, and I cast a look over my shoulder through the back windshield. My house got smaller and smaller, and I wondered if I'd ever see my parents or Pleasant Valley again.

"You're very brave."

I blinked, regarding Leo with surprise. His golden eyes had softened with empathy, and he offered a small smile. It wasn't a lot, but it was enough. Enough to keep me together.

When we got into New York City, it started to rain. We didn't hit a single red light, and every car in front of us *magically* got out of our way, which is how we managed to get to the tower in record time.

Leo parked at the curb and tossed another man his keys to park the vehicle.

Standing on the sidewalk in front of the tower, my stomach twisted. *Here we go again.*

I tilted my head up toward the rain. How had I not seen it before I'd met Death? How the infamous tower's matte-black exterior and tinted windows gave it a menacing appeal that practically screamed, *Run away!* Like everyone else, I'd been brainwashed by the Stars.

I tried to stay calm as I rode the elevator up to the top floor, but my legs were shaking so intensely that I had to press my knees together to keep myself upright. Leo walked ahead of me like a soldier with long, assertive strides. The hallway closed in like a tunnel with no way out but toward the monster.

"Faith Williams, my lord," Leo said, and then I was striding into Devin Star's office.

Star's spacious office was dimly lit, and he sat in the throne-like chair behind his desk, facing the windows. The panes weren't tinted like Death's office, but there wasn't much light anyway as the storm raged outside. I could see the tops of Star's shoes resting on a filing cabinet, the rest of him blanketed in shadow. As I waited for him to speak, mute lightning crackled outside, angry fissures breaking apart the sky.

"I know we didn't end things on the best note," I began as I hugged my upper body tightly, "but I need your help—"

Devin lifted a hand to cut me off. Silence blanketed the room. That shadowed hand turned over in a casual manner, two fingers beckoning me closer. I swallowed down the wedge of fear in my throat and stepped forward.

"Groveling," he said. "It's seductive, is it not?"

I stiffened at the deep, cultured, accented voice.

Little prickles of ice shimmied down my spine. *No.*

The chair spun around, and I swear my heart was visibly pounding through my chest. The man sitting on Devin Star's throne sat halfway in the shadows, his face concealed by darkness. Apart from a small, malevolent grin.

"Welcome back to Hell," Death purred. *"Cupcake."*

XIII

Blood pulsed in my ears as Death crinkled a candy wrapper in his hand, drawing my attention to the sharp points of his talons straining against black leather gloves. Broad shoulders and sinewy muscle filled out a lethal leather jacket. Beneath it, he wore a plain black T-shirt. His long, powerful legs were clad in dark jeans with heavy combat boots planted firmly on the ground.

Even dressed casually, he intimidated.

"I know what happened with your friend," Death said, tossing the candy into his mouth. "Leo informed me—"

"I'm not doing this again," I said, keeping my voice as steady as possible. "I'm here for Devin, not you."

Shadows shifted over the upper portion of Death's wicked features, revealing those sharp teeth again in an unfriendly smile. "I'm afraid my *father* took a jet to Japan earlier this morning." A strong sense of déjà vu overcame me. He'd recited nearly the exact same words that "David Star" once had. "Meanwhile, he's put me in charge. Why don't you tell me more about this 'help' you seek?"

"Please, don't do this. Marcy's life has nothing to do with us—"

Death cut me off with a raised hand. "Agreed. Which is why I'm certain Malphas will be lenient with your insignificant friend's life. He was, after all, so *generous* with Thomas Gregory, no?"

I took a step forward, forcing myself to be strong. "Calling on Malphas was a mistake. I have no connection to him. Marcy being kidnapped proves that."

"All it proves is you failed him," Death said, his voice low and cold. "You failed to stab me and paralyze me at the Halloween ball, and Malphas failed at getting the *Book of the Dead* for Ahrimad. Now he's retaliated to weaken your will. The way I see it, this is a lesson learned."

"You can't possibly be this heartless."

The vicious grin that sliced across his face said otherwise.

"Don't do this, Death. Don't let her die because you hate me. She's my best friend. My *sister*."

"You want my help, Faith?" His deep, velvety voice had slipped into a predatory growl. "Then I'm afraid you're going to have to beg. Fall to your knees and get those tears going. I do revel in a mortal's desperate cry."

Pain radiated in my jaw from clenching my teeth. He was using this opportunity to hurt me again, toying with me like I was his plaything. I couldn't hold back.

"Not in a thousand years," I seethed.

"Oh, I've got time, cupcake. I've got forever. But what about your mortal friend?"

Death's gloved hand lifted to his lips. He bit down on a wrapper and slowly slid another candy into his mouth. His veiled glare pierced mine as I battled internally to hide my frustration. There was no reasoning with him, and I couldn't be selfish. Not when it was life or death for Marcy. Denying him was a privilege I didn't have.

For Marcy. With my chin lifted high, I strode forward. My knees hit the ground, the thin material of my leggings allowing no cushion against the cold, unforgiving marble floor.

"Look at me," Death demanded.

The monster before me embodied pure, unfeeling evil. Shaking with mortification, I refused to give him the satisfaction of my defeat.

I slowly tilted my head up to glare at his tattooed throat.

Death's long leg stretched out, the heel of a black, worn-out leather combat boot slamming into the floor like a hammer and startling me as it came down right beside my body. The throne-like desk chair slid against the floor, slowly dragging him closer until the apex of his thighs nearly touched my chest.

"*In the eyes.*"

I lifted my chin. Shadows fell away from his features like tendrils, and I ceased any movement.

Death's true identity drew me in like a predator luring in its prey. He was a monster in an angel's skin. His lighter green eye sported a long, jagged scar that stretched from his eyebrow to his high cheekbone. I imagined something with hooks for nails had ripped into his face and not even immortality could heal it. He kept his hair shaved short on both sides of his skull and longer at the top, his thick midnight mane of loose curls shaped into a messy faux-hawk. Stubble shadowed a masculine jaw, and his nose was strong and Roman. That harsh scar over his eye, paired with a few piercings scattered around his carved features, made him look vicious, like he'd scalp a guy for looking at him sideways. Fit his personality to a T.

His expression held not even a flicker of humanity or emotion. No amusement in his eyes, no arrogant twist to his mouth. Nothing.

A blank slate—an empty canvas daring the interpretation of my brush. The careful intention of this communicated a high level of intelligence, a self-awareness beyond my years of experience, and a terrifying level of control. Control that had saved my life once or twice—if *saved* was even the correct word. Control that could flip on a dime and put the whole world in peril.

Death could be the poison, or he could be the cure. Maybe that was why he was such a beautiful yet frightening sight to behold.

He reached toward me, holding my jaw in place to keep our eyes connected. Another piece of my heart fragmented beneath his touch as he whispered, "Now say please."

A few tears that I'd desperately tried to hold back came forth, despite my best efforts to keep them in. "Please," I said tightly.

His gloved thumb dragged across my wet cheekbone, curiosity mingling with wicked intentions as he studied my face in the palm of his hand. I pictured the inhuman strength behind his touch, how he'd torn Malphas's underlings apart in the alleyway, and the vicious power beneath the thin layer of his glove. He intercepted a droplet as it slid down my cheek, my lips. His mouth tilted up at one side before he aggressively swiped away the tear.

He rubbed the moisture slowly between his thumb and middle finger. Fastening his eyes on mine again, he then dragged his wet thumb over his tongue.

"That will suffice," Death decided. "For now."

Whatever spell he'd had me under shattered as his boots landed on the ground on either side of me. He lifted his enormous frame from the chair, and I had to sit back on my heels to avoid his legs hitting my face. He towered over me like a brutal god.

I crawled backward and hurried to my feet, but standing did very little to close our height difference or ease my anxiety.

"Stop crying," Death said. "It's time for solutions."

He prowled away without warning, heading to the glass meeting table. Hugging my arms, I followed him. Death peeled his leather jacket off and dumped it haphazardly on the table, knocking over a container of pens in the process. I tried and failed to not notice the way his long-sleeved T-shirt clung to his powerful upper body. He plucked a black pen from the mess, uncapped it with his lips, and spit the cap out like a bullet to the floor.

"Sit."

Sit. Like a dog. I lowered into the modern swivel chair opposite him, simmering with rage on the inside.

"Malphas will not kill your friend," Death said, countering what he'd said earlier, to my surprise. His voice had slipped back into that cold, predatory growl, the magnetic pull between us gone. "When he killed all those guardian Light Angels, it was strategic. They were sacrifices to resurrect Ahrimad's soul from the Underworld. What Malphas wants now is power over *you*. He has less of it if Marney—or whatever her name is—dies, because losing leverage over you lessens his chances of getting the *Book of the Dead*. Which is something he cannot afford."

"But why would he take Marcy? I don't have the *Book of the Dead*, and neither do you."

"Yet," the Grim Reaper said. "Your aunt is the current protector of the grimoire; therefore, she knows its location. I suspect that Malphas or Ahrimad have figured out her connection, and that's why Malphas had an interest in you all along."

"That's where Lucifer is right now, isn't it? Prying the location out of my aunt."

Death gave away nothing.

"If he hurts my aunt . . . " I began.

"If I were you, I would worry less about your aunt right now and more about *you*," Death replied. "Sarah may have been in possession of the book, but you're potentially the first mortal in three hundred years who can read it."

Blood pulsed in my ears. Just like Aunt Sarah's letter. I feigned surprise the best that I could. "How do you know that?"

Death leaned back in his chair like he had all the secrets in the world and unwrapped another candy from his pocket. A blue Jolly Rancher. This guy had one serious sweet tooth.

"About nineteen years ago, a powerful clairvoyant came to Lucifer with a vision given to her by the Fates," Death elucidated. "She said a girl—spared by, well, *me*—with a luminous soul would mature into a great power." His mismatched eyes snapped to mine with a sharp intensity. "And with that great power, the Chosen would be able to decipher the *Book of the Dead*."

I couldn't believe it. Death was giving me answers. Answers that I knew were true because Aunt Sarah had confirmed them.

"Lucifer believes you're the one who was prophesized," Death continued. "He's much older and much more powerful than Malphas. Which is why, if you want your friend back, you'll do what he wants and sign over your soul to me. He can get her back unharmed."

Death fired his gloved hand toward the table, shadows dispersing as a pile of documents now lay on the table. A contract. *My contract.* My mouth popped open. "You can't possibly expect me to read all of this."

Death's mouth curved into a fleeting smirk. That was precisely the point.

"What about you?" I asked. "What do you get out of all of this?"

"Irrelevant."

"That's not an answer."

He *winked.* "It's the one you're getting, cupcake."

I shoved the ridiculous mountain of pages across the table to him. "Forget it. I'm not signing this shit until you tell me about your part in this."

"Then you die, along with Mercy."

"*Marcy*, you son of a bitch. *Marcy!*"

"I'm not the one who will have to spell it for her tombstone."

Throwing back my chair, I stormed toward the exit, but Death suddenly manifested in front of me, darkness pooling off his shoulders as he strode forward with his gloved hand clutching the air. "*Sit. Back. Down.*"

With each word, there was a tugging sensation deep within my chest, and my breath came out in shallow gasps. My soul. *He was clutching my soul.*

My eyes widened as the tugging sensation turned into a *shove*. I staggered backward to sit down. He kicked my chair in, and I braced my hands on the table to stop myself from slamming into the glass.

"Where would you go?" Death asked. "*Home?* Yeah, because that really worked out great the first time. Don't be a fool, Faith. You're not in control anymore. Besides . . . " He leaned in over my shoulder to murmur, "*I know something you don't know.*"

Moving into my line of vision from the right, Death grinned and crossed his arms, cotton stretching against muscle.

"Your expiration date was Halloween," he said. "At eleven-fifty-nine p.m."

My heart fell to my stomach like lead.

"The only reason you're still breathing is because I was sent to Limbo," he continued. "All priority deadlines from Hell were automatically extended. So, in case you thought you had an option here, *you don't*. You leave, you die."

Death had said I would drop dead if I reneged on his agreement, but that hadn't happened yet. In all the chaos that had occurred since Halloween, Aunt Sarah had forgotten about that bit too. The only thing keeping me alive was the possibility that I could read the book.

Otherwise, I was a dead girl walking.

"Holy shit," I said.

"There's nothing holy about my shit, sunshine." The words grated through his serrated teeth. Death leaned his gloved hands on the glass table. "You leave, you die. You die, your *friend* dies too. Your choice."

He shoved the contract closer.

My hands grasped the end of the table with a white-knuckled grip. "You said you'd leave room for negotiations. I sign, my family and everyone I love will be protected. And you'll help me get Marcy back."

"No harm will come to your family." He steepled his gloved fingertips together, contemplating. "As for your friend, we have very skilled trackers that I will employ to find her for us. We don't want you caught in any . . . crossfire. It's best I stay by your side for now."

Taking a deep breath, I tucked a flyaway strand of hair behind my ear. "I have one more request. I want you to teach me how to control my . . . um, light . . . thingy." Under his intense and judgmental stare, heat flooded my face. "I don't have a name for it yet, okay? I want to learn how to control my power."

"Do I look like a fucking sensei to you?"

"Next time I'm up against Malphas or Ahrimad, I want to know how to protect myself. Doesn't that benefit both of us?" I left out the fact that not being in control of my power had resulted in Marcy being taken. It's not like he would have given a damn.

"I'll consider it," Death said.

"Did you just 'nes' me?"

He leaned his head to one side, like an animal.

"The noncommittal answer between yes and no," I seethed. "You did. You just nesed me. Bro, this is a contract, you can't just—"

"I'm not your bro." He flicked his fingers, shadow swirling amongst the papers. "I've added in a trust clause. I said I'll consider it. Anything else?"

Another dodge. All right, so it was going to be like that.

"I sign this, I don't want to hear any 'I own your mind, body, and soul' lines from you. You only get my soul out of this, and no other sneaky benefits."

"I'm not catching your meaning."

I knew damn well he understood. "You can't use me for sex, Death."

A vein in his jaw pulsed. "I don't fuck women who don't want me, and I never have."

I don't know why, but I believed him for once.

"Write in the clause," I said firmly.

His laughter had an edge. He made a gesture with his finger, black smoke swirling around the contract as words inserted themselves into the document. Death's expression was passive again, but by his careful, controlled posture, I could tell I'd offended him.

"Guess I found the one despicable thing in this world that's beneath you," I said, adding insult to injury.

Death worked his neck to one side, as if he were trying to keep a vicious comment at bay. He failed. "The second despicable thing would be having *you* beneath me. Besides the unwilling, I don't fuck awkward, geeky virgins."

"And I don't sleep with two-faced zombies." The bitter words flew out before I could stop them.

Death barked out a laugh that startled me, the mere sight of his fangs making my heart palpitate. He stood and rounded the table, his amused chuckle slipping into the low, sinister rumble of a seductive villain. That was when I realized I couldn't move my feet. Looking down, I could see his shadows had latched to my ankles, and my heart hammered into overdrive.

Death's gloved fingers swept over each chair as he passed, beginning a mental countdown as he neared my chair. I kept my eyes focused forward, averted from him to show no fear.

Whistling, he tore out the chair next to me, straddled it backward, and rolled it into me. Every fiber of my being was aware of his presence. The heat of his body, his cologne, even the lingering fruity scent of cherry cigarettes. Death stretched out his long legs so that one leg trapped the back of my chair and the other trapped my legs.

"You know what I think?" he asked. Heat licked up my body as his hand gripped the back of my chair and pinned my braid beneath his hold. "I think," he whispered in my ear, "you're a *bad liar*. I think I'm in your head. You try so hard to fight me. Then the light fades, and it's night. You're alone in bed, all those dark fantasies coming out to play. I'm there, aren't I? I'm there with you, while your sweaty thighs twist and writhe in your sheets."

I kept my attention forward, my posture unflinching despite every part of my soul electrifying as his breath caressed my throat once more.

"I've got you all wound up tight, cupcake . . . "

"I'm sure you have balls of yarn that are more wound up than I am."

Death laughed again in a low, alluring manner. "Balls of yarn don't shout my name over and over again while I pound into them."

I turned toward him. "Which name?"

Death pulled back sharply, and his nostrils flared. "Ha." Reaching into the front pocket of his black jeans, he flipped open a small pocketknife and slapped it onto the table. "Sign. In your blood."

"Excuse me?"

He gave a half-shrug. "It's an evil thing."

"Yeah, no. You're going to have to accept a normal red gel pen—*OW!*"

Death snatched my hand in his strong, gloved fingers and bit down on my pointer finger. Did I mention he had a mouthful of *fangs* instead of normal teeth? When he unclamped his jaw, my poor finger was all disfigured and bloody, and my eyes were wide with disbelief. The shock of the situation took precedence, and bile rose in my throat.

"*Yes*," Death said, red staining his bottom lip, "or *no?*"

"Yes."

Death carried my hand to the contract and let go so that my finger fell onto the paper. A burn went up my thumb into my arm, then to the center of my chest, lingering over the phantom scar over my stomach. I choked out a cry as my lungs tightened and my bones locked into place.

I stood up sharply from my chair, my chest heaving as the blood from my finger soaked into the parchment, forming my signature in a haunting crimson.

Then the contract was gone in a billow of smoke. I hadn't even read it.

"Oh God," I whispered.

"*He* can't save you. I'm your god now." Death spun me around to face him. He lifted my bloodied hand to his face to inspect the wound. When I tried to tug away, he held it firmer.

"Your soul, rightfully mine." He placed two kisses down my wrist, and it shouldn't have been so arousing to feel his lips brush against my skin. "And yet . . . the greed in me craves more."

My mouth popped open as his tongue swept along my cut, his catlike eyes swimming with mischief. He slipped my injured finger between his lips, sucking gently. Desire shifted to fear as he sipped my blood. I tried to pull my hand away from him, but his other gloved fingers clamped down on my forearm in warning. He took two more hard pulls and *moaned*, deep, low in his throat, moving over my skin like a warm, sultry caress. His eyes briefly fluttered back before his mouth lifted.

I snatched my hand back and cracked it across his face. His head turned to the side slightly, as though intentionally, to give me the brief illusion that I could hurt him, and my palm stung. He gave a dark snicker as he slowly swiveled his head toward me again. His face was a sight I would never forget.

"Again," he dared in a velvet-clad purr.

Death's ruthlessly beautiful features sharpened to something *else*. His mismatched green eyes had been consumed by black, just like his father's. They were like mirrors opening into his dark soul, and their reflection was ruthless and sinister and *hungry*. The tattoos crawling up his neck and jaw shifted, slithering like snakes as they spread out across his face until his tan skin began to turn to night.

I stared at the monstrous sight of him in horror, blood dripping from the corner of his mouth. His tongue slid out, and he bit down on it, drawing blood.

"Come here, mortal," he commanded in a husky drawl. Then he snatched me by the back of the neck and slammed his lips against mine in a searing kiss. A branding mark. A fever rolled over me as his sweet blood dripped into my mouth, a soft moan carrying me away into the moment as he parted my lips, his tongue rolling over mine in a slow, ardent caress.

When he stepped into me, his leg speared between mine, pinning my thighs back against the table. Large, gloved hands gripped my hips and lifted me onto the meeting table with ease, and I buried my fingers into his surprisingly soft hair and tugged hard, eliciting a gruff noise from his throat.

When I slipped my touch down the broad expanse of his back, he stiffened.

"Hands to yourself," Death hissed against my lips.

I gasped as his shadows sprung from his body and pinned me flat to the table by the wrists.

"M-m-my lord," a shaky voice announced.

Death tore away from me with a vicious foreign curse. The spell had been broken, but I remained possessed. I took in Death's appearance, his lips and jaw dripping with the blackish-red mix of our blood, before quickly sitting up from the table.

A little man with a clipboard stood in the room with us.

"My apologies for this intrusion," the little man said. "You w-wouldn't answer your phone, and you k-k-k-k-kept kissing—"

"Antichrist," Death growled. "Spit it out, Glenn!"

"It's the warlock, Ace!" Glenn's throat bobbed down a nervous gulp. "He's recovered and sent a message about an urgent matter he needs to discuss with you." His beady eyes darted to mine. "*Both* of you."

XIV

Ace had recovered from Death possessing his body.

I could only imagine what this meeting would entail and how pissed Ace would be. After Glenn had informed Death that the warlock was located at some club called Spades, Death dismissed the little demon with a vicious glare and gripped my bicep.

Shadow consumed us both, and my equilibrium vanished as we dematerialized. When my feet hit the ground, everything spun like a merry-go-round. I held on to Death's arm for dear life, but he shoved me off of him like a stray dog. I hit his black leather couch at a clumsy angle, sucking in large gulps of air as David Star's office came into full focus.

"Seriously?" I sneered.

Death struck a match against the heel of his boot and lit a rolled cigarette. "I forgot to tell you to inhale, didn't I?"

I scowled. "That—that *blood exchange*. What did you do to me?"

"It'll help me track you down easier." He didn't explain further and tilted his head back, exhaling smoke as he strode away. "You'll stay here while I meet with Ace."

"But what *about* Marcy?" I demanded.

Releasing an aggravated breath, he turned around. "What about Marcy?" His tone was mocking and viciously moody.

"Marcy is the whole damn reason I signed your contract. You said you'd find her."

"I never said *I* would. Semantics, cupcake." When I just stood there, shell-shocked and thinking I'd made a huge mistake, he brushed past me. "Relax. I'm sending a few of my subordinates to start looking for her tonight."

Tonight?

"Why not now? She's in danger. Every second we wait, she's in danger. Send your people now!"

"I know what I'm doing, Faith. You don't call the shots." He slammed his palm into a panel on the wall, and a door opened. He disappeared inside, returning with a blood-free face and a black sweatshirt. His shirt rose slightly up as he pulled the garment over his head, and I caught a glimpse of black tattoos snaking up his lower abdomen as he rolled it down.

"Bye." He chucked a pack of open D&S Tower travel tissues in my direction and slunk past me to palm his phone on his desk "Don't touch any of my shit while I'm gone."

Shadows slunk from the corner of the room, crawling over his massive frame as he started to wane away. I launched forward and grabbed his hand before he could. *"Wait!"*

The mist absorbed back into him, and he became fully solid. Death's hooded head tilted down to our linked hands, and a chill slid up my spine. His fingers flexed as he tore from my grasp.

"I'm going to pretend you weren't just holding my goddamn hand, cupcake."

"You can't leave me here alone," I whispered. "Not after what happened. Ace called for both of us."

"We aren't an *us*. You aren't in control of your abilities, and I can't risk another slipup. As hilarious as it would be, you could kill somebody. Then you'd be a blubbering mess, and maybe you'd—whoops—accidentally flash my dick off next."

"I can assure you, that wouldn't be an accident."

The corners of his mouth *almost* turned up. "Ace is at his club. There will be hundreds of people there. I'm in enough shit with Rainbow Hair as it is. I don't need you burning down his place the second you have a little panic attack on top of everything else."

"The only way I'll learn how to control my power is with experience."

His jaw flexed. When he went to turn away from me, I grabbed him again, and he whirled back around to shove his muscular chest in my face. "Touch me again. Watch what happens."

My whole body tingled from head to toe, but I knew he wouldn't hurt me. Not physically, at least. "What if something happens while you're gone? What if Malphas breaks into the tower like he did last time?"

At the mention of his father, Death averted his eyes and snarled out a foreign word. Guess I knew the Grim Reaper's trigger now.

"What if you mess up again," I continued slowly, "and Lucifer finds out?"

His obedience to Lucifer was a weakness that we both knew he had. I could see a vein pulsing in his neck now. My next words had to be the final nail in the coffin.

"Or maybe you can't handle being around me," I said, letting my voice drop to a sultry murmur. "Maybe I make you lose control—"

"*Stop.*" His face snapped toward mine, and I stiffened. He stalked a slow, calculated circle around me, his mouth dipping close to the wild pulse in my neck. "It's a bad idea to taunt me, Faith."

I turned over my shoulder, our lips a breath apart. "Since when has a bad idea stopped me from doing stupid things?"

He arched brow, as if to say, *You have a point. You are the dumbest individual I know.*

And I knew I was wearing him down.

I pouted. "Pwease?"

Growling, Death clutched my wrist in a rough, viselike grip. "You screw up again, it's your ass and my palm."

His shadows consumed us both.

We landed in the alleyway beside the D&S Tower. As I gasped for air against a wall from the lack of oxygen on that manifesting journey, Death yanked on a leather jacket and straddled a black motorcycle. It roared to life, and he shoved a tinted helmet over his head.

At the front of the bike was a symbol. A black stallion. My attention lifted to the other end of the alleyway, where the massive black stallion Death had called had saved us from Malphas's demons. *Cruentas.* That was his name. Upon closer inspection, the symbol on Death's bike had red eyes. *There's no way . . .*

Death revved the engine to a roar, scaring the bejesus out of me.

"Get on, chicken," he said with a gruff snicker.

My mind briefly shifted to the time Marcy and I had been watching *Buffy the Vampire Slayer* and Buffy had gotten on Spike's bike after driving home from a demon bar. I'd told Marcy jokingly that it'd take more than a hot guy to get me on the back of a death trap. Now Buffy's life didn't seem all that different from mine, and motorcycles were the least of my worries.

I took the second tinted black helmet from the Grim Reaper's hand and straddled the bike behind him. He was burning hot beneath his leather jacket, like the flames of Hell lingered beneath his skin. I looped my arms around his waist as he booted the kickstand to tear into the street.

Death drove like a maniac, and I held on for dear life. We weaved between cars and broke so many traffic laws that I gave up counting and squeezed my eyes shut. By the time we reached our destination, I was a sweaty mess, and my thighs were tense from squeezing his legs so hard, but I was alive. Death drove his motorcycle up onto the curb without a care in the world and parked it. Even though it was barely noon, the line to get into Spades stretched out as long as I could see, roped off by red velvet and monitored by intimidating men in suits.

I tore my helmet off. "What kind of private club is open this early? Don't these people work?"

"They are working," Death said, removing his helmet only to tug up the hood of the sweatshirt over his head. "Blood whores. Mortals who offer their necks and bodies for a paycheck."

As I pieced together what that could mean, Death kicked the stand of his motorcycle out and shut off the bike. Leaving it on the curb, he prowled toward the club, forcing me to hurry to keep up. Not even the autumn wind dared to embrace Death as it picked up, tossing my hair around me but leaving him untouched. Looked like Mother Nature had a more complicated relationship with the Grim Reaper than I did.

"Wait a minute, Ace owns a *vampire* club?"

Death stopped hard in his tracks, and I nearly crashed into his chest.

"No socializing," Death said, ticking off his gloved fingers in front of my face. "No drinking or eating, and no *Faithing*. Until we're alone with Ace, your name is Hope. Just Hope. But you shouldn't have to introduce yourself because then you'd be chitchatting and breaking my first rule. Now, what's your name?"

I smiled sarcastically. "Hope."

Death clutched my wrist again—a move I was getting really tired of—and hauled me to the front of the line. He came face to face with the bouncer, who immediately let us enter. The pounding bass and colorful beams of light enveloped me, and my eyes roamed over the intimate private club. The walls were dark-purple with lighter purple accents and a sleek black floor. Lavender curtains revealed the silhouettes of individuals sitting in private booths.

Death stood directly to my left against a shadowy wall. He was so in tune with his surroundings that he'd found the perfect spot to lurk like a predator, just beyond the reach of any lights. As I stared at him, the darkness shadowing his body peeled away and his furious, striking eyes radiated like two mismatched green gems. For once, his wrath wasn't aimed at me but at the bloodsuckers mingling around us.

He slunk further into the club, not bothering to check if I was following. *Asshole*.

I turned back over my shoulder toward the entrance of the club, wishing I had the option to run away.

Luckily, Death was seven feet tall and easy to spot in a crowd. I was moving toward him when someone slammed into me, their drink spilling all over the floor.

"I'm so sorry!" I shouted, then recoiled as the woman hissed at me.

I hurried away from the vampire, but Death was no longer in sight. Thinking it was better to get to high ground, I hurried to the top of a set of spiral stairs, the strong odor of copper hitting my nostrils. Pulling at my sleeve, I felt bile climb up my throat as I realized that what had spilled onto my arm had been *blood*.

And now everyone was looking at me. Wherever I went, I felt the weight of hungry eyes.

This was a horrible idea. A horrible, horrible idea.

It was time to get the hell out of there.

I turned fast to make an exit down the stairs, but I slipped on something wet on the floor, nearly falling on a topless woman making out with a gorgeous man with shoulder-length black hair. The air rippled over the couple, and the attractive man grew paler, then gray, with foul, rotting skin that triggered my gag reflexes. Fangs extended as he ripped into the flesh at the woman's neck.

The vampire's eyes met mine. I couldn't move. His pretty illusion strobed in and out. Beautiful man. Monster. Beautiful man. But I hardly cared, as I was consumed with an indescribable heat. A spell glued my feet to the ground.

The dark-eyed vampire tossed his topless woman to the side and stood, closing the gap between us with a few swaggering strides. One sultry smile and I fell deeper into the trance.

"So beautiful . . . " The vampire lifted my hand to kiss it. "So pure . . . "

"So pure," I murmured.

His nails were long and sharp as glass as he brushed my cheek. "So . . . delectable."

The vampire's mouth parted, long canines extending. He was leaning in close when a large, leather-gloved hand shot out from over my shoulder and enveloped his throat. The vampire's eyes bugged out like one of those eye-popping stress toys.

"So . . . *not happening*," Death hissed and snapped the vampire's neck in one sharp, vicious movement before throwing him over the glass railing to our right. He fell a whole story down onto the dance floor.

I leaned over the railing and stared numbly at the horrified reaction of the crowd below.

Black leather stepped into my line of vision. Death wedged himself between the railing and me, leaving a portion of his sharp, tattooed features exposed to the light.

"No socializing," Death said, ticking off his gloved fingers in front of my face, "no drinking, and no Faithing. You had three rules. Three. You have the attention span of a squirrel on crack, and you . . . *Hello?*"

I sighed. "I want to be ravished by a vampire."

Death let out a monstrous, frustrated noise and leaned down so that his mouth was at my ear. "I'm naked and dripping with sweat."

I was torn from the spell. I blinked up at the Grim Reaper, whose furious cat eyes were glowing and drilling into me. The vampire. The neck breaking. The spell. The swooning. *Oh God.*

"Hell's prince," a voice declared. "In a demon club?"

Death's fangs gnashed together, and he slowly turned around to face a group of beautiful, pale vampires.

"Yes, Hell's prince indeed." A tall vampire with slivery hair and eyes to match stepped into the space the others had cleared. He was the only vampire with color in his irises.

"I'd know those dishonorable markings anywhere," the silver-haired vampire remarked. "Enlighten me, Angel of Death. What is the penalty for attacking a newborn of an affiliate of Lucifer's comity?" When Death said nothing in response, that silver gaze slid to mine. "I am Duncan, by the way. Master of the Crypt clan."

"Nobody asked, Dunkin' Donuts," Death snarled.

"Cheeky," Duncan said dryly, while his focus remained on me. "Goddess, you are a sight for sore eyes."

I looked down at my baggy sweatshirt and leggings. "Um."

"Not the outfit. Your essence, love," the vampire said. "It's luminous."

"I'm blushing," Death said and then clutched my arm to tug me past the vampires. However, they shifted directly into our path.

"Not so fast, Grim," Duncan said. "Where is your pet's mark?" He held Death's simmering stare. "Or is she something to hide?"

Death slung a heavy, leather-clad arm around my shoulders and pulled me into him. If a neon sign hovered over my head, it would have had an arrow pointed toward Death, and it would have read: "HIS."

"She doesn't need a mark," Death said. "She's my girl."

My stomach flipped. As strategic as the gesture might have been, Death was an intoxicating presence, and I had to stop myself from huddling closer.

The master vampire smiled thinly. "*Your girl* isn't my type any-way." His tone betrayed him. If anything, we'd piqued his curiosity. "She's skin and bones."

Death's arm tightened around my shoulders. I felt my fingertips tingle as a surge of sudden energy built inside of me. They must have started to glow, because Death clamped down on my hands with his free glove.

Duncan arched a brow at our joined hands. "He should keep you on a leash, love." He switched his gaze to Death. "He might lose you like he's lost his scythe."

"Let me be clear," Death snarled. "I will respect Lucifer's rules, but you are not above me, and you will never insult what's mine again." In an instant, Death's pupils consumed both of his eyes. "Otherwise, I will tear your fucking head off, you menial parasite. Now get out of our way."

Duncan's bland expression cracked slightly. He took a step back, as did his clan of beautiful creatures. Keeping me on the opposite side of the vampires, Death strode confidently past them.

"What was that about?" I asked.

"That leech is on Lucifer's comity. He represents the rights of his large clan of vampires. The vampire species has been around since the beginning of time, and they're highly respected by Hell. Let's just say they have a lot of connections in the mortal world that Lucifer uses to his advantage, but they're a bunch of entitled, soulless pricks. They chronically abandon their newborns, which leaves a bloody, gory mess for Hell to clean up, and they're constantly demanding special treatment."

"Sounds like a rocky alliance."

"Even rockier now." Once we were away from Duncan's vampires, Death hooked his fingers into front of the sweatshirt and pulled me to a halt like a feline capturing a mouse. In an instant, my body was flush against his. His silver piercings winked under the lights. "I turn my back on you for *one* second."

"It was a *mistake*—"

"You tend to make a lot of those. It is too bad stupidity isn't painful. Perhaps you'd learn your lesson and listen to me for once."

"Maybe you should take some accountability. You left me alone in a vampire club. What did you expect to happen? That I'd make friends, and we'd all sit down around a campfire singing 'Kumbaya'?"

His eyes narrowed to harsh slits. If he wanted me to be his doormat, he would be sorely disappointed.

This incident only further demonstrates your impertinence, I imagined Death would say next. And then he'd read off a recipe he'd created for a clambake, which substituted clams with diced-up pieces of Faith Williams.

Because you're so flawless in every way yourself, right? I'd reply.

I wouldn't say in every way. One of my fangs is slightly longer than the rest. Would you like to see? It's all the way in the back, so you have to lean in real close.

You're insufferable.

"And you only annoy me when you're breathing, cupcake," Death hissed out loud.

My mouth gaped. "You just read my thoughts!" Great, now I needed an ad blocker to keep the Grim Reaper out of my mind.

"No, your thoughts are still difficult to decipher. I can only communicate with you in your head. Very clearly, as of recently." He arched his scarred eyebrow like there was so much more he was capable of now.

I thought back to Death biting my finger when I signed his contract, and then the black blood from his tongue mixing with my own in a sweet concoction in my mouth.

"What did you do to me?"

He winked. "Nothing you didn't deserve."

"Look what the cat dragged in," a voice intervened, and we broke apart.

Trixie. Ace's assistant. The last time I'd seen her had been in Ace's bookshop in Pleasant Valley when she'd pointed a gun at my head. She flaunted a slim brown corset and matching leather pants. I eyed the strap along her waist that held a walkie-talkie and a gun holster, which her right hand rested on.

"Trixie the Pixie," Death said. "It's been a long time."

"Not long enough," she sneered. "You know, despite everything that happened between you, Ace has never spoken ill of you. What you did to him was despicable and vile, even for you."

Death shifted on his feet. I couldn't believe it. *Death*, uncomfortable? If only I had a big tub of popcorn because this was going to be good.

"I see you're still suckling on Ace's staff for his magic," Death noted. "Only a pixie leeching off a warlock can keep that much glamour in place."

Trixie roared in another language, her eyes igniting to white. Then she turned to me. "I remember you. Don't tell me you're sleeping with this parasite, or worse, dating him."

"Do your job and take us to Ace," Death said.

Trixie pivoted on her heel and led us to the back of the club, opening a door for us to walk through before locking it behind us. We followed her down a long hallway, the sultry, pounding music in the club beginning to fade until it disappeared completely.

She parted a deep purple curtain and stepped to the side. "Get in."

Death moved first, and when I came through, a rush of energy in the air tickled my skin as I took in the lavish room. There was an old Victorian-style desk with a purple velvet chair. A folded changing curtain partially hid a few selections of lavish clothing, and one side of the room was dedicated to jarred herbs.

Death slunk away from the chandelier at the center of the room and positioned himself between two old bookshelves, where the light barely touched.

"Bienvenue."

The warlock had appeared from nothing. He stood to the left of the desk and placed a dark mauve bell hat on it, drawing attention to his shoulder-length white hair with various colors at the ends. He wore a Victorian paisley vest with hints of purple in the pattern. It fit tightly around his lean torso. The golden dress shirt beneath had purple accents as well, and it was unbuttoned partway down, offering a peek of smooth, pale skin and various pendants around his neck.

Ace's violet eyes met mine, and he smiled warmly. Leaning on his cane, he limped closer. *"Ma chérie."* He took my hand and kissed it.

Heat climbed to my face. "Um, hi," I said with a flustered laugh.

The warlock's smile only grew. Until, that is, he turned his head toward Death, who had prowled lazily from the darkness like a predator that had gotten bored waiting in the grass.

"Death," Ace clipped.

"Ace." Death returned the same.

"You're underfed," Ace said, lifting his chin. "It's rather careless of you to travel with her when you're weak."

"Weak, not so much. Hungry, always." Death pinched a rolled cigarette between his lips. "Mind if I smoke?"

"Yes."

"Wasn't asking you." Death's voice was a cold knife whenever he spoke to Ace, but when addressing me, it slipped into that velvet purr. "Princess Narc gets her panties in a twist and makes a face whenever I light up."

"I'll twist something on you, all right," I muttered.

Death snickered but tucked the cigarette back into his pocket. "All right, warlock, we're here. What do you want?"

"You and Faith were both in my vision," Ace said, and suddenly he had our full attention. "The most powerful one I've had in a long time. One of the future. One that may determine whether you ever hold your scythe again."

Death was silent as the two beings had some sort of cowboy standoff. Ace's mouth curled into a small, vindictive smile. I was either missing something here or, as my gut told me, this standoff had everything to do with me.

"Well, since he isn't going to say it," I said, gesturing to Death, "the suspense is killing me."

Ace turned his head slowly toward me. "I will tell you the vision, *ma chérie*. For a price. The price is your time for two dates."

An inhuman growl vibrated the room in a frighteningly low pitch.

"Unless, *Death*," Ace added quietly, holding up a paperweight, "you can cross the glare wall in front of my desk and take this from my hand."

Death approached the desk without hesitation and froze. White bolts illuminated the air like spiderwebs and latched on to him like hooks. His muscles stiffened, his jaw locked, and Ace's mouth curved with pride. Eventually, the force released Death, and he relaxed as if nothing had even happened.

"Impressive," Death said, working his neck to one side with a crack. "But I like a little pain."

The Grim Reaper glided forward, striding through the glare wall with a leering grin that communicated it had been a piece of cake, until Ace took out a spray bottle and spritzed it right into his face.

"Motherfu—!" Death moved in a blur and darted to the other side of the glare wall, darkness unveiling from his shoulders until his entire silhouette was hidden. Low, chilling hisses unleashed from the darkness.

"What the hell did you spray him with?" I asked.

"Water," Ace said with a sly smile. *Genius.* "Same way I keep the strays from sneaking into my greenhouse and eating my valerian root. Those darn cat behaviors just sneak up on you sometimes, don't they, Death?"

Death wiped a gloved hand over his wet face and shoved the bookstand behind him, knocking it down with a crash. "I'm going to wring your neck," he snarled.

"One more step and she dies." There was a clicking noise as Trixie aimed her gun at my head.

"Why are you always pointing that thing at *me*?" I shouted.

"Now, now," Ace said, holding up his palm for Trixie to lower her gun. "No need to get violent. Do you both agree to the terms of me telling you the vision or not? Two dates. That's it. Agreed?"

"Agreed," I said.

"Never," Death snarled at the same time.

Death's face snapped in my direction, and he wore the most imperturbable mask. His jaw clenched tight as he turned back to Ace. "Two dates. We're listening."

"As we speak, Ahrimad is forming an army to retrieve the *Book of the Dead*," Ace began. "An army of Forsaken."

"What are Forsaken?" I asked.

"Lost souls," Death said curtly, like the question irritated him. "Wandering, forgotten souls that abandon Limbo and stray into the realms of the Unknown. The magic that binds each realm together mutates their essence and turns them into . . . monsters."

Holy shit.

"I don't know if he's creating new Forsaken or if he's binding the existing ones to his command," Ace continued, "but either way, I know what I saw. In about two weeks' time, when the moon is full and the ripple between our world and others is at its weakest, Ahrimad will open a portal and return to the mortal realm. If you should fail to destroy him, I fear he will unleash this army of Forsaken onto the human realm and irreparably damage the balance between good and evil."

"Ahrimad's soul won't be able to keep together much longer," Death said. "He needs a new vessel. A powerful one. For that, he'll need a forbidden spell."

"Found only in the *Book of the Dead*," Ace said. "Do you have possession of it?"

"No." Death clasped his gloved hands behind his back, his jaw clenching. "We have a lead, though."

"So, we find the book before he does," I said, "draw Ahrimad out with it, take back the scythe, and say screw your solidifying spell. Problemo solved."

"Stop with the *we*," Death grated between clenched fangs. "*You* can't protect yourself. Therefore, there is no *we*."

"All the more reason to teach her," Ace said, lifting a white brow. "I asked both of you here for a reason, Death. Not just because of our deal but because you were both in my vision and together at the portal where Ahrimad will return to the mortal realm. Telling you all of this is a risk, but the consequences of not telling you felt much more damaging."

Death stared hard at Ace as if trying to determine if the warlock was being honest. And what he found made him slam any emotion behind a wall of wrath. "I will take your warning into consideration."

"You do that. Our conversation is over now." Ace's violet gaze flickered with lightheartedness as he angled himself toward me. "I hope the atmosphere in Spades didn't traumatize you too much, *ma chérie?*"

"Besides the frightening creatures and random naked people, it wasn't too bad."

"What did you expect at a demon club?" Death noisily unwrapped a piece of gum. "A cotton candy machine and a fucking ball pit?"

I tucked my tongue into my cheek.

"Do you kiss on the first date, Ace?" I asked with a wink to play along.

"Always."

The temperature in the room plummeted.

The warlock laughed in a soft, amused way. "I will see you on our two dates, *ma chérie*. However, if you would like to see me sooner, please do not hesitate to call on me." Ace made a small gesture with his hand, and a poker card was now wedged between my fingers. On one side of the card was the ace of spades, while the other read *Qui vivra verra*.

"*Qui vivra verra,*" Ace said. "Who shall live shall see. It's my lucky card."

"As handsome as you are sweet . . . " I looked pointedly at Death before stuffing the card in my pocket, but his attention was trained on the exit. Death shot toward the curtain back into the club, and I followed him with the strangest feeling that there was something Ace had left out of his vision.

When we got outside, it was drizzling. Droplets of rain cascaded down my face as I watched Death swing his leg over his motorcycle.

"You should listen to Ace," I told him. "I sense he's telling the truth about the vision."

"Your sense is wrong." Death turned his head toward me, and I could feel his glare beneath the tint of his helmet. "Never trust a man who doesn't like cats."

"And why's that?"

"Dogs listen to their owners' commands. Cats bow down to no one. Draw your own conclusion."

Two men slunk out from the club, and Duncan's silver eyes slid directly to mine. Death revved the engine again, and I got the message. Get on or get left behind.

Buckling my helmet, I straddled the bike behind Death, and he tore into the street. Rain pelted down, but that slowed neither the beast beneath us nor the beast that I held tight in my arms as we sped through the miserable city.

XV

The rain showed no sign of stopping as Death pulled up onto the sidewalk. I got off the bike, soaked, freezing, wretched, and overwhelmed, but that didn't stop me from noticing where we'd stopped.

Billionaire's Row.

We were on Billionaire's Row.

Aka the most expensive real estate in New York City.

Death stood up to take off his helmet, and his motorcycle completely dissolved into black smoke like some epic magic act. The shadowy substance absorbed into his jacket. His helmet vanished too as he yanked up his hood.

"Now wait a second," I said as Death stalked toward me. "You're telling me we were riding a *shadow* that whole—"

Death clamped his giant hand down on my shoulder. I only managed to suck in the tiniest breath before the world went black around us. We emerged elsewhere, and I collapsed against a black door.

"You . . . could at least . . . warn me," I gasped.

Death grunted a word under his breath and punched a passcode into a lock right beside my head. I moved to the side as he opened the door. The dark void of a room opened like the mouth of a monster, and cold tingles raced up and down my legs.

Death's apartment.

I could only imagine what was inside. Swinging blades as you walked in, mortal souls screaming in the walls, a bed with spikes for a mattress, freezers filled with the heads of his enemies, and a blazing fireplace that led into Hell.

"Stop daydreaming and get in," Death growled. "I don't have all day."

Grumpy bastard. I entered the dark space, and the lights slowly came on by themselves.

"Holy moneybags," I blurted.

A gorgeous open-concept penthouse unveiled itself. Death's place was, of course, dominated by black. Black marble flooring, massive black leather couches in front of a flat-screen television, and a black marble fireplace. No Hell entrance, as far as I could tell, though.

Every aspect of his space gave off an intense, overtly masculine energy. Dim lights hung like daggers over a medieval-looking dining table. A high ceiling with a skylight captured the gray sky above. Another floor was visible past a glass railing, accessed by spiraling modern staircases beside the foyer.

"Wow," I said in awe. "This place could house a whole army."

"Welcome home, King D," announced a seductive woman's voice. A touchscreen to my left blinked as she spoke, and I realized it was some sort of high-tech computer the penthouse was hooked into.

I rolled my eyes. "King D."

"Damn right." Death tossed the keys to his motorcycle into a black and gray checkered dish by the door. I shadowed him into a magnificent kitchen. If there was a magazine for villain kitchens, this one would make the cover page. Was that . . . a battle axe hanging over the stove? He yanked open one of the two industrial-sized fridges, pulled out a carton of chocolate milk, and chugged down at least half of it. Dude was a sugar maniac.

"You'll be staying here with me," Death said, wiping his mouth with the back of his gloved hand as he put away the milk and closed the fridge door. "Indefinitely."

Living in a penthouse.

With Death.

Indefinitely.

I took in the stunning apartment again. Didn't seem all that bad, all of a sudden.

"There are four floors." Death yanked a little on the waistband of my leggings to get me to face him, and I jolted in surprise. "We're on the main floor. There are two kitchens, but you will only use this one. Two living rooms, and a media room."

"Why can't I use the other kitchen? Keeping the frozen heads of your enemies in the freezer?"

"What a fantastic idea, cupcake." He gave me a pointed once-over that made me sweat a little before he jabbed a leather-clad finger down a hallway. "Bedrooms. Pick whichever guest room you want, I don't care. Just know that Cruentas has a thing about the ones to the right."

I blinked. "Cruentas, as in, *your horse?*"

"Any door that's locked stays locked," Death continued like I hadn't even spoken. Somebody was running low on his social interaction battery. "All calls coming out of here are screened, and you'll be provided a new cell phone."

I patted my pockets. "Where's my phone?"

"I yoinked it from your pocket an hour ago and crushed it."

"What?"

"RIP." He checked his watch. "As of thirty minutes ago, a few of my subordinates went to your parents' home and changed their memories. They believe you're away at an accelerated program for the arts where you have little reception. When shifting the memories of a mortal, it's best to give them something believable to replace reality. Hence, why we sent you to Dweeb University."

I gave him a flat look. "Will you send those subordinates to find Marcy now too?"

"Didn't I already tell you I would?"

I really wished I could use my power at will, so I could fry his ass.

"TV is loaded with all the boob tube mortal crap. HBO Max, Prime, Netflix. Video games. Password for the fridge and any pantry doors is 666. No, I didn't pick that, and no, I don't have any kids. Cruentas can open doors."

The second mention of his horse had me spinning around as if the giant stallion would come charging out of nowhere.

"If you need me, don't," Death said. "Call Leo instead."

"And how do I call Leo?"

"There's contact information on the touchscreens, located in every room. Use those until I get you the new phone."

Then he just turned and walked away from me.

He started to fade, but I picked up a ceramic vase and chucked it him.

Death turned, his body almost entirely shadow as his hand snatched the vase in midair, and he became corporeal again. "You better have a damn good reason," he snarled.

"Sorry," I said quickly, wetting my dry lips. "Actually, no, I'm *not* sorry. You were about to leave again without giving me any closure, and I'm not going to stand for it." It felt like my skin was slowly simmering underneath that hidden glare of his. "I—I need to have a conversation with you about what happened at Spades."

Death went quiet for a long, dangerous moment. I imagined he was contemplating grating me like a block of cheese in the kitchen.

"You know Ace was telling the truth," I pressed on. "We both were in that vision. If we don't go together, couldn't that affect you getting your scythe?"

Death's jaw tightened. "Since when do you care about my scythe?"

"You seem to be the only one who can face off against Ahrimad and Malphas. I don't want anyone else getting hurt or taken like Marcy."

Death flexed his gloved hands and lowered his head so that his hood shadowed his face like an assassin.

"I really think Ace is trying to help you," I pressed.

"We only gave Ace the time of day today to ensure he stays in line. He could have reported me to the Elders in Heaven and screwed me into another punishment. If he truly wanted to help us, he wouldn't have humiliated you by forcing you on dates with him because he thinks we're fucking."

"He's hurt, and yes, he's clearly feeling vindictive. But can you blame him?"

Death took a step forward. "Let me be perfectly clear," he growled. "I work alone. And if I wanted a sidekick, which I don't, you would be the *last person* in this entire irritating realm that I would choose. You're emotional, stubborn, soft, and . . . *friendly*." He made "friendly" sound like a dirt sandwich between two pieces of wet cardboard. "Not to mention, you have the coordination of a puffin."

"What the hell is a puffin?"

"I'm not your Google."

At approximately two thousand years old, he might as well have been.

"Doubting our own trainer capabilities, are we?" I taunted.

Death closed the distance between us in a few strides, and I gasped as his darkness pinned me to the wall without him touching me. "Maybe you haven't put two and two together, but I'm starving right now. Far too hungry to be ping-ponging with you back and forth like a sitcom. So, unless you have something *else* to offer me . . ." His velvet voice slipped over my skin like warm wax as he flicked his gaze over my body. My face felt hot, and I dropped my gaze to his chest. A low, gruff laugh huffed out of his nostrils. "Yeah, that's what I thought, cupcake."

Then he stalked past me.

"I want to know where we begin," I snapped at his back, hurt wobbling my voice.

Death halted but didn't face me. "You can't begin with someone who ends, Faith."

"Then meet me halfway," I said. "I'm not a child, so don't treat me like one. You brought me into your world. All I'm asking is that you don't leave me defenseless in it."

"Putting you up against Ahrimad and my father is a death sentence." He turned his hooded head slightly over his shoulder. "I need to protect you."

"For your and Lucifer's sake?" I spat. "That's not protecting me, that's—"

"Keeping you in one piece for our own personal gain," he finished. "You're finally catching on. This is the end of the discussion."

But I wasn't done with him, and I sprinted forward to block his path.

"You little—" The rest of the sentence was cut off in another language, one that I'd begun assuming was Latin.

"Train me recreationally," I said, spreading my arms out to appease him. "On a trial basis, and then you can decide if I've made enough progress. We have about two weeks, don't we? What if you gave me one?" When he just scowled down at me, I got the sense that I was wearing him down. "What if I need to protect myself against Ahrimad or Malphas again? You can't just hold me prisoner here and take me out to play with whenever you want. I know you don't want me to hate you."

He leaned into me. "What makes you think I *care* if you hate me?"

My throat felt thick with emotion as I couldn't think of a single reason. "I'm teachable. Give me a chance to prove it to you."

Death straightened and ran his gloved hand over his jaw. "Are you going to make a huge fuss out of this?"

"Yes, yes I am."

Death growled deep in his throat and crossed the room to pick up the vase I had thrown at him. When he came back, he grabbed me roughly by the arm and hauled me over to stand in front of his dining room table. He set the vase on the table and stepped back.

"Break the vase," he grumbled.

"I'm sorry?"

"Break it. With your power."

"Oh," I said. "Right." I lifted my hand, narrowing my eyes at the vase for about twenty seconds. "Can I have a little space here? And maybe some hype?"

"Break the vase, or you're ugly."

His sarcastic sense of humor always surfaced at the strangest times, and I couldn't help but snort. Focusing on the vase again, I strained to make something—anything—happen. The tiniest ache of a headache began around my eyes before I let my arm fall with a frustrated sigh.

"Guess I'm ugly."

Death edged closer, and my heart picked up speed. His belt

buckle brushed my back as he lifted my arm back up to point at the vase. "Relax," he murmured. "Picture your light coming forth at your command. Think: *break*."

Easier said than done when all I could focus on was his grip, the memory of the heat of his body beneath his clothes on his motorcycle, the notes of leather, earthy woods, and smoke in his cologne, and the distinctive scent of *him* tying it together in a bundle of enticement. I felt ashamed by this relentless, undeniable attraction to him. Even after everything he'd done, all the pain he'd caused me, it remained. Not to mention Marcy—

A bullet of power unleashed right into the wall of his penthouse, and I quickly wiped away the tear that had rolled down my cheek.

"Hmm." Death analyzed the tiny hole I'd made in his wall. "Pitiful."

"Pitiful! Look, man, it *came forth*, didn't it? And in only five minutes."

"You *shut your eyes*," Death hissed, "and you shot with a *finger gun*."

I winced. "All right, that is pretty cringe. But it worked, didn't it?"

I couldn't see his face, but I could feel his stare as he returned to his spot behind me. "Try again."

I hid my surprise as I got into position again.

He ended up coaching me for the next fifteen minutes with the same drill. Over and over again, I lifted my hand with the visualization he instructed of firing my light at the vase. And over and over again, nothing happened. It was embarrassing and frustrating, but for some reason, Death hadn't left. No, he just kept pacing. Pacing back and forth like a panther.

"Focus," Death snapped. "You're distracted."

By you.

Death strode into my line of vision and leaned over the dining room table. "Sinning on the mind, cupcake?" He tilted his head, and I could see the sly grin on his mouth. "Maybe your light isn't what you want to explode."

White sparks ignited my fingertips, and I yelped in surprise. Death pushed off the table, his hooded head aimed like a hawk at the light growing in my palm. My gaze flicked to the vase ahead, but I struggled to multitask holding the light and firing it at the same time.

"You're thinking too much," Death said. "Let the power come to you."

The more force I put into it, the more it seemed to want to burn out, but I held on. Sweat dripped down my spine, and my teeth were clenched tight. "I don't . . . have control."

The air shifted, and suddenly Death's breath fanned the back of my neck. "I could always take the lead," he whispered in a low, sultry purr.

"Stop," I seethed. "I'm going to . . . lose it."

"I haven't put it in yet."

"Shut . . . *up!*"

"You're all red and sweaty."

His tongue touched my ear, and I flinched.

"You better cut it out!" I cried in a laughably high-pitched tone.

"Or *what?*" he growled, slipping back into exasperation as if the flirting tactic hadn't gotten the reaction he'd wanted. "Finish the threat and show me what you're made of."

"If it's so easy, why don't you do it?" I shouted, pivoting to jab his chest with each word. It felt like I'd jammed my finger into steel. "Sweet peaches in a pie . . . that's a ton of muscle."

Death looked down at his chest. Then he flicked my finger away like it was a piece of lint on his shirt. For a second, I thought he would reach for my neck and wring it for touching him. Instead, he raised his gloved hand and made a small motion. Shadow fired from his fingers into the vase, shattering it into a million pieces.

"My vase!" I hurried to the table, collecting the broken pieces into a sad pile. "I was being hypothetical!"

"Could have been you breaking it if you didn't have the attention span of a goldfish."

I whirled around to find him crossing his arms over his chest in a cocky manner. "Whoop-de-doo, you can break a vase. Can do you do card tricks too?"

Death dangled a pair of underwear from one gloved finger. "I can make your panties disappear."

My mouth went slack as I looked down at my pants. Of course, the pair I'd put on were borderline granny panties. Mortified, I let out an inhuman noise and went to snatch them, but he extended his arm, dangling them over my head. He teased me a few times before tossing them in the air, where they vanished in a puff of smoke. "Oh, darn. Where on earth did they go?"

"You son of a . . . " I shouted. "I ought to fry your stupid hooded face off with my—*my*—!"

"Aw, how adorable. She doesn't have a name for it." Death circled me in a slow, calculated way, and I followed his every move. He stopped and shoved up the sleeve of his sweatshirt to check the time on a high-end watch. "I'll be back in three hours to train you."

I blinked. "I passed your test?"

He held up a gloved finger. "One training session. One more chance to prove me wrong. That's it."

I threw my arms outward, a celebration dance in my wake, when it dawned on me that he was leaving me alone.

"Hold on, where are you going?"

"Take a wild guess, cupcake."

He was going to collect. And some of the souls he feasted on would die differently than they were supposed to. Because that was just the kind of monster he was.

Death leaned into my ear. "I'll think of you when I feed," he whispered.

When I turned back, all that was left of him was a black mist.

XVI

Being in Death's penthouse piqued my curiosity, but I was dog-tired and anxious about being alone. The only way to keep my mind off the uncertainty of Marcy's situation and the insane happenings of my life was to focus on a purpose; otherwise, I knew I'd lose my grip. Getting Death to train me seemed like the perfect distraction.

Walking down a long hallway, I found four open guest rooms and a closed door at the far end. I had a feeling it was Death's bedroom. Slowly, I padded down the hallway and tried the handle. Locked. Not surprising.

I entered the guest bedroom on the right of his. Dark-gray flooring led to a queen-sized bed with light-gray sheets. There was a glass dresser in the corner of the room, a closet that would currently be useless to me, and my own bathroom. Every aspect of the furniture and decor reflected Death's cold, hard nature.

The bathroom was larger than my bedroom back home, with a luxurious rainfall shower and a massive tub. There were a couple of high-end shampoos and conditioners lined up on the edge of the tub. The counter held lotion, hand soap, toothpaste, and a sad, lonely toothbrush.

I showered quickly then looked in the dresser, where I found plain underwear, two bras, two pairs of leggings, and T-shirts. I sat on the edge of the bed and stared at the dull clothes in my lap.

The world began to close in. I'd never feel at home in this dead penthouse. Tomorrow, I wouldn't wake up to the sound of Mom doing dishes and frying bacon at an ungodly hour because that's what the best moms do, or hear the coffee pot sputter to life as Dad made a thermos of coffee with milk for me to take to school. I wouldn't eat tacos at Manuel's every Tuesday with my best friend and gossip with her about all the stupid drama that didn't matter much before, and—*Oh God, Marcy.*

On the edge of losing my identity forever, the only thing that pulled me back from the ledge was hope. Hope that this all wouldn't end as horribly as I was imagining. Hope that I would survive and so would Marcy, that I would win this battle. Giving up meant giving in. It meant saying goodbye forever to everyone I'd left behind.

I pulled on the clothes and lay down on the bed. Mentally exhausted, I figured I'd try to take a short nap, and by some miracle, I dozed off.

I woke up to darkness, except for a thin line of yellow light under the door. How long had I been asleep? Where was I?

The bed shifted. Something lay beside me. Whatever it was, it was too small to be a person and too big to be a cat. I reached out with a tentative hand. My fingers pressed against short, velvety hair. When I flatted my palm against its body, I felt warm muscle twitch against my touch. It snorted, and a wet nose pressed against my arm and nuzzled. *Sniff. Sniff. Sniff.* It licked me with a coarse tongue.

It was just a dog.

A dog?

Wait a minute.

Death had never mentioned anything about a dog.

Two big, fiery red eyes burst through the darkness in front of me.

"Neerggghhhhhffff!"

I shrieked and fell off the bed, my pillow thankfully falling with me and protecting my head from the ground. Rolling over, I crawled rapidly across the floor toward the crack of light under the guest room door, threw it open, and raced into the penthouse.

The front door was locked. I banged on it nonstop.

"Let me out of here! Death! *Death!* Somebody better get me out of here right now!" Rage overtook me, and I tugged on the door handle. "Death, if you don't let me out of here right now, then—so help me, *God*—I will kill you! I will make you deader than you already are! I'll—I'll *double* kill you!"

"Neerggghhhhhffff!"

I spun fast and plastered myself against the wall.

A miniature black stallion appeared out of thin air in the foyer and came galloping toward me. In his mouth was a blue ball, which he dropped at my feet. He looked up at me, tail swishing rapidly back and forth, and I just stared. And stared.

I picked up the ball, and the mini stallion whinnied, stomping his hooves. The creature was about three feet in length. He had a silky black mane that blew back as he raced around me like an excited puppy. Dark markings and fading scars riddled his body. The resemblance he had to Death's demon stallion was alarming, but this tiny stallion couldn't have been the ginormous horse from the alleyway . . .

I fished for his name in my racing mind. "Cruentas?"

The tiny stallion nickered, black eyes glowing red, and a puff of smoke and a bit of fire blew out from his nostrils. I jumped back, startled by the flames.

I threw the ball. The stallion dashed across the room at lightning speed and caught it. Ball in mouth, he trotted back to me with pride.

"This is so freaking weird . . . " I reached out and patted his neck. He whined softly, dropped the ball, and lay on his side so I could scratch his belly. "But you're so *cute*. What a good boy!" I cooed as his tail thumped against the carpet. "Who's a good—?"

He vanished.

"Boy," I finished to empty air.

Two black gym shoes stepped into my line of vision. Tilting my head up, I slowly raised my face to the Angel of Death. He wore a baseball cap that cast the tiniest shadow, shading those glowing green eyes. A devastating smirk sliced across his mouth.

"Let's put you to work, cupcake."

He placed me in the corner of his personal gym, where I alternated between hitting a punching bag, squatting with weights, and doing push-ups and sit-ups. This went on for *hours*, while Death read a book on the opposite side of the room. He didn't give me any instructions, except for a few corrections about the form of my punches. I didn't feel like I was doing anything right, and I'd never worked out that hard in my life. Despite him appearing absorbed in his book, I knew he was testing me. Testing to see if I would give up.

At the end of the training, I couldn't tell if I'd passed or failed his second "trial" of the day. My legs felt like noodles as we climbed the staircase from the gym to the main floor. I had to hold on to the railing like an old lady, still wheezing from Death's merciful command to do a finishing move of twenty burpees.

"We'll regroup at five a.m.," Death boomed from the top of the stairs.

I couldn't hide my excited grin as I raced up the last five steps. "Really?"

He nodded once, albeit reluctantly and with an annoyed grunt.

"Yay!" I performed a little victory dance by tucking my hand behind my head and fanning out my other arm horizontally to mimic the movement of a sprinkler with dub music sounds. *"Mm—mm—mm—mm!"*

Feeling Death's judgmental stare, I swiftly composed myself by smoothing a strand of my sweaty hair back from my face. "I mean, cool," I said with a jazzy snap.

Cringecringecringecringe.

"Five a.m.," Death repeated.

Then he turned sharply and vanished in a black mist.

In the shower, all I could think about was what I could learn. Maybe I'd finally feel in control of my ability and be able to protect myself! I also wondered where Death had gone away to this time. All those thoughts distracted me from thinking about being alone again. I changed into an oversized shirt and underwear and passed out within minutes in my new bed.

A wave of raw heat jolted me into awareness. I was hanging halfway off the mattress. Panicked, I pulled myself up and swatted at my *smoking* black wool socks and locked eyes with the blazing red eyes of the supernatural creature at the foot of my bed.

The culprit.

"Cruentas!" I shouted, shooing away the miniature stallion. He hurdled over the mountain of blankets and stomped playfully toward me. "What are you, my alarm clock?"

Air pushed quickly out of his nostrils in a high-pitched whine. Sounded a lot like laughter. Speaking of alarm clock, the one beside my bed read five-thirty.

"Aw, crap," I muttered, throwing my blanket off.

"You're late," Death said as I raced into the training room. He sat in his usual place in another set of dark gym clothes. "Start running laps."

There was almost no conversation. Once in a while, Death would turn down the hard rock blasting from the gym's built-in speakers and bark out a short order. I bit down on my lip multiple times to keep from cursing at him.

I'd thought he was pissed because I was late that day, but when I arrived earlier at the gym the next day, his mood had only worsened.

The next three days of my life were, to put it lightly, horrible.

The good news was Death always made sure I ate, although his concern (if we even want to call it that) began only when I felt faint during our gym sessions. He'd take me to the refectory in the building, which never had any people in it, at least during the day, and would sit silently across from me with his hood drawn over his face. He wore black aviators there and sometimes in the gym, which I knew was because the lights bothered his eyes. It was also a way to avoid interacting with me.

"Why don't you eat with me?" I asked after swallowing a huge mouthful of mac and cheese. Day four of working out had consisted of upper body, and I swear my fork was shaking in my hand from all the push-ups I'd done. "Candy and chocolate milk isn't the most nutritious diet. Well, I guess you don't *need* mortal food to survive, but you said it helps, right?"

Grouchy remained silent in response. If I didn't know any better, I'd have said he'd fallen into a deep depression because of his scythe.

"What's the update on Marcy?" It was a question I'd asked him every single day, nagging him for an answer.

"They're close. I feel confident they'll recover her soon."

Later, alone in my bedroom, I realized that for that entire day, Death had said only those two sentences to me. The whole not-talking-to-me thing was starting to feel vindictive, and that feeling drove me crazier than the arduous workouts, but I was too stubborn to bring it up at first. Was he seriously still mad at me about his father? What about everything he'd done to me? What the hell was going on in his head? I shouldn't have cared so much, but he was my only point of contact. Stockholm syndrome was looking awfully fashionable these days.

This was probably another one of Death's games, but I wanted him to train me, not play games.

"I quit," I said on the fifth day of doing the same boring, repetitive workout and getting the same evasive answers about Marcy. I wiped sweat from my forehead and marched toward the exit. "This is pointless. And the silent treatment you're giving me? Childish. I'm going to go eat a big, fat chocolate bar at the refectory and then take a twenty-eight-hour bubble bath."

The gym door was locked.

Death bookmarked a page in his book. "You have five hours in here with me every day. No bitching. No whining. And no chocolate." He pushed his aviators down his nose and gave my body a once-over. "You can have a salad after your workout."

My jaw hit the floor. *"A salad?"*

"Yes, a *salad*. It's pointless to work out as long as you do and then eat junk food. Pizza, mac and cheese, donuts. Do you even eat vegetables?"

I stormed over to him. "Are you calling me fat?"

"The only place you're fat is your ass." His voice hit a new deep, raspy low that enticed a dark part of me. He studied my hands, which were in tight fists and unusually hot. If I didn't know any better, I would have said Death was purposely trying to get me angry.

I ripped his stupid book out of his hand and heaved it across the gym with a grunt. Death sat back in his chair and crossed his thick arms, and I desperately tried not to pay attention to the fact that his long legs were lazily spread open on either side of me.

"Doesn't take much to get you fired up, does it?" Death asked. "We need to work on that, bubble butt."

Bubble butt!

He *was* trying to provoke me. Another one of his tests.

Inhaling slowly, I crossed my arms over my chest in an attempt to look unfazed. "You can't just stick me in front of a punching bag for a week and expect me to learn something."

"You need discipline and patience. I've seen little progress with either of them. You held out longer than I thought you would, but you're not ready to move on."

"*Show* me what I need to do, and I'll do it. These simple workouts you're giving me are pointless. Sit-ups and push-ups won't help me control my power. I'm ready to jump into the next step. Why don't you teach me more of what we were doing in your dining room with breaking the vase?"

Death rose to his imposing height in a slow, lazy way. He was so close that I had to tilt my head back to meet his glare, and I swallowed a dry lump in my throat. "You think you know better than me?" he growled.

"Yes," I said.

"Then congratulations, you're fully equipped to get yourself killed."

"I've controlled the power before," I maintained. "I'm determined to learn, and I learn fast. I can do this, Death. I'm ready to jump into it."

"Then leave this place and kill a demon," he seethed. "Show me you're ready to 'jump into it.' Because let me tell you something." He leaned in, and it took everything in me not to lean away. "If you're so naïve that you think you can just *jump into* this, then you're in for one hell of a rude awakening. You need to train at a realistic pace to succeed against an enemy. In this gym, I'm your enemy."

He bared his fangs in a vicious smile. He and I both knew he was my enemy outside of the gym too.

"I won't go easy on you," Death purred, and a chill crawled up my back. "If you don't like my methods, leave. Go stare at the wall in your guest room for all I care. If you stay, leave your Googled training tips and positive mantras outside of my gym. They'll only convolute your preparation and make me laugh harder when you prove yourself wrong and I knock you down on that perky ass of yours."

My mouth popped open to defend myself, but he was right. Especially the positive mantras bit, which I'd been vocalizing . . . often out loud . . .

"When I give you a task in this gym," Death said, "it's for a reason. I've been exactly where you are. I've made the mistakes that you're capable of." He faltered a bit, as if regretting admitting that last part. "In my world, you need to strengthen your resilience to face things most mortals can't mentally handle. You'll need patience to get there, and I'm not seeing any of that from you."

His words left me silent.

"When you get that through your little mortal brain," Death continued, as he began to stalk away, "then we will move on."

My fingers rolled into fists. *Jerk.* "Einstein's brain was the size of a cantaloupe, you know!"

Growling, I turned on my heel and stalked toward the punching bag to whale on it.

When I got back to my bedroom later, I was a sweaty, sore mess and horribly moody. I couldn't sit on my bed, considering the fact that I probably smelled as bad as I looked. So I sat down on the floor, leaned my back against the wall, and had a proper pity party by crying my eyes out.

Afterward, I unwrapped the pre-wrap from my hands. My knuckles were split and had blisters underneath. I winced as I removed the final strip of cloth and flexed my fingers. As I stared down at my hands, I attempted to trigger the healing trick I had done before. After a few minutes of concentrating and letting out frustrated breaths, I gave it a rest.

"This is so hopeless," I said.

But I wouldn't give up. No, I had a point to prove, and a prophecy that I couldn't forget. I wouldn't stay behind while Death retrieved his scythe. I needed to be strong enough to fight alongside him and stop Ahrimad and Malphas.

That way, when the time came, I would be strong enough to do the same to Death and Lucifer.

After a nightmare-infested four hours of rest, I lay in bed staring at the ceiling. In the silence of the dark room, low vibrations of music shook my headboard. At two in the morning, I kicked off my blanket and slipped a sweatshirt over my camisole to find out where it was coming from.

The hard rock grew louder as I approached the gym, and when I peered inside, I saw what all the commotion was about.

A pile of mauled practice dummies were heaped in the corner, and a shirtless Death stood in the center of the room. He had his back to me, and when he rolled back his shoulders, corded muscle shifted massive, jagged scars that came together at his lower spine in a V. He wore obscenely low-riding sweatpants and held what appeared to be a black bo staff in his right hand. I had to remember to duck behind the doorway as he rotated in my direction and twisted the staff with him.

I watched him methodically set up six new dummies around the room. His skin glistened from exertion, painting a portrait of a Fallen angel in the rain. Locked in concentration, his chin pointed down slightly, he circled one of the practice dummies. He snapped out his staff like a whip, striking hard and fast, slamming his first target to the ground. Shadow poured off him, pooling across the floor as he kept up the momentum and rotated the weapon around his body. Flashes of the gruesome battle in the alleyway came to mind. How he'd torn and sliced apart Malphas's underlings in a matter of minutes.

He executed like a trained killer. As Death methodically defeated his imaginary enemies, suddenly a surge of emotion overcame me so intensely that it was hard to breathe. I was *anger*. I was *chaos*. I was *grief*.

I was Death.

Death stalked across the floor, consumed by darkness. It pooled in the mismatched greens of his eyes, poured off his shoulders in the form of shadows like weeping branches. He glided with the grace of a panther between the remaining practice dummies, weaved and bowed, shuffled and blocked. *Strike. Strike. Strike.*

Snap. His staff broke in two, and he discarded it. He flexed his talons, working his neck. Muscles shifted in his immense frame as he lashed out with his talons and his legs in unrelenting swipes, punches, and kicks.

Anger. Chaos. Grief.
Punishment.

He was punishing himself, but why?

Perspiration dripped down the sides of his face. It curled his black faux-hawk into a wet mess, slipped down the edges of his chiseled physique to the dusting of dark hair that trailed down his ripped abs. Hair like an arrow on a map, pointing toward those godforsaken pants and the treasure outlined underneath.

"Get back to bed, mouse," Death barked.

I startled. He was glaring right at me.

I scurried to my room like the scared little mouse that peep show had made me.

The next morning, I hid in the gym closet and wrapped and rewrapped my hands exactly twenty-two times.

"Playing hide-and-seek, are we?"

His deep voice trailed down my spine like a caress. I slowly turned around, praying I wasn't acting as awkward as I felt. Death towered over me, blocking the light from the gym. He stood with his arms folded over his chest and wore a cold, menacing expression that I'd learned was his resting face. For someone who had slept even less than me—or *not at all*, for all I knew—Death looked frustratingly sexy in black sweatpants and black pullover with—plot twist—a forest-green collar.

A splash of color today, I see.

A small, nervous man with spectacles peered around Death to look at me. He held a clipboard in his hands, and there was a stopwatch dangling from his wrist.

"Glenn," Death said, still glaring down at me with those catlike eyes, "once Faith stops cowering in here, remind her of the drills she's scheduled to complete today." Then he pivoted on his heel, vanishing into a black mist.

"He thinks he's so cool with that exit," I muttered, walking out of the supply closet.

"It is rather cool, though," Glenn commented, "how the shadows embrace him like he's a part of their 'squad,' as the kids say . . . " The demon noticed my sharp stare and coughed into his fist. "Anyway, Ms. Williams, I'll be timing you through the Graveyard today."

"The *what*?"

Glenn pushed his glasses up his nose. "Oh, apologies. It's an obstacle course he created for you. Located in another gym in this building. He calls it the Graveyard."

Just one day of navigating the Graveyard and I felt like I'd dropped thirty pounds. After just a few rounds of tire jumps, sprints, cone drills, and bodyweight training, I was flat on the mat with my mouth open as I wheezed like a fish out of water.

A shadow appeared, haloed in the light of the ceiling as Death's upside-down face loomed over me. "On your back for me again, cupcake?"

He circled around me once, letting out a low purring noise as if he'd discovered his prey sleeping soundly with no way to escape. Dark aviators shielded his eyes, but I could tell he was livelier and *fuller* than usual by the golden-bronze tint of his skin.

"Just taking a quick nap with my eyes open," I said. "Back from pawing at your ball of yarn and coughing up hairballs?"

Death slapped his combat boots on either side of my body and grinned down at me with those pearly white fangs. Then he lowered himself to a low squat, balancing on the balls of his feet. He had fantastic hip mobility. *What a weird*, weird *thing to think*.

"You think you're cute, don't you?" Death asked.

"I know I'm cute." I smirked.

"Tomorrow, you train *with* me," he said. "I won't be going easy on you."

I sat up on my forearms and felt my shoulders shake with the small movement. "I don't recall asking for you to go easy on me."

Death's lip lifted in a snarl, as if he were frustrated that his bullying hadn't worked. Surprisingly, that frustration transitioned into something else. And he looked almost . . . impressed.

"Hmm," Death said. He rose to his feet and stalked away. "Peel your swamp ass off my mats, cupcake. Class is dismissed."

"I'll bring catnip tomorrow in case you get tired!" I called after him. I could have sworn I heard Death laugh as his darkness devoured him and he left again.

XVII

The rest of the day came and went with the excitement of finally training *with* Death. I imagined we'd go right into hand-to-hand combat, which was what I'd been looking forward to all along. If there was anything I trusted Death with after seeing him fight in the gladiator arena and in the alleyway against Malphas's underlings, it was hand-to-hand combat.

Unfortunately, the training session began like any other. Except this time, he was alongside me, performing the exercises too, or directly in my face, coaching every step of the way.

"Faster."

"Pull your knees up higher, so they're aligned with your hips."

"Again!"

"You knock over a cone, you pick it back up, and you start over!"

"Fist up, head tilted down. Protect your face at all times."

"Are you *napping*?"

"I don't know what that was, but it certainly wasn't a *goddamn push-up!*"

My back hit the mat with a cringe-worthy wet slap.

This whole "proving myself" thing had spiraled out of control.

"I am absolutely blown away," Death seethed, still in full critical-coach mode, "that you made it halfway through the Graveyard yesterday."

"Actually, I made it one-fourth of the way through," I corrected snootily. In my defense, the Graveyard looked like something straight out of Ninja Warriors or a boot camp, with its monster tires, swinging spikes, ladders, ropes, and a warped wall. It was a miracle I hadn't just keeled over at the beginning.

"Glenn was gracious to you, then," Death said. "He told me you made it halfway through. One-fourth is absolutely fucking pathetic."

I pulled my aching body up so that I leaned on my forearms. "I'm so glad you accept me for who I am. Please, tell me everything you feel!"

"I *feel* you would lose at an arm-wrestling match against my pinky."

I scanned his muscled frame. He wore a faded gray T-shirt, the lightest color I'd seen him in, with a typical pair of black joggers. Lord Almighty, did he look good . . .

"Are you listening to me?" Death growled.

Oh, right, he was talking. While I'd been blatantly checking him out.

"Yes. No. Maybe. Nes."

"Nes?"

"Yes and no. I—I zoned out, okay? Can't a girl have a little zone-y sesh every once in a while?" I wanted to bang my skull against the wall for how awkward I sounded. "I'm trying the best that I can here."

"Then try the worst you can," Death hissed, "because clearly it must be opposite day."

Grumbling under my breath, I peeled myself off the mat and stood with an energetic hop, feigning a second wind. "You know, you could at least try to empathize with me and interact with me normally sometimes. Instead, you're always in this robot drill sergeant mode." I wiped at the sweat on my forehead, my throat tight suddenly. "I get it, your scythe is gone, and you're *big mad*. A lot has happened to me too, you know. Things that I don't know how to deal with like you do. I can't just . . . turn it all off."

To my utter disbelief, Death had listened intently to my rant. I waited for him to yell at me to run more laps, but he put his gloved hands on his hips.

"All right, come on," Death said with a jerk of his head to follow him. "Let's take a break."

I stood there for a moment, wishing he'd acknowledged my emotions. At least he hadn't shut me down. I followed him to the side of the room, where a mirror lined the whole length of the wall. I noticed he didn't look at himself as he bent down to get my water bottle.

"Sit down on the floor and start stretching your right shoulder. You keep favoring it. I'll massage your legs."

Our eyes connected, and I swear my heart did a thousand somersaults. "Um. Okay . . . "

What the hell? Did I just agree to Death himself massaging me?

I watched his titanic frame cross the room to get a small black container. He opened the latch and pulled out a massage gun. I felt like an idiot for thinking he'd use his hands or that this would be even remotely sexual. He lowered to the ground in front of me and plopped my leg into his lap.

"You still have that knot in your quad," Death said, deep in concentration as he worked on me with the passiveness of a clinician. "Didn't I tell you to use the roller yesterday?"

"You mean the cylindrical-looking thing with the knobs on it?"

Death glared, and I gave him a sheepish smile. Screwing an attachment that looked like a torture device on the massage gun, he went to town on the knot on my quad.

"Recovery is just as important as the workout," Death said a minute or so later, dumping my leg out of his lap to work on the other one. "Explains why you're moving so slow today."

"Listen, dude, you don't even have to breathe. It makes keeping up with you—oh, I don't know, impossible?"

"Just say the word and I can stop you from breathing too, cupcake." He arched that stupid scarred eyebrow with the stupid hot piercing.

Every day, something seemed to change about him. Today it was his eyes. They weren't shielded by aviators and were therefore slightly squinted against the gym lights. One eye was darker than normal, a deep, woodsy green. His other, the one with the horrific scar slashed through it, glowed a livid mint-green. The only part of his eyes that always seemed to remain the same were his pupils—thin horizontal slits, trapped in their catlike way.

He flashed his fangs in a foxlike grin, and I realized I was staring.

"You like my hands on you?" Death asked in a coarse voice, drawing my attention to his gloved hand resting on my thigh.

I ripped my leg out of his hold and kicked toward him, but my foot went through shadows as he evaporated. He had the audacity to *laugh* as he reappeared standing in front of me with his hands casually in his pockets. The rich, deep sound of his laughter was something I hadn't heard in a while, and it tickled my ears.

He offered me a hand. "Don't be so uptight."

You're one to talk.

I reached for him, but he pulled his hand back and smoothed it across his hair. "Ooooh, too slow. Oldest trick in the book."

"You would know." Evading his second offer to help me up, I pushed off the ground by myself with a string of curses. "For a two-thousand-year-old dead guy, you're an utter child."

"I'm rarely bored," Death simpered, pleased with himself. As we headed to the refectory, it dawned on me that he was a little too sprightly.

Which of course meant Death was up to no good.

In the middle of the night, I felt Cruentas's hot breath on my face, and I petted his silky coat.

"Hey, buddy," I said in a sleepy voice. "Where do you go when you disappear? Hay Island?"

Cruentas whinnied, making me laugh.

I sat up and decided to get a snack. I was leaning over Cruentas with my hand on his coat to turn on the lamp on my nightstand when he lunged forward and took off, and I went with him.

The world spun . . . and I was thrown into oblivion.

My shoulder hit hard concrete, and white-hot pain exploded in my arm. My surroundings had shifted. I was in a spacious warehouse with a blacked-out glass ceiling, except for a few holes that let in the rain. I'd been here before. Death had taken me here after Malphas's demons had attacked me in the alleyway.

I rolled over onto my stomach and found a weapon beside me.

A hunting knife.

A thunderous roar echoed from somewhere, chilling me to the bone.

What the hell?

My heart was a jammed trigger on an automatic machine gun. To stop my fingers from shaking, I gripped the hunting knife tightly and rose to my feet.

This had to be a test. But Death was nowhere in sight.

I tensed as a creature emerged from the shadows to my left.

Its body was bulging with muscle and covered with black quills like a porcupine. Its ears were flat against its head like an aggressive dog.

As the creature herded me into the center of the warehouse, it fell under a ray of light, and its features came into focus. My stomach churned. Leathery gray skin stretched tight against its bones, and its muzzle was stained with blood. When it snarled, chunks of flesh were wedged between its teeth. And its teeth—God, those razor-sharp teeth—dripped a greenish liquid that sizzled like acid.

A monster straight out of a nightmare. Sweat poured off me. I looked down at my little blade, up at the massive creature, then back at the blade. It was starting to look more like a toothpick than a weapon.

The creature's quills expanded before pressing tightly against its body like armor. It barreled toward me.

"Shit!"

I spun out of the way before it rammed into me with its horns. The creature wasn't very smart, considering it kept running for twenty feet and smashed into a wall.

It charged again. This time, I only barely got away, since the black quills on the side came to life. They reached out and hooked onto me like small fingers, dragging me with it. I cried out as the creature picked up speed and my legs crumbled underneath me.

My arm swung out with my hunting blade, digging into the beast's side. With no luck at stopping it, I ripped the knife from its muscular flesh and stabbed it again. The creature howled, and the quills released. Oily blood slicked my fingers, and I lost my grip. I skidded across the ground, rolling a few times before I landed on my back.

The old lights on the ceiling of the warehouse were spinning, rotating. My vision blurred, flickering in and out of blackness. Everything pulsed with white-hot pain.

I rolled over onto my stomach, lifting myself with bloody hands and breathing hard.

I blinked, as if that would wake me up from this sick nightmare.

I spun around and faced the dying animal. The tendons of his legs were all screwed up and shredded, and his abdomen wound was far worse than mine. I raised the blade to end its misery.

A sob lodged in my throat. In spite of my training, I couldn't cross the line to kill.

The creature let out a raspy howl. Its head thrashed side to side, as if it were fighting an invisible force. The cords in its neck strained. Its skin drained to a light gray.

Horror washed over me as I raised the dagger and plunged it deep into the center of its chest. It didn't explode into ashes. Its eyes softened, then the beast slipped away.

My eyes welled with tears. The ghost of its cries rang in my head, and the fright and sadness at what I'd done spread through my body like ice. I forced myself to stand, keep moving away from the scene, and turn my back to it. Left. Right. Left. Right. My emotions caught up with me, and I started to hyperventilate, collapsing to my knees.

Everything felt slowed down. My wounds, they weren't healing. My tongue swelled. My head lolled on my neck. I fell forward and surrendered to the silent warehouse.

Footsteps approached. I could not move.

The heavy toe of a boot rolled me over.

"Your *first* kill," purred a voice. "Congrats."

I felt a sharp prick in my arm and shot up with a jolt, inhaling sharply. My hand gripped a hard bicep, and I stared wide-eyed at Death. He was crouched over me, his face shadowed by a cowl, except his short, dark facial hair and the outline of his full lips. He wore black leather pants with various straps for weapons fastened around his muscular thighs and calves.

"You hesitated," he said, dropping an empty syringe into a bag.

I scrambled to get up and shoved at his chest. "Get off me!"

"Now there's a sentence I seldom hear." Death stood, while I forced my legs to cooperate with my brain.

"What the heck did you inject me with? And what—what *was* that thing?"

"I injected you with an antidote. *That* was a breed of hell hound, and they're poisonous." I could feel him staring at me as I tried to keep myself together. "You need to table your precious morals and commit to ending an enemy that wants to end you."

"I killed it, didn't I?"

"You got lucky," Death said coldly, stepping up to me. Usually, when he did that, I had to fight the urge to step back. This time, I was fighting the urge to sway forward. "You wasted too much time finding a box of Kleenex to finish the beast off."

My face flushed with heat.

"Heed my advice," Death said firmly. "Give your enemies the opportunity to hurt you, and they will. They will drag you around like you're their bitch, then bury you six feet in the ground like you're their bone. When it's life or death, *truly* life or death, you don't have time to decide. It's them or you."

"Killing doesn't come second nature to me like it does to you."

"Agreed. I'm shocked you didn't politely ask the hell hound if you could end its life." He had the nerve to smirk. "Aw, does that piss you off? Good. Maybe it'll trigger your power, which I didn't see a single spark of."

"We haven't been *training* with my power," I grated. "I worked with what I had, which was that ridiculous toothpick of a knife you left me. What the hell is your problem?"

"My problem, Faith, is you. You keep defending yourself, leaving no room for improvement." Death pulled back his cloak, revealing a metal scabbard at his side. "You want to handle something bigger than a toothpick? Then here." He unfastened the weapon and tossed it to me.

I caught it by the handle. It was much heavier than I'd expected. "This is a sword."

"Nothing gets past you." Death tilted his head up. "I've been meaning to give it to you. Go on. Unsheathe it."

The sharp gleam of metal reflected my tired blue eyes in its glossy surface. "It's stunning. Thank you."

"Don't thank me. You'll need it so I don't crush you into the floor."

When I looked up, Death was gone.

I spun around and he was right front of me, twisted in mid-motion as his body cut through the air. I blocked his hard first strike with my sword out of reflex. He carried only a metal bar. He maneuvered it around his body, and I was struck hard enough to stumble back. He halted with the pole tucked under his arm. I followed the line of muscle up his leg to his bicep and broad shoulders.

"Focus," he hissed.

Death punched forward with the bar and performed a series of strikes at the air, corralling me like he was herding sheep. He moved faster and faster, spinning the weapon around his body like it was second nature.

"Get one finger on me, and I'll give you anything you want,"

Death said. "If I knock you down on your ass, the same condition applies. Yes or no?"

I'll admit that thought of him owing *me* something for once intrigued me. But I knew better than to fall for it. "Not happening."

He inclined his head to the side. "Scared?"

"I've made enough deals with you."

We started to circle.

He tossed his metal bar to the side with a loud clatter. "You have a weapon, I don't."

"You have claws."

"They retract."

"You have *fangs*."

Death paused, baring his sharp teeth like a wolf. "I won't use them either. If only I had a blindfold and binds to hogtie my arms and legs together. Then it'd be pretty even."

I spun and slashed the air. He dodged it easily, laughing low in his throat.

"I hit a nerve."

"And I'm going to hit your dick," I growled, slashing again.

"Dick on the mind, cupcake? At *four* in the morning?"

I punched forward with my weapon, missing him by a hair. I swung out again. Death glided around in teasing distance, evading me. He was like a cobra waiting to strike. And I was getting dog-tired already.

"Somebody needs a nappy," Death taunted in a sing-song voice.

"Shut the hell up."

His sardonic laugh echoed through the warehouse before he fell into a deep crouch and swiped hard at my feet with his leg. My back slammed into the ground, knocking the wind out of me. Over. Just like that.

"I won't sugarcoat how an enemy would treat you," he said.

"Picture the strongest fighter you know. They had to be kicked while they were down to rise up to their greatness."

In his own twisted, ruthless way, I knew he was trying to help me, but I couldn't mask the pure hatred I had for him. "Whose *masterpiece* are you, then?"

His stare was lethal.

"You said picture the strongest fighter I know," I bit out, "because you know it's you. But you fell from your greatness, didn't you? So, whose masterpiece are you? Your father's?"

Death bent down and fisted my shirt in his big, gloved hand, lifting me off the ground so that we were face to face. "Striptease."

"What?"

"Strip. Tease." This time, he purred it out. "That's what I want for knocking you on your ass."

We stood up together, and he began to stalk around me in a slow, calculated way.

"In your dreams," I hissed.

"You should know better than to back out of a deal with me," Death said in a low, enticing voice. "I won, fair and square. Moving on. Feeling tired, mortal?"

Coldness slipped down my spine at the downgrade to *mortal.* "Never," I said, mostly out of pride. I regretted my answer as soon as he disappeared into a black mist. I heard his laugh at my back, raspy and deep in his throat.

His mouth brushed my ear. "Look alive."

The lights went off.

Fear clicked into place. There wasn't even a sliver of light in the warehouse, and my heart began to pound like thunder against my ribs.

Welp, we'd definitely never done *this* before.

I knew that Death was no longer standing behind me. But his

sinister laughter lingered in fractured echoes that bounced off the high ceiling. The sound tricked me into turning toward different parts of the warehouse. At some point, I fisted my hands and tried to create my own light. I let out an exasperated noise and rubbed my hands together as if it would make a fire. Nothing.

"Seriously?" I picked up my arm and let it fall with a slap. "Turning the lights off to make me rely on my senses? You're skipping over at least thirty stages of hand-to-hand combat for a novice." *I would know, I Googled.*

I got no response.

This was another one of the Grim Reaper's games. I felt his gaze on me in the darkness like a beacon. He could see me, but I couldn't see him.

I started to move, slowly, feeling with my senses and hoping I didn't trip over anything. I wouldn't rush. That was exactly what a predator like Death wanted: a runner.

While my vision was gone, my hearing was heightened. I focused on things I hadn't noticed before. The small, occasional crack in my left ankle. The clicks from the vents steadily blowing heat into the space.

No matter how hard I strained to listen for Death's footsteps, I heard nothing. He was too good at skulking in the dark.

I shuffled into something sturdy and nearly fell over. I felt a brief presence at my back and something wet caress my neck. A tongue. It licked up my throat, fangs grazing my skin. I bottled up my shriek, my head flinching away out of instinct, followed by a slow burn of heat that shimmied down my body. I spun on my heel and took a swipe at the air with my fist.

"Your instinct is to react with emotion," Death's deep voice instructed from no particular spot. But I couldn't focus on anything except the idea of strangling him. "This is purely instinctual. Feel me in the room with you."

I let out a frustrated noise. "This is pointless."

"Pointless, until you don't have perfect lighting during a fight. Until you can't see your opponent, but they can see you. And you . . . look . . . *tasty*." I felt the air get colder to my left and took that as a hint that he was there and snatched empty air again. Something tripped me, and I lost my balance, crashing to the floor with a grunt.

"That's what happens when you don't focus," Death said.

"I'm not like you," I seethed, picking myself off the ground. "I can't see in the dark."

"I understand this is difficult, but it's not impossible." His voice moved to my left. "Not for you. You may bleed and breathe like humans, but deep down, you know you're different. You feel it."

I stood still. "What am I, Death?"

"Definitely not a creature with night vision." If I didn't know any better, I'd say he was perched somewhere above me. "You can control your power to come and go at will. But first, you need to build mental resiliency."

"Don't I already have resiliency to be where I am now?" I demanded, emotion breaking through my words. "Maybe I should just become immortal. You guys all seem much harder to kill."

"Immortality comes with a price. A price you should fear more than death."

"I'm not afraid of death. Not anymore." I pinched my lips together as those words hit me harder than I expected. "I've been thinking about it. Immortality can be a choice, can't it? Ace must have found a way with magic to extend his life."

"You want to live forever, Faith?" I felt the air shift and drop to a frigid temperature. The closeness of his voice indicated he was standing right in front of me. "I will assume you wish to be immortal in *your* world. Well then, let me paint the picture for you."

His voice circled around me.

"Imagine all the mortals around you dying while you remain the same. You'll seek a companion in this endless time, someone to fill the void in your heart, but they'll all be temporary and abandon you, until you don't have much of a heart left anymore. Imagine starting over, creating a whole new identity once people begin to notice your differences. You'll have to change your name and appearance constantly, or risk exposure and hunters who seek people with your gifts. Eventually, you'll kill someone." He ran a gloved hand along my braid as he continued his stalking. "Maybe you'll like killing, Faith. Maybe you'll become *obsessed* with it. You'll lose yourself to the madness of it all. Time will fly by like a merry-go-round at a carnival. It'll just circle and circle, and then one day, finally, you'll see the truth."

I felt the heat of his body behind me, his breath tickling my ear.

"You'll realize how selfish immortality is. How wrong you were to ever want it in the first place. But you're not the person who made that decision anymore. That person is long gone. You *killed* her."

A life of loneliness, death, repetitiveness. Insanity . . . It wasn't what I wanted. Nevertheless, I couldn't escape the feeling that something terrible was about to happen. Each day, it weighed heavier and heavier, like a foreboding presence, making me increasingly aware of my own mortality.

His gloved fingers gripped my chin, turning my face toward his in the dark. "If you sacrifice your identity out of fear, then you will never recover it again. Isn't that what you fear the most, Faith? Losing yourself?"

Yes. But I also fear losing you nearly escaped.

And it stunned me.

"Do you know what I wished for on my eighteenth birthday?" I whispered. "I wanted to know who I was. If you think I'm anywhere near existing in that wish, you're dead wrong. I can't lose something I never truly had."

My hands felt hot, and when I looked down, flickers of white were leaping from my right hand, lighting up a section of the dark warehouse. It was scorching hot, and as it burst, a small piece of light burned my cheek. I stared down at my hand in horror, and my throat tightened at the thought of losing control again. The more scared I became, the more violently the light ignited.

Death's gloved hand curled around mine, capturing the light.

"This power can rule you," Death said as I watched the light radiate through the cracks of our fingers. "Time and time again, you have allowed yourself to be its victim. But look at it now, trapped in your palm. Do you wish to know where it came from?" He stepped closer to me, keeping our hands together. "It waits in your eyes. Always with you, lingering in your soul. Vibrant, mighty, beautiful. Do you understand, Faith?"

When I just stared at him in disbelief, he tightened his hand around mine.

"I understand," I said softly.

It was me. *I* was the light.

Death let go of my fist, and my knuckles glowed like a lightning bug. Carefully, I pried my shaking fingers open, palm up. A small orb had formed there, hovering like a calm, compressed star.

I looked up at Death. If he was as astonished as I was, it didn't show. He was great at that. Still, his eyes met mine, steady and intense in our small cocoon of light in the warehouse.

"What are you waiting for? Let there be light, lamp girl," he said. "Imagine it rising and lighting up the ceiling as you release it."

In my head, I imagined the orb rising from my fingertips. It rose so that it hovered a few inches beyond my middle finger, and then it grew, expanding, charging, vibrating my veins. I lifted my hand and pointed to the sky, flinging the light up into the air. The orb shot upward and exploded into webbed electric currents on the ceiling, curling around the old light fixtures above and igniting them back to life.

"I think there's hope for you yet, cupcake."

Death's face had moved closer to mine. Close enough to kiss me. And then he did.

One of the light fixtures above us burst into flames, cracking a part of the ceiling and crashing down to the floor twenty feet from us. We broke apart as a fire alarm went off. The kiss had been so brief that there was hardly any trace of it left behind except a warm tingle on my lips.

Glenn appeared out of nowhere, nervous and sweaty, with two fire extinguishers strapped to his back like he was a Ghostbuster. "I got it, my lord! I got it!" He circled the flames in a low squat, aiming at the root of the fire with the extinguishers.

"Whoa!" Glenn miscalculated a step and somehow caught his pant leg on fire, which resulted in him rolling around the ground and shrieking. "All . . . under control . . . my lord!"

We watched Glenn put out the inferno we'd caused in silence.

Getting on the back of Death's bike had become instinct. We rode to his building, and he walked me to his penthouse.

At my guest room door, I looked over my shoulder to find his shadowed silhouette hovering at the other end of the hallway. We were spending so much time in the dark that I was adapting to it.

"It won't happen again," Death said.

I knew instantly he was talking about the kiss.

Any feelings he'd resurfaced in me extinguished like the flames before us. "Nothing happened anyway," I replied, bitterness dripping off my tongue. "You don't have to worry about me getting attached. The walls you've built are too high to climb, and now so are mine. Lonely people just love convenience."

He said nothing.

"I need an update on Marcy," I said, crossing my arms. "I gave up everything for her, and I'm sick and tired of your wishy-washy answers—"

"Your friend is fine," Death interjected. "I was notified this morning."

My heart raced. "They found her? Where?"

"Malphas dumped her off at some motel. He got bored of her, just like I said he would. She's safe, unharmed, and her memories have been erased."

I could barely think straight. "I want proof she's okay."

"Here." Death slid out his cell phone and showed me a picture of Marcy climbing the steps of Pleasant Valley High School. The bottom was dated yesterday morning.

"I—I don't understand. You heard about this yesterday? You knew a whole day ago that she was okay, and you didn't tell me? Why wouldn't you tell me right away? You know how worried I've been."

Death went eerily still amongst the shadows.

I couldn't explain it. How it hit me then, like a sixth sense.

He'd kept this news from me for a *reason*.

I went into my bedroom and slammed the door.

XVIII

David Star was on TV.

Which meant Death was back to his double life.

This was a rerun from an interview earlier in the morning, a press release for the D&S Tower about their supposed art program for New York City's youth. David's chestnut-brown hair, much longer than Death's black faux-hawk, was styled messily over his forehead, and he wore a dark-gray dress shirt and medium-wash jeans. Handsome features, unmarked by any cynical tattoos or scars, bore a close enough resemblance to Alexandru, Death's old human self, that it was disturbing.

One devastating smile, and he effortlessly controlled the room. Little did they know that beneath that pretty façade was a green-eyed monster. One that hungered for the very people he sought to manipulate, including me.

Pointing the remote at the flat-screen over Death's massive fire-place, I angrily changed the channel to an action film and turned up the volume. Then I dumped a few more kernels of popcorn on the floor for Cruentas. He inhaled them like a vacuum. Since he appeared to be trained not to jump on the leather couches, he plopped back down on his dog bed, which I'd placed on the floor by my feet.

"He seems to like you."

I startled at the voice and swiveled my head. Leo stood behind the couch. Cruentas sprinted to him and began furiously sniffing his knee before jumping up on his hind legs for a pet.

"Cruentas can be a little shy around strangers," he said.

I reached for the remote to turn the TV down. "You scared the crap out of me. What are you doing in here?"

Leo's amber eyes scanned the food on the coffee table then shifted to the guns blazing on the television in a James Bond movie. "Checking in on you."

"He gave me a babysitter? Since when?"

"Since day one," Leo replied. "I normally stand out in the hall-way or stop by in the middle of the night."

"While I'm *sleeping*?"

"It's not like that. I don't enter your bedroom. I can hear your heartbeat from the outside. Just like I heard a bunch of guns and violence on the television from the hallway outside . . . "

"And what, you thought there was actually World War Three in here?"

"No, I . . . figured I'd make sure everything's all right. With you."

I set my ice cream and popcorn on the coffee table. "Maybe you haven't heard, but I sold my soul to the Harbinger of Doom and Beelzebub. So no, nothing is all right."

The words came out nastier than I'd intended, but it's not like I owed this guy anything. He was one of them.

Leo slid his hands into his pockets and sat down on the couch beside me. "Getting locked up in here all alone must be a real joy, huh?"

"I feel like a caged animal."

"I may be able to help with that."

I looked over at him. "You can get me out of here? Can you take me to visit my family?"

"I wish I could," Leo said, and the earnestness in his eyes was refreshing and more human than anything Death could offer. "It's not safe for you to leave the premises. I was talking about something smaller. A birthday party."

"For you?"

"For my brother. He's one of the Seven."

I blinked. "Oh. Will there be food, or am I the food?"

Leo arched a brow. "You never have to worry about your safety around me, Faith. My brothers and I, we have one job and one job only: collect the souls we are assigned. I think you'd get along great with them, and there will be an obnoxious amount of food. Interested?"

The way he talked about the Seven intrigued me. I wanted to know more. I also wanted to get the heck out of this penthouse, even if I had to hang out with a bunch of soul eaters to do so.

"This is going to get me in trouble, isn't it? The last thing I want to deal with right now is another one of Death's mood swings. Or Lucifer getting pissed and sticking me on the end of his freaky tail to dangle me over the pits of Hell like a marshmallow over a bonfire."

He chuckled. "Damn. That was very descriptive."

"Thanks, I'm quite creative when I'm spiraling." When Leo clearly didn't know whether I was joking or not, I smiled to ease the mood. "But really, what if Death finds out?"

"Then I'll take the blame," Leo said. "Listen, Death's two thousand years old, and he's clearly forgotten how to treat people because *this*"—he motioned to the empty apartment and let his arm drop—"*this* isn't healthy. You, cooped up here all alone. It's messed up." He opened the apartment door. "Let me break you out of jail."

I joined him at the door. "Where's the party?"

"It's a surprise," he answered with a slow grin.

I smiled and tucked my hair behind my ear. "I do love surprises..." I stepped out into the hallway after him. "Lead the—" My breath caught in my throat.

"Surprise," Death said.

The Grim Reaper leaned against the wall in the hallway. His complexion wasn't pale anymore, and the sharp bronze planes of his face were less skeletal.

"My lord," Leo said with a bow of his head. "I had no idea you were . . . Had I known—"

"I haven't forgotten how to treat people, Leo." Death glanced at me. "I just don't care enough to put the effort in."

Ouch.

"That was out of line," Leo said. "I apologize."

"Where are you taking her?" Death asked with a casual, calm curiosity. Call it a sixth sense again, or some kind of strange connection due to the weird bond he'd created between us, but I knew Death was concealing something. He had, after all, been lingering *outside* his own penthouse, which was odd . . .

It was then I noticed that he was hiding something behind his back.

"The den," Leo admitted. "We arranged a small gathering for Gunner's birthday."

"I see." Death went quiet for a moment. "Well, what are you waiting for? Go have fun."

Leo regarded him with disbelief. "Are you sure, my lord?"

"If she is," Death remarkably said.

"I am," I replied.

Death and I stared at each other before he pushed off the wall and stalked past us to his apartment door. He maneuvered his arm in front of him so that I couldn't see what he was holding, and then he threw open the penthouse door and shut it. No slam. No vanishing. No dramatic exits.

He was not okay with this. The furthest from okay. But I was. I was definitely okay with this. After everything I'd been through, Death was respecting my choice, and I appreciated the compromise.

I followed Leo.

XIX

DEATH

Hundreds of feet below, a pedestrian shuffled along the sidewalk. I sat on the edge of the roof with the neck of an empty whiskey bottle clutched in my fist and stretched out my arm, swinging the bottle slowly back and forth like a pendulum.

"Bye, bitch."

I dropped it and leaned over the edge to watch it fall and shatter right behind the man. He startled, glanced at his empty surroundings, and booked it down the sidewalk.

"Damn," I muttered. "I'm getting rusty."

"M-my lord?"

I turned back to peer at a little man with glasses.

"Glenn!" I shouted, beaming at him. "My trusted—" Glenn's eyes went wide as he jumped back with a scream that made my ears ring. "What the hell is the matter with you?"

"Sorry, my lord!" Glenn exclaimed. "It's—it's just you *smiled* at me."

I unscrewed the cap of another bottle, taking a long swig. "For once, I'm happy to see you. Sit with me, pal. Drink with me."

"Uh, okay . . . my lord." Still hesitant, Glenn climbed up onto the edge, his anxious eyes glued to the drop below. "I can't believe you called me pal—"

"Arm's length," I snarled.

Glenn scooted down a foot. "How long have you been up here, my lord?"

"An hour. Maybe two."

"This is a-a-awfully high."

"Indeed, the perfect height to push an idiot off." I clapped Glenn hard on the back, making him yelp and start to fall over the edge before I grabbed his shirt to pull him back. "Kidding."

Glenn clutched his chest. "Good one, my lord! Always the jester!" Probably remembering last month's *incident* when he hadn't laughed at my joke, Glenn forced out a high-pitched laugh until his face turned purple.

I cringed. "That's quite enough. And change your laugh next time; that one's hideous."

"Right. Of course. My apologies, my lord." He took the bottle from my hand and downed a large gulp. Coughing, he handed it back. "Hellfire, this is diabolically strong, my lord! May I ask how many of those you've had?"

"Enough to come to you for advice," I replied. "What's it called when you want to possess something entirely, but there are obstacles in the way? Obstacles that are both internal and external?"

"I believe that's just life, my lord?"

"Life. How repulsive." My lips peeled back from my fangs in a sneer as I gulped down more whiskey. "Are you surprised I summoned you, demon?"

"Very, my lord." Glenn's eyebrows were drawn together, and he looked stiff as hell. "Especially since you summoned me away from my sudden . . . execution."

Ah, right. The execution. "Listen, I know we've had our differences, Glenn. I ripped your tongue out; you screwed me over and virtually aided in the release of Ahrimad and the abduction of Scytherella. We've both wronged each other rather equally, have we not?"

"I'm not too sure about that, my lord. You did sever my body in half one time . . . "

Now I was intrigued. "Truly? I don't recall that."

"It was thirty years ago, my lord. You said you were 'practicing your back swing,' I believe."

"You healed, though, didn't you?"

"Six weeks of raw agony later, yes." Glenn wiped his nose and sniffed. "You've also tossed me into a tank of hungry sharks . . . "

I snickered. "Oh, yes, that was hysterical."

"Indeed," Glenn muttered. "There's also the fact that you stripped me of my previous identity by renaming me."

"Your name isn't Glenn?" I scratched at the stubble on my jaw. "Huh. Anyway, back to me. I summoned you here for a reason. To tell you that Jerry was the worst punching bag I've ever had."

"Who's Jerry?"

"Your replacement, of course."

"I've been fired for less than a day, and you already replaced me?"

"Jerry's been working on a trial basis at the office for a week. Today was his first official day as my henchman. He sucked. And, damn it, I cracked and slit his sweaty nerd throat. The guy bleeds out like he's auditioning for a goddamn slasher movie. Gruesomely entertaining, but a whole unnecessary mess." I pointed in the vague direction of the shadowy part of the roof. "He's somewhere over there."

"Is that him . . . choking on his own blood, my lord?"

"It relaxes me." I slugged back more whiskey. "I can't deal with Jerry anymore, Glenn. And you're . . . well . . . " I took in Glenn's appearance, struggling not to grimace at his blotchy, ruddy, sweaty face. "*Somewhat* more tolerable than he was in comparison. When you worked for me, a small fraction of the things you screwed up were perhaps partially my fault. I understand that I can occasionally be difficult to work with. Overbearing, a tad psychotic, not to mention all my masochistic tendencies. Those are some of my finest qualities, if you ask me, but I digress. The point is, you mean something to me, Glenn. As insignificant as that something may be, I . . . I . . . "

"Need me?" Glenn offered.

I pounded my chest with my gloved fist to free a belch. "Yeah. Sure."

My kick-around demon inhaled shakily. "My lord, that is the nicest thing you have ever said to me."

"Don't make this fucking weird, Glenn. I still have my front-row ticket to your execution."

Glenn quickly wiped at his tears with his sleeves.

"I want you to work for me again," I continued. "Do my bidding. Ding-dong ditch my enemies. Spread my wrath amongst the living. Either you take your job back or you get executed. Your choice."

Glenn looked off to the side.

My lip curled. I smashed the neck of the whiskey bottle against the roof with the intention of cutting his throat. "That was *hypothetical!* Are you seriously contemplating an execution over working for me again?"

"Of c-c-course not, my lord! I was only zoning out, as idiots do!" He wiped his hands on his slacks. "However . . . " Climbing down from the edge, Glenn jumped to the roof, puffed out his chest, and looked me directly in the eyes. "I want a raise," he squeaked.

"A *what?*"

Glenn cleared his throat. "A *raise*, my lord. I want a raise. You are simply horrifying to work for."

"Thank you."

Glenn's brows creased together. "Do we have a deal or not, sir?"

I swung my legs over the wall, dropped down, and towered over the little demon. He backed up but held his brave face. Snarling, I bent to snatch up the large paper bag I'd left on the ground and handed it to him.

Glenn stared at the parcel like it would explode. "Is this for me, my lord?"

"Yes, it's for you, you twit." I shoved the bag into his chest and patted his shoulder. "Happy . . . Welcome Back Night."

Glenn slowly opened the bag to peer at its contents. "My lord, was this for the girl—"

"No."

"But it—"

"It wasn't for the girl!" I exploded, feeling the numbing effects of the alcohol slipping away. "It's for you, so just take it! Sell it, keep it, toss it, take it back whence it came. *I don't give a shit.* Just get it away from me and you'll get your raise, all right?"

This time, instead of shuddering under my glare, Glenn calmly looked me in the eyes again and just nodded. Nodded like he understood. "Have an unpleasant night, my lord."

He vanished. I fumbled with the pocket of my sweatshirt for the note I'd written Faith. It was gone. *Damn it.* I must have dropped it.

Wind snapped at my face as I furiously paced the roof. The more I thought about the gift, the more I thought about *her*. And the more I thought about *her*, the more I thought about *him*. Leo, my second-in-command. Kissing Faith, touching her. I hadn't set boundaries for him; I hadn't thought I *had* to. I never thought they'd actually—

Kill.

A headache stabbed at my skull, and I doubled over from the agony.

We aren't consuming enough, the beast purred. *You're concerned about the girl; meanwhile, you're withering from the inside out without your scythe. What happened to screwing the whole world and never looking back?*

"Nothing has changed," I hissed out loud. "Doesn't mean I have to like the thought of her with someone else."

Then claim her.

"Shut up," I snarled.

She belongs to us.

My eyes shut as I worked my neck to one side. "Until the end."

I realized my lips had moved in sync with the monster in my head. The madness was surfacing bit by bit, day by day. The only thing that kept me rooted was the blade and my motivation to break the Seven Deadly Sins curse once and for all. Now I had neither in my grasp.

I was impatient. Putting so much trust in Ace's premonition felt risky, but despite everything, deep down, I somehow still trusted him, so now I was sitting on my hands waiting for his deadline to arrive. The issue was that after tonight, after imagining Faith kissing another man and barely containing my reaction to it, I wasn't so sure I'd last two more weeks.

A sense of dread dropped into my stomach like lead at the thought of losing complete control of my *other side.* I manned up and shoved the fear away.

There. Gone. Time to stop thinking about Faith with Leo too.

I turned away from the dusky city and manifested back into my apartment.

How the hell long was a birthday party anyway?

Fuck!

Thirty minutes later, I was molded into the black leather couch watching last night's Chicago Bears game. I'd finally run out of whiskey, so a carton of milk lay on my bare chest, and I was absently scratching Cruentas with my big toe.

"Hell's Bells" blared from the coffee table, the rock riff going on and on. It ended. Then the phone beeped with a voicemail. Groaning, I sat up and slapped the coffee table for my phone, grabbing a Reese's peanut butter cup instead. I popped the candy, wrapper and all, into my mouth and chewed before slumping back into the couch.

When my phone buzzed with a text message, I unleashed a growl and shoved a bunch of Skittles off my phone to check my screen.

My office. Now.

"Grrrreeeeat." I peeled myself up off the couch and dropped a bunch of crumbs off my stomach that Cruentas would vacuum up. I bent down to give him a few firm, affectionate thumps on the side. "Watch the house, boy."

Cruentas whinnied.

I stormed toward a clearing in the room, shadows peeling off the walls and launching onto me as I manifested on the roof. The darkness formed my cloak, the fabric pressing tight to my skin as I sprinted across the roof and leapt, wings unfurling. I tore into the night toward D&S Tower.

Lucifer stood on the roof waiting. *Must be important.* I dove down, coming in a little too fast. I stumbled as I landed, rolling it off with a slow jog toward him. "Yeah?"

"Don't *yeah* me," Lucifer said. "You took your sweet time getting here." His nostrils flared as I neared. "You reek."

"Got thirsty."

"Just get inside." A doorway of flames appeared behind him, and we both walked through it to get to his office on the other side. Lucifer stepped up onto the raised platform beneath his desk and plucked a cigar from a golden box.

"I got it, kid," he said. "I got the location of the book."

"*Already?* I didn't think Sarah would break so easily."

Lucifer clipped two cigars and lit them with his thumb, tossing me one.

"It wasn't entirely a matter of breaking her as much as a matter of persuasion." He gave me a leering look, and I assumed he'd had sex with her.

"Who knew you'd dick your way to getting the grimoire," I said with a wry smile.

Lucifer grinned back around a plume of smoke. "Don't be a jackass. We talked at length about Faith's situation. Her niece is her weakness. It's a shame, really. She always wanted a child, and she sees Faith as the daughter she never had. Little does Sarah know that when she begged me to save her fiancé's life all those years ago, her fertility was my price."

My head snapped up. He'd never told me that. "Why? You could have taken anything from her."

"And you could have scared Faith into complacency rather than making her fall in love with you," Lucifer countered. "We're Fallen. It brings us pleasure to make mortals suffer. It's our nature."

I couldn't deny that characteristic in my own black heart. "What's the plan now, old man? Where's the grimoire?"

"She hid it. In the floorboards of a church."

I snickered, smoke escaping my mouth. "How unoriginal."

Neither of us, nor any other creature of the night, could cross into hallowed ground.

"The church was abandoned after Hurricane Sandy," Devin

continued. "The flooding blew open the front door and broke the hallowed seal."

"Perfect." I grinned.

"Not quite," Lucifer said, resting his cigar on an ashtray. "When Sarah disappeared, the Guild acted fast. Only a Chosen can hold the book for any length of time, but they must have gone to the church and jinxed it, just in case. It's been housing a nest of more than thirty harpies for two days now."

I released a violent curse in Latin. "We'll need at least ten Fallen for a job like that."

"I only require *one*," Lucifer said. "*You.* Tonight, you will go destroy the hive and bring me the book. Complete this task and I will overlook your dalliance with the girl."

Unease darted down my spine, and I gripped the armrests of my chair.

"I know you've been training her," Lucifer said, leaning his forearms on his desk. "I know the two of you have been getting . . . *closer*. As you know, Faith is practically my daughter, so I will warn you one last time. Keep your dick in your fucking pants. Because if I find out you've tarnished her or she gets pregnant, I will tear off your goddamn wings with my bare hands."

Rage tightened my throat. The implication that I was some lowlife punk getting scolded by a protective father ticked me off. Lucifer was paranoid that Faith losing her virginity might affect her precious pure power.

I was getting tired of him treating me like some low-level subordinate because I'd screwed up collecting Faith's soul. I was *Death*. A force of nature. Our Fallen soldiers kneeled at my command, and I'd become the mortals' worst fear.

Maybe you're his *too*, purred the voice in my head. *That's why he prefers when you're weak.*

"Here." Lucifer stood and chucked a bag at my chest, which I snatched in midair. Inside, there was an address on a piece of paper and bulky gloves. "Wear those when you handle the book, and don't hold it for long. I expect the grimoire on my desk by the break of dawn."

Without another word, I manifested to the roof of the D&S Tower.

I took another pull from my cigar before smashing it to the ground and crushing it beneath my heel. *"Pregnant?"* I scoffed. "He says that as if my pull-out game hasn't been strong for over two thousand years."

I wasn't physically strong enough to take on thirty harpies without a little extra oomph. I'd need a good hunt before collecting the grimoire.

I stepped onto the ledge of the tower. Two hours of murder would do the trick. Perk me right up, just like old times.

A plane overhead drew my attention to the night sky, and I scowled. Drawing attention from the Elders tonight would be reckless, though. Miraculously, the reapers and I had been able to get back on track with the dead without any probing, and Lucifer and I had managed to keep Faith under Heaven's radar. But we'd be complete morons to let our guard down. Those dusty, goody-two-shoes pinheads in Heaven were planning something. But until we could confirm that, I had to *behave*—even when I needed a quick pick-me-up the most—and collect the dead as I was supposed to.

I summoned my to-kill list, the old scroll unraveling and filling with names at an infuriatingly slow rate. Selecting my first victim, I dove off the tower headfirst, like diving into a pool, and then I heard it. Her voice.

Death!

Faith? My wings stretched, catching the air the wrong way as

I glided to wrap around the tower. The sharp change in trajectory nearly slammed me into the skyscraper, but I turned over and shoved forward, my stomach grazing the side of a building. Five sharp strokes of my wings and I rose into the air until I narrowed in on my apartment building in the distance.

Faith? Can you hear me? What's wrong?

When there was no response, my stomach clenched. There was a sliver of doubt that I'd heard anything at all. The weak whisper of her voice might be a symptom of the madness within me.

No, I'd heard her. Faith had called to me through the bond, but now she was silent. Her mind barriers had slammed closed.

Or worse, I thought as I plummeted down to the rooftop of my penthouse like an avenging god. *She's dead.*

XX

FAITH

Three floors down from Death's penthouse, Leo and I got off the elevator. We walked down a sleek hallway with windows looking out onto the city on one side and simplistic modern art on the other before stopping at a door. Leo opened it and ushered me inside. We entered a cozy, masculine apartment with worn-out couches and beanbag chairs, a pool table, a dartboard, and a pinball machine. Against one wall was a long bar with drinks being mixed by a bartender. Rock music played through extra-bass speakers, but not at a volume where people couldn't hear one another talking. Along another wall was a popcorn machine and a table laden with food: sandwiches, pizza, various chips like Doritos and Cheetos, candy, sodas, and water . . .

There were only six men in the room. All of them were attractive, imposing, mysterious. They wore outfits ranging from casual to elegant, and each of them had vibrant, different-colored eyes.

There was a connection linking them. I'd felt it the moment I'd entered the room. A palpable, deadly energy radiated off these seven men. Beneath their pretty façades were cold-blooded killers.

"Faith," Leo began, "these are my brothers."

"Pleasure to meet you, love." A grinning man with a pink Mohawk sauntered over. "I'm Romeo. We're the Seven Sins, but there's an eighth one just for looking at you, you exquisite little treat."

"And a ninth for when I wedge my foot up your ass," I said.

"Wowza." Pink Mohawk backed up a step, and a few of the reapers heckled in amusement. "You're dangerous. I think I'm in heat."

"Romeo's sin is obviously lust," Leo said. "I won't be letting him within six feet of you. You might catch something with an itch." He motioned to the man stuffing a sandwich down his gullet. "That's Gunner."

"Gluttony?" I guessed.

"'Hat would be me," Gunner said around a mouthful of food. "Nice 'o mee' you." He reached for a handful of Red Vine licorice, but the bowl was snatched away by a tattooed arm.

The thief with the tattoos sported gelled-back black hair. Real Mafia-esque. He tore at the Red Vines with his teeth and snarled like an animal. "I'm Wolf." He held out the licorice like a saliva-drenched bouquet, and when he grinned, his canines were unnaturally sharper than the rest of his teeth. "You want some?"

"That's okay." I laughed.

"Keep your valuables away from that one." My attention was drawn to a gray-eyed reaper with ebony skin and a baritone voice. When he stood up, he towered over the others. His dark hair was shaved close to his head like a soldier's, and I could see an intricate black mark on his bicep. Death had a similar tattoo in the same spot. Now that I thought about it, Wolf's tattoos reminded me of Death's as well.

"Denim," the reaper said, and then a polite smile softened his severe face. "Pride."

"Nice to meet you, Denim," I said, returning the smile. "You guys part of a motorcycle gang with these badass names?"

Denim gave a great, unexpected chuckle. "Funny. Death mentioned that you were eccentric."

"You're saying it like a compliment, but you know damn well he meant it as an insult," chimed in another reaper. He wore wire-rimmed glasses, and his sandy-brown hair was combed in a prim style. He sat back on a brown leather couch with his feet crossed at the ankles.

"That's Flash," Denim said when the reaper didn't introduce himself. "Sloth. In Latin, Sloth means 'lack of care — in the world, in themselves, in others.'"

The reapers all grunted in agreement, evidently teasing Flash. He flipped the room off, and it made me laugh at how sibling-like these guys acted.

"It is not just lack of care but resentment that curses me," Flash elucidated, sloshing the drink in his glass thoughtfully. "I'm multi-layered, complex. The Roman poet Virgil described me as 'the effect of an insufficient amount of love.'" He looked out into the distance with a somber expression and sniffed. "I'm misunderstood, really—"

"Get your head out of your arse!" barked a thick Irish accent. "Nobody cares."

"That would be Blade," Leo said with a sigh, motioning to the guy sitting at a table with a whetstone, sharpening a knife. "Wrath, if you couldn't tell."

Blade narrowed his eyes at us before returning to his knife.

"Lovely group," I muttered. "Lust, Gluttony, Pride, Avarice, Wrath, Sloth . . . " My eyes swept the reapers at each sin and then landed on Leo, who was watching me very peculiarly with those amber eyes illuminating like an owl's. "You're Envy."

"I must be," Leo replied, "because I'm jealous how quickly my brothers were able to make you smile."

My face grew hot.

"*Suaaave*," Romeo sang sarcastically.

Leo rubbed the back of his neck. "I think that's enough with the introductions. Who else wants some bland human food?"

The next two hours were the most fun that I'd had in a while. I ate my fill of sandwiches, chips, and root beer. I kicked Leo and Romeo's butts in *Disco Rebel*, since they had all the versions on the PlayStation in the den, and I almost got the new high score. After my victory, there was ice cream cake.

Gunner came forward, his light-green eyes shy as Wolf and Flash clapped him on the shoulder and encouraged him to stand in front of the cake.

"Ah, so you're the birthday boy," I said to Gunner. "How old are you today?"

Gunner scratched his head with a sheepish smile. "I lost track at year two hundred thirty-two."

Dang. Two hundred and thirty-two. I glanced around the room at the seven's young faces. They all appeared to be in their early to mid-twenties, around Death's age. Guess it made sense that they were a bunch of old souls too.

After we sang "Happy Birthday," Gunner closed his eyes theatrically for a wish as his sparkler candles flared like the Fourth of July. I got quiet as I remembered my own wish not too long ago. *I want to know who I am.*

"Birthday boy gets the first piece," Gunner said, smoke drifting from the extinguished candles as he triple-stacked his paper plate. He cut a third of the giant ice cream cake for himself and licked his fingers as he hauled it protectively to his spot at the other end of the table.

"Geez," I muttered to Leo. "Guy can eat."

"I have to make three turkeys on Thanksgiving," Romeo chimed in, leaning over the chair between us to talk to me. "Your birthday just passed last month, didn't it, love? The ol' prophecy and matured-soul situation and all."

"Yep, my birthday was the twentieth," I muttered.

"Congratulations! One year closer to death," Romeo said cheerfully. "Or one day closer to *me*, if you're lucky. No soul leaves the Love Machine unsatisfied."

"Bye," Leo said, shoving Romeo's face as he moved to sit between us.

Laughing, I brought my root beer to my lips, then paused. A high-pitched ringing sounded in the distance, growing louder the more I concentrated on it. I cast my gaze around the room to see if anyone else noticed it.

"Do you hear that?" I asked Leo.

He frowned. "Hear what?"

"That ringing."

Where had I heard it before?

"What ringing?" As Wolf pulled out his phone to check if he had a notification, the ringing seemed to rise, and I rubbed at my ears with a wince.

Leo reached out to touch my arm. "You all right?"

The ringing came to an abrupt halt, leaving me with what could only be described as a claw raking over my brain. I looked down at my forearm, where the ghost of the scar from Malphas's underling still marred my skin.

"Faith?"

Bile climbed up my throat. "Excuse me, I—"

Shoving my seat back, I hurried into the bathroom, barely making it to the toilet before I threw up everything I'd eaten. I flicked on the lights, acid burning my throat and my nostrils. I went straight to the sink and splashed water into my mouth. When I looked up at my reflection, I went rigid with terror.

Ahrimad stood in the mirror, amber eyes flaring with rage.

Bring it to me. His pale lips moved in sync with his voice in my head. *Bring me the book, Faith.*

A scream tore from my throat as I slammed back into the wall behind me and collapsed. The lights flickered violently as the sensation of claws tore into the inside of my skull again. Energy surged down my arms, snapping out my hand as I fired uncontrollably into the toilet, exploding a water pipe.

Leo broke in to the bathroom. His eyes went wide as he took in my crumpled form on the ground and the uncontrollable light gathering in my shaking hands.

"I can't stop it," I said with ragged breaths. The energy kept coming, the blue-and-white orb as wild as an unstable star. I rose onto my knees and turned toward the wall to shield it from Leo. The paint on the walls on either side of my hands began to peel back from the heat of my light.

I know you feel me, Chosen. Ahrimad's voice hissed inside my skull. *I know you hear me.*

I know you hear me.

I know you hear me.

You can't hide forever. You can't outrun destiny . . .

"Go away!" The lights flickered back on with a buzz. A migraine split my skull as warm liquid rushed from my nose to my lips, until I tasted blood. "Leave me alone!"

Light filled my vision and exploded outward in a sonic boom, and I yelped as it knocked me flat on the floor. My ears rang uncontrollably. I covered my head with my hands as bits of ceiling rained down. Leo pulled me across the floor before a piece of it slammed into my leg and barked out orders to the reapers. His voice was muffled as my hearing warped in and out.

You cannot fight me.

Your mind is too weak.

Power raced down my arms. I shoved both of my palms into Leo's chest to try to keep him back. I hit the floor on all fours with a scream, light consuming my surroundings.

Death! Panicking, I roared his name in my mind. *I need you!*

He can't save you from me, Ahrimad seethed in my head. *I am the ultimate death. I am his maker. Feel what I am capable of. See it with your own eyes.*

I was paralyzed: my spine bent back, and my arms went stiff at my sides. My eyes rolled into my head as my worst nightmares came to life. I watched Ahrimad slaughter my family one by one: my mother, my father, Aunt Sarah. Gruesome, unspeakable executions.

Bring me the grimoire! Ahrimad thundered.

I collapsed to all fours again, hyperventilating. Everything merged together, and the room spun in a blur.

"I can't control it," I gasped at the reapers standing in the doorway. "Get away! Everyone get back!"

I raced out of the bathroom. I had to get the hell out of there. I had to—

I crashed into a hard, masculine frame. Strong hands caught my waist, securing me in a tight grasp. *Death.* His nostrils flared as he rapidly scanned my features, those vertical pupils dilating as shadows crept into his irises. I was a live wire buzzing with adrenaline until he laid his gloved hand against my wet cheek.

My knees buckled from exhaustion. Death caught me and held me upright against him as I sobbed uncontrollably.

"What happened?" he thundered. "Someone speak the fuck up! *Now!*"

"I don't know," Leo answered, sounding both worried and in pain. "She was fine, and then—"

"I left you. To *protect* her!" Death snarled.

"Death," I whispered, snapping his attention to my face. "It's not his fault. Please . . . just take me away from here."

A muscle flexed in his jaw. Without a word, he bent down, carefully hoisted me into his arms, and carried me to his penthouse.

XXI

I woke up in the Ferrari of all beds—a king, no, a *castle*-sized mattress on a raised platform with a thick black comforter and matching velvety soft pillows. When I flicked on the lamp beside the bed, it illuminated the tall ceiling above. My mouth fell open. Sheer shadow cascaded from the ceiling in beautiful lacy designs, draping around me like a protective canopy.

I brought the comforter up to my nose, breathed in the familiar scent of *him*, then an icy sensation pricked the side of my face.

"Get a good whiff?"

"Ahh!" I jerked back, hitting my head on the headboard.

The shadowed canopy dropped like a curtain falling to the floor. It gathered together in a hissing, whispering cluster of sinister voices as it absorbed back into the Grim Reaper. Death lounged in a leather chair beside the bed. He rested his arms over the length of the armrests with his legs spread out in that obscenely masculine manner. His short-sleeved black T-shirt exposed his tan biceps and the exotic markings etched all the way down to his wrists. A beat-up, vintage baseball cap shadowed his eyes.

I crumpled the comforter in my hands, my stomach fluttering with nerves as I took in the spacious, masculine room. "What happened?"

"You went through some sort of power surge." The long-gloved fingers of his right hand curled tightly around the chair's armrest. "Don't you remember?"

Thinking about the party with the reapers triggered a tingling in my limbs. I'd felt helpless, terrified, suffocating in my own body, in my own light.

Ahrimad . . .

I gripped the comforter with white knuckles as I tried to calm myself. When I exhaled, my breath caught in the air like a fog. The temperature had plummeted to a bitter cold. I turned accusatorily to Death, whose body was tense and stiff.

"I intended to take you back to your room," he explained slowly, "but you started to violently shake. You had a fever of one hundred twelve degrees Fahrenheit. It didn't drop for two hours."

"That's impossible. A fever that high would . . . it would—"

"Kill you?" Death offered, pushing up from the chair. He closed the distance between the chair and the bed with two smooth strides. "Or at least leave you with severe brain damage, wouldn't you think?"

"Yes," I whispered.

We stared at each other.

"Headache?" he asked.

"No."

"Chills?"

"No."

"Seeing double?"

"No."

"Pain anywhere?"

I did a quick assessment of my body. "Um, no."

He pinched my arm.

"Ow!"

"You still feel pain. Good. When's the last time you had your period?"

"What?"

"Well, you see, Faith," Death began in that husky, monotone way he spoke when he was being sarcastic, "when it's that time of the month, a woman begins to—"

I reached back and whacked him hard with a pillow, which curled his lips into almost a smile. "I'm getting the heck out of here."

When I attempted to sit up, he pushed me back down with a single poke to my chest. "Not until I say so, cupcake."

With a growl, I swatted his hand away and yanked the covers off me.

Death kept his eyes on my face even as I felt a breeze on my legs.

"Holy—!" I pulled down the oversized shirt I was wearing and then yanked the covers back up. I had on cotton underwear but no pants. "You changed my clothes."

"Had to," Death said. "You were soaked in sweat and threw up all over yourself—and me, for that matter." He stretched out his gloved hands. "Ever try to get vomit out of leather? Fun time."

I glanced down at the crumpled blanket around me, trying to wrap my head around the fact that *Death* had taken care of me.

"Take my word for it or don't," Death continued, "but I didn't look at anything or touch any inappropriate areas. You weren't naked either."

"Thank you," I said, "but couldn't you have at least put some pants on me once the fever broke?"

"What do I look like? Goodwill? Besides, all my sweatpants are in the wash, and you don't want my wash mixing with yours. All the blood and gore I get on my pants never comes out in one cycle."

I blinked. *Good God.*

"Get me a pair of clean pants before I scream," I said calmly.

"Fine. Slip these on for now." He strode to the top drawer of one of his dressers and tossed me a pair of black boxers before facing the door. It felt so weird to wear his underwear as shorts, but the band could roll up, and with the length of his legs, his pants would have been a joke on me anyway.

"Tell me what happened in the den," Death said, crossing his arms. "Leo said your power was triggered and you couldn't control it. Did you have a vision or something?"

My chest tightened at the memory. The lack of control I'd had over my power had almost killed me.

"There was this ringing." My fingers absently touched the faded scar on my forearm. "And this scar, it started to, um, hurt . . . "

"Where Malphas's underling infected you." Death reached for my forearm. The warm, firm touch of his gloved hands massaged my flesh; I felt an electric sensation that lifted the little hairs on my arms. But I had a feeling it wasn't from the mark.

"It wasn't Ahrimad," Death murmured, running his finger down the faded pink line, the only reminder of the horrifying day in the alleyway. He lifted his catlike eyes to mine. "This has Malphas written all over it."

"But . . . I saw him. I saw Ahrimad."

"What you saw could have been a hallucination Malphas conjured. Either a hallucination or a mirage of some sort. He's a master of manipulation. I'm not saying Ahrimad wasn't involved, but he's very weak. I don't think he would have risked communicating with you like that."

"What about the ringing?" I inquired.

Death tilted his head to one side thoughtfully. "When a portal splits open, the void between worlds creates a tiny rift in time. A whistle can occasionally be heard. That's where Ahrimad would come in. Given the circumstances that I met him in, trapped in that mirror under the willow, I would assume he has a vast amount of knowledge about the Otherworlds and how to generate portals. Malphas was able to create a mental bridge to you that was secured through your scar and the portal. It must have been a very temporary portal, like the communication one in Limbo that I used to contact Ace. Lucifer's wards are far too strong for them to have physically crossed through it to get to you, so it appears Malphas found a way around that."

As I watched Death piece this all together, I couldn't help but admire his intelligence.

"So, now what do we do?"

Death looked at me like I was insane. "*You* don't do anything. I've already rid the penthouse of all the mirrors, and we're removing any other mirrors in the building today."

"Geez. Even the ones in other people's apartments?"

"Everyone in this building belongs to Hell. Therefore, they belong to me, and so do their belongings. They will do what I say." He took off his cap and raked his fingers through the loose midnight curls of his faux-hawk. "This is the first time you've seen Ahrimad or Malphas since the ball, correct?"

I let my eyes drop. "No, it's not."

Leather creaked as Death clenched his hands. "You saw him before this incident? A vision—"

"Not exactly—"

"Then what was it?" he demanded.

"The night Marcy was taken, I had this dream. Ahrimad and Malphas, they were in some sort of . . . mausoleum."

"You kept this to *yourself*?" His facial features began to sharpen right before my eyes. "Why wouldn't you tell me?" he growled with a sudden ferocity.

Because I don't trust you. Because I've learned the only way to protect myself from you is to keep my secrets, and because I'm afraid, and denial is my favorite coping mechanism.

"Because I didn't think it meant anything," I answered, since I was too stubborn to admit I'd made a stupid mistake. "What happened in the bathroom, I had it under control."

He let out a harsh laugh. "Clearly. Let me go get your wheelchair so you can reenact this 'control' you speak of."

"Your precious cargo is safe and sound," I snapped. "There's no need to be an ass."

"You don't use your damn head, Faith. What happened to you in the bathroom could have been prevented—"

"A *lot* of things between us could have been prevented!" The words exploded out before I could stop them.

"Like if I'd let you die from square one?" Death suggested, his own voice rising. "It's time to be a big girl and move on from the past."

"Oh, screw you!" I seethed. "You're just mad I won't bend over and take it from you like your demon slaves."

I instantly regretted my choice of words. I also regretted getting off the bed, because now we were toe to toe.

"Don't act like you aren't the cause of this whole situation, because you are," I said, burning everywhere. "You're two thousand plus years old and can't handle basic emotions. So don't call *me* childish."

His lip twitched in a brief snarl.

"You're not perfect either," I went on. "You certainly don't have all the answers, and *you*," I added, daring to move into him, my tongue dripping with venom, "you have *fears* too. Or else you would have your precious scythe back by now. Whatever is going on with me, I'll figure it out by myself. You're the last person I want help from."

I strode past him with every intention of leaving, but the room spun.

Death wrapped his arm around me before I could fall, and my heart fluttered as he hoisted me up onto his bed. "I couldn't hear you," Death said, growling the words through his fangs. His hands were firm on my waist, his body standing between my legs. "You called out to me. Then you shut me out, and I couldn't feel you through the bond. I felt *nothing*. Don't do that ever again, Faith. Next time something awful is happening to you, you keep up those walls, and you keep calling out my name. No matter how much you hate me. Swear it."

The way his hands clung to me. The hoarse drop in his voice, the concern in his eyes. It was a rare glimpse of humanity, and I was stunned.

Was it possible he cared?

"All you do is lie to me and play mind games until you create massive rifts in my trust," I whispered. "You didn't tell me Marcy was safe until it was convenient for *you*. And you wonder why I keep my secrets?"

"Swear it, Faith."

"Fine," I said, utterly exhausted. "Fine, I won't shut you out again. You're not going to punish Leo for what happened, are you?"

Death's features shifted and grew colder. "Leo is the incarnation of envy. He wants what he can't have."

"You didn't answer the question." I slid off the bed, and the dizziness didn't follow this time. All I could feel was the pain in my jaw from clenching my teeth. The burn in my stomach. A hunger so relentless, it made me want to *harm*. When I stepped toward Death, those sensations only intensified, and he took a step back. "You're jealous."

"Faith," Death warned in a low gruff, "get out of my face—"

I clutched his shirt to keep him in place, and his menacing glare promised violence. "You're *jealous* that I spent time with Leo and the rest of the Seven."

Death ran his tongue over his teeth with a dark laugh. "You are getting some real heavy iron balls on you, cupcake."

"Deny it."

Darkness consumed us both.

We manifested across the room. My breath caught as he slammed me to the wall beside the bed, stealing my breath away. "I have nothing to deny," he growled. "If you knew what goes on in my head when you're around. If you were brave enough to cross into the shadows of my twisted mind, you'd see. I have no competition."

Death moved his lips down the column of my throat. "Because any man can make you laugh," he whispered in a velvet-clad voice, my pulse pounding as his bottom lip brushed my bare skin. "Any man can tell you all the sweet, romantic folly you think you need, but none of them can shake the ground beneath your feet. None of them could go against nature for you. Shift a storm, darken the moon, beckon the night." His tongue traced the sensitive part of my ear, sending chills down my back. "Make you feel so good being very, very bad . . . "

It took everything in me to move out from his grasp, and when I did, Death's seductive expression easily shifted to boredom, like a lazy cat that had had all its fun anyway. Still, I could feel his warm presence lingering against my skin even as he slowly slunk toward the bed. He lazed back against the mattress, a strand of black hair falling over his forehead, and leered at me from beneath thick lashes.

A villain's open invitation.

"*Good night*, Death."

His mouth curved. "Sweet nightmares, cupcake."

I walked out of his bedroom and into mine. The bedside lamps were on, and a black box secured with beautiful black ribbon lay on my bed. I felt lame that my heart fluttered just at the sight.

I ran my fingers over the silken ribbon. I glanced over my shoulder. Death lingered in the doorway, his mouth slightly parted with words he never said. He stared down at the present in my hands in blank surprise.

"Is this from you?" I asked.

Death went quiet, but those mismatched eyes darted to mine.

He vanished into smoke.

"Okay," I said to the empty room. What the heck was happening?

A minute or so later, Death reappeared. His cheeks were slightly flushed, and his hair was sticking up. Like he'd run his hand through it. In his fist, he held a folded piece of paper.

"Here," he grunted.

He placed it awkwardly on top of the present.

I smiled. He'd gotten me a gift.

"Lucifer wants to meet with us tomorrow morning," Death said, his voice tight and unlike him. "Be dressed by eight."

Then he was gone again.

I reached for the card and tore it open, recognizing Death's neat script: *It wasn't all a lie.*

I sat down on the bed, feeling as though I was floating. The present was heavy. My fingers shook a little as I pulled the silk ribbon, and it all fell away. I popped the lid to the box, and my hand slowly rose to cup my mouth.

Inside was a clear glass display container with a teddy bear inside. Not just any ordinary teddy bear, though. It was Mr. Wiggles, my childhood teddy bear from home. I knew it was him because of the red heart sewn into his chest, a patch that my grandma had made after Aunt Sarah's dog got hold of him and tore out half his stuffing in seconds. I remembered how devastated I had been that day as I opened the glass container to run my thumb over his heart. The teddy bear's left arm, which had been hanging on by a thread, was properly attached now, and his torso was plumper and softer, like he'd been filled with new stuffing. The big, red bow tied around his neck was rich silk.

I thought about my family and the life I'd left behind. I missed my parents so much. They were safe, and Marcy was too. But that didn't change the fact that nothing would be the same again. And all at once, this silly old teddy bear was my everything again. I hugged Mr. Wiggles hard, bursting into tears. Imagine my surprise when his voice box, which had broken years before, went off as I squeezed him.

"I'm Mr. Wiggles, and I love to sing this song! Clap your hands and you can sing along. Be my friend and I'll be yours. Hug me when you're feeling blue . . . "

The exhaustion of the night overcame me, and I slept with him clutched in my arms.

A loud crash jarred me awake.

Cruentas sat at the foot of my bed, his tail anxiously swishing back and forth. I groggily checked the alarm on the nightstand and set Mr. Wiggles aside. Three in the morning.

I heard another slam that sounded like it was from the kitchen.

Jumping from the bed, I crossed the room and unlocked the door. A month ago, I would have hidden under the covers. Now I was creeping down a dark hallway to see what all the commotion was about.

Shuffling. Cabinets rapidly opening and shutting. The sound of a glass shattering. A deep, baritone voice cursed, followed by a cold sensation shimmying down my spine. I relaxed marginally.

Rounding the corner, I peered into the kitchen. Blacker than the darkness of the kitchen, he continued rifling through cabinets, searching for something. "What are you doing?"

Death stiffened. Lowering to a hunch, he leaned over the sink and kept his back to me. "Go back to bed."

The tension in his voice undeniably conveyed pain. I went to the wall and turned the dimmer light on halfway, my eyes widening at the mess of paper towels crumpled all over the counter.

Blood. Blood as black and oily as his demigod father's.

Death had turned his face from the light, but not before I caught the blood streaking his cheek.

"Oh my God! What happened?"

"I'm handling it."

He tried to maneuver past me, but I blocked his way. The fact that he didn't try to manifest around me set off alarms in my head.

"You're bleeding all over the floor!" I cried. "Why are you holding your stomach like that?"

"Because if I don't my *intestines* will fall out," he snarled. "Now *move*."

I blocked his way again. A low warning growl sounded from his throat, but I stood my ground. "I know you don't want my help, but you *need* my help. Now stop being a stubborn ass and tell me what you're looking for."

Death released an aggravated noise, evidently too incapacitated to fight me. "First aid kit," he muttered. "I thought I had a clotting dressing in the one under the sink to try to stop the bleeding, but I don't."

"I'll find it for you. In the meantime, please sit down."

Death made another disgruntled noise, like he didn't want to be ordered around. He stepped forward to bulldoze past me and staggered. I gasped as he suddenly toppled to the side and sagged against the archway. Reaching out fast, I grabbed his arm and slung it over my shoulder, then hooked my arm around his waist, careful not to touch where his hand was clutching his gut.

"To the table," I ordered. "Lean on me."

We made our way into the dining room, until Death was close enough to a chair to dump himself into it. His massive body hardly fit in the seat, but now wasn't time to get Goldilocks picky on our seat choice.

"Downstairs," Death breathed, his deep voice ragged and weak. "In the closet where I keep the wrap for your knuckles. Large first aid kit. It's blue."

He'd hardly finished, and I was already sprinting to the gym.

With all of the gear and equipment we had been using recently, it took a minute of scrambling and moving things around in the closet to find the kit. When I got back to the main floor, Death was hunched over and worse for wear. He'd managed to shrug out of his cloak and drape it over his chair, but he appeared to be struggling to take off his tattered black shirt.

"You might want to look away."

But I didn't. I set down the first aid kit, taking in the ghastly sight of his injury.

"That looks horrible."

"It'll heal." Using one hand, Death wrangled his T-shirt the rest of the way over his head and then peeled off his right glove with his fangs. He reached for the first aid kit and popped it open. His nails were black and pointed at the tips, like deadly blades prepared to unleash. "Need to sew it up to speed up the process, though."

"I'll call for help."

"*No,*" Death said firmly. "Don't call anyone. This stays between you and me."

"Okay," I said. "But you can't sew yourself shut, can you?"

"I've done it a thousand times before." I watched him attempt to thread a needle with his enormous, bloody hand and noticed the slight tremble to his fingers. Evidently, asking for help was not in his nature.

"Give me that." I plucked the needle from his grasp and threaded it for him. Then I bit the bullet and pulled up a chair to sit in front of him.

"Faith . . . "

"It can't be that difficult, can it? At least not this part." I pointed to the part of the wound where the skin hadn't torn as far apart. "My mom's mom, Grandma Evelyn, she was a seamstress and taught me how to sew when I was a kid." I took the plunge and started to stitch up the wound, and Death didn't even flinch. "She still makes her own clothes, and whenever I see her, I like to watch her work. I've just never sewn up a . . . well, a *body.*"

I was babbling, but I was focused, and I could do this. I could feel his stare on me as I worked. Suturing a wound was trickier than patching up a pair of jeans, that's for sure, but with his occasional guidance, I got much further than I thought I could.

"So," I said. "You gonna tell me how this happened?"

"Harpies."

"*Herpes?*"

Death laughed unexpectedly, then hissed with a curse. His first outward sign of pain since I'd started suturing. "*Har*pies," he corrected through clenched teeth. "With an a."

"Ah, see, that makes more sense. Your accent got a little thick there." I wonder if he knew I'd heard him correctly and had just tried to lighten up the mood.

"Harpies are avian monsters." Appearing to be gaining strength, Death carefully took the needle from me and finished the suturing. "Violent, temperamental creatures that manifest from the Underworld through storms. I had a run-in with a group of them in an abandoned church. Harpies are notoriously unlucky, and there was a whole hive of the damn vultures."

"Can I ask what you were doing in an abandoned church? Other than being insanely cliché?"

Another brusque noise that resembled a laugh. "I'd tell you, but I'd have to kill you." On that enigmatic note, Death closed the wound. While I was impressed by his rapid needlework, it was also disturbing that it seemed to have been learned by rote. "The harpies pinned me down and ripped out half my bowels before I managed to get free."

"Ow."

Death cut the string with his talon. "For a mortal who threw up after running half a mile, you have an iron stomach. That was gruesome."

"It was three miles, you jerk," I replied. "And I'm just as surprised as you are." The truth was, I'd been so worried about him that nothing else had mattered. "Let me, um, get some soap and water to help clean you up."

"I don't want—"

"*Eh!*" I held up a palm for him to shut it, already backing out of the room. "Sit your undead ass down."

The kitchen was an utter mess. I gathered as many dirty paper towels as I could and threw them in the trash. I washed my hands first, then got a roll of paper towels and three bowls. Two of the bowls I filled with clean, warm water, one with added soap, and the third was empty for dirty water.

When I carried my supplies back to the dining room, I saw

Death had discarded the rest of his mangled shirt and was lounging back in his chair. The stitches had done their job to aid his supernatural healing, and his skin had already miraculously mended back together. I tried and failed not to ogle the hulking breadth of his shoulders, the obscene swell of muscle in his thick biceps and pecs, and the deep ridges of muscle in his abdomen. An *injured* abdomen. One I shouldn't have been checking out, let alone been attracted to, all things considering.

Wetting a paper towel in soapy water and internally scolding myself, I began to wipe away the blood from his skin. Keeping my mind out of the gutter was virtually impossible when my hands were rubbing suds all over his body like a freaking car wash. My hand shook as I ran a fresh damp paper towel over his stitches to try to clean the area. When I brushed his lower stomach, he straightened in his chair with a jolt and gripped my forearm tightly.

I looked up at him, those magnetic eyes clashing with mine. Steady. Imploring. Wanting.

"That's enough." His voice had reached a low timbre, and his accent had thickened. "I . . . *appreciate* your assistance in cleaning the blood off," he continued, the grateful words stumbling out inelegantly as he released his hold on me, "but there's no need to disinfect the wound. I'm not prone to mortal illness."

"Oh. Right." I prayed that my face wasn't as crimson-red as it felt. "In the alleyway," I began, "when all those demons were attacking you, weren't you injured badly like this? You were wearing your cloak, so it was hard to tell, but I swear you didn't seem hurt in the warehouse."

"It's because I don't have my scythe," Death elucidated, lifting his hips off the chair and reaching into the back of his pants to retrieve a new pair of black gloves. "The blade helps me collect at a much faster rate. I'm not as satiated as I normally am. It affects my ability to heal, and it's why the harpies managed to pin me down in the first place."

He stood up slowly and walked to the couch, where he collapsed onto the cushions with a groan. "You should get to bed. It's late."

Sending me off to bed like a child. Was that how he thought of me? I was about to retreat into my bedroom when I thought better. I strode into the living room and stood in front of him with my arms folded.

Death wiped a gloved hand over his face. "Yes?"

"What you did . . . with my teddy bear," I said, "I didn't expect it. It meant a lot to me."

Death shifted in his seat and adjusted a pillow.

"And I need to know . . . " I stepped closer to the couch. "Did you mean it? What you wrote in your note?"

His mismatched green eyes flicked up to mine and lingered. I had my answer.

I closed the distance between us and bent down to press my lips against his. At first, his lips were firm and unyielding against mine, but then he let his guard down, and what I had intended to be brief peck burned to a fiery, aching caress that vowed to ruin me.

I pulled back to find that I'd ruined him too. His eyelids were half-lowered, his mouth parted, his dangerous expression torn between wanton desire and a monstrous hunger. I wasn't sure which side had overcome him the most.

The Angel of Death beckoned me closer with a single inclined finger.

Suddenly, I was in his arms, my knees indenting the soft leather couch on either side of his waist. He clutched my hips with his large, demanding hands and yanked me down to his lap. Our hips ground together, and I could feel his chest hitch as he hissed in pain.

"Your wound," I gasped. "I shouldn't have—"

Death's gloved hand collared around my throat. "Kiss me."

A soft sigh escaped me as we ruthlessly made out, his mouth roughly seizing my lips over and over. My fingers slid up his solid chest to his neck, weaving into his hair and tugging. It drew a growl out of him that rumbled his chest, and his fingers dug greedily into my ass. I felt the sharp points of his talons pinch into my skin through his gloves and gasped. He swallowed my breath in another dizzying kiss as his hands lowered to the back of my thighs and then slid up to my waist, our lips exploring, hot, tasting, battling in the war we had started long ago.

He lifted the fabric of my shirt, warm leather grazing my bare skin as he teased his way up my ribs like climbing a ladder. When he cupped my breasts, my heart beat faster than a hummingbird's against his deadly palms. Nothing but him. There was nothing but him.

Then he was gone in wisps of black smoke.

I fell forward onto the cold, empty leather couch. Death had materialized across the room, panting hard. He had his back to me, a hand braced on the wall.

"*Fuck*, Faith."

He moved in a blur, threw open his bedroom door, and slammed it behind him. Beyond the door, I heard something crash. I don't know how long I stared at the door in disbelief at what we'd done before I went off to bed.

Whatever we were, it was sick, twisted, sinful. He was dark and I was light, and I wouldn't be foolish enough to let my heart fade into the obscurity of the gray between us.

But now, soon to be fighting side-by-side, I wondered if, like the madness of our bodies pressed together, we would be a force to be reckoned with.

XXII

"Cute drool."

Having almost fallen asleep, I jolted at the deep voice in my ear and smacked my spoon on the table into a flip.

Death rounded the dining room table, twirling my once-airborne spoon between his fingers. I did a double take. He prowled across the room with the glide of a panther, muscles shifting beneath a sharp black dress shirt and black slacks. Tailored perfectly to his menacing frame, the ensemble both attracted and intimidated with all the lethality of an apex predator.

"Cat got your tongue?" Death purred.

"Remind me to put a bell around your neck," I seethed.

"Someone's a wittle cwanky."

I bit my tongue. He knew damn well *he* was the cranky one ninety-nine percent of the time. After helping Death with his harpy wound last night and sucking his face off, I hadn't slept a minute. He, on the other hand, seemed well rested and unbothered. By the touch of a healthy tan in his complexion and the spry gleam to his catlike eyes, I could tell he had collected souls that morning.

Death sipped from the large black mug in his hand. I wondered if it was coffee in his morning cup or something villainous, like gasoline, liquid souls, or the blood of his enemies. He lifted the mug away, and a small white crescent lingered on the dark stubble along his upper lip.

"Cream?"

"Warm. Four sugars," Death said with a wink. Then he downed the mug like it was a shot and licked away any evidence with a swipe of his tongue. "Grab a jacket, cupcake. It'd be a shame if you froze off those perfect tits."

I choked a little on my cereal and glared in his direction. "What exactly is this meeting about?"

"You'll see."

Death parked his motorcycle illegally at the entrance to D&S Tower, and an employee rushed out to move it. The cryptic nature of this meeting had launched my imagination into overdrive, and I instantly thought about the reason Lucifer had wanted my soul in the first place.

When we entered the lobby, a nervous, uneasy energy settled sourly in my gut, labored my breath, and formed a small, throbbing headache behind my eyes. The lobby was eerily empty, without the usual frenetic energy of employees rushing about.

Death punched a gloved finger into the elevator door and checked the time on a black Rolex on his wrist. I cast a look over my shoulder: the glass doors through which we'd entered were now guarded by four armed men.

As per usual, the long ride up to the top floor was torture. I hated tight spaces. But this time, when the elevator walls closed in, I felt a different sort of apprehension. The nausea blooming in my stomach swelled, and I put a hand to my neck as the sensation climbed up my throat.

The elevator doors opened with a chime. I did not move. The nervous energy had magnified until it became external, until it became a tether. An invisible force reeling me in. I stepped off the elevator, the pristine marble entryway pulsing to the rhythm of my heart. Dissociation numbed all thought as I felt detached from my body, an onlooker watching myself trail behind Death's long strides.

The Grim Reaper pulled open a glass door and gestured me forward. "After you."

Heading into a small waiting room, the air went static, raising the hairs on my arms.

I took a deep breath and entered Devin Star's office.

The Devil poured a drink at his personal bar, wearing a perfectly pressed navy suit. He had his back to me and didn't turn as I entered.

Sitting at the long glass meeting table was Aunt Sarah. My heart clenched. Her red, inflamed eyes indicated she had recently been crying. When she saw me, she snapped out of her chair to stand, her weary face wracked with worry. A moment of conflict passed between us before I raced toward her for a constricting hug.

"Oh, thank God," she whispered against my hair. Then she held me at arm's length to clutch my face in her hands. "Are you okay? Has he hurt you?"

Not in the way she was asking, at least. "I'm fine." There was so much to tell her, including the fact that I had read her note about the Guild, but we weren't alone. And I had a feeling it wouldn't matter anyway. "What's happening? Why are we both here?"

"I'm so sorry, Faith. I did everything I could—"

"Have a seat, ladies." Devin's smooth voice cut through our moment, and I jumped. He was standing directly behind me.

I glanced back at Aunt Sarah, who sat obediently at the head of the table. *What the hell?*

I remained standing, my eyes trained on Devin as he sauntered over to his desk.

"Now, Faith," Devin began, "I'll save you some anxiety and cut to the chase. I know your aunt debriefed you about the *Book of the Dead*. Told you her little tale about the Guild and then shared *our* belief that you are the Chosen who can read it."

At *our*, my attention shifted over to Death. He was a dark presence in the room, peering out a floor-to-ceiling window and into the city while he smoked a cherry roll-up. The brooding storm outside matched his mood.

"With Sarah's gracious help, we were able to recover the grimoire last night," Devin Star continued.

My attention snapped to Devin. To my aunt. *"What?"*

Aunt Sarah had given him the book.

"How could you do this?" I cried.

But as I stared into her wide, terrified eyes, I understood. She had been willing to die to stop this, until he'd broken her. Somehow, he'd broken her.

"I felt it would be best to test our theory straightaway," Devin said.

My heart beat a thousand times per minute. "You have the *Book of the Dead*? In this room?"

"Indeed," Devin murmured, those sharp, glacier eyes unblinking. "Although, you already knew that, didn't you?"

Coldness slipped down my spine. I could sense Death slinking somewhere nearby, the shadows in the room shifting with him.

Thump.

I looked down at what the Devil had dropped on the table in front of Aunt Sarah. A small, pocket-sized book. Devin distanced

himself a few feet. He wore thick gloves on his hands that were disintegrating right before my eyes with a yellowish smoke.

"Sarah," Devin said in a velvet voice. "Your turn."

Aunt Sarah lowered her eyes to the book, a tear sliding down her
cheek. She took a deep breath and laid her hand directly on it.

"I, Sarah Pierce," she began, her voice tremulous, "your loyal
protector, pass you to my blood, Faith Williams."

My heart fell.

She slid the *Book of the Dead* across the table, inches away from
me. Stones swirled in an intricate design on a black leather cover, and
four old latches bound the pages together.

I couldn't help but laugh.

"*This* is the *Book of the Dead*?" I asked. "It's just a diary."

But as I continued to stare at the little book, an eerie feeling
came over me.

It was watching me too.

Devin and Sarah were speaking, their voices fading into the
distance. The air crackled against my fingertips, that odd tethering
sensation snapping suddenly like a rubber band. The *Book of the
Dead* slid sharply across the table to me, and I froze.

Everyone fell silent. Aunt Sarah had gone pale, and the Devil
was grinning from ear to ear.

"Please," Devin said, motioning to the glass table before us,
"have a seat."

"Hell no," I said. "You can go pound salt."

Devin arched a golden brow. "Excuse me?"

"If I can read this thing, then you'll make me your bitch," I said,
rolling my shaking fingers into fists. "You'll use me for whatever sick,
evil plan you have, and I'd rather die than be a part of it."

Aunt Sarah smiled with unspoken pride at my response, though
her mouth turned down as the Devil sauntered closer to the table.

"I'm afraid, my dear," the Devil drawled, "*you* dying is not on the schedule for today."

A snapping noise whipped through the air from behind him, and Aunt Sarah cried out with a gurgling choke. My eyes widened as I realized it was a long, ropy *tail* that had impaled her throat, the deadly arrowhead embedding into her carotid artery.

"*No!*" I started toward her when leather bit into my forearm. Death manifested beside me and pulled me sharply into him. And what I found in his face was frighteningly cold and monstrous. Darkness spread out from his towering frame, and the tattoos along his neck slithered up his face like deadly cobras.

I writhed against Death's hold, but it was like trying to bend steel.

"What are you doing?" I shouted, my chest heaving. "Let go of me—!"

"*Faith!*" Aunt Sarah gurgled, snapping my attention to her in horror. "I love you—"

Devin released her throat with a snarl, blood pouring from her neck. I screamed at the top of my lungs. He quickly waved his hand, and she faded into nothing with a wisp of fire.

"I'll kill you!" I roared. "I'll fucking kill you!"

The Devil's tail whipped behind him, his expression utterly fiendish. Like he wanted *more*.

And I'd give him more.

I thrashed against Death harder, my arms burning hot as a rage unlike anything I'd felt before took over. Somehow, I shoved the Grim Reaper away with every intention of charging at Lucifer, but Death manifested back into my path with a wicked grin and snatched me around the throat. His other hand cuffed my wrist, and I could feel my power radiating off my palm.

"*Obey.*" The slits of his pupils dilated, the single command snapping my spine ramrod straight as I felt a hard tug inside my chest. My *soul*. My breath caught in my throat, tears sliding down my face. *"You will sit down at the table and behave."*

The low drawl of his velvet-clad voice hypnotized me, and through a dreamlike haze, I obeyed. I lowered into a chair, vibrating with anger.

Death stalked around the table, roughly grabbed a chair across from me, and sat down with his dress shoes kicked up onto the table. He pulled a lollipop from his pocket. "See what happens when you fuck around, Faith?"

I could hear Devin snickering, but I couldn't remove my glare from Death. He unwrapped the lollipop, dipped it into the crimson pool on the table, and licked it off.

He was just as bad as Lucifer. A heartless monster.

"Now," the Devil said, "will you cooperate? Or must we bring another mortal pig to slaughter?"

Seething, I turned my fury to Devin, who was standing casually with his hands in his pockets again. Like he hadn't just slaughtered my aunt.

He loves her.

Death's unexpected voice in my head made me pause. He subtly slid the lollipop from his mouth and pressed it against his lips as though to indicate that was our little secret.

Lucifer loved my aunt.

Death was telling me he wouldn't let her die.

Incredibly relieved, I showed no outward reaction.

"What do you want?" The question grated through my tight teeth, directed at the Devil.

"Open the book," Devin said.

My vision pounded to the beat of my heart. In the seconds since I'd last looked upon the *Book of the Dead*, it had transformed and swelled six times its original size. And the locks, they were unlatched.

Slowly and unsurely, I reached toward the grimoire to lightly brush its obsidian cover. The smooth, waxy texture deeply disturbed me. It almost felt like . . . human skin.

Chosen.

A force heaved into me, knocking the wind right out of me, but I didn't fall backward. A phantom yanked me forward instead. The book flew open on its own, my palms slamming against the pages. Pages that melted to hot liquid, seeping through my fingers like lava.

A vapor rolled over my surroundings in chaotic whirl, and suddenly I was no longer in Devin's office. I was . . . somewhere else . . . trapped in endless darkness. In front of me, the book lay open, hovering in the empty air. My stomach twisted into knots, the black murkiness on the pages melted away, revealing words and pictures like cryptograms.

Words fluctuated along the parchment, a Rubik's Cube shifting each row of blocks until the puzzle finished and it all translated to English. The book came to life again, feathering out with endless possibilities . . .

Footsteps. Movement snapped my attention to the side, but nothing was there.

"Hello?"

Slowly, I turned back to the book. Instead of finding the grimoire, I found myself. Standing right in front of me. She stood perfectly still, a lifeless doll with glossy, dead eyes.

When I turned my head to the left, she mirrored me. To the right, the same. Then a sly smile unlike my own curved her mouth, and she stopped following my lead.

"I have waited for you, Chosen," it said. "Tell me, Faith Williams, what do you seek?"

It all warped away, and I was screaming. Devin had slammed the book shut, the thick glove disintegrating into smoke as he hastily tugged it off.

I sagged in my seat, trembling, utterly exhausted.

Doomed beyond belief.

It was true. I was the Chosen.

"Excellent," Devin said, clearly having arrived at the same conclusion. "I will need more equipment to move the book to a safer location."

"I hope it melts the scales off your nasty lizard face," I spat.

Devin leaned back, though he appeared more amused than insulted. "You have quite the spirit in you, Faith," he observed. "I do admire aspects of it."

"I don't," Death grumbled as he slowly licked the pink lollipop he balanced casually between two fingers. "In fact, I often think of something she could wrap her mouth around to shut that spirit right up."

My face burned.

Devin's lip curled with a low hiss, and the room's temperature rose a few notches. "Now that we have confirmation that she's the one," he said, speaking to Death as though I were no longer in the room, "we need to discuss where you are with regard to recovering your scythe."

I looked over at Death in confusion. They hadn't discussed recovering his scythe this entire time. Weren't Lucifer and Death a team?

"I have a source that is confident that Ahrimad will open a portal into the mortal realm in a week and a half. All I need to do is narrow down the location."

"How many soldiers will you require to resolve this situation quickly?"

"Not sure yet."

"Very well," Lucifer said with a dismissive wave of his hand. "I'll watch the girl while you're gone."

"Wait, what?" I exploded. "What about Ace? What about his vision?"

Death slowly turned his head toward me, his jaw twitching, like I'd made an enormous mistake. He bit down on the lollipop with a crunch.

Lucifer's sharp gaze snapped to Death. "What is she talking about?"

"May I speak with you in private?" Death asked Devin, his politeness carefully masking what I knew to be rage. He hadn't told Lucifer about Ace's vision. But why?

"What you have to say to me, you can say out loud," Devin said. "I wouldn't want to be rude."

"The warlock," Death began begrudgingly, "had a vision. He said a portal between this world and where Ahrimad is located would open, and that is when Ahrimad would unleash his army."

"And you didn't tell me this," Devin questioned, biting the words out, *"because?"*

"Your Majesty, you indicated on multiple occasions I was to recover my scythe on my own."

To this, Devin said nothing. "And what about the girl's training?"

"What *about* the girl's training?"

"If I didn't know any better," Devin said around a hostile grin, "I'd say you were training her to come with you."

"Because he is," I said, and suddenly all eyes were on me.

And Lucifer began to laugh. I waited for Death chime in. Instead, he lit up another cherry cigarette and snickered under his breath.

"Is that what he told you?" Lucifer asked. "That he was training you to *fight with him*?"

"Yes," I whispered. "That's what was implied, at least."

Lucifer clucked his tongue. "Well, that's just cruel. Tell her the truth, Death. Tell her why you're *really* training her."

Death wore a bored, passive expression. "If you insist . . . " He dragged his gaze across the table to meet mine, smoke escaping his nostrils. "Training you has been the only way to get you stop bitching and moaning about your old mortal life."

I stared at him. All this time. All this time training, and he'd never intended to take me with him. He'd lied to avoid dealing with my emotions.

Rage simmered inside me, until I reached my boiling point.

I had to get out of this office. *Now.*

I sprang to my feet, heading toward the door.

"Go after her," Devin said in an amused drawl. "Make sure she doesn't do anything stupid. We need her alive."

XXIII

Outside D&S Tower, I immediately turned on the Grim Reaper and felt myself detonate. "What the hell did your boss do to my aunt?"

Death sauntered to the curb with a lazy arrogance and stomped out his cherry cigarette. He materialized a tinted helmet from nothing before shoving it unexpectedly onto my head and swinging a long leg over his bike. "Not here; you're drawing attention to us. Get on."

I managed to contain my rage the entire drive back to his apartment. The second his front door shut, I zeroed in on him like a bull about to charge a red cape.

"All right," Death said, dumping his keys into the usual dish. "Let's talk—"

"Yes, let's!" I exclaimed. "If I could bring you back to life, I would! *To kill you again!*"

"Are you going to keep screaming at me, or will you hear me out?"

"Tell me my aunt is okay," I growled.

"Your aunt is fine. Lucifer used an illusion to persuade you to cooperate. But I wouldn't count on being so lucky next time."

"I need to see her. Now."

"Not happening."

"Why? Because you're scared shitless of Lucifer?"

Death laughed and ran his tongue over his teeth. "Keep it up and I'll kill her myself, sweetheart."

I lost it.

"Argh!" I pulled back my arm and pitched my power at his face, but Death swiped out his hand in a blur and captured it in his gloved palm. Shadow consumed my light into a mini vortex, extinguishing it.

Oh.

He came at me like a bullet. Tendrils of darkness slammed me up against the wall, shackling my wrists and ankles to the door.

"Do. Not. *Ever*," Death snarled, his accent thickening as he loomed over my restrained body, "do that again."

I took a breath to calm myself. Trying to assume a reasonable tone, I asked, "Did you mean it? When you said you trained me to get me to shut up about my mortal life?"

He turned his face away, stalling.

"I thought I was going with you. I thought—"

"Be realistic." Death flattened his hand on the wall beside my head. "No amount of training would allow you to win against an ancient creature like Ahrimad, or a demigod like my father, or, for the matter, *me*. If I can take my scythe back on the full moon, I can avoid entering the otherworld altogether."

"And what if you fail? What if you epically fail like you did in the corn maze against your father? What if the consequences are greater than the risks? Did you ever think about that?"

His temper flared. Shadows bit into my wrists and ankles like thorns on a rose. I writhed against the darkness, but to my frustration, it didn't budge. Death's mouth quirked up on one side as he witnessed the struggle.

"I told you," I said in a huff, "I've had a gut feeling we're supposed to follow Ace's vision. I'm supposed to go with you. You might think you're so high and mighty going up against fate, but some of us can't afford the repercussions. I have a family to think about. I have *myself*. I'm not immortal like you are."

Death's jaw tightened. "You're not strong enough to fight against Ahrimad. End of story."

Neither are you! I so desperately wanted to scream.

"All this time, you never intended to take me with you to fight Ahrimad. You toyed with the idea of it to keep me complacent!" My fingers tingled, power rushing through my veins. Shadows hissed against my hands, retreating down my forearms and freeing my wrists from the wall. Death must have known that I was about to explode again because he struck like a viper and snatched my hands in his.

"Enough," he warned in a low, authoritative voice. "You've only been training defensively for a short time. As long as you have the one thing Ahrimad needs the most, as long as you're the Chosen, the one who can read the *Book of the Dead*, you've got a massive target on your back."

"You want to talk about risk? All of evil wants a piece of me. I'm not safe anywhere I go. But you, you've kept me . . . relatively safe." *Give or take a few villain-esque instances . . .* "Even if it's for your own benefit," I added, mostly to remind myself. "And now you're going to hand me off to Lucifer when everything is at stake? You lose your scythe for good, you're donezo. Then what? Everyone gets so hung up on the consequences of magic, but what happens when *Death himself* is gone? Open your eyes, Death. Every time we are apart, things take a turn for the worse. We're stronger together."

Death released my hands at once and took a step back.

A lump formed in my throat at the rejection. "You saw what Malphas was able to do to my mind. Who's to say they won't figure out a way to reach me from inside this penthouse? Who's to say Ahrimad won't make his move the *second* he knows you've handed me off to somebody else?"

Death raked a hand through his hair. "Even if I wanted to take you with me," he said, biting off the reluctant words, "Lucifer would never allow it."

"Ah, so that's why you didn't tell Lucifer about Ace's vision. Lucifer's got you with your tail between your legs—"

"Watch it." Shadows curled over Death's broad shoulders and cracked at the air like whips. His deep voice altered to a monstrous, otherworldly snarl. "I obey Lucifer's command out of respect. A concept you, an impertinent little mortal brat, know nothing about." A sharp smirk edged his mouth. "I am pleased to see that I've finally broken you down to anger rather than pitiful tears, but I would think twice as to what you do with this anger next—"

Death's sentence cut off as I placed my hand on his chest. Meeting the intensity of his gaze, I slowly lifted my fingers up to his face, swiping my thumb over his velvety soft bottom lip. His mouth parted under my touch, revealing the tips of serrated teeth.

"You'll *never* break me," I whispered. "Not when I own you as much as you own me."

Blackness washed over Death's catlike eyes, dispersing from his vertical pupils into the white sclera. He inhaled a rough breath. The darkness swiftly retreated to where it belonged, but it was never far away.

He moved closer. He must have because I was suddenly consumed by him. My fingers shifted from his mouth across the rough stubble on his jaw and into the back of his silken hair. He was a god up close. A masterpiece. A poison. He was everything, and no matter how much I tried to deny it, I wanted all of him and, selfishly, more. His head dipped until his mouth hovered over mine, his undead heart pounding against my palm.

"If you ever lay a claim on me like that again," Death said, "be prepared to prove it." The low, dangerous rasp of his threat dripped with a dark, carnal intention that speared my core.

But I wouldn't let him get the upper hand. "All this time, you were training me for nothing. You lied to me, but that's not what hurts the most." I stared deep into his wicked eyes, daring to meet his evil soul. "It was the look on your face when Lucifer commanded you to tell me the truth. It was the second of hesitation where you didn't know which secret to share."

Death's face remained unmoved, but the knob in his throat dipped as he swallowed.

"Someone is at the front door, King D."

The panel beside the door lit up as his security system notified him. Frowning, Death jabbed a gloved finger into the screen. The camera pointing into the hallway outside his penthouse displayed footage of the entryway. All we could see was a playing card in front of the lens.

"Ace of spades," I said with a smile.

Death released a small snarl and stormed down the hall. He threw open his front door so hard that he broke the doorstop.

"Ah, I sense I am interrupting an important conversation!" announced a familiar French-accented voice. "Allow me to, how you say, *stir the pot.*"

Ace shouldered Death to the side as he swaggered into the penthouse like he owned the place. Wearing an oversized white-and-gray faux-fur winter coat over an all-white suit, the man dripped lavish elegance.

"*Ma chérie*, you look magnificent." He bent over my hand to kiss the back of it. Over the warlock's shoulder, Death's eyes went feral. As if sensing the Grim Reaper's rage, Ace lowered his sunglasses down the bridge of his nose to give me a playful wink. "Ready for our hot date?"

Ace's timing could not have been any more perfect.

"Sure am!" I said cheerfully.

Death produced an inhuman noise that landed between a bestial growl and a menacing hiss. "The fuck she is. Get out of my goddamn house."

Death stormed toward the warlock, but Ace turned sharply around, striking the Grim Reaper hard in the side. Power exploded. Death grunted as his massive frame was thrown back, magic bolting him to the wall behind him.

I covered my mouth with my hand to suppress a gasp.

"Tsk-tsk," Ace said. "A deal is a deal, *Alex*."

God, this was perfect.

I put a finger to my chin, appreciating how similar this was to the position Death had had me trapped in moments before. "Karma is a bitch, ain't it, big boy?"

Death strained against the binds on his wrists so hard that the tendons in his neck and shoulders bulged. "You wait until I get my hands on you, cupcake."

His untraceable accent had thickened, and the threat swept over me like a stroke of heat.

"Our carriage awaits," Ace said, ushering me forward. "Should you need us, don't. I'll be wooing Faith tirelessly until midnight."

Death spat a foreign sentence, at which Ace laughed. He twirled me into the hallway like we were dancing, slamming the penthouse door closed behind us.

We rode the elevator down, all smiles and giggles. Outside, a limo waited. Ace opened the door in a gentlemanly manner and helped me inside.

"He's going to kill you, you know," I said.

"Eh, he can get in line. I'd give him an hour or two until he breaks free of those bonds. By then, we'll be in my shop, safe and sound." Ace shrugged out of his fur coat. "Gods, that thing is hot."

"All this just to piss Death off, huh?"

"Absolutely." Ace snapped his fingers, and the limo rolled forward. "I'm embarrassed that I was ever friends with the selfish prick. Death possessing my body was low, even for him, so I appreciate your assistance in settling the score."

I wanted to know more about Death and Ace's feud, but my own emotional distress from the day caught up with me. "Anything to get the hell away from him."

Ace hung his arms over the seats behind him. "Trouble in paradise?"

"If by 'paradise' you're referring to my prison sentence with a psychotic Grim Reaper, then yes, loads of trouble." I tucked a strand of hair behind my ear. "Your vision didn't land well. He had me convinced he was training me to go with him to get his scythe."

The rest of the car ride to Pleasant Valley, I gossiped with Ace about how Death had wasted my time, leaving out everything about our meeting with Lucifer and the *Book of the Dead*. Frankly, the book was the last thing on planet Earth that I wanted to talk about. I told him about Marcy and how she'd been the only reason I'd signed with Death in the first place, and at least now she was safe. When I mentioned her kidnapping, Ace jutted his head forward and frowned in puzzlement.

"You will have to tell me more about this friend later," he said.

When we arrived at Ace's shop in Pleasant Valley, he took me by the elbow to guide me inside. Warmth passed from his body to mine, and oddly it calmed me.

"It must be difficult for you, coming back to Pleasant Valley."

"Death said that they brainwashed my parents. Made them think I'm in an advanced college art program. Do you think you can take me to visit them?"

"The mind is a delicate place, Faith. I could take you to see your parents, but you would risk confusing them to an unsurmountable degree."

I took a long, deep breath. "I don't think now is the safest time to see them anyway."

We strode through the shop, entering the cavernous space of his library. The only sound between us was the clack of his dress shoes against marble.

The warlock slid my arm from his elbow and held my hand. "All of this stress and emotional turmoil is affecting your mental health. I am sure it is affecting your ability too. I'm sorry I cannot be more helpful with your situation."

"It's not your fault I sold my soul," I said bitterly. "Very little *doesn't* affect my ability these days. Death has barely taught me to control it. We've mostly been practicing self-defense so I can protect myself. Death's boot camp, if you will."

Ace turned toward me before parting the curtains in front of his séance room and arching a brow. "Has Death been patient with you?"

I burst out laughing. I mean, I had to. "Hell no! The guy went on a wild rampage the other day because I drank *half a glass* of his chocolate milk. He's literally just a bigger, cloaked, more terrifying version of a bitchy old cat, and nobody can convince me otherwise."

"Why do you think Death isn't helping you with your power?" Ace asked.

Turning toward the warlock, I had a strong feeling that he already knew the answer. "Besides the fact that he likes to watch me suffer, has no emotional empathy, and is literally the second-in-command of Satan, so he's still my enemy? No idea." I heaved in a breath. "It's like he's . . . " Everything seemed to click into place, stunning me into silence. "Afraid. Afraid to get too close. When he's teaching me self-defense, it's so second nature to him that it's predictable. Everything is calculated. Especially the distance he puts between us."

"And the light that comes from you is more unpredictable," Ace reflected. "It requires a more personal, unique approach."

"Exactly. I think he's afraid my power will get into his head again, so he's wary of getting too close. He's afraid to . . . to even touch me."

"Well, that may be for the best. If Death touches a living creature with his hands for too long, it dies," Ace elucidated, and I felt my heart sink into my stomach. The reminder of why he wore those black leather gloves was depressing.

A figure skirted my peripheral vision. I turned my head to look down the aisle of books behind us, and I stilled as I caught the silver eyes of Master Vampire Duncan, the vampire Death and I had crossed paths with in Ace's club.

"Get a good earful?" I sneered before I could stop myself.

"Just enjoying some literature, love. Say hello to your zombie boyfriend for me, would you?" He pushed a book, which I was certain he hadn't read, back into a shelf. Then he strode to the other end of the library and shoved open a velvet curtain against the wall before he disappeared inside.

"Stupid fang-face," I said. "He was totally eavesdropping."

Ace folded his arms, his head still turned in the direction the vampire had gone. "It appears so . . . "

"Aren't you going to do something about it?"

"Can't. He's a member of Spades; he's allowed to visit my library." Ace didn't seem happy about that rule as he threw open a different set of purple velvet curtains against the wall. "Let us continue our conversation in my séance room, where it's private. Also, have you ever had the Taco Bell?"

While Ace placed our order on his phone, I wandered around the room looking at all the ancient-looking artifacts. I stopped in front of a glass case and leaned in, taking in the small pendant inside. I'd seen this the last time I'd been here.

The warlock limped over to me and leaned on his cane. "The barracuda," Ace said, sliding his free hand into his pocket. "Beautiful as it is dangerous. Suits you, *oui*?"

I could feel him staring at me intently, and I laughed shyly. "Suave."

Ace's smirk broadened, illuminating his handsome features. "Barracudas are notorious for intensifying emotions, which is why many novice magic users give up on them. But given some adjustment time, they become one with their wearer. They are incredible conduits of inner strength from the heart chakra." He touched his own chest and smiled down at me. "Wear it well, *ma chérie*."

I frowned, then looked back at the glass case. The pendant had vanished.

Something cold pressed against my cleavage. The barracuda was now around my neck below my communion cross.

"What's the deal with you and Death?" I asked later, as Ace and I feasted on our smorgasbord of Taco Bell. "I know you two aren't on the best of terms, but he must trust you if he called to you for help from Limbo."

"Due to moral clashing between magic users and humans in this realm, there aren't many neutral warlocks like me anymore. See, in my business, the good guys would never involve themselves with Death, and the bad guys, they're too greedy to trust to get the job done. Therefore, I'm one of the finest, most convenient options."

I narrowed my eyes and took another bite of my Crunchwrap. "You know I'm not an idiot, right? You evaded my question."

Ace sighed and sipped his Baja Blast. *"Ma chérie . . . "*

"What? *You're* the one who teased me about being his friend once."

"Because I knew the only way you would trust me quickly was to make myself relevant to your problem."

"Why does everybody insist on keeping things from me?"

"I am more than happy to answer any questions about wielding your power. Other than that, there are some stones better left unturned."

"Oh, come on!" I exclaimed. "I played along with you at the penthouse and riled him up about this date. Now I gotta go *back* and face the psycho. The least you can do is give me some juicy gossip out of this."

Ace unwrapped a supreme taco, not meeting my eyes. "You're telling me, in all the time you've spent with him, he's told you nothing about me?"

I nodded. Ace scoffed and muttered a bitter phrase in French.

"Death doesn't exactly enjoy talking about his past," I said to soothe his hurt.

Ace raked a hand through his colorful hair. "Getting him to trust anyone, let alone open up—"

"Is like pulling fangs," I finished. "Oh, I know. Death opening up means all of his cryptic intentions could get exposed too. Hence, he doesn't tell me shit."

Feeling much more trusting of Ace, I finally told him about the meeting with Lucifer and Death, and how Death had lied about training me to come with him to stop Ahrimad. "When Lucifer told Death to tell me the truth, Death hesitated, like he didn't know which truth Lucifer wanted him to share. I can't shake the feeling that whatever he withheld, it's important."

Ace absently drew a shape on the table with his finger. "I believe I can help you."

"Really?"

"Yes, but I need to tell you my own truth first." Violet eyes flicked up to mine. "Every spell I cast has a consequence, you see. With the smaller spells, I am able to swiftly redirect those consequences the best that I can to ensure the safety of others. The larger spells aren't so easy. Redirecting their consequences takes a lot of patience and research, and I didn't always have the luxury of patience. My father taught me the craft of magic at a very young age, back when we would only use minor spells for medicinal purposes. He was my only family, and then he was taken from me suddenly. Murdered, by witch hunters . . . " Ace shut his eyes, as though reliving the anguish all over again. "I will spare you the details of the macabre story."

"I'm so sorry," I whispered.

Ace rubbed the heel of his palm against his heart. "I tried to bring my father back from the dead and failed. In my desperation, I conjured a dark spell far beyond my capabilities, and that too failed. The consequences of that spell transformed into a severe psychosomatic injury." He kicked out his weaker leg. "When I use this leg, I feel nothing but pain. It is not an ailment of the body, but of the mind. Whatever this is, I've managed to slow down the progression, but as of late it has worsened. I need your help, Faith."

"How?"

Ace laced his fingers together, leaning forward on the table. "I know you can read the *Book of the Dead*."

"Oh my God. You too?"

"Listen to me: I will not take advantage of you," Ace insisted. "I need only one page. One page to reverse this injury and rid myself of this damned cane. I've been in pain for so long. So long. There are days where I feel like I am a prisoner in my own body, and those days have outnumbered the ones that I don't. You can free me, Faith."

I felt for him, really I did, but I didn't know what to think. What if he was lying? What if this was another trick?

"At what cost?" I whispered.

"All I would need is for you to translate the page," Ace explained. "You would write the spell on a piece of paper. I would handle it from there."

"Are you sure this is a good idea? Not for me, but for you. You're seeking an answer from a book that's forbidden for a reason—"

"Do you want to know Death's secret or not?" Ace pressed.

When I said nothing, the warlock rose from his seat and limped over to a stove. He flicked on the burner and took a pitcher of water from the fridge beside it to pour water.

"What are you doing?" I asked.

"Making you tea. One that will help induce your visions. You may make your decision by the time I've made the cup."

I stood, curled a stray piece of hair behind my ear, and crossed the room to him. "Is that ginger?" I asked, pointing to a light-brown root-looking thing.

"That would be galangal root," Ace answered as he crushed ingredients with a mortar and pestle of brown stone. "It's in the ginger family." He paused his crushing to tilt the bowl toward me. "I will also add kava kava."

"Kava kava?"

"Oh, yes." His violet eyes flicked to me, mischievous. "Kava kava is abused as an aphrodisiac by some magic users. I will only use it to induce visions in you. I drink this all the time, no worries." He reached for a plant under a pink grow light and plucked out some leaves.

"Mint?"

"For taste," Ace explained. "I'll put it in a tea bag and steep it, just like a normal tea. This is a much better alternative than our last encounter in the séance room, *oui*?"

I agreed. The gladiatorial memory with Alexandru Cruscellio and what happened afterward had been utter chaos.

Ace pointed to a small pot that sat over a flameless burner next to a whistling kettle. "I'm also making a valerian and skullcap tea." He stuffed the smashed ingredients in the bowl into a tea bag. "If you come off the potion in a panic, this tea will relax you."

"What if I want to stop the effects of the potion immediately?"

"You cannot stop it once it begins." Ace poured some boiling water into a cup. "You must let it fade. Should I take your interest as a yes, Faith? Will you help me if I help you?"

Taking the tea from Ace, I made my decision. "Yes."

His eyes crinkled as he smiled, and he bent to briefly kiss my hand in a gesture of appreciation. "You might feel loopy. Then you will succumb to the spell, and I will walk you through a visualization. Now to activate the potion."

Ace cupped his hands around the top. He murmured some words, and his eyes flashed white. He pulled back sharply from the mug, and the drink roared. Threw-my-hair-back roared.

"Quelle horreur!" Ace exclaimed. He combed his fingers through his wind-blown hair to fix it and then grinned. "It's perfect!" He picked up the cup and held it out for me. It was a little milky, with specks of gray.

"No freaking way, man."

Ace chuckled. "You must take a sip quickly, before it congeals."

I couldn't stop grimacing. "Can you maybe give me a countdown?"

"*Three, two, one,* now," Ace said quickly, then cupped the back of my head and brought the drink to my lips. I took a big gulp.

The acidic, slimy texture caught in my throat a little. I heaved but managed to keep it down.

"Disgusting," I coughed out. "Mint . . . did *nothing*. Dizzy. Room is spinning."

"I have you, don't worry," Ace said, taking my elbow in a firm hand as he guided me back to my chair. "In order to unravel a secret through your power of sight, the Spirits will need the context of a specific moment between you and Death. One where you questioned his intentions."

"Jesus. Help me narrow it down, will you?"

Ace worked his jaw. "All right, I will. How about when you lost your friend Marcy and signed the contract? Do you remember how he was behaving that day?"

I remembered his surreptitious grin. The one Death wore as I'd signed away my soul. He'd acted so strange afterward. Like there was no sense of urgency to save Marcy.

Marcy.

My vision strobed in and out.

And then I was elsewhere.

I was standing on the roof of the D&S Tower. Death stood about ten feet away with his back to me, and in front of him loomed a figure in red.

Lucifer.

The scene warped nonstop around the edges, and I could barely hear their quiet conversation. Only a single sentence before the scene dissipated.

". . . stage an attack with Malphas and frighten her," Death said.

Now I was standing in my front yard watching a menacing, hooded figure approach my bedroom window. Judging by his broad back and immense frame, it was Death. He wrenched open my bedroom window with ease, as the lock had already been broken.

Peering into the dimly lit room, he paused, his head turning toward my bed. I could see myself stir. I was asleep.

Death held out his gloved hand toward Marcy, shadows pooling like wisps in the air. She awakened with a start.

"Come to me," Death commanded in a whisper.

Marcy crawled through the window obediently, her eyes glazed over. Dawn began to break as she crossed the dewy lawn. Death murmured foreign words beneath his breath, and the surroundings shifted like a mirage. Ravens. They were all around, circling like vultures. Looking up at the sky, Death slowly pulled down his hood, his mouth still moving in what appeared to be a spell. Mismatched green eyes were consumed by darkness as his appearance altered to his father's . . .

"Faith," cried a voice in the distance, and I watched myself run across the lawn after Marcy. The raw panic wracking my expression brought me back to all the pain and anxiety I'd felt that day. The desperation of signing my soul over.

And it'd been a trick.

Another twisted trick.

Another lie.

"Faith!"

My entire body jolted. My surroundings strobed in and out between reality and the past. Violet eyes. I warped back to the present, crouched over Ace's body with my fingers curled tightly around his throat. White glowed from my fingers, burning into his flesh.

"Ma chérie," Ace choked out, helpless beneath me.

I managed to tear myself away from Ace, my chest heaving. "I can't . . . control it."

Clutching at his bloody throat, Ace cautiously climbed to his feet. His violet eyes widened as he took in my power. "You're okay, *ma chérie*. You're safe."

"No, I'm not okay!" I gasped, tears raining down into my sweat-soaked collar as I squeezed my eyes shut. "He *tricked* me! *Again!*"

Ace rubbed my back in soothing circles. "I can help you get through this, but you need to take a deep breath. Take a few deep breaths with me, then we'll get the calming tea."

But *I couldn't breathe.* I couldn't breathe. Hurt. Betrayal. *Fury.* Heat fanned the side of my sweaty face, willing me to open my eyes again. The room. It had been set ablaze with a rampant fire as fierce and violent as the energy within me.

"Did I do this?" I whispered in horror.

"You unleashed your light during the vision," Ace replied grimly. "It appears the barracuda is enhancing your emotions. This is the rare side effect that I mentioned that will pass, but it's best if you take it off." He held out his palm, his voice softening. "Unclasp the necklace, *ma chérie.*"

Black dots splotched my vision as I held up a fist of fire instead. "Get back. *Get back!*" And Ace did. "All you people do is use me. You're just like him!"

"*Ma chérie*, please." Ace clutched his heart in earnest, and we both coughed wildly from the rising smoke. "I understand you are in pain, but you are not yourself right now. I would never hurt you, not like he would. I am your friend. We need to leave this room."

My attention snapped away as Trixie burst into the room. Ace's bodyguard. Her ferocious eyes ignited as she took in the flames before narrowing in on me with a snarl.

"Trixie, *no*!" Ace shouted.

Trixie's fingers flung two knives in my direction. Time seemed to slow as I lifted my palm, white light expelling from my hand. The first knife veered off course, landing in the wall beside my head, while the second ricocheted off my power and came back at her.

Shock turned into anger as the knife cut deep into her bicep.

When she went for her gun, Ace launched into action. Magenta magic swirled into the air like a whip as he knocked the weapon from her hand. "You'll *kill* her!" he reprimanded.

Pulling Trixie's knife out of the wall, I vaulted over the séance table and hurled myself toward an exit. I cast one last look at the burning room and Ace's disturbed violet eyes before shouldering open the scalding metal door and booking it to the back parking lot.

Rain speared down as I sprinted through a tight gap between two buildings. The feeling that I was being followed clung to my spine, shadows crawling down the brick walls on either side of me. I broke free into the street. No matter how fast I ran, darkness followed.

I tore into a walking path between a pizzeria and a thrift store. There were apartments above each building, with fire escapes. Stuffing the knife in the waistband of my pants, I sprang up onto a dumpster and jumped onto a fire escape ladder, pulling it down with an upper body strength I'd once lacked. I climbed up high, the barracuda burning against my chest as my rage took me higher and higher. When I looked down past the railing of the metal stairs, whatever shadows lingered below vanished like smoke.

Footsteps echoed on the rusty metal steps below. Slow and calculated, akin to the sly grace of an alley cat slinking behind a dumpster to hook a mouse.

I backed up to the center of the roof. Rain misted my eyelashes, and an eerie haze curled over the black tar like a scene from a horror film.

The rain curiously slowed. Cold slipped down my spine as I sensed his presence behind me.

"What happened?" The deep snarl of Death's voice carried with it a clap of thunder in the night. "What did he do?"

"*You*," I seethed. "*You did this to me.*" My throat felt so tight, I could hardly get the words out. "Lucifer told you to tell me the truth, but you left out your favorite part, didn't you? The part where you tricked me into signing away my soul."

The silence that ensued confirmed he knew what I meant. My limbs vibrated with the anticipation of unleashing my violence.

"I swear to God, if you lied to me about Marcy being safe . . . if *anything* happened to her at your hand—"

"Marcy is fine," Death said. "She is unharmed and in Pleasant Valley. She never left." Darkness swallowed the roof around my shoes, and I could feel him closing in like a shark. "I will remind you that despite your little date, I *warned* you about going to the warlock for information on me. Tell me what you offered him."

"Go the hell." I spun and slashed the blade as I went. He was gone.

Motion in my peripheral vision caught my attention. Death manifested a dozen feet away, casually leaning against the door to the roof. His mismatched eyes, iridescent in the night, narrowed to the barracuda around my neck.

"Cupcake," he purred.

"Asshole."

He raised the scarred, pierced brow. "Did you just try to kill me, pumpkin?"

I ran my finger over the blade. "I tried to slit your throat."

Death strode forward and circled me at a distance, and I fell in step, countering his predatory dance. "Ah, a *barracuda*. Explains your bizarre affect. Let me guess, a bonus after your exchange with the warlock?"

My molars ground together as I tried to keep it together.

"You denied Lucifer," Death continued. "What did you expect would happen? He'd let you go on your merry way? He gave me orders to make you compliant. I implemented them."

"You . . . had . . . *a choice*."

"Yes, I did," Death admitted. "Getting you to sign with a lie was a mercy. Would you rather I'd harmed someone you loved? Be grateful I didn't."

"Don't act like you have any compassion in you," I hissed. "You have no heart, no spine, no feeling. You're an undying freak of nature!"

He flinched, a sliver of emotion slipping through his mask before his features hardened to cold marble. My pendant burned so painfully that I gasped and clutched at it. Death's gaze clung to the movement like a hawk.

"Here's what's going to happen," he said in a low, commanding voice. "I'm taking you back to my apartment. Then I'm going to rip off that necklace. I will give you *one* chance to come willingly. Otherwise, I will drag you kicking and screaming."

"Oh yeah?" I picked dirt under my nail with the blade, unbothered.

"Yeah," Death growled, the air crackling from his irritation.

"You're going to have to make me, then," I said as the pendant burned against my throat again. "Because I'm not going anywhere with you, and I'm not resting until I hurt you. Hurt you like you've hurt me."

Death's beautifully constructed façade cracked a little again. A mistake on his part. I could feel the anger come alive within me, and I captured the vulnerability.

"You want to hurt me, Faith? Fine, I'll let you. But not here. We'll do this at my penthouse, where it's safer."

"Clean out your ancient ears, Alex," I said through a tight throat. "I'm not going anywhere with you. We're done."

Death's head dipped down at my use of his mortal name, and a chill climbed my spine. Against the moonlight, his fangs flashed like serrated knives. "Kicking and screaming it is, then."

I launched toward him first. He expected my attacks, anticipating them faster than humanly possible, allowing each assault and then dodging them accordingly. My blade swung faster and faster. We fought to a rhythm, a dangerous dance akin to our sparring sessions.

When I reached peak exhaustion, he swatted me away in a casual manner, like a fly.

"It *is* a barracuda," Death commented, folding his powerful arms as I struggled to catch my breath. "And to think I was almost stunned by your boost in coordination."

"Fuck you," I hissed.

Without Death moving from where he stood in front of me, I felt his breath fan the back of my neck, his rasping laugh like a dark melody. "You'd like that, wouldn't you?"

I spun around with my weapon, metal slicing into cold air as I tried to stab his duplicate. Gone. *Both* of them were gone, but his scent lingered. My chest heaved with each violent tug of air into my lungs.

"Over here."

I slashed out to my left. Death's massive fist caught my wrist before the blade came down at his throat. He bent my hand backward, black claws extending from his fingertips, shredding his leather gloves like they were made of tissue paper.

We remained stuck in the air, my dagger aimed at his head and his claws aimed at mine.

"Where did you get this dagger, anyway?" Death asked, his manner of speaking infuriatingly casual.

"I stole it off Trixie. Right after I lit Ace's palm-reading room on fire."

His eyes widened. "You *what*?"

"Guess that squashes all your jealous fantasies of me and him together, huh? Unless we were having hot pyro sex."

"Give a girl a shady necklace and suddenly she has all the confidence in the world," Death growled. "Barracudas notoriously have adverse side effects, which explains your delusion that you can hurt me."

He shoved me back, and the fight resumed. Where I was furious and lashing out wildly, he was calm, calculated, like he was *allowing* this to keep going. Then the moment arrived where he stopped playing around and took me down with one quick, hard hit to my neck with the side of his hand. I collapsed to my knees, gasping for air.

"Need a break, baby?" he taunted.

The next time I was up, Death was mine. Light unexpectedly ignited as I struck him hard in the chest. He stumbled back a few feet, and for the first time, the impact of my punch actually landed on the Grim Reaper. Either it had caught him off guard or my power had affected him, because he wheezed in a ragged breath.

"*You* need a break, baby?" I asked, flipping a piece of hair out of my face. "You can go get another lip piercing and then come back."

He lifted two fingers, inclined them toward himself, and gnashed his fangs. "I'd rather give you one right now."

I charged. He threw up his forearms like an offensive lineman's block. We were close to the edge of the roof. I took my left hand and held on to one of his arms. Then I used my right hand to strike first his elbow joint and then his neck, as he'd struck mine. I slipped to the side, pushed his elbow down and away, caught his head, and used all my strength to drop my weight, flip him over, and roll us both back onto the ground. Now he was beneath me, and I was straddling his waist.

"I thought there was a chance," I said, too pissed to be pleased with myself. "I thought that deep down there was still life in you. But you're a cold monster from the inside out. Pure evil."

Death slid out from beneath me and enfolded me in his massive arms. My weapon vanished. He crushed me against him and held me down with his weight, strong hips digging into mine.

"Does *that* feel cold to you?" Death growled.

Heat splayed over my sweaty skin, the feeling of his body against mine almost too much to bear. "Don't ever, ever expect me help you again," I seethed. "Because the next time something doesn't go your way, I'm going to step back . . . and *let it happen!*" I used all my strength to shove his heavy weight off me, reached for my weapon on the ground, and wrestled him onto his back again.

"I was willing to help you," I continued as we grappled for the weapon. "I wanted to *help* you get back that damned scythe. But all you care about is yourself and Lucifer—"

"Yeah, you got me pinned down, cupcake," Death said sarcastically. "I don't give a *shit* about Lucifer, and he doesn't give a shit about me. That's why he hasn't lifted a finger to help me get my scythe."

I stilled at his words, my hair falling around my face and curtaining around his head. "Then why are you working with him?"

Death stared at me, like he'd said far too much. My heart fell into my stomach. His answer was about me.

"Because I keep my enemies close, Faith." Death sat up, and I inhaled sharply as the change in position made me fully straddle his lap, but when I tried to get off, his hands clutched my hips. "You're not so innocent in this game either, you know. All you've wanted is to feel like you're not different. You joined me because you had to, but you kissed me because I'm your favorite poison. I'm so screwed up and fucked in the head, it makes you feel better about yourself. What kind of person does that make you? Desperate? No. *Cruel.* Lonely people love convenience. Isn't that what you said?"

Then he grinned, and I felt like his best creation yet.

"I know you," Death purred. "Better than you know yourself—"

"Then you should know that I loved you!" I said fiercely, and his smile fell. "Despite it all, I was stupid enough to care, and you cut me deep anyway."

Tears ran down my cheeks, but I didn't care.

Death vigorously shook his head, his hands sliding to my waist. "What do you want from me, Faith?"

"I want you to *feel*. You pierced your knife straight through my heart and you keep twisting the blade. Do you have any idea how that feels? *Do you?*"

Death clutched my hand in his and punched my fist forward. My eyes opened wide, darkness pouring off his body as the shock of the moment registered. He lowered his upper body to the ground so I leaned over him, and we both stared at the blade I'd buried deep into his heart.

"Now I do," Death growled tightly. "Twist it."

I couldn't have imagined a more deranged way to apologize than to stab yourself in the heart.

Suddenly, his muscles tightened, his head thrashed back against the roof, and the muscles in his neck strained. His eyes rapidly dilated, filling with panic. "*Shit*, Faith."

"What's happening?" I demanded.

"Losing control." He tossed me off him. I rolled onto the ground and stayed there, my head turning toward him in confusion. "*Run!*" Death snarled, his deep voice undulating with something monstrous beneath it. "Get back!"

But I couldn't move. Death writhed and groaned in agony, and I grimaced at the sound of joints and bones shifting within him. His shirt stretched and tore as his muscles bulged and his already massive physique *grew*. When he lifted his head, his features were too sharp, too wicked, too alien to resemble a human. His tan skin had almost entirely turned the color of coal, and his mismatched green eyes glowed with power.

I scrambled backward and tried to get up to run, but the monster lunged forward and grasped my ankle, talons digging into my flesh. I hit the ground. My lower back skinned against the pavement as he dragged me toward him and crawled on top of me like a big, muscular cat.

I slammed my fist into Death's concrete features. The bones in my fingers shattered with a sickening crunch, and my breath caught in my throat in a choked sob. I opened my hand, dizziness overcoming my vision as broken bones slid right back into place.

The discoloration on Death's skin began to fade, as if he were snapping out of it, but then the darkness returned, and his mismatched eyes glowed like firestorms. He pinned me down and roared into my face with a mouthful of fangs. This wasn't Death. I found my fear, abandoned at the bottom of my soul, and it surfaced at full force. He *would* kill me.

My fear triggered my power: my light shot him directly in the leg, and the monster cried out. Then he grabbed me in a way that left me defenseless and tossed me like a rag doll. I slammed into the small wall at the edge of the roof with a sickening smack and rolled off the ledge, dropping, then luckily—but painfully—landing on the top platform of the fire escape.

White-hot pain sparked from my back, my shoulder, my arm, and my wrist, which was bent at an awkward angle beneath me. Bile rose in my throat. I was certain my arm was broken, my shoulder had popped out, and my wrist had snapped like a toothpick. I clamped down on my bottom lip with my teeth. I tasted blood. The platform shifted. I stiffened. Something had broken loose on the old, rusted fire escape.

I slid down as the platform tilted until the fingers of my left hand, my good arm, latched into the gaps in the metal and held on. My legs dangled over the side of the fire escape. I looked down at the ground below, and a droplet of rain hung from my nose.

"Now would be a great time to save me!" I exclaimed.

The fire escape dipped to the left and tilted significantly, and I held on for dear life. My fingers bled, and my arm was beyond tired. I swung my injured arm up from its awkward position and latched on to the fire escape. It felt like my arm had been ripped out of the socket and someone was jackhammering my shoulder blade and my wrist.

"Jesus . . . *Christ! DEATH!*"

Two marked hands smacked down the platform in front of my face, and the fire escape hit the point of no return. It let loose from the wall, and I lost my grip and fell into the alleyway. The ground came at me at fast, but I never hit the pavement. An arm caught me around the waist and cradled me against a strong chest.

"Wrong." I looked up into two mismatched green eyes. He wasn't all there. The night was still washing away from his beautiful features. "Let's go home."

He summoned his motorcycle from the shadows of the alleyway and rode it out onto the street. We sped out of Pleasant Valley toward New York City. The long, exhausting ride seemed to go faster on the back of his bike. We were both still seething from the argument and soaked by rain.

Back at the penthouse, I tried not to cry as I nursed my injured shoulder.

Death bit down on his wrist and poured his black blood into a shot glass.

"Drink," he said gruffly. "It'll heal you."

The last time he'd given me his blood, I'd gotten high as a kite. I hesitated, but pain radiated through almost every part of my body. I brought the glass to my lips and downed it fast. Pain shifted to pleasure, but I shoved it down.

"What about you?" I asked tightly.

"I'm fine." He slammed the fridge door, having taken out two plastic-wrapped T-bone steaks in one hand and two cartons of chocolate milk in the other. He cut open the plastic with a talon and stuck a knife in the steak like he was planning on eating it raw. I wanted to ask him about what had happened back in Pleasant Valley. How he'd almost lost control, and I was starting to see more of that beastly side of him than, well, *him*.

"I want to keep training," I said instead. "Now that I can read the *Book of the Dead*, it's more important than ever that I'm able to defend myself." I took a deep breath. "But I think it's best we stay out of each other's way."

With his back still to me, Death set aside his bizarre meal and braced his gloved hands on either side of the sink. "Long as you stay out of mine."

XIV

The next morning, I woke up with my socks on fire.

"Not today!" I ripped the white tube socks off and quickly dunked them in the glass of water on my nightstand. Throwing a pillow over my face, I flopped back down on the bed to wallow in my depression.

Cruentas had other plans and nickered at the end of the bed, performing a little dance around my body with his hooves.

"*No*, Cru."

He dropped his blue tennis ball on my neck. I peered out from under the pillow at him. His muzzle hovered inches away and snorted hot air into my face.

"Fine." Gripping the tennis ball, I hurled it across the room. He raced off the bed, leapt, and vanished, reappearing at the end of the ball's trajectory to catch it.

Guess I was supposed to meet Death after all. Groaning, I threw off my comforter. It wasn't like I could fall back to sleep or avoid him all day. We lived together. *Unwillingly* so, but still.

I dressed in a plain sports bra, a tank top, and shorts. After brushing my teeth and washing my face, I left the room and halted in the middle of the hallway.

Leaning against Death's dining room table was an unexpected face. Dark-amber eyes lifted to mine, glimmering to a brighter gold as a charming grin crossed his mouth.

"Morning," Leo said.

"Good morning . . . " I glanced around, expecting Death to make his usual cryptic grand entrance. "What are you doing here?"

"Keeping you company for the day. I'll be overseeing your training."

My brows lifted. "Where's Mr. Harbinger of Doom? Mauling a scratching post and coughing up a hairball?"

"Any pressing issues you want to communicate to Death can be forwarded through me," Leo answered, as if he were a programmed like a robot. "I will direct the message to Glenn, who will in turn deliver the message to Death. Would you like me to send anything?"

He had to be joking.

"No, thank you," I said and crossed my arms. "Actually, *yes*, thank you. You can tell Glenn to tell Death that he's an *asshole*, both as an individual and as a parent, and he should pay attention to his horse-dog. Cruentas is a sweet, cutie little baby and is clearly neglected. Also, tell Glenn to let Death know that we're out of Chunky Monkey ice cream, so he should get on that."

Since I binged it all last night, I didn't add.

"Told you she'd be cranky," Gunner said, exiting Death's kitchen with chocolate milk. He wore a gray T-shirt with a mini grilled cheese sandwich on the right breast pocket. "The Prince of Insomnia must be shitting on her sleep schedule too." He drank greedily from the container, pausing as Leo shot a disapproving look in his direction. "What?"

"You're an idiot," Wolf growled, materializing from the darkness behind Gunner like Dracula. Must have learned that from Death. He snatched the carton from Gunner's grasp. "*Never* drink Death's milk."

"It was a sip," Gunner said with a laugh. "It's not like Death keeps tabs on who drinks his milk." He paused. "Right?"

"Of course not," Wolf said with a straight face. "That'd be psychotic."

Gunner would be an outline on the floor by morning.

The rest of the Seven were waiting for us in the gymnasium where Death had built the Graveyard. The obstacle course from hell filled half the room, but there was plenty of space to train around it. I'd just started my warm-up when someone tapped my shoulder.

Glenn stood directly behind me. "Hi, Ms. Williams." He handed me a folded note. "From His Highness."

"Uh, thanks."

Glenn didn't move and remained fixated on the note. Realizing he had probably been ordered to wait for a reply, I awkwardly peeled it open.

You're mistaken. Cruentas is spoiled rotten. He spends time with you because he thinks you're clever and funny.

— D

P.S. I've settled on black lace.

My mouth hung open as I read, a slow burn making its way down my body. It took me a moment to remember he was talking about the striptease.

Glenn was holding a notepad for my response to Death. I

crumpled the letter in my fist and flipped it the bird. He got the memo and gave me a sheepish smile before vanishing.

"Ah, love letters." I looked over at Romeo, who was leaning against the wall beside me and shaking his head with pride. "An almost forgotten and yet insurmountably effective method of wooing a woman and exposing a man's heart."

After a water break and a protein-packed salad (boo), I returned to the gym with hand-to-hand combat with Wolf, Gunner, and Flash. These reapers really were Death 2.0 except with less callousness. Gunner, a stickler for correct form, made me do push-ups whenever I dropped my left punching arm and left my face vulnerable. Wolf was an expert on reading an opponent's body language to predict a counterattack. Flash played the role of the pretend opponent who would attack me or Wolf and Gunner during demonstrations. Leo stood off to the side, watching me from afar like a lifeguard the entire time.

After the sparring session, I followed Romeo to a back room to learn about various weapons and equipment.

"Come one, come all, come up and take a look at the table!" Romeo shouted in an announcer's voice, gesturing at items with his hands. "Here we have body armor, headgear, shields, gauntlets, daggers, swords, and some miscellaneous . . . "

The stuff on the tables made my eyebrows go up above my hairline. I dangled a pair of fancy-looking handcuffs from my finger. "These are yours, aren't they?"

Romeo snatched the cuffs away. "Careful, sweet cheeks, these aren't your standard handcuffs." He held out his arm to snap one of the pairs of cuffs down onto his wrist, and suddenly the cuff transformed into a rope-like object that curled up his arm and tightened like a boa constrictor. "Get these on the enemy and you'll incapacitate any powers they may have for about thirty minutes. The more they struggle, the tighter they get. Kind of like sticking your fingers in a novelty bamboo finger trap." The veins in his arms protruded as the cuff jerked around, and he grappled to get the key in the lock to free himself. "However, that's if you can get these on the enemy. Cuffs come with a matching leash too. Why walk your dog when you can walk your enemy, am I right?"

I eyed the handcuffs with interest.

"Let's see what the boys are doing, love. I'm starving." Romeo swaggered out of the room, whistling. I quickly stuffed the handcuffs into my sweatshirt pocket and followed him to the main gym. Gunner and Denim were sparring on the mats, while the rest of the Seven watched. I went to stand next to Leo.

"What's Death's plan for killing Ahrimad?" I asked.

"If you have any questions for Death, you need to leave a message with Glenn," Leo replied.

"I've about had it with this 'leave a message with Glenn' game. I want to know what's going on."

"Mind your business, mortal," sneered Blade to my right. "You're not entitled to any information; you're a prisoner."

The rest of the reapers shot him glares of disapproval.

"It's not like you all weren't thinking it too," said Blade. "Why should we walk on eggshells around her and treat her like a princess? She's beneath us."

"Blade," hissed Wolf, "*don't* start."

"Why don't you make me, *boyo*?" Blade challenged.

"Someone didn't take his meds," muttered Flash.

Blade turned his fury on me. "Want to know why Death didn't show up today, lassie? He's out *beggin'* the warlock for forgiveness so that Ace doesn't lash out and obliterate you for injuring his precious pixie. See, you don't stand a chance against Ahrimad or Malphas or any of their soldiers. Your silly power is an unpredictable mess. You're a liability. Death knows it, and we all know it."

My breath hitched at the fact that none of the reapers seemed to disagree enough to defend me.

"What if you have to take on a demon by yourself?" Blade said as his eyes flickered red. "You gonna throw out your hand and *hope* your prophesized light beam shoots out? Preparation means nothing if you can't find your block. Nothing."

"That's enough," Leo said, stepping up so that he was between us. "Go cool off."

"You don't know me, Blade," I said. "I don't give up, and I still have time."

"Did Death not tell you *that* either, lassie?" Blade laughed bitterly. "*We* are the ones who don't have time. Death's Seven Deadly Sins curse controls our inner animals. Without his scythe, we're all more screwed with each passing day. Time is the last thing you have. By the looks of it, you're a walking time bomb. Better start looking for another dick to suck to save you from yourself—"

Leo punched Blade square in the face. Blade's head snapped backward, and his eyes flared from a dull maroon to crimson. He lashed out, hurling his entire weight into Leo. Black blood splattered the ground as Blade stabbed Leo with a knife.

"Guys, stop!" I shouted. *"Stop!"*

Denim, Wolf, and Flash grabbed Blade and threw his body against the wall with inhuman force. They held him there, shouting expletives. Romeo and Gunner helped Leo to his feet while at the same time making sure he didn't go after Blade again.

Coldness darted down my spine.

"Am I interrupting?" growled an accented voice.

Death came forth from a black, swirling mist like a god summoned from the night.

And he was *pissed*.

XXV

"Why is it," Death began as he stalked a slow circle around his reapers, "whenever I leave one of you *idiots* alone with the girl, chaos erupts?"

When nobody responded, Death glared at Wolf. "Were my instructions not clear?"

"You were perfectly clear, my lord."

Death prowled past Wolf and stopped at Gunner. "Have I not been a generous and merciful master to you all?"

"You have always been generous to us, my lord."replied Gunner.

"Are you not all indebted to me?" Death asked Denim, face to face with him.

"We are forever indebted, my lord,"

"Then why the *fuck*," Death roared, now standing before Leo, the cords of muscle in his neck protruding like a drill sergeant's, "did I just walk into goddamn World War Three?"

This was hard to watch. In a matter of seconds, Death had made seven incredibly masculine men transform into terrified puppies with their tails wedged between their legs.

Blade muttered something vicious under his breath.

Death vanished in a mist of black and reappeared in front of Blade like a monster straight out of a nightmare. He grabbed the reaper by the shirt, fangs lengthening in his mouth. "*What* did you say?"

At the sight of Death's own wrath, the crimson in Blade's eyes extinguished to a dark maroon. "I said somebody isn't getting any ass from the virgin," he muttered.

A muscle in Death's jaw twitched. "Am I to assume you're the cause of all this, Blade?"

The reapers shifted as Death calmly slid off his right glove. The sight of his black markings and deadly pointed nails unnerved me. Talons extended like knives from his fingertips. and I braced myself for a gruesome execution.

Leo moved to stand between Blade and Death, holding his bandaged side. "It's the curse, my lord," he said imploringly. "It's affecting all of us, including you, and especially Wrath. I implore you to take a moment and not do anything rash. Especially with the girl here."

As nasty as Blade had been to me, I knew I needed to step in too.

"Don't you think you're worsening the situation with your scare tactics and tyrannical speeches?" I asked.

As I spoke, Death straightened, but he kept his gaze drilled into Blade. "Keep your smart-ass comments to yourself, Wrath. This is your final warning."

He shoved Blade back in line with the other reapers. My heart pounded a thousand beats per minute as Death turned his anger on me. The room darkened like an impending storm. Our eyes connected, and I wished I could pull my head into my shell like a turtle.

"You're all dismissed," Death ordered.

The reapers left.

I could cut the tension between us with a knife.

Death glanced at his watch. "You have another date with Ace in three hours."

"Really?"

Was this what resulted from Death begging for Ace's forgiveness for me? Damn, Ace was petty as hell, and I loved it.

Death glared at me in the large gym mirror. "I offered Ace money for the damage you caused to his property, but apparently, he values your presence more."

I fought back a smile, but Death caught it and narrowed his eyes. He brushed past me and approached the shelves holding various weapons.

"What are you doing?" I asked.

"I want to see if you've made progress today."

"Sorry, I'm done for the day."

Death shrugged off his cloak, thick muscle shifting beneath his shirt.

"I'm *not* fighting you," I added, since the guy was clearly not taking the hint.

Holding two swords, Death prowled under a light at the center of the mat. His alien eyes shifted colors, like iridescent green kaleidoscopes. "Stop crying, cupcake." He threw me my sword. Fortunately, I caught it by the hilt. "You knocked me down last night, didn't you? Now we're even." He arched that scarred eyebrow. "Don't you want to know who'll come out on top?"

"I'm not fighting you," I repeated firmly. "Your mood is volatile, your fangs are, like, six feet long, and you look like you want to eat me. More than usual. Besides, I got my revenge."

"Did you? Because you still seem pissy to me." Death rotated his sword in a skilled motion around his body, bringing my focus back to the training. Metal clashed. We moved around the mat as if it were choreographed, his mismatched eyes never leaving mine.

A dangerous grin spread over his face like venom. "You made the correct decision to keep that barracuda. It's tamed down, and your footwork has improved."

"Uh, thanks."

We continued this adrenaline-filled dance. Death came at me with his blade in various movements, and I struggled to keep him off me. My arms felt heavy from all my training with the Seven.

"Stay focused," Death muttered.

"I am."

He moved faster than usual. Metal whistled through the air. I saw the blood before I felt the pain. It gushed down my bicep like a river and splattered the mats. Panic took over. My heart slammed into my ribs. I covered the wound with my palm and stared up at Death in horror. He was breathing hard, the catlike tilt to his irises violently stuttering. Jesus Christ. He looked positively monstrous.

"Death," I panted, "I think we should stop."

His expression went distant. "Stay focused."

A horrible feeling settled over me as I realized he was talking to himself. I thought back to Blade's comment about Death's scythe affecting the reapers' inner beasts.

Death lunged for another attack. The clash of metal against metal rang out. The monster laughed and countered my attack, knocking the sword out of my hand like a toothpick. His pupils expanded over the width of his eyes as he snatched my bicep in a viselike grip and then wrapped his other hand around my throat.

"Death! Death, you're losing control!"

"Stop me," he purred. "*Fuck*, your scent is so sweet, cupcake. You have no idea what it does to me."

His fingers gripped my jaw, prying it open. His power seeped into my skin like a hot oil, and I sank into it. His magnetic influence. His mouth parted above mine. I imagined Death inhaling and ripping my essence from my body, ending my life, and something triggered inside of me. A will to live. Light cast across Death's face. Shock rippled over his expression as my fist connected with his face. A blinding light ensued, and the stench of burning flesh filled the room.

Death released a bestial howl and reared back, clutching his cheek where the outline of my knuckles was engraved like a branding iron.

I looked down at my hands in awe. A bluish-white fire licked up the length of my fingers. Turning my head, I saw that Death had sobered up. He grinned like a cat. Shadows expelled from his body, flooding the floor. I kept my hand up and imagined a shield around myself. His darkness hit my light like a wall, recoiling back with hisses.

"That's my girl," Death said. He was nearly obscured by his darkness: a mighty creature of the night firing everything he had at me. "You don't need a weapon to protect yourself. *You* are the weapon."

You are the weapon.

I stood in front of the mirror, nervously playing with the chain of the barracuda around my throat. I wore an oversized Def Leppard T-shirt dress I'd paired with fishnet stockings and low-heeled combat boots. I checked the time.

Thirty minutes until my date with Ace.

Wandering into the main living room, I felt the chill in the air that always seemed to follow Death. I tilted my head to peer at the upper-level glass banister before climbing the staircase and stopping at the top step. Death sat cross-legged on a large area rug. His eyes were closed, and he sat with perfect posture. I shamelessly studied the markings that resembled tattoos across his bare skin, then the curve of his full lips, those long eyelashes brushing against his cheekbones.

He had great cheekbones for a "don't look at me wrong way or I'll skin you alive" kind of man.

The calm state made him appear gentler, softer—two words I would have never expected to use to describe Death. Seeing him like this felt strangely intimate. Like I was watching him sleep.

He was clearly deep into some sort of meditation, and here I was gawking. I started to retreat down the stairs.

"Don't bother tiptoeing," Death said. "Your crackly ankles disturbed me the second you left your bedroom."

Rolling my eyes, I turned toward him. His eyes were still closed, and he hadn't moved an inch. Slowly, I made my way to him.

"Never pinned you as the 'balancing my chakras' type," I said.

"I'm not meditating. I'm sending my duplicates to do their tasks. Takes a deeper level of concentration."

"So . . . meditation."

A gruff noise. "You're wearing perfume."

"I am."

His eyes slowly opened, lingering for a long, leisurely time on the fishnets before flicking to my face. He said nothing. He didn't have to. He said it all with his hungry eyes.

A coy smile curved my mouth as I took a folded blanket from a black basket. Carrying it to the area rug where he sat, I placed it on the floor like a cushion and sat down so I was directly in front of him.

"Thought you don't wear dresses," he muttered.

"It's a long T-shirt."

"With no shorts underneath." He played it off with a nonchalant tone, but I knew better. It had been a question in disguise. One he wouldn't get an answer to.

"It's not every day I get to leave your penthouse. I wanted to look pretty."

"For Ace."

"For me."

"Hmm." His stare was unflinching.

"How would you know if Cruentas thinks I'm funny and clever?" I asked.

Death tilted his head to the side.

"The note that you had Glenn send me," I explained. "You said Cruentas thought I was funny and clever."

"Because he talks to me. I understand every language. I'm Death." His mouth curved into a slow smirk. "Impressed?"

"A dead guy who can talk to horses and squirrels but can't apologize to a woman. Yeah, real impressive, buddy—"

"I'm not your *buddy*," Death snapped. "And I'm certainly not your friend."

Touchy about the friend zone. Made me want to keep pushing his deadly buttons.

"Relax, I'd never be your actual friend anyway," I said, and his eyes narrowed slightly. "A friend of mine wouldn't have kept half of himself from me because he thought I'd run away screaming at the sight of his beast. A friend wouldn't cut another man who hurt me down at the knees but never hold himself accountable for all the pain he's caused me himself."

He said nothing, and my eyes unexpectedly stung.

"One moment you're kissing me, making me think there's something there," I said, "and the next, you're lying to me again. I sold my soul to you because I thought Marcy would die."

"I let you bury a knife into my chest," he growled. "That was my apology."

"You and I have two *very* different definitions of an apology."

"It appears so."

"I don't know why I even came up." Rising from my blanket, I started to get up, but a hot, leather-gloved hand encircled my wrist.

"Don't go," Death said stiffly. "Stay."

My chest felt so tight. Coming to my senses, I ripped free of his grasp. "How do you sleep at night?"

"I don't." His laughter had an edge as he turned his face away from mine. "If you only knew what goes on in my head when I'm around you."

"Tell me," I said. "Tell me what goes on in your head. Tell me *anything*. You used to hide under the hood. Now you hide in plain sight. What don't you want me to see? How many more secrets can one person possibly keep?"

His cold, marble features shifted through several emotions, but he remained silent.

"How am I supposed to trust someone who won't let his guard down for five seconds? Isn't that what you and Lucifer want from me? *Trust?* You barely tell me anything about yourself."

"It's better that way."

"Another half-assed answer."

"You know what your problem is?" Death asked.

I stared at him, shocked that he was deflecting this back to me. "I'm looking right at him!"

"You lead with your emotions," Death said gruffly. "Your feelings guide you through life. That's your downfall. That's your Achilles' heel. When you're upset, you leave all reason to the wolves. Logical decisions are cast aside. There's no balance between what you feel and what you need to do, and that's why your power is so unpredictable."

"What exactly are you asking me to do?" I climbed to my feet and stood over him. "You want me to stop feeling? Smother all of my mortal emotions? Or do you want me to stop seeking answers and stop holding you accountable for your actions?"

"Get out of my face, cupcake."

The threat was calm and quiet. I backed off a bit, but I wouldn't back down.

"You can't handle me, can you? It frustrates the hell out of you. Hate to break it to you—I'm not going anywhere. If I could, believe me, *I would*. But I can't. I'm stuck here with you and your ancient, decrepit ways. So, suck it up, asshole."

"Watch," he snarled, rising to his commanding height, "your mouth."

"Or *what*?" I asked, jabbing at his chest.

Death glared down at my finger through slitted eyes, as if he wanted it to shred it apart with his fangs. Instead, he rolled back a broad shoulder and stalked closer until he loomed over me.

"Or I'll pop the cherry between your legs and shut you up myself," Death purred.

A slow, ruthless burn settled in numerous locations of my body.

Death's mouth cranked up into a wicked, twisted grin. "I wanna ask you a personal question."

Flustered by the way he was staring at me, I intended to put distance between us, but with every step back, he only prowled forward, pursuing me in a slow, predatorial manner.

"What have you done?" he questioned.

"W-what have I done?" I stumbled back against his bookshelves. How had the tables turned so fast?

In an attempt to hide his smirk, Death wiped the thumb of his gloved hand across his bottom lip. "Sexually, Faith. What have you done *sexually*."

"You already knew I was a virgin because I wore slacks to the interview. Why don't you figure it out?"

His arm shot out, trapping me in a corner between a wall and a shelf. "So, nothing." His grin widened, showcasing white fangs. "You've done nothing." *Like I already assumed*, added his wicked eyes.

"My personal life is none of your business," I said, trying to sound as unruffled as possible. I'd never been obsessed with boys and sex the way other girls at my school were. I was pushing the concept of dating to the side until college.

Death reached for a book next to my head, reading the title as if he were interested in it. "Have you ever touched yourself?"

I straightened, burning hot. "I think that's enough questions."

He shut the book with a thump, catlike eyes gleaming. "You *have*."

"It's time for my date with Ace," I said and tried to maneuver around him.

Death shelved the book and lowered his arm to block me, while his free hand gripped the shelf next to my head to cage me in. "Now who's running away, cupcake?"

Swallowing a lump in my throat, I tried to concentrate on anything besides how strikingly handsome his face was, or how the delicious, crisp scent of his cologne was like a freaking sex-bomb air freshener. Or the way he had to bend when he loomed over me because he was so damn tall.

"I'm running away because you're a deceitful pig." God, it was so nerve-wracking to look at him when he was this close. "You run away because you're a coward. Two very different things."

"I never run from you," Death said, his voice slipping into a velvet tone. "I run from myself because I don't want to lose control. But then that enticing, delicious scent of your soul reels me right back, and I . . . can't . . . help myself."

I could feel the madness surfacing before I saw it brimming in his eyes. He raised his gloved hand, and I shivered as he brushed the communion cross above my cleavage with a leather fingertip.

"The Fates are laughing at me, you know," Death murmured. "Those twisted three have poked and prodded at their favorite plaything for two thousand years. They know I have a godforsaken sweet tooth. So, they put you in my path. To torture me." His catlike eyes flicked up to pierce into my soul. "To *ruin* my every waking moment with the temptation of having you. I try not to blame you for what you are, and if you can imagine it, a sliver of myself occasionally wants to even make amends . . . "

Then he moved in for the kill and turned his head in to my neck. My hand braced against his chest, and my breath escaped in a rush.

"But then you go and torment me all on your own," he growled against my throbbing pulse, his gloved hands sliding down my waist to the hem of my T-shirt. "Wearing sexy fishnets for your silly fake date with Ace, and I know you're not an innocent after all. Not in your heart, not in your soul, not in the war between us."

The cold, silver loop piercing on his lip brushed my bottom lip, and his tongue followed in a slow caress that sent chills throughout me. I couldn't breathe. The back of my dress clung hotly to my skin. The fine line between fear and arousal had burned away a long time ago.

"Don't you dare kiss me," I whispered.

"I appreciate your faith in my restraint."

Then he kissed me anyway. His lips brushed mine with a soft, velvet touch, his tongue skimming the seam of my lips in a gentle nudge for more. I opened for a tiny taste. He grabbed my jaw with a gloved hand and deepened the kiss with a slow, erotic caress of his tongue, and I met him halfway, chasing the high. The flavor of him was too addictive, a forbidden nectar awakening a dark, carnal need.

Death broke apart from me and wet his bottom lip. "You kiss like a slut."

I grabbed his shirt, light electrifying my palms. I turned and shoved him into the bookshelf. Death slammed into the shelves with a groan, books raining down. I took a step back with my chin lifted, my arms to either side of me as my power flickered away.

Leaning back against the broken wooden shelves, Death breathed raggedly and watched me from under half-lowered lids like a taunt. *"Ow,"* he purred with delight. "If you wanted to make a mess, you could have said so . . . "

An evil, devastatingly beautiful grin crossed his mouth as I charged toward him. He grabbed me as I lunged at him and crushed me to his strong frame. We made out at a feverish level until he stifled a deep groan that made my knees wobble.

Flickers of images darted in front of my closed eyes, memories like colorful lattice reaching out to me from him. I pushed them away to make a new memory. Death hoisted me off the ground and hooked my legs around his waist. I locked my arms around his neck as he carried me to the couch and sat down so that I was straddling his lap.

His legs were long and powerful between mine, his skin burning hot through the cotton material of his sweatpants. Breaking away again, Death arched his head back against the couch and tilted my body forward. His gloved hands dragged up the back of my thighs to the curve of my bottom beneath my dress.

"You naughty little cupcake," he growled in a deep, rough voice. "No shorts indeed."

Our lips kept at it, our fingers gripping each other's clothes. He kissed a trail up my neck as I bit back a moan that escaped with a gasp as he sucked on the sensitive flesh. As he dragged the tip of his tongue to my collarbone, I lowered myself flatter into his lap and could feel the large swell of him pressed against my inner thigh. The film of what could happen next played out before my eyes, and doubt swam to the surface of my consciousness.

I braced my hands on Death's shoulders, pinning him back against the sofa.

Death looked up at me with wild, lust-filled eyes. At the sight of my face, he instantly sobered and dropped his gloved hands to the sides of my knees. "You all right?"

"I can't." In my heart, this didn't feel right. What he wanted and what I wanted were physically the same, but our emotional needs were so imbalanced. My feelings had yet to be reciprocated the way I needed, and I realized they might never be.

Suddenly, I felt so small and awkward, enclosed in my own inexperience. "I don't want to get things out of my system," I said slowly so that I didn't cry. I felt everything so intensely, so fully, and sometimes I couldn't help but burst into tears. "I'm not . . . I'm not that type of girl." *I want to be loved in a moment like this.* "I want more than this. More than what you would give me right now."

Death went quiet, staring at me for a long beat before he put his hands on my waist and set me down on the couch beside him. It felt like we were a mile apart.

"Say something," I whispered. "Are you mad?"

"No." Death raked a hand through his hair and dropped his arm over the back of the couch. "I know better. I know you're a certain kind of girl."

"Clearly I'm not because I all but attacked you." Hadn't he felt me dissolving into his touch? "I don't want to regret anything intimate. I want . . . I just . . . "

"You want to feel reciprocated." He answered the unsaid, reading me like a book. "You need this kind of stuff to feel special."

"Yeah," I said, tucking a strand of hair behind my ear.

"Then I'm glad we stopped when we did," Death said. "Emotional stuff, I'm shit at it. Everything besides anger and basic instinct feels so manual, so unnatural, as if I have to learn it all over again. I can't give you what you need. Not without hurting you along the way." A wave of anger flickered over his features with an upsurge of something suppressed. "Don't you understand that I've kept myself from you not for my sake but for yours? That it's the only selfless thing I can remember doing in centuries? If you only knew what I've done to be where I am right now, reigning beside Lucifer as his dutiful prince. If you'd only seen me take the lives I have, all for sport. If you knew the friendships and trust I've broken. I've learned the value of shutting everything out, shutting *myself* out. I'd break all my rules for you, Faith. Just don't be surprised if you don't like what you see once we're finally introduced."

I realized I was clutching at my chest. It felt like I'd had the wind knocked out of me.

Death rose to his imposing height and extended out a gloved hand. "Come with me."

"Where are we going?"

"To the roof. I want to show you my wings."

XXVI

I placed my hand in his, and our surroundings washed away. The roof of his apartment building towered over New York City with a breathtaking view of the skyline at night. I expected the cold air to be freezing all the way up here in November, but the temperature was the same as inside, and there was no wind.

"Why isn't it cold?" I asked, turning away from the view.

"It's the ward." Death reached down and picked up a rubber doorstop. He flung it high into the sky, and it ricocheted off an invisible dome—the "ward," as he'd put it—that made itself visible with electric blue fissures that stretched down to the edges of the roof. "It acts as an insulator. I put it up a few years ago when I bought the building. It notifies me when anyone unwelcome tries to breach the barrier."

My thoughts snagged on *bought the building*. I couldn't fathom how much it had cost to purchase all the open space below us. If he'd acquired it legally, of course . . .

Death inclined two gloved fingers to himself.

With my heart in my throat, I strode closer, an innate warning of danger licking up my spine.

"Stop right there," he commanded.

I glanced up at the sky and laughed. "Is a piano going to drop on my head or something?"

Death grabbed the back of his long-sleeved shirt and pulled it over his head.

He might as well have dropped a piano on me because I was deceased.

I took in his herculean frame. His broad shoulders, powerful arms, and outrageously defined abdominals. He tossed his silky shirt on the ground like a model in the middle of a photo shoot and stood in a relaxed way. Intricate black markings covered his torso and drifted into his sweatpants. The sweatpants hung low on his hips, and now I was picturing yanking them down a little further . . .

"I will remind you," Death said in an alluring, velvety voice, "that allowing you to view my wings is equivalent to showing you my . . . well, my *dick*. See, angels rarely expose their wings for long periods of time, especially as a demonstration. It can be considered a grand display of intimacy." Then he looked meaningfully at me, as though seeking permission for what could happen next.

"How are your wings even remotely comparable to the male genitalia?" I wondered with a coy smile. "Do they have testicles at the end of each feather?"

"Say that last part again." His eyes darkened to a sultrier deep-green, crackling the tension between us. "Slower."

"In your dreams."

"They're comparable because of their impressive size," Death answered. "At least, in my case. I suffer terribly from TBDS."

"TBDS?"

"Too Big Dick Syndrome."

My mouth fell open.

Death barked out laughter. "Priceless. Don't worry, cupcake." He gave me a slow, deliberate once-over. "I'll make sure it feels good."

Heat flooded my cheeks. "What makes you so certain I'll give it up to you?"

"I'll arrange my long list of reasons and get back to you. The first one is the most obvious though: your incessant flirting."

"You're the one who's always staring at me with your freaky cat eyes."

"See, now that's hurtful. And flirtatious."

I punched his powerful arm, and he released a hearty laugh, which in turn made me laugh too. When our laughter faded, there was a shift in the air. We looked at each other with such intensity that everything else washed away.

"Show me," I said.

I could see the vulnerability in him as he stepped back. He lowered his gaze as he pivoted, showing me his broad back.

My hand crept up to cup my mouth. Two violent, jagged scars marred either side of his spine. The gruesome remnants of a pain unlike any other, tombstones where wings had once been embedded. Beneath inky markings and bronze skin lay the bone structure of another species. His shoulder blades protruded out a little at the bottom, like . . .

"Don't come any closer," Death said.

Confusion knit my brows. I thought maybe he was self-conscious of his scars. That he didn't have wings after all because he was a Fallen. But then his skin darkened, ink slinking over his bronze skin until he was one with the night.

"Angels are built differently than humans." His voice had morphed from man to monster, deepening to a low, primal husk that sent chills down my spine. "Our bones are larger, stronger, though less dense than a mortal's, so it's easier to take flight. Some angels were once mortals that died, others are purebloods born from other angels."

"How did you become an angel?" I wondered.

He went quiet for a short time, hesitating. "A long time ago, shortly after I became a creature of death, the Elders in Heaven took notice of my . . . bad behavior. They knew they couldn't destroy me, not without disturbing the balance between good and evil, but they wanted to keep me close, utilize my death power and my gift of seeing into souls to help the afterlife. When I agreed to this, they transformed me into a Light Angel with magic. If you can imagine it, I once helped guard the Gates of Heaven, determining which souls could enter."

"Holy crap."

"The job didn't last long," Death said in a grave voice. "They banished me, tore off my wings, then cursed me with the Seven Deadly Sins curse. To limit my capabilities. Or, at least, to try to." He turned his head over his shoulder with a sly smile. "All angels, including Fallen, are reborn with eternal wings, which we conceal with magic."

Lightning fractured the sky. Death's head tilted heavenward as he flexed back his arms, and enormous wings unfurled from his back. They extended in seconds, until they reached nearly half the width of the entire roof.

"Whoa! You weren't kidding, these are *huge*!"

Death's laughter rumbled like the thunder above. "Thank you."

My jaw gaped as I analyzed the rows and rows of midnight feathers. "Incredible . . . "

"Feel free to get a closer look." His wings fluttered as though to shake out a cramp before curling inward with the arch of a vulture.

My eyes followed the line of his wing to his lower shoulder, where the crease of the wing ended. Death dropped to his knees so that he faced away from me. While this gave me a better view, it also made my heart hammer in my chest to have such a powerful being kneeling for me. *Again.*

My fingers hovered over the base of the wing. His wings shifted, bending in a way that reminded me of a demonstration in my high school anatomy class. My teacher had stood beside a model of the human skeleton and bent his own arm alongside it, pointing at the various bones underneath his skin.

"Humerus bones," I said in awe, following the bone that attached from Death's back to the thick extension of his wing. "The anatomy of your wings is nearly identical to human arms?"

"Correct," he said. When my finger brushed one of the silky feathers, his wings flinched reflexively and contracted marginally. *Careful.* "Someone paid attention in anatomy."

"I'm a nerd," I admitted.

"You say that like it's a bad thing," he said, eying me sideways. "Besides, being a nerd means you struggle less to keep up with my extreme intellect."

"Always humble."

He spent the next few minutes explaining the musculature of his wings and their ligaments and joints. He angled his right wing closer in my direction. I felt like I was in anatomy class all over again, except this time, the sexiest man on the planet was teaching it.

"What about the connection to your body?" I wondered as my attention slid over his back. I wanted to run my hands across the thick cords of muscle there.

"A scapula sits on either side of my spine, and sockets are connected to the arms."

Coldness built in my core as I thought of the V-shaped scar on his back. "So when an angel becomes a Fallen . . . "

"Two of my limbs were essentially torn from my body," he confirmed through tight teeth. I wanted to understand the purpose of Heaven ripping off his wings, but the stiffness in his shoulders and his overall body language told me to back off.

"Do you mind if I feel them?" A flush crept up my face. "Or is that . . . too sexual?"

His husky laugh rolled out like a purr at the back of his throat. "You can do whatever you want to me, Faith, but know my wings are sensitive in certain areas. My alulae are extremely ticklish."

"Your *what*?"

"Feathers," he muttered. "They're feathers. Be gentle. Don't do anything weird, like pluck out a quill."

"There goes my shot at an authentic calligraphy pen aesthetic."

My fingers brushed the soft feathers directly on either side of his spine. An energy, a power that I could only describe as ancient coursed throughout me like hot oil, and my mouth parted. Death must have felt it too because he tensed.

"Those are called scapulars. Down feathers, essentially."

My arm spread up and out until it extended to a different shape of feather along the top of his wing. "And these?"

He shuddered. "Marginal coverts."

I lowered my hand, and gooseflesh burst across my skin. Death turned curiously over his shoulder, and our eyes locked. Beneath the light of the moon, his vertical pupils were dilated.

"Secondaries." The low rasp to his voice beckoned me closer. My touch affected him, and that gave me a strange sense of empowerment.

I ducked beneath his wings so that I was now in front of them. From this angle, Death wouldn't have to crane his neck to look at me as I explored his wings.

"I want to see the layers from this side," I explained with a shy smile.

He said nothing. Only watched me with a perfectly composed face. My fingers trailed over the bottom of his feathers.

"Primaries."

I raised my fingers higher, stroking the length of the longest feathers of his wings. This act no longer felt innocent. His wings weren't just feathers and bones and joints: they were a part him, a part he hid from the rest of the world. Death closed his eyes, his jaw pulsing as he slowly tilted his head away from me.

"Primary coverts . . . " He released a ragged breath. "Faith. Careful—"

I brushed the top right, and suddenly his wings jerked and sliced inward, launching him six feet into the air. I lurched back and ducked, although I wasn't low enough, and my hand instinctively lifted toward him. A sharp pain carved across my hand like a knife before I yelped and pulled it back, cradling it to my chest. The wings came back, as wings naturally did when they flapped, the sheer force of their power hurling wind into my body and knocking me hard to the ground. Good thing too, or those lethal things could have lopped my head off.

Death planted his heavy boots on the roof, his wings curling inward. "You alive?"

"By the grace of *God*!" I screeched. "What was the hell was that?"

He shrugged. "Reflex."

"A flinch is a reflex. That was a full-on attempt at a wing bitch slap!"

Death laughed hysterically, and I mean *hysterically*. The booming sound made my ears feel hot as I glared up at him. "You almost cut me in half!"

"Shhhh." Grinning, he offered a gloved hand to help me to my feet, and I took it, but not before flipping him off first.

I checked off all my body parts and then peered down at my sliced hand. My fingers trembled as blood oozed from the deep gash. *Don't cry. Don't cry. Don't cry.*

Death prowled closer, shadows dripping off of his wings and pooling across the ground as he walked. "You're hurt."

"It's a scratch," I said in my best tough-girl voice.

Lowering to the ground, Death sat back on the balls of his feet. He raised a gloved hand and motioned me closer. "Doesn't smell like a scratch. Let me see it."

My heart pounded. I approached him cautiously, my gaze sliding down the length of his deadly wings as they tucked in neatly behind him.

He was another version of Death, his inner beast showing through with unnaturally sharp, demonic features and glaringly cat-like mismatched eyes. Seeing him like this, crouched and monstrous, staring unflinchingly at me, was frightening. And a little thrilling.

"You're going to need a big bandage for that *scratch*." When he touched me, my whole body burned to life. His leather-covered fingers held the sides of my hand as he inspected the wound. "Try to heal yourself."

"I don't know how," I said. "Can't you fix me?"

"You need to know how to survive on your own, Faith. I won't always be around to protect you."

I caught the strange lilt in his voice. "Why are you saying that?"

He rose to his full height. "My wings grew back," he said, rather than answer my question. "It was a slow and excruciating process, but that pain was nothing in comparison to the day Heaven damned me to the human realm. I was alone, in an unfamiliar era, with no connections to the humans. I had to adapt to survive. It's not always going to be the best-case scenario. Sometimes, it'll be the worst. You must be prepared for the worst."

I looked down at my hand in his to find the wound already healed.

"Time to go," Death said, his voice bitter. His wings dissipated into shadow, then into nothing. "I've made you late for your date with the warlock."

XXVII

When my hand touched the door of the Crossroads, an awful sensation landed in my gut.

I looked back over my shoulder. Death was parked on the curb, straddling his motorcycle. A tinted helmet veiled his face as he waited for me to go inside.

"Could you walk me in?" I asked.

Death tugged the helmet off, a few locks of dark hair tumbling over his forehead. "Can't. It's hallowed ground. Nervous about your date?" I could tell another hostile comment had been chopped off at the end. I cast an uneasy look through the window of the shop.

"I got a bad feeling," I said. "When I touched the handle of the door. Are you sure there isn't any way you can come inside? Make sure Ace is okay?"

"Ah, let him die. He's lived a long life."

"Death."

Death shut off his bike with an aggravated groan. "Since when are you getting 'bad feelings,' cupcake?"

"Since I met you."

Shooting me a flat look, Death closed the distance between himself and the store and stopped at the entrance. Before we left the apartment, he had swapped his black t-shirt for an armored black chest piece that laced down the front to his tapered waist. Paired with a long leather coat with a cowl, he looked like an assassin ready for battle. Death lifted his gloved hands slightly out at his sides, darkness collecting in his palms. He sent the shadows forward, and when they connected with the door, a web of energy revealed itself. The magic crackled and sparked, and the shadows hissed and howled before tearing themselves free and retreating back into Death's hands.

"Ace must be in the process of resetting his ward," Death said. "This one is weak. Temporary. I can break through it, but it may cost me a hand. Stay back."

He gripped the door handle before I could process that statement. His enormous frame stiffened as if he'd stuck his finger into an outlet. Tendrils of violet light pulsed to life around the store and latched on to Death's gloved hand. Leather and flesh seared.

"Oh, crap!" I lurched toward him, but Death ripped the door open with a menacing growl and loosed a ragged breath. The magic died off.

Under his hood, Death had an untamed look in his eyes. His monster side had awakened again. He blinked, and he was back.

Baring his fangs in a smile that was a distant cousin of polite, Death made a show of holding the door open and gesturing inside with his charred hand. "Ladies first."

I stepped past him into the Crossroads, my eardrums popping like bubble wrap.

Death pulled a new leather glove from his pocket. I grimaced at the sight of bone along his fingers. "Ouch."

Right before my eyes, he began to heal, pink stretching across the bone before he shoved the glove on. "Barely feel it," he growled. "It's the constant hymn music in my ears that's pissing me off."

I frowned.

"Hallowed ground," Death said, as if that were the obvious answer. "Let's go find your new boyfriend."

We passed crystals, meditation trinkets, and other paraphernalia before entering the vast library. As we traveled down a row of bookshelves toward Ace's séance room, someone slunk into our path.

"Evening," said Master Vampire Duncan. His silvery hair was pulled back in a low ponytail, and he wore a tailored suit. "Fancy running into you two again."

"You again," I said in disbelief. "You're not even trying to be subtle. Don't you have anything better to do than creep on me all the time?"

Death swiveled his head in my direction.

"Duncan was here last time," I explained. "Watching me and Ace while we were hanging out—"

Death shunted me behind him, and my eyes widened as darkness consumed the tall shelving on either side of us. He prowled toward the vampire. "*Stalking*, are we, leech?"

"Now calm down, Your Highness." Duncan showed his palms as he backed up. "I'm browsing some reading material. Last time I checked, this property doesn't *belong* to you. Ace is a neutral warlock, mate."

Death halted in his steps, albeit reluctantly. Light slowly returned to the room.

"Touchy. Very touchy." Duncan reached a long-fingered hand to a random book beside him. "You're in enough shit with Lucifer already; best to play nice with others, hmm? I *am* on Hell's comity."

"Enjoy it while it lasts," Death seethed.

"You think you can remove me? Yes, I'm sure Lucifer completely trusts your opinion on business matters as of late. All of Hell knows you dropped the bag winning over your precious mortal prize, and that's why you lost your scythe. I wonder . . . " He tapped his chin with a pointed nail. "Is that why Lucifer's been traveling all over the world as Devin Star, continuing your little Hollywood ruse rather than helping you find your scythe?"

Death fell silent, and I could tell this guy was getting to him.

The vampire turned toward me. "Your *pet* remains in pristine condition and unmarked. How come? Have you gone soft, and now she wears the trousers in the relationship?"

"We're not in a relationship," Death growled in a low voice.

"And yet you laid claim to her in Ace's club," Duncan sneered. "Right after you killed one of my vampires."

"He died?" Death flashed his fangs in a broad grin like a wolf baring its teeth. "What a crying shame. I was only testing his elasticity."

Duncan's expression hardened to granite. "You humiliated me, and you humiliated the Crypt. I expect a formal apology. Unless, of course, you're willing to offer this tasty morsel to me for the night? Pass her along and I'll let bygones be bygones."

Death unleashed a terrifying noise at the back of his throat.

I grabbed a fistful of his jacket. His spine straightened, and he glared over his shoulder. I imagined he wanted to whirl around and bite off my hand, but he appeared to receive the message: *He's baiting you.*

I didn't know why, but the vampire was trying to trigger Death.

"Don't you have anything better to do than pester us like the annoying mosquito that you are?" I inquired.

"What a cheeky mouth you have on you, love," Duncan said. "Can't blame a vampire for being curious. Your soul is deliciously vibrant. It's unfair that Death gets to keep you all to himself. By the looks of your unblemished throat, he hasn't even had a taste of your blood. Has he at least shagged you?"

I stepped forward to punch him, but Death gripped the back of my dress and yanked me to his hip.

"I recognize my newborn was out of line in Spades," Duncan said. "Although, there's such a thrill in an authentic hunt. Taking your prey by force. Drinking your fill . . . "

"And chasing it down with a garlic milkshake?" I offered, earning a low, sinister laugh from Death.

"The good old days were more fun, don't you agree, *Your Highness*?" Duncan pressed. "Back when evil could shag and eat any human they wanted without any repercussions."

The implication that Death was like Duncan made me sick.

"You'll find no common ground with me, leech," Death growled. "Get out of my way."

"Don't you think it's unfair for the girl," continued Duncan without any fear, "to keep her so freely, yet under control, at your side? Lively things like her don't last long around you."

Death cocked his head to the side, muscles ticking in his jaw like a bomb counting down. Earlier, he'd lost his grip. Now that madness had resurfaced as he prowled forward to leave a massacre in our wake.

Jumping ahead, I physically put myself between him and Duncan.

"*Stop*," I said, planting my hands firmly on Death's shoulders. "He's not worth it."

Death shrugged sharply out of my grasp. "Don't touch me."

"Yeah, don't touch him, love. He's a lunatic, just like his psycho father." When I turned around to face Duncan, he flashed his fangs in a slow, gummy grin. "I'd hate to see you draw your last breath without me getting a taste."

I had to think fast to get us out of this.

"You should work on that enigmatic grin," I said. "That gummy smile you've got is cringe."

Duncan's silver brows furrowed. "Gummy smile?"

I glanced at Death, winking for him to play along. He arched a brow.

"She's right," Death said. "That was one weird smile."

"What the bloody hell are you talking about?"

"Maybe he has high gums?" I casually grabbed a book off a shelf.

"Some things even immortality can't fix," Death said, the lapels of his leather jacket brushing against me as he remained close.

"I most certainly do *not* have high gums," Duncan insisted.

"Okay, but you definitely have something between your teeth," I said.

Duncan prodded at his teeth with his pinky. "I do? Where?"

I moved toward him. "Right . . . there!" I smashed the book in my hands into his pale face. His hand shot out toward me, but I dodged left and whipped out a set of handcuffs from my bag and snapped them around the vampire's wrist. The device spiraled up his arm like a snake and constricted. Duncan reeled back with a hiss, his arm limp at his side. Death kicked his boot into Duncan's side and knocked him into a bookshelf. Books tumbled off the shelf and onto the floor. Death threw his whole weight onto the vampire, slammed him into the ground, and wedged his knee between his shoulder blades. I scrambled to gather his wrists together and cuffed them together behind his back.

Duncan hissed, his facial features sharpening unnaturally. "Get off of me, you wanker!"

Death stood with his boot pressed against the vampire's spine. "Shut the hell up," he snarled. Then he cut his stare to me. I smirked.

I held out my arms as I rose to my feet. "Amazing, aren't I?"

Death ripped down his hood. His mismatched eyes held mine. I expected him to rip into me with his words, to chastise me for attacking a master vampire.

Death bowed his head at me, an oddly intimate, unexpected acknowledgement of respect. I felt all warm inside, like I'd achieved a pivotal moment.

"You can't do shit to me, mate!" Duncan shouted, writhing on the ground like a big baby. "I'm an affiliate of Lucifer's comity! I'm a pure-blooded vampire, and you're a bloody bastard question mark. You don't deserve your position in Hell, you good-for-nothing mutt!"

Death smashed his boot onto Duncan's arm. Bones crunched. The vampire released a comically high-pitched wail.

"What is going on here?"

Death and I turned our heads to find Ace standing at the end of the towering aisle of books. His magenta alligator-skin shoes clacked against the marble floor as he strutted to the ticking of an old clock resounding through the spacious library.

"Unbelievable," Ace said, stopping before us to lean on his cane. "Why is Master Vampire Duncan hog-tied in my library like a Christmas ham?"

Death crossed his muscular arms, silent.

"He doggy-ears his book pages," I blurted, earning a look of confusion from everyone, including Duncan. "What? It should be a crime."

"They ganged up on me!" Duncan snarled. "That crazy bitch hit me with a giant book!"

"Aw, did the poor little baby get a boo-boo from the mean girl?" Death leaned against a bookshelf as he dug into his pocket.

Duncan's fangs lengthened. "You wait until I'm free, you bloody repulsive *thing!*"

With a crinkle of plastic, Death popped a piece of blue candy into his mouth. "I'm quaking."

Ace raked a hand aggressively through his hair. "Why is it everywhere you two go," he said, splitting his attention between us, "*une tornade* of chaos follows? You could have handled this *outside* of my store. These books are invaluable, hundreds of years old. Also, if you had listened to me when you were here earlier, Death, you would have known to knock thrice on the door before entering instead of completely demolishing my ward."

"Why isn't anyone freeing me?" Duncan thrashed on the floor. He managed to knock a book off a shelf, and it thumped right onto his head. *"Arghhh!"*

Death rested his boot on the vamp's throat. "One more sound out of you and I'm sticking your goddamn head on a wooden peg and feeding it to my hounds."

"What Death means to say," I said to Ace, "is we apologize. We're both a little volatile with all the stress. I also want to say how sorry I am about your séance room. I hope you and Trixie are okay after the—er—the accident. I feel really bad about what happened."

When Death remained silent beside me, distracted by a ribbon hanging out of a book with a bead at the end of it, I nudged his side. "What she said," he growled.

Ace cleared his throat. "I appreciate your apology, *ma chérie*. Trixie is already recovered. I'm glad to see you are in good health too. The last time I saw you, you were certainty not yourself . . . " His violet eyes lingered on the pendant around my throat. "How is the barracuda treating you today?"

"I haven't noticed anything strange." I touched the pendant with my fingertips. "I think it might be working."

"Placebos do tend to work on weaker minds," Death muttered, and I shot him a look.

"I've been an associate of Lucifer for more than three hundred years," Duncan seethed, "and this inbred Venom wannabe and his stupid big-bosomed slag dishonored my entire clan! Now the tattooed delinquent with daddy issues is threatening me on neutral ground, and nobody is doing anything about it? I am a pureblood! I am an immigrant of the Netherworld! I will not stand for this—"

Ace snapped his fingers, and suddenly Duncan had a wad of cloth in his mouth. "*Quel emmerdeur!* Does he ever shut up?"

"Say the word and he'll be disposed of," Death said with dark smile.

The vampire whimpered.

"There will be *no* murder in my library." Ace put his hands on his hips. "These floors were just mopped. I'll have Trixie escort Duncan out. Come along now; the three of us shall gather in my greenhouse for tea and a chat."

My skin prickled as Death bent down to my ear. "I'll pick you up later." Then he stalked off the way we'd come.

"I said the *three* of us, did I not?" Ace exclaimed. "It is imperative that you both meet with me tonight."

Ace's mouth had flattened into a firm, grave line, those ominous words landing like lead in my stomach. He pivoted and hobbled down the aisle of books, pulling open a door and disappearing into another room. Death and I shared a perplexed look before following.

XXVIII

Past heavy glass doors reared a greenhouse straight out of a garden magazine. Hundreds of feet above us, forty massive beams came together across a glass-paneled ceiling to create an intricate design. Rays of light slanted through the glass, twinkling off the reflection of a magnificent pond with lily pads, water hyacinths, and foliage along the rim. A fountain with scattered bubblers added a tranquil backdrop.

"Beautiful," I said breathlessly.

The heat and humidity in the air had increased. We followed Ace down a leafy path. I'd entered a fairy tale. Tropical plants and trees stretched up as far as I could see, rooted around potted herbs like peppermint, witch hazel, sage, and lavender. Strange flowers with petals in blues, purples, yellows, reds, and oranges gleamed and glistened as if painted with glitter.

I reached toward a plant to trace the moisture of a leaf when Death's warm, gloved hand closed around my wrist.

"You can look, but don't touch," Ace said from ahead of us, as if he had eyes in the back of his head. Given the supernatural things I'd encountered, I wouldn't have been surprised if he really did. "My garden is enchanted. Some of these plants are carnivores, I'm afraid."

I gulped. "Like that piranha plant from *Super Mario*?"

"Precisely." Ace performed a dramatic spin to disappear behind foliage. "Except my carnivorous plants expel a bubblegum fragrance when blooming!"

"Bubblegum," I repeated. "That's very specific."

"It's how they attract their prey, *ma chérie*," Ace replied from somewhere far away. "What mortal doesn't enjoy bubblegum?"

I edged away from the creepy plant and pressed my hands to my sides. Death faced off with a prickly plant that snapped at him like an animal and latched on to his cloak. With an irritated growl, he opened his jaws to hiss with a sound unlike any other creature— bared fangs and all. The plant released a high-pitch shriek and shrunk down to an itsy-bitsy trembling flower.

Death turned his glare on me, fangs retracting into smaller, human-sized teeth. "What?"

We approached a Victorian-style wrought iron gazebo with thorny vines and roses tangled in the framework like a fairy's home. The inside had ancient iron furniture with cushions, and at the center of the space sat a small table for two. I sat across from Ace.

Death ducked underneath the archway of the gazebo, shrinking the space to the size of a dog crate. He kept his head bowed to avoid hitting the ceiling. "Cozy," he mumbled sarcastically.

"I can't believe I missed your garden from the road," I said to Ace. "It's huge."

"You cannot see it because it is hidden. I concealed my green-house with magic to protect it," Ace explained, pouring three mugs of tea. "There are thousands of different species of plants in here, most of which are endangered in other realms."

Death dropped his colossal frame onto the couch beside my chair, shaking the floorboards beneath our feet. I was shocked the antique hadn't pancaked beneath his weight, smashing him through the gazebo's wooden floor. He adjusted himself as the poor little cushion flattened beneath his butt, then draped his long arms across the back of the couch and spread his legs.

"Let the record show," Death said, "you *willingly* let Pyro Girl into your second most flammable room."

Ignoring Death's taunting, the warlock held out a cup of tea. By Death's instantly disgusted expression, I expected him to strike it from the warlock's hand.

"To relax your . . . other side," Ace explained.

Death's eyes narrowed then darted to mine as he reluctantly took the drink. *Death holding a little teacup. I never thought I'd see the day.*

I eyed my own tea skeptically. "This isn't anything funky that will roar, right?"

Ace chuckled. "It will not roar, *ma chérie*. It is called cinnamon bird tea, a very mild sedative for anxiety, kind of like chamomile. Give it a whirl."

"I do like cinnamon," I said and sipped it. Milk, cinnamon, and some other flavorful spice soothed my dry throat. "Not bad."

Death gazed inquisitively down at his tea like a cat watching a goldfish swimming inside a glass bowl. "There's a bird in this?"

"No, but there is a shot of my best fifty-year-old whiskey in yours."

"Hell yeah." Reaching a long arm around me, Death grabbed the ceramic bowl of sugar cubes off the gazebo's table and dumped the whole lot of them into his drink. Then he tipped the scalding tea back and devoured the whole thing in one gulp, making my jaw fall open.

Death aggressively tugged at the neck of his vest and set down his cup. "I'm trapped in a carnivore's nightmare right now. Starving and surrounded by endless goddamn shrubbery. You still preserve raw crocotta meat?"

I shook my head at his blatant rudeness.

"I see your beast is rearing its ugly head," Ace said. "Are you ingesting those soporific herbs that I prescribed you?"

"I don't want sedatives, I want *meat*." Twiddling his gloved fingers, Death used one of the prickly ends from the flower he'd battled earlier to pick between his fangs. Ace gave Death a scornful look. "What? Your tomato plant started it."

"I don't have raw crocotta meat," Ace said, "but I do have prime rainbow serpent that I've been meaning to thaw. I've sent a telepathic message to my chef. Faith, would you like anything?"

"Got any plain ol' tortilla chips?"

"Yes, I'll send for some." Ace leaned his cane against his chair and crossed his arms over his chest. "Death, I'm sure you're wondering why you're here. Frankly, my dates with Faith were never intended to be dates *per se*. I want to help her refine her gift so she's strong enough to go with you when collect your scythe, but it's been brought to my attention that you—"

"This is an *intervention*?" Death hissed. "As we discussed earlier, Faith is not coming with me."

"My approach is simple," Ace continued without pause, and I could *feel* Death's temper flare. "We must find the trigger that is blocking Faith's ability. For example, a bottled-up or unreciprocated emotion."

I choked on my tea. "Oh my God."

He was couples therapy-ing us.

"Hell's horns . . . " Death speared a hand through his hair. "The last thing I need is for you to convolute our situation any further."

"He's right, Death," I said.

Death's harsh glare landed on the side of my face. The tension in the room was unbearable, but the hot-and-cold relationship between us had without a doubt affected my power.

"I will leave you two to discuss!" Ace said chirpily. "I do suggest a resolution, for the sake of your fates. Not to mention, I've locked you two inside, and Death won't be able to manifest out until I feel you've resolved this." Before either of us could protest, Ace tapped his cane against the gazebo. "Toodle-oo!" Violet magic swirled around him like a tornado, and he vanished.

"Great." Death lowered his hood and leaned forward with his elbows on his knees, lighting up a roll-up. "This blows—"

"What do you get out of it?" I asked.

His eyes snapped up. "What?"

"The whole ordeal with me, Lucifer, and the *Book of the Dead*," I said, feeling as though I'd been holding back. "You get something out of all this at the end. I know you do."

Death slung his arm over the back of the couch again and inhaled from the cherry cigarette. "You're sharp as a tack."

I grated my teeth at his sarcasm. "I want to know what it is. You owe me that much information."

"Did you forget the blood exchange, cupcake? *You* answer to *me*. Not the other way around."

I stood up sharply, knocking my chair over. "Let us out, Ace! This isn't going to go anywhere." When there was no response, I released a huff. "I'm finding an exit."

I stormed from the gazebo, only to find Death standing outside, exhaling smoke into my path like a barricade. "Where are you going, mouse?" he purred, that unmarked accent thickening. "We were having a conversation."

"Wow, you want to have *another* conversation? Looks like

306 KATARINA E. TONKS

I broke the back of the beast! When we first met, I could barely exchange three words with you without you vanishing inexplicably into black mist."

I barged past him toward a path through tropical plants and vines, but he grabbed me around the waist and spun me around. A lusty fever dizzied my vision at the sight of his beautiful, poisonous features inches from mine. "There are a thousand *other* things that affect your focus other than us. Like you missing your family, or Marcy, or your home. Or wanting a friend to confide in about all of this."

"All of which you can't give me. All of which you used against me—"

"I told you, I'm not the one in charge," Death suddenly snarled. "I have orders and obligations . . . and . . . " He worked his neck to one side, as though contemplating what he could reveal. "The truth is, Faith, I have been seeking something for a very long time. Now it's finally within my reach, and there isn't a force in this entire realm that could stop me from attaining it."

His cold confession shouldn't have surprised me, but my throat felt tight.

"I can't give your old life back," Death said, his voice slipping to a warmer velvet. "But I can give you something else. I can give you me. For one night."

"You're kidding, right?"

Those mismatched eyes drifted down my frame. "Serious as a heart attack."

Burning from head to toe, I backed away from him. "Thank you, *Your Highness*, for your gracious offer," I said sarcastically. "Are you *cracked in the head*? Did you even hear yourself?"

"Yes or no, cupcake?"

"*No!* I'm not desperate for your glorious dick, and I already told you my feelings about sex."

"Who said anything about intercourse?" His grin was slow, arrogant, and stupid hot. *Curse him.* "And you wouldn't be so sarcastic about the glorious part if you saw it up close."

"Unbelievable." I turned sharply on my heel. "You are the epitome of an egomaniac."

"I don't understand what the problem is." Death was right on my heels again. "You have urges, I have urges. It's because I'm a dead guy, isn't it?" I could *hear* the amusement in his voice. "Necrophilia is nothing to be ashamed of."

I pivoted to punch him in the face, but he was gone.

Death's laughter startled me as he materialized to the left of me, tendrils of dark matter expelling from his frame.

"I like you better when you're cranky and hardly talk!" I shouted, then started down another path. "What is this, freaking *Labyrinth*? There's no way out!"

"That's the whole point, cupcake," Death said silkily. "He wants us to resolve our issues, and I'm the one being solution-oriented. You, on the other hand, keep running away from me. But I can't complain about the view of you from behind."

My libido performed a series of backflips into a split at the thought of him checking me out. God, what was *wrong* with me? He'd basically confessed to having no problem ending any innocent life that stood in his way. What if one day that innocent life was mine?

"We both know our 'tension' isn't going to be solved in a magical rainforest," Death continued. "You want me, and I'm game. The sooner you see the simplicity in what I'm offering, the sooner we solve your block, don't you think?"

"You're disgusting, and you know that's not why Ace trapped us in here. He wants us to resolve our emotional issues and defeat Ahrimad together, but you're too thickheaded and stuck in your old ways to see that." I strode quickly away to split us apart, him on one side of an iron fence covered with vines, me on the other.

"You asked me to open up; I showed you my wings," Death said, stalking parallel to me from the other side of the fence. "I did that for you."

"Bull," I seethed. "You wanted to show off."

"I mean, *yeah*, but that wasn't the only reason. I am, perhaps, the tiniest bit . . . " Death cleared his throat into his fist. "Remorseful. About my behavior toward you. Although, you are rather sensitive, don't you think?"

I gave him a vicious look.

"Nix that last part," Death growled with a frustrated swipe of his hand. "Listen, I'm trying here, all right? I told you; I'm shit at this. The last time I talked about feelings was—oh wait, I *don't* talk about feelings, and I'm never concerned about anyone because I'm the Grim Reaper. Yet here I am. Feeling like a bitch because I'm imploring you to understand that I . . . " He stopped and glanced around. "Do you think Ace is listening in on this entire conversation?"

The rational part of me knew this ridiculous attempt at an apology from Death was a sign of progress, but the stubborn part wasn't satisfied. "You said showing me your wings was the equivalent to showing me your"—I waved my finger toward his general crotch region—*"thing!"*

He visibly fought back a smirk. "And?"

"*And* I think you and I have two very different definitions of opening up! Just because you showed me your wing-dick doesn't mean you can get into my pants. And getting into my pants doesn't fix the broken trust between us."

"Wing-dick."

"When's the last time you were in a serious relationship?" I interrogated. "When's the last time you were called a *boyfriend*?"

"Me? Tied to a silly mortal label? Don't make me laugh."

"Why not laugh? Have a big chuckle. It's so funny, leading me on, lying to me, and then trying to solve everything with sexual favors. Ha ha! Har har!"

"Am I wrong, then? Do you not want me?"

"Are you even hearing yourself? Do you not know me at all? I am not going to be your sex buddy, your sex slave, and wherever the hell else your sick fantasies lead! In fact, I think we should be platonic!"

Death's eyes darkened, raking a scorching path up my legs. "Is that so?"

"Yes, that's *so*," I sassed. "Welcome to the friend zone, angel. Population: you. The last thing I want to do is waste my time and energy getting involved with an immortal fuckboy."

"How can so much annoying be packed into one mortal? It's beyond comprehension. I'm curious, how the hell do *you* know what a fuckboy is? You sleep with a teddy bear and own more cartoon pajama bottoms than a Disney gift shop. Not to mention, you cerebrally explode at the mere insinuation of sex."

My cheeks burned.

"Nothing?" Death held out a leather-gloved hand. "Not even a laugh? You know that was funny."

"I think it's *funny* how you think you can keep me around like a prisoner and toy with my emotions when I had every intention of helping you get your scythe back!"

"Believe me, if it were up to me, you wouldn't have been *my* prisoner at all. You've managed to make three weeks feel like a millennium of agonizing, unrivaled torment from a termagant misandrist."

My jaw fell open. "How dare you use complex offensive words that I happened to learn for the SAT! I apologize for not living in Death World, where women fall to their knees before you in ecstasy and scream, 'Take me, D!' I apologize for the fact you're a two-thousand-year-old antisocial jerk who gets exasperated like an old fart after only a brief conversation with someone who was *forced* from her normal life, *forced* to live with you, and *forced* to deal with your infuriating personality!"

Death leaned into the fence so that our faces were close. "Get off your high horse, Faith," he seethed, his voice fluctuating between man and beast. His pupils were merely slits, and sweat misted the edge of his hairline. "I don't need you and your precious morals and your ridiculous giggly laugh and your naïve perception of how life is supposed to be constantly reminding me that I'll never be good enough for you. I'm already well aware!"

He blinked. He couldn't believe he'd said that, and I couldn't either.

"I abjure any inkling of interest I ever had in you," I said. "You're a coward."

Death manifested in front of me like a violent storm in the night. A cynical smile showed his razor-sharp teeth. He grabbed me, and everything whirled. We landed somewhere else in the greenhouse, the darkest part, I assumed, where shadows collected from snakelike plants that reminded me of Death's shadows. He backed me into the hard bark of a tree, his head stooped to reach my height, heat firing out of his body like a furnace.

"I am not a coward," Death said, his accent velvety thick. "Do you want to know what I am, Faith? If I will a creature with all of my might to cease its last breath, it dies. If I *barely touch* a living creature without these damn gloves, it dies, and if I hate a living creature and have even the tiniest slip of control, it's dead. Everything I am leaves destruction and pain in its wake. Peel away my skin and see what little lies beneath. I'm a monster with a razor-thin layer of control and a selfish, deep-rooted hate for a world that keeps saving me."

I turned away, unable to take the intensity of his soul staring into mine.

"That's not true," I whispered, despite all the hurt I felt. "You're more than your curse."

"What you see is an illusion of a man," he said coarsely. "All I am is death."

"Then why do I feel your heart beating when we kiss?" I pressed my hand against his chest. All I felt were the cold buckles of his intricate armored vest and the hard wall of muscle beyond it. Death went rigid beneath my touch, and my whole body felt electric from the strange energy charging between us.

He reached up a gloved hand and started unbuckling his vest beneath my fingers. One by one, the clasps undid. I forced myself to look away from the trail of dark hair leading into his leather pants.

"What are you doing?" I asked breathlessly.

Death's head bent down, his cheek nuzzling the side of my face. "Making amends," he said hoarsely.

I tried to remember why we'd fought and the things he'd said, but all was lost when I felt his fingers gently encircle my wrist and guide my hand back to his stomach. My fingers trembled as I pushed the rest of the clasps aside and spread the material until the scorching, bare skin of his tattooed abdomen met my fingertips. He released me, and my shaking fingers spread out, sliding down his taut stomach. To his belt. His zipper. To the place my mind went to in the dark, no matter how hard I tried to deny it.

He inhaled sharply.

The stubble on his jaw grazed all the way down my neck as I explored him through his leather pants. "Faith . . . " My name left his mouth like a prayer. He kissed my throat and then licked a slow path up the hollow of my neck to my ear. "Keep doing that and you'll lose your virginity against this tree."

I shivered so hard that my teeth rattled. "We shouldn't be doing this . . . "

"What's a few bark splinters in your ass?"

He swallowed my laughter with another kiss. His mouth sought mine and devoured it like a punishment. My chest arched toward him as his hands slid down my spine and pulled our bodies together. Our tongues crashed in a fierce battle, tasting, wanting. His kiss was my favorite toxin, a slow, agonizing poison. When I bit down on his lip, he released a throaty growl and grabbed my butt with both hands.

Death hoisted me up into his arms like I weighed nothing and slammed me back against a tree with his hips. "Like that," he said, demonstrating again. "Except your panties are off and in my mouth."

I couldn't help but laugh again as he kissed down the hollow of my neck to my collarbone. He slowed to a sizzling caress as his lips brushed mine once more, a good night kiss. The need for more friction overcame me as my mouth came down on his again and sought him in a darker, rougher way. I took control, crazed and fascinated by the monster holding me. He made me feel like I was sinning, permitting my lips to possess him over and over again. A fever spread throughout my body, the need to dig my nails underneath his clothing, rake my fingers through his soft hair. The crowding presence of his strong, protective body cocooning me in desire. His hips ground into mine again, and my palm spread out over his pounding heart.

And that's when I heard it. That strange ringing cutting through the greenhouse. It was soft at first, but then it grew louder, and I winced.

I fisted the back of Death's hair and pulled his face up from my cleavage to look at me. His wicked eyes bored into mine like liquid fire. He looked positively elated and erotic. His eyes were lustrous and wicked like two stolen, radiant emerald and peridot gems.

"Do you hear that?" I asked.

He peered around. "No, and neither did you." He tried to face-plant back into my breasts, but I tugged on his hair again.

"That ringing, Death . . . "

The same ringing as when Ahrimad had appeared in the bathroom mirror.

I clamped my hands to my ears as the panic set in.

"Faith? *Faith!*"

In an instant, everything changed. Death's voice faded into the distance. The garden altered like I had taken a hallucinogenic drug. I turned in a circle. Exotic plants melted away, the ground stretching and shifting to wild grass.

I tilted my head up and fell to my knees.

It was the dead of night, and I was no longer in Ace's greenhouse. The moon shone through weeping shadows of branches that reached like roots across a starry sky and arced down like fallen angels. Wind caressed the willow leaves, swaying them softly.

The sound of footsteps edged closer.

I lurched onto my feet, my heart hammering.

"Who's there?" I demanded.

"This is certainly unexpected," said a bored, raspy voice.

A figure emerged from behind the willow tree. Moonlight slanted over Malphas's unforgettable features, creating a doll-like gleam to his stark black eyes and forcing the illusion of life within their cold, bottomless depths.

"Hello, Faith."

Fear slammed into me. I grabbed a rock off the ground and held it up between the raven demigod and me like weapon. "Don't come any closer!"

Malphas raised an eyebrow at the rock, then calmly slid his hands into the silken pockets of his pants. "How did you do this?"

I viewed him as if he were crazy. "Do what?"

"Find me," Malphas said, staring at me for a stretch of time. "*You* came to *me*."

I couldn't breathe. What. The. Hell.

"Accident, was it?' A grin revealed Malphas's white teeth, which weren't dripping with black venom for a change. "Must have been because of the scar that marks your arm. Near-death experiences can form powerful bridges, you know."

"Am I . . . unconscious?'

"If I were to guess, yes. The strange part is . . . *I'm* not." Malphas corralled me back a few steps. We both knew the rock wouldn't save me from him. Tossing it to the side, I raised my fists. My heart was thrashing a mile a minute. Malphas showed his palms, amusement dancing in his eyes. "I'm not going to hurt you."

"Why the hell should I believe you?"

"Because even if I wanted to, I couldn't," he explained, as if already uninterested in this interaction. "I believe you're having an out-of-body experience. It's called astral projecting. Your body remains on Earth, but your soul is here with me. At least, it appears that way, based on the glowing aura around you. Now I see what the big deal is. Your soul is indeed light itself."

I looked down at myself. Sure enough, I was a freaking glow stick. *Great*, I thought. *I'm a lamp on Earth, and I'm a lightning bug here.*

I gazed at the willow tree behind him. The same willow from Death's memories two-thousand years ago. "Where are we?"

"The Unknown," Malphas said. "It's a realm of time beyond Limbo, where forgotten souls and memories come to fade away."

"Where's Ahrimad?"

"Elsewhere." Malphas crossed his arms. "Preparing our army."

"Okay." I was going to have a heart attack. "Could you, um, help me get back? Please?"

"No. I don't think I will."

Ah, shit.

I needed to stall until I figured out a way out of this. "What were you doing before I came here?"

Malphas glanced over his shoulder at the willow. "I wanted to come back to a specific night. Traveling in the realm of the Unknown is a dangerous feat, but I learned a few tricks from a realm jumper in the Underworld." He stalked a half circle around the willow tree, inspecting it as if it would divulge something to him. "The particular moment I wanted to go back to was by our old family home. Alexandru's childhood home. I wandered through the forest to the willow nearby, and then you appeared."

I didn't know why he was telling me all of this.

"Has Death found a secure portal into the Otherworlds yet?" Malphas asked, deep in thought. "To retrieve his sickle-majiggy?"

"Why the hell would I answer anything you ask?" I snarled. His expression turned amused again. "All you've done is try to pit Death and me against each other, or screw with my head."

"All gods are tricksters; I await your point," Malphas sassed.

No DNA test needed. He was one thousand percent Death's father. "All you're planning to do now is get whatever info you can out of me to run back to your buddy Ahrimad with it and get a gold star."

Malphas gazed steadily at me in a way that made me think he was contemplating snapping my head off. He walked closer. Although he was shorter than Death by a handful of inches, that still landed him well above six feet. Add in the venomous look on his face and he was a nightmare come to life.

"Little girl, I must inform you, before you speak so openly again, that you are currently *stuck here*, and that mouth of yours won't bode well with me." He tucked his lower lip over his bottom teeth and bit down, pausing before deciding to admit more. "For your information, I have only seen Ahrimad once since the D&S ball, and it was in passing. I complete my tasks for him, and I wander wherever I please. Frankly, he is insufferably annoying to be around."

"You're telling me that you're *avoiding* Ahrimad?"

Malphas said nothing.

"That doesn't make any sense," I continued. "You're his—his second-in-command."

Malphas narrowed his eyes. "Where were you? Something must have triggered this new ability of yours, yes?"

I thought back to my make-out session with Death, and my eyes went wide. "None of your business, Polly Wants a Cracker."

Malphas cocked his head. "Have you forgotten how fragile your life is? How skinny and *breakable* your bones are? Perhaps I will remind you."

He took one forceful step toward me, and I reeled back.

"That's what I thought," Malphas muttered. He turned his head slightly toward the willow tree, and his even expression seethed into frustration. "Now," he said, walking toward the tree, "to figure out why you've come here—"

Those black eyes focused on my neck.

"That gem."

I absently touched the barracuda around my throat. "I'm sorry?"

Malphas lifted an arm as though to reach for the necklace but decided against it. "Your pendant. His mother wore one like it."

"Death's mother?" I inquired.

Malphas nodded, his eyes still trained on the necklace.

"It's a barracuda—"

"I know what it is," Malphas said sharply. "It has the classic serpentine shape around the gem. Hers was . . . different, though. There was no cross. It was only a blue gem and a serpent. An amulet. Hers contained a Familiar too."

"A Familiar?"

Malphas finally lifted his black gaze from the pendant and blinked at me. "A Familiar is a species of demon. An entity that follows witches. It was trapped inside her necklace."

We stared at one another for a long, confusing moment. "Did . . . she trap it there?"

"No." I almost missed the small flare of anger that sparked behind his cold, dead eyes. "The Familiar was put there as a price. A consequence."

"A consequence of what?"

Malphas shifted his attention to the willow. "I have done unspeakable things in this world that have left me entrenched in sin, but my greatest offence is my most painful secret. A secret that I will take to the grave. You must discover these answers on your own."

A riddle.

He'd given me a riddle. Just like he'd given Alexandru a riddle in the gladiator arena two thousand years ago.

"Your warlock, Ace," Malphas said at last. "You trust him?"

I nodded once.

"You shouldn't. Let's just say Ace and I crossed paths recently, and his mind had a lot of secrets to share with me."

I turned my head to follow him as he moved around me.

"There is a glimpse into the future that the warlock has kept from you," Malphas said in a solemn voice. "A fate only you can stop. Ahrimad will destroy him, Faith. He will kill my son." Wind swirled suddenly and threw his warrior braids to the side. It coiled around us, the cold slate of his face unflinching against our chaotic surroundings as they faded. "Unless you jump."

The world was melting away like a dream, and coldness washed down my spine. *Death*. He was close. But I was far away, and I didn't know how to get back.

My breath came out fast and unfulfilling as I swung my gaze around the shattering world, searching for a way out. Suddenly, I heard a clicking noise and whirled around. My scalp prickled with fear. The creature standing before me had reflective skin like a mirror, with no visible features. Gazing at me with its eyeless face, its body swayed like a charmed snake. All at once, the mold of its face shifted, and it opened a large jaw filled with piranha teeth and howled.

I jumped back and hit a warm body. I turned, and violet eyes met mine.

"Return," Ace commanded.

I awoke with a sharp inhale.

XXIX

As I came to, Death's furious features hovered over mine, and I knew I was in trouble. "Welcome back."

I rubbed my forehead, feeling a stabbing headache. "Lovely to be back. Feels like a hydraulic press is smashing into my brain."

We were in Ace's library. Books upon books surrounded us, and the lights were dim.

"How long was I out?"

Death breathed hard through his nose like a dragon. His fingernails grazed my shoulder, the ends of his gloves hiding razor-sharp talons primed to release. "Two hours."

Damn.

I put a hand to my throbbing skull and looked down at the black blanket strewn over us both. His cloak. *Oh my God.* The firm pillow underneath my head was his muscular thigh. We were on a couch made of blue velvet, *and my head was in his lap.*

And I was way too comfortable to get up.

"You fainted in the greenhouse," Death said in a gruff voice.

"So you carried me all the way here and wrapped your cloak around me? How romantic." I thought a playful smile might crack the irritated expression he'd loved wearing lately, but all it did was train his vicious gaze onto my mouth.

"I thought you were dying," he said, grinding out the words between his fangs. "Your scent changed. Your pulse was almost non-existent. And your mind slammed closed."

At the thought of the whole astral projection thing and Malphas, I snapped out of what felt like a nightmare hangover as sobriety slammed into me. My heart started to pound a million miles a minute.

"Where's Ace?" I asked.

A muscle pulsed in Death's jaw. "He had to talk to one of his employees." He re-tucked his cloak around my side. We made eye contact. He stopped tucking and stabbed his glare elsewhere. "Tell me what happened. Now."

"I went . . . somewhere else." I felt my breath choke as a sob lodged in my throat. Suddenly, I couldn't stop the fearful words on the tip of my tongue from tumbling out. "Oh God, Death. Your life is in danger."

He laughed derisively. "My life?"

"Listen to me: you're going to die," I said, sitting upright with his cloak clutched to my chest. The room swam a little, and his arm curled around my waist. "You're going to die. You're going to die, unless . . . " *I jump. Whatever that means.* I shook myself, confused as to why I was believing all of this in the first place. It sounded so ridiculous when I said it out loud. "Ace. I think he's playing us. He knew something was going to happen to you, but he kept it to himself."

Death focused on the bookshelves ahead of us.

"I don't know if we can trust Ace," I whispered.

"*Ma chérie,*" announced a chirpy French voice, and I jumped a little. "I'm so pleased to see you are awake. How are you feeling?

Death dumped me to the side and pushed off the couch to storm toward Ace. *"You told her?"* he boomed.

The warlock glided a few nonchalant steps back and lifted his chin. Turquoise swirls of electricity formed a wall between the pair. "Do calm yourself in my library, or I'll have to contain you."

"You swore an oath you wouldn't tell her." Death's broad shoulders tensed, and his fists clenched until leather creaked. "Now she knows, and she's stoned out of her mind from whatever the hell you slipped in our tea!"

"What do you mean he swore an oath?" I demanded. "You kept this from me on purpose?"

"*Silence*, woman," Death hissed. Under his cloak, my right hand sparked a little with light. *Silence, woman?* What was this, the medieval era? His cloak smoked a little in my lap, and I swatted it with my hand.

"Just because you don't have your scythe," I said once the small fire was discreetly out, "and you're more 'pantherine' than usual, or whatever the hell your otherworldly ass is, it doesn't give you the right to act like an animal." I frowned. "That sounded much more coherent in my head, but you get my point!"

Death narrowed his eyes into slits and faced Ace again. "How do we put her back to sleep?"

"I'm a part of this conversation whether you like it or not," I said, throwing his cloak off as I stood.

Death glanced at his cloak on the ground, then glared unblinkingly at me. That look could have literally wilted every single plant in Ace's greenhouse. I picked up the stupid fancy garment, folded it haphazardly, and tossed it back onto the couch. "There. Happy?"

"Neither of you are stoned," Ace said, crossing his arms over his chest. "Your teas had cream and sugar and a slight dash of magic, perhaps." When he saw our faces, he quickly added, "I kept to our blood oath. I didn't tell her anything of your foreseen death."

I felt my heart fall into my stomach as my eyes met Death's. "You knew?"

Death became unnaturally still. "Yes, I knew."

"For how long?"

Death's gaze dropped to the ground, yet another betrayal wrenching me apart. "When we first met with Ace in his club, I could tell he was withholding information. I had a hunch. When I met him earlier today, he implored me to see the vision of you and me through. Said I was risking too much by going against the glimpse of the future he'd shared with us." A grim smile lifted the one side of his mouth. "And I knew my hunch was correct."

I felt like crying. Instead, I retreated inward, slipping into some dark place. When I spoke, my voice didn't sound like my own. It was hollow and empty.

"You weren't going to tell me, were you?"

"He couldn't," Ace said. "*We* couldn't, and for that, I must defend him. Death understands the cost of overriding fate more than anybody. It could be destructive to the balance between good and evil—"

"*Screw* the balance between good and evil!" I shouted. After everything we'd been through, he was going to let fate have its way with him? "I was supposed to die, and here I am!"

"That's not the same, Faith," Death said. "Your soul, your gift, it never weighed on the balance between good and evil because I was meant to save you. I'm meant to be destroyed, and the consequences of stopping that would be drastic."

Ace nodded. "He's right, *mon ange*. You were destined to live, through the Kiss of Death. It was not a direct act against fate. Telling Death his fate has a much smaller impact on the balance than physically changing what the Fates have woven for him. He *must* die." He looked to Death. "And she *must* go with you to the battle." Then he spoke to us both. "Or else I fear what I have seen will be gravely worse—"

"You don't get to decide anything about his fate!" I exploded, jabbing a finger in the air toward Ace. "I trusted you. This whole time, you've done everything in your power to make sure his death went according to plan! What kind of friend does that?"

"Faith," Death said firmly. "You need to calm down."

My surroundings warped in and out. I was so confused. And angry. The kind of anger you keep tightly bundled inside you so nobody else feels the burden of your pain, but it lingers right below the surface, ready to erupt. Why was Death so willing to accept this fate, and why, *why* hadn't he told me?

"No!" I cried, backing away. "I will not calm down. This is bullshit. You're the Angel of Death. You can't die. Don't you have some sort of way around this? A trick? A spell?" When neither of them responded, I pressed a hand against my breastbone and held my frantic heart. "I refuse to accept that there's nothing we can do to save you. Not when Malphas told me otherwise."

Ace's eyes went wide. "Oh. Oh, no."

Death's expression closed up until something terrifying and inhuman was left in its wake. "You were with *Malphas*?" The black tattoo snaking up his strong neck came to life and bled into his face like wicked ink. Right before my eyes, his skin was shifting color to obsidian. "After I kissed you in the greenhouse, you went off to meet with *my father*?"

"I can explain," I said quickly. "Well, maybe I can't, since it was an accident and doesn't make any sense to me either, but Malphas claimed that I astral projected to him."

Death stepped toward me, incensed. "Did he now? You two are super close?"

"No, it's not like that—"

"Then *tell me what it is like.*" His catlike eyes scanned every inch of me, his tongue poking against his cheek. "Why the fuck," he growled out, his voice more monster than man, "were you in contact with my father again?"

"Let's not jump to conclusions," Ace said, holding out a calming hand to Death. "She's in shock, and she hasn't fully explained herself."

"You shut up!" I screamed at Ace. "I don't need you to defend me!"

The warlock's eyebrows bowed together. *"Ma chérie . . . "*

"I await your explanation," Death hissed. "This is the second time he's approached you. The *second time* you've interacted with him behind my back."

"I can't control what Malphas does," I said, "let alone these mysterious powers I'm developing. I don't know why I astral projected to him, but last time I was alone with Malphas was different. Last time he screwed with my head. This time . . . he didn't seem to want to hurt me. He warned me. Warned me that you were going to die. Unless . . . " I frowned. "Unless I jump."

Death stared at me, his eyes stony.

"I think he's trying to save you," I said softly.

In what felt like a heartbeat, any imitation of humanity in Death had vanished again, leaving behind the face of a cold, detached creature.

My chest tightened. "Death, please, I know how this all sounds, but you have to listen to me—"

"He's a lying sack of shit," Death snarled, the whites of his eyes consumed in black. "End of story."

Ace shifted uncomfortably. "Perhaps we should all sit down—"

"I would never tell you something like this unless I thought it was true," I told Death.

"You have no idea how lucky you are Malphas hasn't killed you," Death snarled, darkness rising off his shoulders. "Why he hasn't is beyond me." He laughed humorlessly. "Honestly, knowing him, it's probably because he wants to fuck you."

Behind him, Ace lifted his chin. "Death . . . "

His pain. His anger. It devoured the oxygen in the room until it felt hard to breath.

"I'm not trying to justify what Malphas has done to you," I said carefully. "All I'm saying is there might be a chance that this alliance between him and Ahrimad isn't what it seems—"

"He murdered them!" I stumbled back as Death's enormous body towered over me. "Two thousand years ago, my father killed my mother. Then he killed my wife. She was—she was pregnant." His voice broke with emotion, pure anguish ripping over his features. "I have to go."

Death turned and stalked down an aisle of books. Shadows leapt off the massive shelves around his retreating frame, drowning him in darkness.

"Death!" I shouted. "Death, wait!"

Ace grabbed my hand as I started to run, halting me. "Let him go. Let him go, Faith."

His mother . . . and his wife. A baby? I turned back, tears welling in my eyes. "What have I done?"

It was too horrible to imagine. Too traumatic to comprehend. How did you even begin to process so devastating a grief?

Ace placed his hand on my shoulder. "It's not your fault. You couldn't have known."

I wish I'd known. Then I wouldn't have hurt him.

"If he believes your vision is true," I said, hugging myself with my arms, "then this was a suicide mission all along."

Ace's silence was blaringly loud in my heart.

"You can't run from your destiny," Ace said quietly. "The Fates and the Spirits are spiteful with our glimpses into the future. Premonitions are fragile; they're not supposed to be revealed in full. Not even Death himself can run from what is meant to be. Not without a great consequence, which could impact others, including yourself." He paused. "Although, sometimes consequences are inconsequential. When we meet someone who is worth walking through fire for."

I considered his words. Knowing what I did now, I couldn't stand by and let Death die. Which meant I needed to be in the fight, and I needed to prove that I was ready. Above all else, I needed to be able to protect the *Book of the Dead*.

"I need you to do something for me, Ace," I said. "I need you to help me break the vase."

XXX

Break. Break, damn it.

Ace and I were in an extension of his library, a large, circular area with bookshelves as high as I could see and balconies with doors leading into other secret rooms.

"Try to visualize your light becoming a weapon, such as a fireball or a bullet or a knife," Ace instructed. He stood about ten feet to my right, leaning against a bookcase with his golden cane propped beside him. "Whatever you prefer to wield. That might help you."

I tried to visualize a knife. Nothing. A gun. Nada. One of those medieval spiked ball things with a chain. No dice. I dropped my hand and heaved in a deep breath.

I brought my head back in frustration and looked at the ceiling. "We've been at this for an hour. Doing the same thing over and over again and expecting the same result—"

"Leads to discipline, *ma chérie*," Ace finished.

"*Not* what I was going to say. At some point, you throw the in the towel or try something new."

"Again," Ace said, his violet eyes calm and steady. "You can do this. Don't give up because you are struggling. Stay in the struggle. Move toward it."

Rolling off the tension in my shoulders, I raised my hand toward the vase. In the silence of concentration, all I could think about was Death. I kept remembering our same lesson with the vase. The turmoil of emotions I kept trying to push down resurfaced, and my vision blurred. My fingers trembled before I dropped my arm with a curse.

"Give me your all, *ma chérie*," Ace said. "You can't back down now; you have come so far."

I scrubbed a hand over my face. "You're right. I can't give up."

"Why?" he prodded. "Why can't you give up? Tell me."

"Because," I muttered, "I have to be able to protect myself."

"Why?"

"To protect the *Book of the Dead*. Aunt Sarah passed it down to me, and now it's in Lucifer's possession, but he can't touch it. When Death goes to take back his scythe from Ahrimad, who knows what will happen. All I know is, it'll be up to me to protect the book. I can't let Ahrimad or Malphas get their hands on it."

Ace began a slow walk around the marble platform until he stood on the opposite side of the vase as me. "Your power is energy," he said. "That energy is moved by your will. I have taught others to properly channel their gifts with this same drill, and this is how you will learn too."

My mouth fell open. "You taught Death this, didn't you?"

"This isn't about breaking the vase, Faith. And it isn't about Death. It's about you having agency over yourself."

"Maybe you haven't noticed, but I don't have any agency over myself. I gave that away the moment I pressed my bloody finger down on that contract and signed my soul away."

"Stop whining and break the vase, *ma chérie*," Ace commanded, power vibrating through his voice and pulsing in his violet eyes like electricity. The golden urn levitated off the marble platform. "Or else the vase will break you."

The vase fired toward me. Snapping into action, I dodged it before it shattered against the bookshelves behind me. I whirled around, and another identical vase was halfway toward me. I had little time to react: my hand shot out instinctively, and I fired an orb of light at it, annihilating it.

There were rows of marble platforms. I turned in a slow circle and realized I was surrounded by other vases as they materialized around the room.

"Outstanding," Ace said with a feral grin. "But what if there's more than one obstacle in your path?"

Ace's magic swelled. The vases thumped rhythmically against their platforms until the cylindrical room filled with their drumming. I shut my eyes and tuned it all out, tuned everything out, and pulled all of my focus into my light. Something within me charged back to life, ready for anything.

The urns soared toward me. I smashed two on either side of me with slices of my light from my hands and roundhouse kicked a third. The combinations Death had made me practice tirelessly clicked in like second nature, orbs of light firing out of my fists and attacking each vase one by one.

Suddenly, the vases transformed, becoming people. Faceless enemies coming at me with weapons and fists. I imagined a sword similar to the one Death had given me. My mind whispered for it to manifest, and the light listened as a blade molded from energy appeared in my hand. Books ripped from their shelves and levitated like stairs in the air. I climbed them as I battled the faceless enemies, balancing like a cat on each book as the enemies appeared from nothing.

The books I stood on trembled beneath me, and I nearly toppled before leaping for a balcony beside me to grab the top of the hand-rail. I dangled there, holding on for dear life as my fingers twisted desperately to get a better grip on the slippery railing.

I flung my legs back and then forward and swung onto the second floor, landing on marble. I pushed aside the throbbing pain in my body. My breath heaved, and sweat poured down my face. Muscles I didn't know I had burned, and the room ignited with white as I pushed myself harder.

Hurrying down a set of stairs to the bottom floor of the library, I stilled. The floor was a graveyard of hundreds of shattered golden vases.

I looked down at my hands. Veins beneath my pale skin vibrated with power, my fingertips submerged in white flames. Both of my arms were still consumed with light.

And I wasn't afraid.

I was in full control.

The light dissipated as I grabbed at my neck to find the chain of the barracuda had broken off. Picking it up from the rubble on the ground, I pocketed it with a big smile and burst into a victory dance that involved a mean moonwalk and robot finale.

Something smashed into my back, and I went flying across the room, landing haphazardly on a couch.

"That was *fantastique, ma chérie!*" Ace said cheerfully. "But always stay humble, and always check behind you."

Ace's magic gusted beneath me, and I was back on my feet.

We were sitting on opposite ends of a red leather couch with our feet propped up on a coffee table. Ace was reading an old leather-bound book with a Greek title, whereas I was flipping through an encyclopedia of ghosts.

"I want to know about your friendship with him."

Ace sighed. "You're not going to drop this, are you?"

"Nope."

He pinched the bridge of his nose. "My father was a respected healer in Rome," he began, shutting his leather book with a thump. "Back then, warlocks had much more freedom than they do today. They would claim they were specialists in herbs and would hide their magic while helping patients."

"If you were born in the Roman era, then why the heavy French accent?"

"It adds to my mystique," he answered in a perfect American accent. With a sly smile, Ace propped his head up on the armrest with his thumb and his pointer finger. "I'm a little over the top, but when you're two thousand years old, you tend to get bored. I migrated to France and lived there for almost two hundred and twenty years. Such a beautiful language, French. It's ingrained in me."

"It suits you," I decided.

"When Death enrolled in a high circle of gladiator fighters all those years ago," Ace continued with a casual wave of his hand, "I became one of his closest friends."

"What happened between you two that made you . . . ?"

"*Not* be friends?" Ace asked with a bit of a sad smile. "Malphas knew of my family's paranormal background and hired me as a private medic to tend to his son's injuries, since he was half-mortal and healed differently than other contestants. Alexandru's mother, Phoebe, had taught him at an early age how to cast black magic, but the more we worked together, the more he wanted to know about my own medicinal practices and spells, so I began teaching him everything I knew. And in return, well . . . " He shifted in his seat and coughed into his fist. "If you can imagine, I spent most of my boyhood painfully shy and awkward with *les femmes*. Alexandru helped me—*er*—"

I choked on my spit and laughed hysterically. "Well, well. Once upon a time, the Harbinger of Doom was your wingman, huh?"

"I could tease you too, you know, *virgin*," Ace said.

"You seem embarrassed," I said and playfully placed my hand over his as if to console him. "He made you memorize Roman pickup lines, didn't he?" I looked dramatically into space. "Are you Medusa? Because seeing you makes me hard as stone . . . "

Ace ripped his hand out from underneath mine as I cackled with laughter.

"I should never have opened my mouth—"

"I'll stop," I said, running a hand over my face to clear the slate. "Please continue. I'm sorry."

The warlock sighed and continued. "By the time I'd heard the news of . . . what happened to Alexandru's family, and to Malphas in the gladiatorial arena, Alexandru had already abandoned his childhood home. He'd burned it to the ground."

"Oh my God."

"Alex showed up at my door a few weeks after. He'd changed drastically. He was . . . animalistic. He'd lost all his humanity and wielded all Ahrimad's powers. He was soul-thirsty with no will to live." Ace swallowed hard. "He couldn't end his own life, so he begged me to help him. I was young, naïve, and terrified of what he'd become. To see him in his true form like that . . . he was unlike any creature I'd ever studied in my father's books."

I thought about the pain in Alexandru's face in the gladiators' arena. Had the deaths of his mother, his wife, and his unborn child led him to that point?

"What can you tell me about Death's mother?"

"Ma chérie."

"I know. I know this is a sensitive topic, I'm just trying to understand."

"Alexandru's mother made a bad decision before he was born. She practiced magic she shouldn't have practiced. It brought a curse upon the entire family . . . "

"Are you saying this curse had something to do with her death?"

"All I know is there are many answers the Fates deny me." Ace's fingers fisted on the table. "Death vowed to destroy the men who had killed my father if I helped him try to reverse his death curse, so I did. There were spells to help curb his hunger, and I was determined to find a way around his curse. But deep down, I knew there was no hope of reversing it. His soul was marked by *Dis Pater*. Hades, god of the Underworld. Maker of Ahrimad."

"Holy shit," I whispered.

"Even though I'd failed Death, he kept his promise. He brought me the head of the man who'd executed my father. Then he was gone, and Heaven recruited him. Where I saw a friend who had become a monster, they saw a warrior. They would use his death powers for good. I didn't hear from him for more than four hundred years after that. By then, he'd already fallen from grace. He never told me why, but I have my theories. He's not the same person I befriended all those years ago. He's transformed himself a thousand different ways. He's taken more hits from this life than anybody I've ever known, and he's so entrenched in demise that he's become Death himself.

"Don't get me wrong," Ace added, his violet gaze clinging to mine. "I haven't remained the same either. I've lost twice as much as I've won, and I've suffered the consequences of my own everlasting appetite for power and vices. But I wonder, wouldn't you succumb to your sins too, if you were us? Wouldn't anybody?"

We contemplated this in silence. Hearing such a remarkable story from Ace's perspective was fascinating to me, and I wished I had been there to see how Death used to interact with him. The fact that they'd been *friends*—the fact that Death had had any friends for that matter—boggled my mind. He'd made a huge point of closing himself off from the rest of the world.

"You're the only human left who remembers who he used to be," I said, drawing the warlock's attention back to me. "When he was Alexandru. I think that means a lot to him."

A smile played on Ace's lips. "You give me far too much credit. You're the one who has the most faith in him now, when he considers himself the worst version of himself. With your help, who knows what transformation he could make next."

"You say optimistic things like that," I said, "and I want to believe you. Ever since I met him, our lives have gone to the dogs. I lost possession of my soul and any chance of a normal life." I released a self-deprecating laugh. "Well, I wasn't exactly *normal* before all of this, but I was *me*. I had dreams. I wanted to go to college and pursue art. I mean, what kind of life is this, anyway? I'm afraid. I'm *always* afraid. Everyone around me is a sinner or a villain to an unfathomable degree. The scariest part is that the line between what I thought was good and what I know is bad has blurred, and I don't know what the hell that makes me."

My eyes snapped to Ace's hand as it curled tightly around mine. "It makes you human, Faith. It makes you human."

"There you are," announced a deep voice. "One needs a map to navigate this place."

Leo, Death's head reaper, strode into the room toward us. He wore dark jeans and a casual gray T-shirt that exposed a sleeve of tattoos on his left arm. His amber eyes drifted to Ace as he rose out of his armchair. The two men exchanged a "bro nod" hello.

"Hello, León," Ace greeted. "It's been a long time."

"Two hundred years, at least. Hardly recognized you without your long hair."

"And I hardly recognized you without that ghastly rat on your face you once called a moustache," Ace fired back with a grin.

"You had to go there." Leo laughed, then he slid his gaze to mine. "In case you didn't know, this guy was notorious in the supernatural world for his long hair. I'm talking straight white hair down to his ass and a different woman running her fingers through it every time you saw him."

I burst into laughter. "I hate that I can picture that."

"Ladies loved the hair," Ace said and winked at me.

"They still do," I said good-humoredly. "But I'm wondering how you were so suave with the ladies? It couldn't just be the hair . . . ?"

Leo seemed a little confused by the inside joke, whereas Ace shot me the evil eye and discreetly gave the back of my leg a little whack with his cane.

"I'm guessing you're my ride home," I said to Leo, trying to maintain a nonchalant façade. On the inside, I couldn't help but feel upset seeing him. Because it meant Death was upset with me.

"Until next time, I must say *adieu, ma chérie*."

"*Adieu.*" Not knowing if we were at the hugging stage of our friendship, I raised my hand awkwardly for a high five.

Ace made a face and pulled me into a tight hug. "Remember what I told you, *mon ange*," he whispered into my ear, "about walking through fire."

He kissed me goodbye on the cheek, and Leo and I left.

XXXI

"So, *this* is what you guys do the night before a mission?" I asked as Leo handed me a plastic cup of peach iced tea. The twinkling skyline of New York City winked back at us like stars. "Party on a rooftop at midnight?"

And not just any rooftop. Death's rooftop. Which made me think about when Death had showed me his wings.

Leo grinned. "None of us get hangovers, and it's not like we'd be sleeping right now. We rest during the day. And no, we aren't *vampires*, and we don't sleep in a coffin or on a cold slab in a crypt. This eternal servant of Hell prefers a good ol' memory foam mattress."

"You know, I never got the full backstory on you and the reapers," I said. "Eternal servants of Hell? Sounds like you guys were bad eggs."

Leo took a long sip of his drink. "Speaking of vampires," he said, clearly avoiding the subject, "I heard you cuffed a master vampire at the warlock's?"

"I was a dominatrix in my previous life."

He choked on his drink. "Easily the last answer I expected from you. Especially after the way you eyed Romeo's whip the other day. I thought your eyes would pop out of your skull."

"As would any other woman's if they interacted with Romeo for five seconds."

"You know what? Fair." Leo raised his palm, amusement twinkling his dark amber eyes. "Duncan got what was coming. I've been forced to converse with that pompous prick a few times at social events. Gives his species a bad name." Leo gulped down the rest of his drink. "So, I'm curious. What kind of training did you do with Ace?"

"Nothing too crazy," I answered. "Broke fine china with my ninja skills, levitated books, fought a bunch of magically conjured-up enemies."

"Nice. You nailed the ol' 'break the vase' drill."

Thinking about how far I'd come, I gazed into my cup.

"What's the matter?" Leo asked, elbowing me teasingly. "You're not feeling insecure about your ability, are you? I've seen you explode an entire bathroom with your power. Although, I think Gunner will do that tonight too, if he keeps it up with those mini burgers."

"Sit on it and spin, *León*!" Gunner flipped us off from the table of food thirty feet away.

Leo burst into robust laughter, and I covered my mouth to suppress my own.

"It's the curse," Leo explained. "We're all a little overstimulated tonight. Once we get Death's scythe back, it will be manageable."

"No such thing as *over*stimulated," Romeo jested as the pink-Mohawked reaper sauntered over with a drink in each fist.

"Any idea where His Highness went off to?" I asked Leo.

"No. He just texted me to pick you up tonight."

"Maybe he's nervous for the mission tomorrow?" I suggested to Leo, Romeo, and Denim, who was now looming over Romeo's shoulder.

"Doubt it," Denim chimed in with his booming voice. "Death doesn't get nervous. We were supposed to meet about the plan tonight. He ghosted me."

"What's up?" Gunner asked, looping his arm around Denim and Leo's shoulders. Denim looked like he wanted to tear Gunner's arm off, whereas Leo was passive about the embrace. "Why are we all secretly huddling?"

"Seems like *you're* the last one who saw Death, sweet cheeks," Romeo said accusatorily.

"Why does it matter if I saw him last? I'm not his keeper."

One of the reapers whistled at my sass.

Romeo chimed in again. "Ever since Death lost his scythe, his moods have been affecting our curses. I haven't been this horny since the seventies. The three-hour-long boner twice a day was thrilling at first, but now it's just a pain in the balls."

Gunner made a disgusted face. "How do we always get on the topic of Romeo's dick? I've heard enough stories about that dreadful thing over the past few centuries."

"Maybe none of you noticed," I said, "but Death has a habit of vanishing for no apparent reason. It's his thing. You guys have known him longer than I have. Don't you have cool paranormal ways to track him? Why ask me?"

"Because you're his *inamorata*," Romeo purred.

I choked on my iced tea. "His *what*?"

"Girlfriend?" Romeo offered. "Lover? His main squeeze? His boo-boo kitty? Bae AF?"

"I get the picture," I cut him off. "No, to all the above. We're not together, Pinky."

Romeo narrowed his eyes and stepped up to me, inhaling. "Do you want to bone the vicious bastard or not?"

My face flamed. "I—"

"Suspicions confirmed," Romeo said, turning to the reapers and grinning mischievously. "Pheromones are through the roof on our little lady. And she's exceptionally testy. Conclusion: Mommy and Daddy got in a nasty fight. Never doubt the Love Doctor. Now cough up the dough, boys."

The pink-Mohawked reaper held out a hand impatiently toward Gunner and Denim. Cursing, they each coughed up twenty bucks.

"He's probably with that woman I saw him talking to earlier at D&S," Blade chimed in. He was sprawled out on a cushion with a plate of food balanced on his chest. With a cold look in my direction, he pierced a cube of cheese with his pocketknife and popped it into his mouth. "She was all over him, wearing this tight little dress . . . "

My heart sank. That was the last thing I needed to hear right about now. I'd been devastated and sick to my stomach, concerned for Death's well-being while also feeling betrayed that he hadn't told me about his foreseen death. Now all I could picture was Death hooking up with some woman.

"Don't start again," Leo warned Blade.

"Oh, shove it, boyo." Blade flipped on sunglasses and stretched his arms lazily over his head on the chair. "Wouldn't you want to know if your lover was screwing around? That'd fuck me right off."

"Don't listen to him, sweetheart," Romeo muttered, clasping my shoulder with a look of empathy. "He's trying to get you riled up."

Peering down at my fisted hand, I saw light spark to life in my palm, threatening to unleash. I gritted my teeth and smothered it to smoke before tossing my cup in the trash. "It's been a long day, boys. I'm heading to bed."

"Wait," Leo said, making me turn around. He inhaled slowly and squeezed his eyes shut for a moment. "He's not with a woman. He's alone."

"How do you know?"

"Because I know where he is," Leo said reluctantly. "I physically can't tell you where, and it's better that way. Stay out of his business tonight. Please. For your own safety."

Death had sworn him to silence. My face slackened, and my heart pounded as I visualized the mausoleum and the portal. Surely he wouldn't have gone by himself?

I stepped toward Leo, rage making me brave. "Where is he, Leo?"

The reaper's eyes searched mine. "Summon Cruentas," he said. "He'll take you to Death, but don't say I didn't warn you."

I hurried from the roof and down a long hallway that led directly to the fourth floor of Death's apartment. The lights were off, and the space transformed into a shadowy castle at night.

"Cruentas!" I called out as I walked. The lights came on automatically as I descended the staircase to the main floor. "Oh, Crueeeeeeentas! Where's my handsome boy?"

I'd never summoned Cruentas and had no idea if I was doing it right. Usually, he simply appeared at random times. "Cruentas, if you can hear me, I need you." Sighing, I brushed a flyaway strand of hair out of my face. "Do you want to play fetch?"

A blue tennis ball dropped to the ground behind me. Bending to pick it up, I cracked a smile and spun around in a circle, searching for the miniature horse. Pulling my arm back, I threw the ball down a hallway, and Cruentas manifested mid-leap, catching the ball in his mouth before trotting proudly toward me.

"There you are, sweetie," I cooed, giving him a full-body scratch as he nudged his muzzle excitedly against my shins. With my hand resting on his neck, I lowered myself to Cruentas's level and gazed into intelligent ruby-red eyes. "Leo said you would know where Death is. Could you take me to him?"

Cruentas sneezed. With a puff of smoke, a black studded collar appeared around his neck with a matching leash. He stomped his hoof once then turned to face away from me and nickered.

"Guess we're going on a field trip."

I looped my hand through the leash, and Cruentas lunged forward. Air rushed out of my lungs as my surroundings transformed. "Oof!" I stumbled forward, bracing my hands against a cold brick wall. I took in my surroundings.

Great. Cruentas had taken me to the warehouse where I'd fought that demonic creature.

Cruentas's butt and tail started to shake in delight. He tried to yank me forward to the center of the warehouse, but I held him firm by his leash. "I asked you to take me to Death?"

"Nrrrffghh," Cruentas said and licked my face. He whined and tapped his front hooves hard on the ground in front of him.

"Shh. *Shh* . . . " Tiny goosebumps of fear and uncertainty prickled my forearm.

Shadowy creatures slunk in the dark around us, weaving between crates and whispering. With my heart slamming against my ribs and Cruentas dragging me, I bit the bullet and moved forward.

My ears perked at the rhythmic clank of metal in the distance.

Cruentas nickered and jumped up onto a stack of crates. He shook his head and made a sneezing sound again, shooting flames into the air like firecrackers.

"Get down from there," I whispered with an assertive point at the ground. "Get down right now or you are in big trouble, mister. I asked you to take me to *Death*, not this creepy warehouse. Cruentas. Get. Down. If you think I'm sneaking you another slice of cheese from his fridge tonight, you are *sadly*—"

Cruentas leapt off the crate, ripping his leash right out of my hand, and raced across the large space, disappearing into the endless void ahead.

"Mistaken," I said, swallowing a lump in my throat. With seemingly no way out of this warehouse besides finding Cruentas, I stormed after him. "*Eff* my life, I swear."

I followed Cruentas's damp hoofprints on the concrete floor through a barricade of bricks and stopped at a door with the same type of lock as the touchscreen ones in Death's apartment.

The clanking of metal was coming from inside.

Raising my knuckles, I thought about knocking. What if I barged in on Death and some woman having freaky supernatural sex inside? But I was in too deep to turn back now.

I stared at the touchscreen beside the handle and gnawed on my lip. I was hovering over the screen to try to make an educated guess when blue electricity sparked unexpectedly from my skin into the device. The screen shattered, malfunctioning with a series of distorted beeps and a mini explosion.

"Dang," I muttered out loud. "That little trick could have come in handy with Death's penthouse security system."

I gingerly opened the heavy door and discovered a dimly lit staircase. Hard-rock music crashed through expensive speakers around me, growing louder the further I traveled into the underground area. It dawned on me that this was totally Death's evil lair.

Cruentas appeared at the end of the stairs to greet me, bouncing his front hooves on the bottom step in anticipation. My body relaxed somewhat. The stairs were carpeted, and what I'd expected to be a disgusting basement was a refurbished man cave. I plucked up the courage to stop tiptoeing and reached the bottom of the stairs. Layered over the pounding music was that constant clank of metal shifting around, along with male grunting. I stopped in my tracks at the bottom step.

My heart leapt.

Death faced away from me, lying back on a chest press bench loaded with so many plates on either side that the bar was bending as he thrust the weight up. He had horns, black and menacing, curling up and over the sides of his skull and his clean-cut faux-hawk, as if they were meant for the hairstyle. Obsidian had replaced every inch of Death's usual golden-bronze skin, hiding all his intricate tattoos. Dark-gray joggers hung low on his hips, and he was shirtless.

I watched the monstrous version of Death lift the barbell from his well-built chest and set it down on the rack. He sat up, and my fingers climbed to my mouth. In the mirror in front of him, I saw the panels of his face were sharper, alien, and his mismatched eyes were luminous against the midnight of his complexion.

Oh. Oh, boy. Holding my breath, I anxiously glanced back up the staircase at my way out.

Rising to his immense height, Death attached a belt with weighted plates to his waist and leapt up, gripping a pipe in the ceiling above him. He drew himself up with a low rumble. The muscles in his broad shoulders and back shifted deliciously with each effortless pull-up.

In the midst of drooling, I might have forgotten about my purpose here.

"You must be out of your damn mind," Death said.

My heart leapt to my throat.

I reeled back against the wall like an idiot, knocking into a water cooler. I hugged the big water bottle to save myself from falling, and it bubbled angrily in my arms, leaking all over the carpeted floor.

Growling out a foreign word, Death dropped down mid pull-up and pivoted with a wrathful expression. "What did you do?"

His voice was guttural but still drenched in that usual velvety undertone.

"The water cooler thing," I said, pointing. "I popped it."

"Fucking hell, cupcake." Death snatched a towel off his bench and stormed toward me. My breath caught as he zoomed in, and I glided away to another part of the room. He was the night on foot: dark, dangerous, beautiful. I stared wide-eyed at his large hands, those long talons that gripped the rag as he got down on his knees to mop up the carpet. The jagged V-shaped scar on his back, the slight glimmer of his full-body tattoos now camouflaged underneath his skin.

It took me a moment to remember how to form sentences. "So . . . *this* is your evil lair? I thought for sure there would be a dragon, bear traps, and swinging blades."

"Why are you here?" He slammed the cooler down, and it stopped leaking before he faced me. My mouth went so dry I wish I'd utilized that water cooler while I had a chance.

I mean, sweet mother of God, he was *ripped*. And monstrous. Definitely monstrous.

Death gazed unflinchingly at me for a painful amount of time.

"I came here to talk to you," I said, and my voice sounded hoarse. I cleared my throat. "About what happened in Ace's library."

"Pass." Death stalked away, looped the weighted belt around his narrow waist again, and leapt back onto the pipe with a growl, pulling himself up furiously.

"Real mature," I said, getting angry now. I marched across the basement to stand in front of him as he continued the pull-ups. "Don't go to the mausoleum tomorrow."

He ignored me.

"Please," I said, feeling as though I had already reached a point of desperation. "Don't do this. Don't push me away."

His mismatched eyes seared through me as he fully extended his arms from the pipe to slowly lower his body. I fought the urge to stare at the ridiculous show of muscles in his chiseled abs right above my face, not to mention the clear outline of his *appendage* in his low-riding sweats.

"Isn't it past your bedtime, *cupcake*?" Death asked in that deep, throaty voice.

I hated how his voice alone had an insane effect on me. Like he'd licked an imaginary path down my spine. "I'm not letting you go on a suicide mission."

He leisurely dragged himself back up and continued his upper body workout. "That's what you think this is? You think I'm trying to kill myself?"

"As far as I can tell, you had no problem accepting Ace's vision."

"Here she goes again, storytelling."

"Tell me I'm wrong, then. Tell me you are doing everything in your power to protect yourself."

"You're confusing acceptance with passiveness."

"Passive, like how you say you feel about me?" I challenged.

"I already told you how I felt in the greenhouse." A grin split his cruel, fanged mouth. "Unfortunately for you, that offer has expired."

From his cocky tone, I assumed that he'd satisfied his urges, and a horrible feeling churned my stomach. I glanced back at the rumpled sheets of the bed against the far wall and felt the green-eyed monster scratch its way out. "Wel, I guess old habits do die hard. Glad you took some of the edge off, at least."

"Old habits die hard? What are you talking about?"

I crossed my arms over my chest, burning all over. "I was told you might be with a woman here."

He paused at the top of his pull-up and laughed in a way that made my ears tingle. "Ah, so that's why you broke my alarm system. You thought I was having sex."

"I—"

"If I didn't make it clear enough by my current location," he said, switching his grip on the pipe for another variation of a pull-up, "I didn't want to be bothered tonight. By anybody. But," he continued, with a shit-eating grin, "now that I know how keen you were on getting in here and finding me with another woman, would you have joined in?"

If I could have, I would have breathed fire onto his half-naked, all-stupid body and laughed maniacally as he disintegrated into a pile of arrogant ash.

"You should feel flattered by my offer," Death said, still performing pull-ups like an Olympic athlete. How many of those could he even do? "Would have been a lot of schooling on my part. You probably don't even know what a hymen is."

"Of course, I know what a hymen is."

Death glanced down at me again with those sultry, wicked eyes, while his arms held him up mid pull-up. The swell of his biceps could have cracked my head open like a walnut and I'd honestly have died happy. There, I said it.

He arched a pierced eyebrow. "Enlighten me, Saint Faith. What's a *hymen*?"

"I won't answer stupid questions." I mentally patted myself on the back for standing my ground.

"Look at you, so assertive," Death taunted. His gaze burned into mine before he hauled his body upward again on the

I whirled around to face the mirrored wall, but not before I got an eyeful of his package again. *Dear God, stay focused, woman.* "I know you care about Ace's vision. You wanted to tell me, didn't you? But instead, you pushed me away. Just like you're doing right now. Because you're afraid—"

"Because I know you," Death interjected, any amusement vanishing from his voice. "I know you'll stand in the way, and I'll be damned again before I let that happen. I won't let you lay down your life for me. I won't."

A mixture of emotions overcame me at what he'd admitted.

I gripped my elbows, hugging myself. "Have you at least told Lucifer? I'm sure if you told him, he'd have more people come to the mausoleum to protect you."

Death released another low, bestial noise that echoed off the basement walls, and the hairs on the back of my neck rose. "He doesn't care, Faith. Doesn't matter, anyway; Ace explained to you the consequences of exploiting such visions."

"I couldn't care less about the consequences. Not if it saves your life."

Death dropped down behind me, his naked torso brushing the thin cotton of my T-shirt. I froze, fighting the urge to either run or lean into him as the low timbre of his voice wrapped around me like a toxic sheath. "If you speak one word of the vision to anybody, you will deeply regret it."

"I'm tired of your empty threats."

He spun me around, and I gasped as his darkness leapt from his body and shackled my wrists to the mirror. "They are *far* from empty," Death growled against the shell of my ear. "You've betrayed me in an unforgiveable way. My trust in you ended the moment you said you were with my father."

"I didn't betray you," I said, finding strength within to defend myself. "I didn't voluntarily go see Malphas. One moment, you and I were kissing, and the next, I got swept away and I was *there*, in some other place, and so was he. I may have summoned him somehow, but none of it was intentional. What happened to you . . . All the anger and hatred you have for your father, don't put that on me, because it's not fair. This wasn't my fault." Rolling my shaking fingers into fists, I lifted my chin. "If you expect me to stand back and let you die because you're willing to cut me off so easily, then you don't know me at all. I'm in this fight. If you disagree, then you're going to have to stop me."

His gaze clung hotly to the side of my face. I shivered when the tips of his talons grazed the left side of my hip and slipped underneath my shirt to scrape against my bare skin. He exhaled a ragged breath. "Was that a challenge, Faith?"

"Since you don't want to talk, yes. Yes, it was. and you're going to accept it." I arched a cocky brow at him and slid out from his shadows' grasp. "If you knock me down and keep me down," I said, strutting to the center of the room, "you get that striptease. But if *I* knock you down and keep *you* down"—I pivoted toward him, reveling in his sinful, undivided attention—"then I go to fight with you tomorrow. Yes or no?"

Shadows pulsed off him in wisps and tendrils as he considered my offer. "I don't make deals with virgins anymore. You never paid up on the striptease, and you never planned on it, so what *value* does this deal have for me?"

"How about I throw in something sugary?" I backed away toward the stairs to the main floor of the old warehouse. "I'll make you the best batch of cupcakes you've ever had."

Death's wicked eyes hooded, and he prodded a fang with the tip of his tongue. A part of him was intrigued. But as he slowly pursued me up the stairs, he seemed to hesitate, and his fists tightened against the railings on either side of him. His expression darkened and closed again.

"No," he said.

"How come?" At the top of the staircase, I looked down at him and inclined my head to the side. "Scared?"

His jaw ticked. He ate up the rest of the stairs in a few leaps and trailed after me into the warehouse. It felt like I was luring a beast from its den, and a dark part of me loved the thrill of it.

"Walk away, cupcake," Death growled. "Go back to the pent-house. Keep your pretty head attached to your neck another night."

"Aw, you said pretty." I clucked my tongue, feeling a boost of confidence in our teasing game. "Is wittle Death afwaid to fight me?"

A noise rattled at the back of Death's throat, reminding me of a snake. "Do *not* taunt me," he said, a cord of muscle protruding in his neck. "Not when I'm in this form. Not when I'm this unstable. I could suck out your soul in seconds, and you'd be helpless against me."

I pretended to yawn. "Sounds like you any day of the week, kitten."

Death flinched at "kitten." Freeing a low snarl, he rolled back his right shoulder. I watched his jaw twitch as he considered his next words. "I'll fight you," he decided, circling around me like always. "On one condition."

"What?"

Death continued his predatorial walk, those wicked eyes taking their time as they raked over me. One gliding step and he traveled in a blur, the shadowy warehouse shifting with him as he consumed my space. He leaned his face down to my level, stopping close enough that our noses brushed. I held my breath at the frightening, yet allur-ing, sight of his form up close.

"I want the thong you're wearing," Death said. "Take it off. Hand it to me."

Prickles of heat pulsed between my legs.

"Have some class," I said with a coy smile, *"Grim."* I visualized an orb of light in my palm and threw out my hand. The power obeyed as blue and white fractured the air with a crackle and fired, nailing Death in the stomach.

I'd pictured him flying back like a rag doll and slamming into the metal structure behind him. Metal would ring out, and he'd blink rapidly as imaginary birdies flew around his head. Instead, the energy seeped into his inhuman obsidian skin like a sponge. The only evidence that I'd hit him was a low hiss that escaped from his fanged mouth and the smoke steaming off his abs where I'd burned him.

"I see how it is," Death purred, his head still bowed. Tendrils of soft black hair tumbled over his forehead as he reared to his full menacing height. "Let the battle begin. Don't say I didn't warn you, cupcake."

He moved in a blur. Deadly talons sliced through the air, grazing my throat as I scarcely evaded his swipe at my face. Adrenaline slammed into me, but I couldn't react fast enough as his body twisted in the air, his foot connecting with my stomach.

I went flying, catching myself at the last second on the wooden crates as I collided into them.

Pain exploded. The blow left me winded, and I bit hard on my lip before a howl ripped from my throat. Trembling, I looked down at the wood impaling the back of my right thigh like a shish kebab and saw black splotches. Squeezing my eyes shut, I tried to jerk my leg outward to free myself, but Death's fist wrapped around the spike, keeping me pinned.

"Not so fast," Death rasped against my ear, manifesting beside me in a whirl of shadows. The talon connected to his thumb brushed my upper thigh, and his power sank into me like hot oil, mingling with the pain. My whole body shivered deliciously. "You won't always have an easy way out with the enemy." His lips hovered over my cheek. "Or be unaffected by their allure."

The all-consuming agony of this moment made me aware of my humanity. "You are *not* keeping me impaled here," I gasped out, "like an hors d'oeuvre . . . to teach me a lesson."

He grinned. "How about you hand over those panties, and I promise to only toss you around a little more before humiliating you with a defeat."

"Do those big, ghastly horns . . . get in the way of your brain cells? I'd rather drink bleach than let you win."

"That can be arranged," he purred. "How's it feel to be impaled by my wood?"

"Barely feel it." My teeth grated when he pressed his thigh into mine, making the wood go further in. A nasty curse flew out as my hand smacked into his bare chest to push him away. It was like trying to move a mountain. Layers and layers of rock-hard strength. "Besides the river of blood running down my leg and the splotches in my vision, this is a walk in the park," I panted.

"A little blood is normal during your first impalement," Death said, raising one of his talons to his mouth and making a show of licking away my blood. "Tasty."

"Sleeping during the day, soul-sucking one-liners, hidden lairs, eerie insinuations that my beet juice is seasoned just right. Sure you aren't a confused vampire?"

He scowled. "I am not a tick."

"But you are a prick," I quipped. "Two letters away from a major identity crisis."

He smirked, although I was pretty sure it was to show off his razor-sharp teeth. "Mortal blood tastes like cheap wine. However, if you were to offer a bit of *flesh* . . . "

"My attraction to you is the most mystifying thing of the century."

His eyes lingered on my lips. "Beyond a shadow of doubt."

He unwrapped his hand from the bloody wooden stake and pulled me forward by the hips until they pressed against his.

"Motherfu—!"

Death's laugh boomed as he slunk around my peripheral vision.

"You know, my blood could heal your thigh," Death said, moving toward the clearing in the warehouse. Catlike green eyes burned wickedly bright. "I'll make sure to give it attention when you're sitting on my face later."

Biting the bullet, I gave a warrior's cry and charged while he waited with a shit-eating grin. His whole body vanished right before I hit him, dark tendrils clouding my vision. Coming to an agonizing halt, I grabbed at my leg and tried to breathe through the pain that exploded like firecrackers in my leg and my back.

"That's *it*." I tore a strip off my shirt like a madwoman and secured it around the wound on my thigh. Then I concentrated on my bloody fingertips until blue sparks came to life. Soon my entire fist was made of light and fire. "No more playing with me like I'm your ball of yarn, Angel of Dipshit. I'm going to fry you so good you'll start talking in Shakespearean."

A massive shadow cast over the floor.

"Your analogy is incorrect," Death purred. "I'm much more violent with my ball of yarn."

I tore my eyes up, tendrils of darkness melding back together to form Death's menacing figure. He stood on a metal beam above me, where hundreds of industrial arms crisscrossed and stretched horizontally across the warehouse. His enormous frame blocked out most of the light fixture behind him, giving his dark silhouette an ironically angelic aura. I pictured those inky, wicked wings spreading out on either side of him.

"Why did you fall, Death?"

Death cocked his head as he lowered himself to a crouch on the metal beam. Under the light, his horns had an almost lustrous shine to them. "Why do *you* think I fell?"

"Insubordination. Being good got too boring for you, so you broke the rules." I wandered into the shadowy parts of the warehouse's main floor and climbed a set of metal stairs. I ignored the pain in my leg the best I could. I made it four flights up, but it still wasn't high enough. Standing beneath his spot, I put my hands on my hips in frustration.

"Hmm, you're warm, but be more specific." He sprawled out on the beam and gazed down at me over the side with a lazy smile. All he needed was a catlike tail to complete the visual. "Why would I break a rule in Heaven?"

"Jealousy."

"Warmer, but not warm enough." He snickered in a way that made my temperature rise. It was crazy how he had that effect on me from so far away. "You're going to have to try harder than that, cupcake."

I noticed a stack of crates across from me on a platform that led to one of those metal beams. I started toward it, and the slow smirk that spread across Death's mouth was sinister. He leapt soundlessly to his feet and sauntered across the beam to follow me from above. "What do you think you're doing?" he questioned.

"What does it look like? I'm the firefighter coming to get my big, stupid cat out of a tree."

I got one foot up onto a crate, climbing up and stretching my hand toward a metal beam. The tower of crates wobbled and threatened to fall. Attempting to go up one more step was a mistake as the tower of crates gave way. But before I could fall, a taloned, obsidian hand wrapped around my arm and hauled me up to the beam. My palms leaned against the warehouse wall for support.

When I slowly pivoted on the narrow beam, Death was already so far away it was as if he'd never saved me. His hands were clasped behind his back, one foot behind the other with his spine ramrod straight. He cocked an arrogant brow, confident that he controlled the situation.

"Don't look down," Death taunted. "You might fall. Then you won't be cupcake anymore. You'll be pancake."

When I glanced below us, a sense of vertigo overcame me. My heart pounded as I looked straight ahead at Death.

"It would be wise for you to return to the penthouse," he said. "Let's call it a draw, shall we?"

I edged further along the beam. "I told you; I'm not going to let you die. I'm strong enough to come with you tomorrow, and I'm going to prove it tonight."

"Very well." Death stuffed his hands in his pockets and moved gracefully backward, balancing perfectly. "Tomorrow will be my last chance to enter the portal, you know."

My heart skipped a beat. "What do you mean?"

There was a reluctant pause. "I'm running out of time," he said. "My scythe is my Achilles' heel. There are creatures of the night less civilized than me and Devin, or our soldiers. Night creatures that are more animal than man, driven by primal urges like killing, eating, mating. I've found that my scythe has kept me safe from my own inner . . . " He cocked his head. "*Beast*. But now, the destructive drives of the Seven Deadly Sins that plague me are spiraling out of control. Soon I'll be driven completely mad by my curses, by my hunger, unable to communicate in the mortal language. I'll forget who I am. Ahrimad knows this. He was diminishing in this way when I found him in the willow. Which is exactly why he's in the Otherworlds, so that I can't get to my scythe and stabilize my curse. Portals between our world and other realms are stronger around a full moon. And tomorrow night, by midnight, I must find one of these portals and enter into the otherworld. Or else—or else it'll be too late."

"There has to be another way," I said. "Can't we draw Ahrimad out from wherever he is?"

"The forbidden worlds are difficult to navigate between. Even Limbo is complicated to travel to. There is a razor-sharp line between reality and imitated memory."

I continued toward him. He seemed strangely more composed

in his demonic form than he did in human form. Still, my heart was slamming into my ribs at the thought of him losing control in this monstrous state.

"I'll tell you why I fell, Faith," Death said, staring at me and rooting me to my spot. "I loathed the mortals. I hated how they breathed, I hated how they felt emotion, and I hated how they were all so predictable. Mortality is a miserable element in every human's existence. You fear it, mask it, pretend it isn't there. Here I am, embracing it. Still, I saw the souls of men who lived a thousand lives richer than mine, most of whom had the poorest of circumstances. They had friends, relatives, strangers they left behind, people who loved and grieved to the point of sickness. And I wondered why a part of me envied their pain. Now I understand. Death gives life a significance lost in my eternity."

He held his arms out to his sides, palms out. My heart lurched in my throat as I watched him lean back and fall off the beam. I shouted after him, and adrenaline slammed into me as I rapidly searched the ground below me for his body. I hurried back across the beam to the wall, climbed down, and raced to descend the metal stairs to the ground floor.

His body was nowhere to be seen.

"Are we finishing this fight or what?" his deep, velvety voice asked from behind me. "I'm bored."

I spun toward him. "You idiot! I thought you—*ugh*!" I came at him in full ninja mode, and this time he didn't vanish. But he did fight back. I was quickly on the defensive, blocking his movements. He fought like it was second nature, like a machine calibrated to kill. And even now, in this frightening form, I could feel him holding back. Watching my every decision as if he were fifty steps ahead of me.

I knew I would never amount to his skill level, but it was *so infuriating*. I wanted to impress him, though his hard hits quickly fatigued me, and I was forced to back off and put some distance between us. Light burned out of my hands.

"You're fading fast, princess." He tsked with his tongue. "Never fight a villain half asleep."

When he slunk toward me with his head lowered, I followed my instinct this time and backed away.

Death corralled me away from the light, into the dark. He feigned a lunge and dislocated his jaws with a roar, razor-sharp fangs elongating from his gums and his pupils shrinking to thin slits. I lurched back with a shriek, knocking into a shadowy object. Sharp metal brushed against my arm and tore into my bicep before I caught myself.

Panic pulsed in me as I frantically searched around, but Death was nowhere in sight.

Warm blood poured down my forearm and dripped onto the floor. "Stupid demented angel-monster-panther *thing*!" I hissed, slapping a hand over the deep wound. Now I had two gashes, my arm being the worst of them.

"Klutzy, clumsy, girl. Maybe you're your own worst enemy," Death taunted from the dark. "Did you know your heart quickens when I talk? Sometimes it's slight, and other times I feel it pulse through me like it demands to be heard. And then there's your scent right now . . . "

"Can't say I can smell much of anything except public bathroom in this disgusting warehouse lair," I snarked, tearing my shirt the rest of the way and attempting to tie it over the wound. I managed to loop it around the gash and tighten the cotton knot with my teeth. "Ever heard of Febreze? Or is that your natural form's stench?"

The air shifted as he manifested closer.

A tap on my shoulder. I kicked backward, but his hand shot out and seized my sneaker.

We stared at each other in the dark. Him, a god, with a single hand gripping my foot mid-kick, and me, a helpless flamingo. I watched him decide what to do with me next.

"Hmm." Death hitched up my leg a little, forcing me to hop in a puddle of who knows what with my bad leg. I desperately tried not to cry out. "I believe this requires a witty line."

"You have my *sole* in the palm of your hand?" I offered between clenched teeth.

White fangs gleamed against the shadows of his face. "That's the one."

Death twisted my foot so I rotated around, and I released a small squeal as he spanked my ass. I lost my balance and hit the disgusting cement floor. I was slow to turn over, but he'd vanished anyway. I cursed violently. His laughter thundered around the warehouse, vibrating the metal slates against the walls. This had been a bad, bad idea. As I moved, blood smeared the floor like a trail of breadcrumbs.

My heart pounded as I pressed back against a cement beam to hide and figure a way out of this.

"I must say," Death's deep, velvety voice said, traveling from all directions, "I'm impressed by your rapid improvement since visiting the warlock. What did he teach you, anyway? How to bite off too much to chew?"

"There's strength in fighting against the odds," I said, edging around the cement pillar. I could feel him lingering around the bend and peered around the side. But he wasn't there. Still in the dark part of the warehouse, I reached for a wooden crate beside me and slammed my foot into it, snapping off a piece. Then I pressed back into my hiding spot with the new weapon clenched in my hand.

Shutting my eyes, I listened to the dark.

"Ace helped me see what you have been trying to teach me all along," I said. "I can't let defeat define who I am or else I'll never learn. Who I am is not defined by where I came from, or my past, or another person's opinion. It's defined by who I want to be *now*, and I have to live to fight another day to figure that out. Even if it means sacrificing everything. Even if it means *to beard the lion in his den*."

His lack of response spoke volumes.

"You know what I've also realized?" I asked, creeping around the pillar. "I'm not the one who's afraid to take what I want. A cat in gloves catches no mice."

Death veered around the corner like a summoned nightmare and grabbed me, his hand encircling my throat. He flattened me against the pillar with his muscular thigh pinned between mine. "I'm not wearing gloves," he hissed.

"Guess this means you can touch me, after all."

His expression slackened. He looked down at his bare hand around my throat, and my nerve endings tingled.

Death could touch me.

When he didn't move an inch, I reached up and grazed his black cheek with the pads of my shaking fingers. My palm spread, cradling one side of his face. Patches of his obsidian skin peeled away, the night fading from his features. While the rage that ripped over his expression warned me to remember his unpredictable state, his hand on my throat had other ideas as it slid down to rest on my racing heart.

"Even when I tell you to run," Death said in a hoarse voice, "even when I'm the worst version of myself, you always stay." He leaned his hand on the pillar beside my head and lowered his forehead slowly to mine. "Nobody ever stays."

I lifted onto my toes and brushed my lips gently against his. He tasted like mint and warmth. When I pulled back, his eyes were hooded, as if he were drunk, and his brows slanted inward. He licked his lips, a smirk tilting one side of his mouth.

"Now I could have *sworn*," he began in a low drawl against my lips, "that you said you abjured any interest in me—?"

I wrapped my hands around his neck and pulled him in, crushing my mouth against his. His fingers spread down my spine, pressing me flat against his hips.

"Suck," I whispered in his ear.

He released a soft rumbling noise from deep in his chest. "Suck what?"

"My light beam."

I slammed my ignited fist into his hard stomach, and my light blasted into him with a sonic boom. Death was tossed back, his massive body flying across the warehouse from the momentum and slamming into a metal structure. He fell hard to the ground without the usual perfectly balanced catlike landing. There went a ninth life. Growling out a string of vicious curses, Death rolled over onto his back. His large obsidian hand reached down to fist the splintered end of a piece of wood wedged deep in his stomach, which sparked with light.

"How's it feel to be impaled by my wood?" I shouted, adrenaline pulsing throughout my body as I smiled uncontrollably.

Death crawled onto all fours, keeping eye contact as he pulled the fragment from his stomach and threw it to the ground. Bulging muscles flexed as he planted one foot and then the other to rise to his full height, the wound gradually knitting itself together. He flung his head back and tossed the jet-black hair away from his forehead, then ran his tongue over his fangs.

"You're mine, cupcake," he growled throatily.

A shiver rattled through me.

Death held his hands out, inclining his long fingers toward himself as if to beckon me. Those mismatched eyes blackened as the iris and sclera drowned in the color of the shadows pooling across the floor. The shadows crawled toward me, hissing in low whispers, stretching toward my feet. I tried to conjure up a weapon, but they lurched at me like snakes, wrapped tightly around my ankles, and pulled me down to the concrete.

"Not fair!" I shrieked as a shadow grabbed one wrist, then the other. Soon I was bound by his darkness again, fully restrained on the floor as the shadows glided over every inch of my skin. With every intake of air, they tightened like a boa constrictor. I felt them latch on to the wounds on my bicep and thigh and gasped.

Death approached me with an unhurried swagger and straddled my body with his feet.

"You managed to best me, but where you failed is to pin me down." His shadows peeled away as he grinned and offered me his hand. "Truce?"

XXXII

Death shouldered open a metal door into the parking lot and blew it straight off its hinges.

"Uh." I indicated the fallen door as we left. "Aren't you worried someone will break in?"

"To what? Steal a bunch of plywood?" Death summoned his motorcycle. "My shadows will eat them alive before they get one step inside."

My eyes widened, and I couldn't tell if he was joking or not. "How come Cruentas can manifest all the way to the warehouse, but you can't?"

"Manifesting a long distance like that would compromise my energy," Death said. "I already have thousands of duplicates out collecting as we speak."

"Couldn't we ride Cruentas back to the penthouse?"

"Cruentas can only manifest one person at a time, and although he's faster than my bike, I don't need you throwing up on me your first time traveling on a hell horse." He glanced up at the night sky. "If you're feeling bold, we could always fly back. Weather seems to be holding up."

"Death, I'm *terrified* of heights."

"You were also afraid of riding on a motorcycle. The harder you resist fear, the more power you give it."

I saluted him. "Rain check."

He laughed in a way that made my face burn. "I'll hold you to it, cupcake."

He wasn't wearing a shirt beneath his leather jacket. My chest fluttered as I locked my hands around his bare midsection, his hellish heat keeping me warm the entire ride.

We entered the lobby of his apartment building and took the elevator up.

"You're not healing," Death said, inspecting my arm with the rough pads of his fingers. "Get to it before you lose too much blood."

"I don't know how . . . "

He glared.

"Jesus Christ, I'm tired. Can you just drop some of your blood on it again?"

"What if I want to lick your wounds clean instead?"

My eyes widened, and a slow, devastating grin spread across his wicked mouth.

The tension between us had intensified. The elevator doors chimed open, and he stormed out like a predator.

"Death—"

He grabbed me by the back of the neck and pulled me in for a kiss. The smallest moan escaped me. My hands didn't know where to go and gripped his bare forearms. His tongue flicked against my teeth, and I tasted his blood dripping into my mouth. It poured down my throat like hot, liquid sugar. That strange, sweet, thin texture of a Fallen's blood. The madness of his bloody tongue slid across my lip one last time before he pulled away. He threw open his apartment door with a ragged breath.

"Get in. Now."

I crossed the threshold and whirled around right as his lips crashed into mine. His hands greedily slid up my waist, clutching the back of my head and prying open my mouth as he stroked my tongue. I slid my grip up his powerful arms to the back of his skull to have an excuse to touch that silky-soft hair again.

The sound of male voices and laughter echoed down the entryway.

I felt my strength return full force as I pushed him away, breathing hard. He thumped a little against the opposite side of the hallway with his black hair sticking up from my hands and gaped at me with dark, carnal eyes. He prowled toward me, but I pressed my hands against his concrete chest.

"Stop," I hissed. "There are people here."

"It's the Seven. They each have a key. Probably thought we were spending the night at the warehouse. I'll kick them out."

Death stalked down the hallway, and I followed him.

Imagine our surprise when we discovered the reapers watching *Jurassic Park* in the living room. Death motioned for me to get back behind the wall dividing the kitchen and the dining room, so that we were hidden.

We observed his subordinates as if we were at a zoo.

Gunner and Wolf were sprawled on the large couch facing the TV, fighting over Gunner putting too many "gourmet spices" in the popcorn. Romeo wore a sleep mask and drooped in a beanbag with one hand resting halfway down his pants and the other holding a bottle of liquor. Denim sat rigidly upright watching the television, fully dressed in gear. Leo was playing some sort of shooting game on a Switch that made him rage quit at that exact moment; Blade had situated himself on the ledge of the fireplace, swiping his dagger over a sharpener; and Flash lay haphazardly on the coffee table in the middle of all of them, snoring noisily.

"I can't believe these seven bozos are your reapers," I whispered over Death's shoulder.

"They're focused when they need to be," Death replied.

As Gunner and Wolf's popcorn argument elevated, Romeo, still blindfolded by his sleep mask, slapped his hand against the floor. *"Excuse me!"* he screamed, as if he could hardly hear himself talk over his earbuds. "I'm trying to relax here! Can't an ex-animated creature of the night enjoy his steamy audiobook in peace?"

"Disgusting," Blade hissed. "Didn't you get enough bloody action tonight with those twins?"

"You're jealous because he did, and you *didn't*," Wolf said with a grin.

Blade feigned a laugh. "How about I punch your face down your throat and screw your mutilated head?"

Death looked back over his shoulder with a "we should try that" face. I punched him in the bicep, suppressing my laughter at his silent, theatrical reaction.

"I think you should make your entrance now," I whispered.

Death's fists clenched until his knuckles cracked, and he released a bestial noise. "Well, isn't this *cute*," he boomed, charging into the living room. All the reapers froze like children caught misbehaving. "My seven feared soldiers of death having a slumber party . . . in my *fucking living room*."

Leo stuffed his Switch in the crack of the sofa. Denim, perhaps recognizing he looked overly invested in a dinosaur movie, hoisted himself up too fast, which resulted in catapulting the TV remote off his lap and hitting Wolf in the head with it. Wolf scrambled for the remote to shut off the television as Gunner panicked, tried to hide the popcorn, and lounged on the floor to cover it with a big, goofy grin.

"Before you get mad," Flash said, wiping a bit of drool from his mouth as he jabbed a finger at Gluttony, "Gunner's the one who locked Glenn in the coat closet with a confining spell."

Romeo flipped up his sleep mask. "Mumzy and Zaddy are home!" His neon-pink eyes landed on my torn clothes. "Well, I'll be hanged. That's a lot of blood. Hath the Prince of Darkness slayed the forbidden maiden?"

Curious eyes bounced back and forth between us as they took in my bloodstained clothes and Death's lack of shirt.

"It's not what it looks like," I said. "Death—er—healed me . . . "

Romeo raised a sly eyebrow. "Where's your shirt, my lord?"

"Yeah, where's your shirt, virgin killer?" Wolf pressed.

"We were *sparring*," Death sneered, his nostrils flaring. "Which one of you morons had the bright idea of trashing my apartment? You got shit all over the floor."

"Deflection," Romeo sang.

"Indeed," Denim said, "the subject has been changed."

Death made a monstrous noise at the back of his throat. *"Enough,"* he snarled. "I want all of you out of here, and all of this cleaned up. Tomorrow we meet at the agreed time."

They groaned but vocalized their agreement in unison. Each reaper cleaned up their mess and vanished, while Death stormed to his coat closet and threw it open. Sure enough, the little man with glasses came ambling out.

"My-my lord!" Glenn stuttered, and then he pushed his glasses up. "Ms. Williams! So nice to see you together on this . . . unpleasant night."

Death stabbed his finger toward the front door. "Goodbye, Glenn."

Glenn scrambled to collect himself. *"Goodbyemylord!"* He dove through the front door as if it were a hologram and evaporated.

"I like Glenn," I decided. "He's funny and awkward."

Death lifted his lip in disgust. "He's a disease."

"Your Highness," Leo called from the living room. "May I ask who will be protecting the girl tomorrow while we meet Ahrimad?"

"Lucifer will be."

I looked up at Death, having hoped he'd changed his mind on leaving me behind.

"I'm ready," I insisted. "I'm in this fight too." When Death didn't budge and kept his eyes forward, I looked pleadingly at Leo.

"Perhaps she has a point, my lord," Leo said. "It may be safer for her to stay in plain sight. I can accompany her if you wish."

I looked up at Death again, thinking that was a decent plan.

"No," Death said. And that was that. "You're dismissed."

Leo stood there a moment longer before nodding once. "As you command, my lord." He'd started to turn when he caught my eye and nodded. "Good night."

"Good night . . . "

Once Leo was gone, Death gave me a seething look before stalking away. Frowning, I trailed after him. "What's the matter with you?"

"You put yourself in the middle of my discussion with my subordinate. Don't do it again."

"Excuse me?"

"Don't do it again," he repeated, pivoting to face me. "Or you will be punished."

"Wow. Here come your outdated villainous torture tactics, right?"

"Who said it'd be that kind of torture?" The sinister flicker of desire in his green eyes sent chills down my spine. "Maybe I'll take it out on your soft thighs."

"If you haven't gotten the memo by now, everyone is sick and tired of your 'I lost my scythe boo-hoo' moods. You're mad because I agreed with Leo, and you know damn well you're embarking on a suicide mission. Get over yourself and go take a shower; you smell like the undead."

His face was priceless. Of course, he didn't smell bad, he never did—which was beyond me—but he didn't have to know that. I brushed past him, feeling pleased with myself, and was heading down the hallway to my room when Death manifested in front of me, blocking my way. His arms were spread, his hands braced on either side of the hallway, drawing attention to his upper body and outrageous abs. And he knew it.

"Only if you take a shower with me."

The back of my neck prickled. I tried to keep my utter disbelief hidden, but I knew I was failing.

"My shower is much more efficient than yours," Death explained with feigned concern, stretching his hands higher on either side of the hallway to stretch out his abs. "We'd be saving a ton of water."

All I could do was stare at him, dumbfounded that we were even having this conversation.

"What's wrong?" he asked, his grin widening. "Afraid of what will happen after you see me all wet and sudsy? A certain *appendage*, perhaps?"

"I'm not afraid of your dick," I snapped.

"Whoa there, cupcake," Death said, dropping his arms to stalk a slow circle around me. "Didn't know you had it in you to speak so explicitly."

He flicked a strand of my hair.

"Let me guess," I said, whirling around to face him. "You want to deflower the virgin before you kick the bucket."

"You think so little of me." He lowered his head slightly, looking at me from under his lashes in a mischievous way. "Maybe I want to spend time with you."

"Naked in the shower?"

His sinister laugh made my stomach tingle. "It was a joke; don't get your panties in a twist. Like you'd ever strip down and take a bath with me."

"Ah, the ol' reverse psychology trick," I said. "I thought cats didn't like baths."

"I do. I like to soak." The way a piece of his wavy black hair had fallen into his eyes was driving me insane. "You're looking a little rosy, Lamp Girl. I haven't even said anything that dirty. But the night is still young."

I swallowed the lump in my throat. "I'm going to go take a shower, and then I'm heading to bed. *Alone.*"

Death manifested and blocked my way again, sprawling lazily against the hallway wall with sin pooling in his mismatched eyes. "Honestly, cupcake, lighten up. Everybody gets a little panicked about being naked with someone else for the first time. Except for me, of course, but that's because of my very sad, very rare condition. TBDS."

"You know what I'm thinking right now?" I asked.

"Crickets chirping?"

"I think you need to find a hobby outside of getting under my skin and talking about your manhood like it's the Great Bambino of dicks."

I brushed past him, and he grabbed my hand.

"Wait." When I looked back at Death, he slid his hand from mine and into the pocket of his sweatpants. "Never deny that slice of me inside your soul. It belongs to you. Light is your hope, and darkness is your strength to make the choices nobody else can."

My throat felt tight. Nodding once because I didn't know what to say, I shut the guest room door behind me and braced my back against it.

The thought of losing Death made me feel like I was drowning above water. He'd become the angel before the fall, the darkness I'd forgotten how to live without, and we both stood on the edge of the night with everything to lose. Waiting for the inevitable meant we had time. Time, instead of the threat of destiny and a crooked hourglass ticking away our last few grains of sand.

I took a long, leisurely shower to wash off all the blood and loosen up my sore muscles. Then I pulled on a pair of shorts, soft knee-high socks, and a baggy band T-shirt and paced back and forth. It took a long internal pep talk to muster up the courage to exit the guest room.

Wandering around the penthouse, I sought him out again. Past his gym on the bottom floor of the penthouse was a decked-out man cave. Two pinball machines, a pool table, Skee-Ball, and a dual-shot basketball arcade game. Various old photos of celebrities and a pop-corn machine.

I passed a flashing neon-pink silhouette of the Grim Reaper cutting off someone's head on the wall and rolled my eyes. Past the two side-by-side doors was an explosion of gunfire from an action film. Death sat on an enormous black leather couch in front of a large flat-screen TV.

I padded across the room and peered at him from the side, admiring his sinfully handsome profile.

Taking a deep breath, I came around the U-shaped couch to sit. Death's eyes shifted away from the movie and snagged on my bare legs as I tucked them into my chest.

He paused the movie.

What are you doing? he asked, but his mouth did not move.

Keeping you company, I replied in my thoughts. *But you already know that.*

"How many tattoos do you have?" I asked out loud.

"They're not tattoos." He seemed to hesitate before he pushed up his T-shirt sleeve and laid his forearm on my bent legs. Turning his palm over, he displayed the tribal-like designs from his fingertips all the way up his tan bicep. "They started showing up after I was cursed by Ahrimad, then more when I fell from Heaven. I used to only see them when I was in my full form, but now they've become permanent, shifting around every so often. I've been told they're relics, remnants of old magic or something."

I leaned forward, outlining the curve of one of the markings with my finger. His skin was hot to the touch. "Do you know what they mean?"

He shook his head, jaw tight. "No. I don't want to know."

"Why?"

"Don't care."

I had a feeling he did. Maybe ignorance was bliss.

I shivered at the sensation of his fingertip drawing a slow shape on my bare thigh, and that was when I realized he'd never removed his arm from my leg. "I have a question," he said.

Laughter that I didn't quite recognize tumbled out of my mouth. "I might have an answer."

"You said you wanted to be loved your first time. Why?"

I blinked, totally not expecting that one. The seriousness in his expression was off-putting. Like he genuinely didn't understand. It took me a second to think about what I wanted to say.

"There's a coldness in not feeling anything. I don't want to remember feeling cold. Not for my first time. I associate love with feeling secure, warm."

"Coldness." Death stared into nothing as he sketched small shapes on my thigh. "I think I can understand that."

I tried to articulate my opinion carefully. "People who don't want to have attachments to others, they learned how to flip a switch. They know how to feel nothing. And I . . . can't do that. I feel things fully. Most of the time, I feel too much. When I don't want to feel anything at all, it builds up inside me until it surfaces, until it explodes."

"Because you're young," he said. "The world hasn't had its way with you yet. Nobody is born with thick skin. You're tried and beaten with life's weapon of choice until you decide how much more you can take. True power is controlling how you react. To everything."

"Love isn't just a reaction," I argued.

"It's a mental, physical, and hormonal reaction based on subconscious, innate behaviors."

"You can't be serious, Death. Love is healing and powerful. It's what connects people to others."

Death let out a bitter laugh and shook his head. "Your poetry is cute. If only it wasn't based on the deranged romantic fantasies of mortals and had some merit. I have a hard time believing the worldview of a girl raised in a safe, nurturing family, sheltered from all the horrors of the world. What could you possibly know about life to be so certain about love?"

I knew this wasn't about me, and it broke my heart. "Your mother loved you, Death. I could tell in the memory I saw of you as a little boy. She loved you."

"Sometimes. In a *cold* way, I suppose." He gave me a meaningful look. "My father—well, you've seen how naturally paternal he is. And my mother—she allowed my father to rob me of my childhood, mold me into an executioner. All for power, money, materialistic things to fill the voids inside them both. Children reflect their parents. If I reflect my parents' love, then I am twisted and cruel and vacant. So vacant that I have become nameless."

Feeling like I couldn't breathe, I got up from the couch and stood over him. "Is this the lie you've trained yourself to believe? That you're nothing? You are *not* nothing. Living without any connection to others is a trauma response. You're so afraid of being hurt again that you've convinced yourself that you don't need love. And that's not living. That's just . . . existing."

This dark revelation confirmed what I had hoped was not true.

"In the warehouse," I continued, prying the difficult words from my mouth, "you said you envied mortals because their lives had significance. I saw something in you that frightened me." I halted as my vision blurred and my throat tightened. "You don't care whether you live or you die, do you? You haven't for a long time."

Death shut his eyes and leaned forward onto his knees, raking his fingers through his hair from the back of his skull to the top. "Faith."

"That's why you're afraid to get close to anyone. You push people away because you don't want them to see that you're suffering inside. And let me tell you something. That makes you as human as I am. Your life is *not* insignificant, Alex."

His head snapped up. His expression sent a chill down my spine as his eyes erupted with a glowing kaleidoscope of green. It felt as if I'd wrenched something merciless and haunting out of his soul.

"You matter," I said, finding the bravery to continue. "If you were gone, *I* would grieve you. *I* would miss you. *I* want you to live. You've become . . . everything to me. If that means anything to you, anything at all . . . " My shoulders slumped as a sob shook my voice. "Promise you'll do everything in your power to stay."

Death remained unmoving, gazing up me with slightly wide eyes as I wept.

"Come here." He reached out with both arms, and I let him tug me into his lap. He cradled me into his chest. "You sweet, beautiful, *foolish* little mortal. I'm not worthy of these tears, and you should be frightened by what they awaken in me." He took my hand in his and flattened my palm over his heart. "Until you feel that coldness, I promise."

My eyes drifted closed as I pressed myself deeper into Death's warm embrace. He kissed my forehead and rested his chin on my head, and I knew. I knew he loved me.

Death stiffened. The stench of smoke and burning flesh.

"Isn't this sweet," announced a British voice. "The bitch and the zombie canoodling like it's the end of the world."

My heart plummeted. Duncan, the master vampire, stood in the door of the entertainment room with one hand clasped behind his back. The fabric of his shirt had burned away, leaving a few strands of silky material hanging from his lean, pale chest. The porcelain skin of his face and his right arm were slowly healing from a vicious burn that was so deep, it exposed sections of bone.

Death moved in a blur, placing me behind him. "How did you get past the ward?"

"Oh, you have much bigger things to worry about than your little ward," Duncan said, flashing his fangs. "I come bearing a lovely gift. From Ahrimad." His amiable veneer vanished. "Meet us at the Greywood mausoleum in one hour. *Both* of you. Or the warlock dies."

He thumped Ace's bloody cane to the floor.

XXXIII

T-minus forty minutes remained until Ahrimad's deadline.

I tugged on form-fitting black cargo pants and laced up my heavy-duty black boots. My first layer over my bra consisted of a skintight black long-sleeved shirt made of a heavy material that Romeo claimed was bulletproof. A discreet but rock-hard black armored vest covered most of my torso and chest, designed like a comfortable corset. It zipped up the front instead of having complex laces. Then a jacket with a built-in hoodie thrown over everything. My gloves were simple and black with spikes on the knuckles, and I braided my hair into the usual French braid.

Dang, I thought, turning to look at my butt in the cargo pants in the mirror. I looked like a badass bounty hunter.

A knock on the door sent my pulse rocketing. "Come in."

My stomach fluttered at the sight of Death's menacing form filling the room. He shut the door behind him and locked it.

He wore a similar all-black outfit. His chest and a portion of his arms were covered in that armored chest piece that laced down his torso. On top of his typical leather gloves, combat boots, and black cowl, he also had bunched-up black material around his neck that I pictured he'd pull up over the lower portion of his face. Weapons were tucked into every strap along his legs and waist, and two swords crisscrossed his back.

His cold expression said it all. The moment Duncan had left Death's apartment, any sign of humanity in him had evaporated. His otherworldly side took precedence, and he'd called back the reapers for immediate action. Romeo arrived first with my new gear, and that was that. I was going with them.

Death unsheathed a third sword hidden at his hip—the sword he'd given me, I realized—and inspected the blade before stalking toward me. Even in all the bulky gear I wore, I felt so small in comparison as he towered over me.

"What's up?" I asked, glancing uneasily at the sword. Considering his beast side was itching to unleash at all times lately, him gripping a sword in front of me wasn't exactly comforting.

Death grabbed my belt in a large, gloved hand, and my breath hitched. Weeks ago, he would have picked me up and curled me like a dumbbell to bring me level with his fanged mouth so he could rip my throat out. He would still do that, honestly, but instead, he adjusted one of my straps and slid the sword into an empty scabbard on my belt.

"How does the belt feel?" he asked in a low voice. "Too heavy?"

All I could focus on was graze of his fingers at my hip and his proximity. I thought about our moment in his theater room, how he'd held me as I cried.

"The belt feels fine." I toyed with my braid. "Only thing I'm nervous about is the clothing. Romeo claims my entire outfit is designed with some enchanted fabric that repels most magic, including my own power, but we haven't had time to test that theory."

As if receiving permission, Death gave my outfit a slow once-over, his exotic eyes snagging on the corset. "You've never had that issue before." He glided around me to unzip my backpack and dig around.

"So *far*," I said, chewing my lip. "But the fact that Romeo even brought that up is nerve-wracking. I don't want to accidently char-grill myself in front of our enemies."

"Ideally, you won't be using your power at all tonight," Death said, coming back around to stand in front of me. "Give me your wrist."

"Please," I coached. "Give me your wrist, *please*."

He glared down at me.

I reluctantly held up my arm and watched him clasp a fancy-looking watch around my wrist. "So, we're going to do this together? You know, like in Ace's vision."

"Ace's vision never included himself being abducted. Things have changed."

"As far as you know," I said, irritated by his attitude. "What if Ace gave you the wrong date? What if he omitted the little fact about him being kidnapped because he didn't want to change fate?" Emotion lodged in my throat. "Maybe this was how it was supposed to go all along."

"It's possible," Death conceded. "Doesn't change my decision regarding you. End of discussion."

My fists tightened. I'd give him an end of discussion.

"Take the command," Death said, his voice deepening to a growl. "I'm in charge of this mission."

My face burned under his intense authority. "Do you honestly think Ahrimad will meet you alone? That he won't try to destroy you the second he sees you? It's clearly a trap, and you know it."

The fury that rippled over Death's expression told me not to question his leadership again. Too bad I was too fired up to care, even as the room darkened significantly.

"I didn't come in here to fight." He reached down and grappled with my belt, securing another item onto it. My eyes widened. He'd harnessed the mini version of the *Book of the Dead* to my waist. It was surrounded by its own sheath, so he hadn't been affected by touching it.

Coldness hit my spine as I realized what this meant. Ahrimad wanted one thing and one thing only, and that was this book. The *Book of the Dead*. Infuriated, I shoved Death's hands away.

"You're using me as *bait*?" I exclaimed. "I'm starting to think your English isn't as good as it appears, Roman boy. When I said I wanted to come with you and fight with you, I didn't mean I wanted to be the worm you dangle in front of the king bass."

"We can't keep the book here, not when Duncan was able to enter through the wards."

"Vague and not answering my assumptions. Fantastic. Back to your old ways, I see?"

"If we can take my scythe back tonight, we can avoid entering the otherworld," Death said. "There's a chance you're right about our fate, that it can change. It's happening already. This gives us the best chance of survival." He looked away from me, his jaw tightening. "The reapers and I all agree that you're not strong enough to go up against Ahrimad or Malphas. And I especially don't want you entering the portal."

"Then what exactly is your plan here? Because it sounds to me like you're going to go into the mausoleum by yourself, winging it. And if all else fails, you'll use the *Book of the Dead* as leverage for Ace."

He stretched his neck to the left and growled out an aggravated noise. "I'm not giving them the book, Faith. Giving Ahrimad the book means giving him you, and I'll drop dead before that fucking happens."

I felt a little breathless at his confession. Although, I reminded myself that he'd said that because he wanted me and the book all to himself. "You can't make me hang back and be babysat while you go in there like a martyr. Sure, I might not be a full-blown she-warrior yet, but I want to be involved. Ace needs both of us, and he's my friend. I can do this."

But he didn't seem convinced.

"Ahrimad is twice, maybe three times as old as I am," Death said. "He doesn't give a *shit* about anyone, including me, including the warlock. He's an ancient, evil entity created solely for the purpose of harboring death. If you want Ace to survive, we need to be careful, and you can never be alone. You'll be guarded by the Seven."

I couldn't lose him, but I couldn't fight my way onto the front line and make matters worse. If something happened to Death and I couldn't help . . .

"We need to talk about the worst-case scenario tonight." Death's eyes searched mine as if he were reading my thoughts. I could feel my heart sinking. "If things go south, if things don't work out the way we'd hoped, and I—"

"No, *no!*" I thrashed out of his grasp, but he only grabbed me again. "I'm not listening to this. Let go of me—"

"Stop. Faith, *stop.*" He pinned my wrists at my sides and flattened me against the dresser. His eyes were calm and steady against mine. "I know. I know this is difficult to talk about, but we can't pretend Ace's vision isn't a possibility. If things don't go the way we planned, if Ace's vision comes true . . . I need you to promise me you won't be reckless."

I hated this. I hated that he was even making room for the worst-case scenario. As far as I was concerned, Ace's vision had been wrong from the moment he was kidnapped. We would be at the mausoleum one night earlier than he'd predicted, so fate had already changed.

"I made my promise to you," Death said. "Now it's time you make yours. I've lived two hundred lives. You've hardly lived one. If anything happens to me, promise me you won't get yourself killed trying to be the hero. Promise you won't seek revenge. That you'll choose *you* over me. I need you to choose you over me."

I looked up at him with wide eyes as an invisible fist squeezed around my throat.

He grasped my face, smoothing the pads of his gloved thumbs over my cheekbones. "*Say the words*, cupcake."

"I promise," I whispered.

With my fingers crossed behind my back.

XXXIV

The Seven showed up to travel with us to the Greywood Mausoleum. Unlike Death and the other Fallen, none of the reapers had wings, which meant we had to travel by car.

Leo, Wolf, Gunner, and Flash traveled in one, while I traveled in another, sandwiched between a stoic Denim and an exasperated Blade in the back of a Cadillac. Romeo boasted in the driver's seat about how he'd coined the term *ménage à trois* in 1856, explained why monogamy is a social trap, and expounded on other Romeo-related topics.

". . . and *that* is why I get along so well with gynecologists," Romeo said as we pulled into a bare parking lot.

"Shut," Blade hissed, gripping his head, "the fuck. Up."

Romeo snickered. "Clearly, I'm not the only one suffering from high testosterone levels in this vehicle."

"Enough," Denim warned. "Both of you."

Suddenly, dark-winged angels hit the ground, surrounding the

Cadillac. The shadows of their menacing wings tucked gracefully into their backs. I counted at least ten.

"Death's Fallen," Romeo said and cut the engine. "Just a precaution to protect you, love. Let's do this thang."

Denim and Blade got out of the Cadillac. I scooched out after Denim and slammed the door behind me. The Fallen moved into formation with their hands clasped behind their backs. One with a buzz cut stepped forward as Leo approached.

"I am Reaper León, Lead Commandant of the Seven," Leo said. "What is your status?"

"I am Fallen Morax, Battle Order Lead Commander, Legion Six-Nine," said Buzz Cut. Morax's black eyes flicked to each of the reapers before landing on me with a brief flicker of surprise. "Is that . . . ?"

"Yes, this is the girl," Leo answered. "She is to be protected at all costs."

The horde of hooded soldiers swiveled their heads to look at me, whispering amongst themselves.

"You're kind of a big deal in Hell," Gunner whispered at my ear. "You might want to say something charming for your first impression."

Feeling incredibly under pressure, I raised a hand with a peace sign. "Greetings, Legion Sixty-Nine."

Romeo burst out laughing.

Morax turned his attention back to Leo. "Upon Lucifer's order, I have thirty Fallen surrounding the perimeter of the cemetery. I await orders from His Highness, Lord Death. When can we expect his arrival?"

As Leo and Morax discussed strategy, I heard a slight rustling from above us. My gaze moved heavenward, and I squinted at a small shadow above us, a raven sitting in an old maple tree. My heart rate picked up as I thought of Malphas and our encounter in the projection.

Wolf grabbed me by the shoulder. "You're gonna hang back with Denim and me. In the Cadillac."

"You can't be serious," I said. "We're waiting in the *parking lot* while all of them go in to kick some demon ass? What if they need help?"

"There are thirty other Fallen for backup," Denim said, steering me toward the car. "Neither of us wants to babysit a mortal tonight, but it's Death's orders."

Instead of arguing that I didn't need to be *babysat* and Death was in no frame of mind to be making last-minute decisions about my involvement, I planted my feet and crossed my arms over my chest, trying to look as intimidating as possible.

"Denim and Wolf, I *command* you let me into that cemetery."

They shared a look and chuckled.

It had been worth a shot.

"Get into the Cadillac, pipsqueak," Wolf said. "Before I throw you over my shoulder."

Before I could argue further, Death landed like a cat on top of the Cadillac. His mismatched green eyes were nearly black in the night, the lower portion of his face was covered by that black scarf, and he wore his cowl. He pounced onto the hood of the car and hit the pavement gracefully.

"Faith is coming with us," Death said.

My heart skipped a beat.

Wolf spoke up for us all. "But you said—"

"I changed my mind," Death snapped. "She's coming with us. Got it?"

"Yes, my lord."

Under his breath, Romeo muttered bitterly, "Always a dramatic entrance. Did he have to dent my hood like that?"

Death stalked past the group of hooded soldiers and moved

fearlessly toward the entryway of the Greywood Cemetery. He kicked open the massive black cast iron gate.

"So much for a surreptitious entrance," I muttered.

Neither the stars nor the moon showed up to light the way as we trudged into the boneyard blanketing the dead. The rotting smell of earth brought awareness of the corpses lingering beneath the rows upon rows of tombstones fading out of sight. I'd never been in a cemetery at night, and I yearned for this to be the last time.

"You smell that?" Denim asked Morax.

"Indeed," Morax answered.

"It's getting stronger," Romeo replied.

"Whoever smelt it dealt it," Flash joked.

We approached a fountain at a fork in the pathway leading to the mausoleum. An overpowering metallic odor filled my nostrils. I peered down into the dark water, a chill slipping down my spine.

I looked across the fountain at Death. "Mortal blood," he said. "It's fresh."

Wolf's nostrils flared. "The scent lingers all over the ground."

It was too quiet. With every uncertain step, my boots crunched over dry leaves. The ominous feeling that we were being watched made my heart pound. I kept searching for Death's looming frame ahead of us, finding a sense of security that he was in sight.

"I was starting to think you wouldn't show."

Morax and his Fallen soldiers drew their swords, and the reapers readied their weapons. Leo and Wolf moved to either side of me, but Death remained unruffled, calmly turning to face Master Vampire Duncan. Duncan stood with an arrogant confidence that he was in control of this situation, his hands clasped behind his back. He wore no armor and had no visible weapon.

"Look at what you've brought me," Duncan said, gesturing with open arms. "A whole little militia to pick apart!"

"We want proof of life," Death growled. "Show us the warlock."

Duncan laughed, his elongated canines prominent. "You're getting ahead of yourself, Grim. This cemetery is so magnificent at dusk. Especially tonight when the scent of mortal blood overpowers the decay. Can you tell I started the party already? Apologies, I would have let you watch the massacre of the mortal hogs, but my newborns were so . . . thirsty."

"We didn't come to chitchat," I snapped, drawing Duncan's cynical eyes toward mine. Wolf gave me a swift pinch on my left arm that told me to keep my mouth shut, but I ignored him.

Figures that I hadn't noticed before shifted in the night, darting in and out behind gravestones, leaping down from trees and hovering in the dark surrounding us.

Blade flicked out his hands. Two blades popped into his palms as he fanned out to the left with Gunner trailing right behind him with a crossbow. Gunner aimed at the approaching figures, and the beam of light attached to the rim of the bow illuminated the chilling faces of oncoming vampires. Unlike Duncan, these vampires were gruesomely ugly. Drool seeped down the corners of their mouths.

"Hate to be cliché," Duncan said, "but you've fallen right into our trap."

His smile was broad, smug.

Blade's lip curled up in disgust as he nudged Romeo. "The hell is up with this guy's smile?"

"It is a bit of a quirky smile for a villain," Romeo said. "Very odd . . . and gummy."

Death snickered darkly. "Hardly saw any teeth."

"There's nothing wrong with my smile!" Duncan shouted. "Screw the bunch of you. You're all imbeciles. Slaves to Lucifer and his corrupt ideals of how the creatures of the night should live."

"You fail to recognize the importance of the balance," Leo said.

"Good and evil must have common ground. Without that, the mortal realm will fall into complete anarchy."

"Lucifer does not care about the balance or fairness," Duncan argued. "Otherwise, he would never have smothered the voices of vampires. We were here first. Yet, for nearly four hundred years, vampires have been forced to comply with Lucifer's reign."

"And for good reason," Wolf said. "Vampires have caused more turmoil between species than any other. Quarreling among lycans and shapeshifters."

Duncan cocked his head and laughed. "Lycans are filthy, despicable creatures jam-packed with stupidity from inbreeding—" His mouth parted, and his silver eyes widened slightly as he feigned realization. "Ah, wait. Aren't you that Seven who used to fuck a legendary alpha's mate? Until he found out and put her down, of course." He tapped his chin with a sharp nail. "Say, didn't he rip out her spine and feed her bones to his devotees? What a shame. But it is a dog-eat-dog world."

Wolf lunged for Duncan's throat before Flash and Gunner grabbed him and hauled him back. "At least she *had* backbone, you spineless tick!" Wolf snarled.

Duncan continued. "Vampires have been *forced* into hiding, *forced* to live on limited territory, and *forced* to hunt on certain grounds, all while the Seven and Death's Fallen live like spoiled royalty." Duncan's eyes darkened as they swung to Death. "And you, Death, are responsible."

Vampires emerged all around us. Dread churned my stomach as they surrounded our much smaller army. The reapers and Death's Fallen prepared to fight.

"More vamps coming from the east." Leo's eyes glowed as he held his sword out in front of him. "My lord?"

Death laughed darkly under his breath. "Blood is the only thing that keeps your life essence animated. And you wasted it, decorated this graveyard with it." His voice gradually rose with each word, beckoning everyone to listen. "All to create the illusion you're in control and not Ahrimad's pawn! As if you aren't already a hostage to your own undying hunger, as if your body isn't unbearably thrumming right this second, begging for you to wet your dry mouth and taste the blood seeping into this ground."

A few of the vampires around Duncan became distracted and flicked their hungry, beady eyes to the ground and to their shoes, stained with crimson.

Energy crackled in the air like static electricity, and I could have sworn the ground gave a slight tremble. Shadows slunk across the ground beneath Death, unfolding from the darkness, consuming the pathway to the mausoleum.

"Tonight," Death said, his voice booming over the graveyard, "you have soaked this graveyard in your demise. The mortal lives you have slain shall not be wasted. Not with a god in your company."

The sky ruptured with lightning, striking the fountain between us and the enemy. As the vampires lurched back, Death launched into the sky with a single jump, levitating high over the graveyard. His skin darkened to the color of night, a horrific, hellish silhouette of a monster against the moonbeams. Two enormous wings, concealed in obsidian shadows, beat the air in thunderous, rhythmic strokes, and the trees bent away from the movement as if in fear.

He was a reawakened nightmare: skin like midnight, wicked horns curving down the side of his skull, his bare upper body rippling with lethal muscle. The green hues in his eyes were masked by dusk, a lethal fury pouring outward in the form of a noxious smoke. Darkness expelled from his every pore, haloed the crest of his head like a magnificent crown, and curtained behind his back—a royal cloak fashioned from shadows.

"I call upon the dead of night," Death's monstrous, guttural voice thundered. *"Souls from Hell, I summon. Draw from the crimson life soaking these graves. Awaken, my dead. Crawl from your dark depths and serve me. Awaken, awaken, awaken, bones from beneath. Stir from your slumber and rise. Rise, and serve your master!"*

The ground shuddered with such force that it sent us all off-balance. Stone cracked in the distance, gravestones fracturing one by one, row by row, the bone-chilling moans of the dead unleashing across the graveyard.

How much had Death sacrificed to unleash his full power? All that energy and without his scythe—could he come back from it?

Shadows hissed from all directions, strobing in and out between the shapes of creatures and formless tendrils. They crawled against the ground on all fours, approaching the vampires. One of the vampires dared to attack the darkness, but it latched on to him like a parasite. It plunged into his open mouth and down his throat, and the vampire dropped with a gurgled, painful scream, as if his insides were being shredded apart in a blender. The vampire's body jolted, and skin suctioned to bone as the shadow ripped the life straight out of him.

Death soared over the graveyard with two screaming vampires in his clutches. He tossed their mutilated bodies to the earth and spiraled down for seconds, snatching two more newborns with his massive claws and tearing their heads right off. His enormous wings arched down, pitching his monstrous frame back into the night, the wicked rumble of his laughter thundering over the pandemonium.

He was bathing in the grisly glory of the war beneath him.

The shadow finished as a horde of, well, *zombies* and skeletal animated creatures lurched into the clearing in the graveyard with pulsing auras of dark power.

"Hell yeah!" Wolf roared, holding a vampire head in his hand. "It's Z-War up in here, bitches!"

The vampires sprang back in shock, knocking into one another to get away as the shadows and undead corpses slunk closer. The stench of rot overpowered the air as the zombies opened their decayed jaws with horrifying howls and attacked the vampires in swarms. The shadows and corpses glided where they were needed to imprison and debilitate the vampires enough so that the reapers and Death's Fallen were able to finish the job and decapitate them.

"Party time, boys!" Denim said, cocking his machine gun.

"Yee-haw!" Flash shouted.

Death slashed his hand through the air, and shadows sliced into the blood of the fountain, spraying it everywhere. The newborns lurched toward the fountain to lap at the blood with their tongues. A trap, as Death's Fallen and the reapers slaughtered the bunch of them.

Suddenly, three vampires jumped on Leo at the same time as hands clamped down on my arm and my mouth. The world blurred. Then I was being dragged back underneath the shadows of trees and shrubbery.

Crashing back to earth, I writhed against my captor, the slippery material of my jacket aiding in a miracle as I wrenched free and rolled across the dirt. A foot kicked me hard in the stomach. Romeo's padded vest between the foot and my abdomen thankfully absorbed the impact.

"*This* must be the mortal Ahrimad wants," a vampire hissed.

"She's just an ordinary girl," said another.

They grabbed my ankles and hauled me across the dirt. This time, I writhed against the ground and managed to turn over, kicking out as hard as possible with my free leg. The clink of metal rang out like a bell as the toe of my heavy boot slammed into solid flesh. Chiclet-sized pellets fell into my lap. His fangs. The vampire cried out, and adrenaline coursed through my veins. I fired a beam of power at the vampire, who went airborne and splintered a tree.

DEATH IS MY RIDE OR DIE

I stood up fast. The will to survive took over, but I couldn't see how many vampires were in this space. I couldn't see anything. My mind harked back to training with Death, how he'd turned off the lights and forced me to listen.

Shuffling. I had hardly a second to react to the blur of another vampire attacking. An icy palm cracked across my face. My whole body flipped in midair before I slammed into the frozen ground. I must have bitten down on my lip because I tasted blood. Pain exploded in my face, and involuntary tears sprang to my eyes.

A lone newborn vampire approached with its fangs elongating in its mouth. It reached out, grabbed me by the throat, and squeezed. I struggled with all my might to get one last gasp of air when the vampire cried out and its grip loosened. I landed on my back as blood sprayed over me. As the vampire roared in agony, I realized its hand, which had been wrapped around my throat, was severed completely from its arm, and the limb still dangled from my neck. I shrieked and chucked it off me. It landed with a splat in the grass.

Whoosh! The vampire reeled back again with a choked sound, and through the gaps in the trees, the moon shone enough to show the one-handed vampire clutching at its chest. Another object sliced through the air like a bullet and perforated its neck, with the sickening noise of blood spraying. Still, the creature focused on its task and stumbled toward me with its jaws wide open.

Blade sprinted into the clearing and leapt onto the vampire, tackling it to the ground. His one weapon impaled the vampire's eye, while his other sliced the vampire's neck to the bone.

Two more vampires followed behind Blade, wounded but alive. One of them came toward me, and my body vibrated with fear. Light shone from my right hand before I fired a punch out, slamming into the porcelain jaw of another newborn. I ducked at the sideways swipe of a hand toward my face and landed in a low crouch. Blade dove over me and rolled onto his feet to slice another newborn to pieces.

Another vampire grabbed my armor and threw me ten feet, my teeth digging into my lips as pain exploded in my shoulder. Blade released a howl, and I turned my head in time to see a vampire bite down on his neck and rip off flesh.

Beside me, I found the splintered tree where I'd thrown another vampire. I tugged hard at piece of wood to free it and moved with a newfound madness to kill. Sprinting into a lunge, I drove the spiked wood through the back of the vampire attacking Blade. The vampire released the reaper and spun, just in time to meet my reared-back fist. Gloved knuckles demolished bone with a sickening crunch at the sonic boom of my power.

I turned to look back over my shoulder and arched my leg up in a backward roundhouse, kicking the last vampire in the face. Blade finished him off by ripping his head off and kicking the dead corpse away with a crunching wallop.

With no other creatures to fight, Blade and I breathed hard and looked at each other across the clearing, a pile of dismembered vampires in our midst.

"Jesus Christ, your neck."

He clamped a hand to the wound on his neck with a wince. "Fucking fang-face venom. Makes me heal slower."

I quickly shrugged off my backpack and searched for a first aid kit. When I sprayed some kind of magical antiseptic on his wound, Blade hissed and glared at me like an animal. Like Death. Deciding Blade should take over, I handed him the first aid kit. He took out a big piece of gauze and slapped it haphazardly onto his neck.

"The other six were neck-deep in battle, and Leo got pinned," Blade said. "Somebody had to make sure you stayed in one piece."

"I thought you hated me."

"I hate everyone, lassie. Equally."

"Well, thanks for the help."

"Don't mention it." Blade swiped his knives across his pants to clean them. "You were impressive back there. There may be hope for you yet."

We hurried back to the battlefield and jumped into the anarchy. Gunner took out creatures one by one from his perch in a tree, releasing arrow after arrow from his crossbow, spearing them in their skulls and hearts. Leo was on the ground with Death's Fallen, cleaving away with his sword, while Denim and Wolf sprayed bullets that sizzled as they met the vampires' flesh. Romeo and Flash were tag-teaming with hand-to-hand combat.

Ravens cried out in a frightening chorus, circling the sky in a swarm that drew everyone's attention. Demons re-formed from the ravens, ambushing the reapers with their blackened fangs, claws, and terrifying porcelain faces.

Malphas's raven underlings. Which meant Malphas was close too.

A mighty wind raged as the ravens came plummeting to the earth. I leapt back with a scream to avoid getting speared by their beaks and fell to the ground.

The second my head hit the grass, images flashed through my mind like a dream on mute.

Ahrimad . . . He was in the mausoleum. Death's old cloak hung off his body, but he looked too thin, too sickly, like a parasite had drained him from the inside out. He stood in front of a floor-to-ceiling mirror with a surface like water. As he turned away from the portal, he silently roared, his eyes glowing a wrathful amber. The skin of his face pressed tighter against his skull. His scythe swung out, his face taut with fury, the portal rippling closed behind him—

Suddenly, I was back in the graveyard, my mind scrambling as I hurried to my feet. I was trying to understand what I'd seen when I noticed a wall of shadows in front of me. I was trapped, untouched by the sounds of war around me, surrounded by Death's shadows. A barrier had formed between me and them. Between me and *everybody*. And they all continued to fight, unaware of this.

The shadow prison stretched outward, forming a larger clearing of darkness. When I tried to escape, the darkness hissed and spewed out toward me like claws, and I reeled away from it with a shriek.

The adrenaline shooting through my veins told me these shadows weren't protecting me.

They were containing their prey.

Coldness spilled down my spine. I whirled around as Death's boots touched the ground. He stood tall and monstrous with his wings tucked behind his back, his head pointed slightly down. Posed, like a deadly statue. And for a horrifying second, I didn't think he recognized me.

All I knew for sure was that I had been imprisoned by these shadows. For him.

Above us, more ravens circled like vultures.

Death moved in a blur, sprinting toward me. He picked me up and bounded off the ground, hurling us both into the night before a scream could rip through me.

XXXV

Gone was the sweet, sweet, blessed sensation of earth, as Death's wings took us high into the air. Heights were a bellowing *HELL NO* from me, and this was the unanticipated amusement park ride of the century. I wrapped my arms frantically around his corded neck, holding on for dear life.

We landed on a flat portion of the roof of the mausoleum, where a massive, overgrown oak tree blocked our view of the sky. Well, landed isn't really what happened. *He* landed and then tossed me away from him. I rolled over twice and ended up on my back.

Death stood over me: horns, wings, demonic eyes.

My mind whirled as he flexed those lethal talons.

"Um, hey," I said, rather awkwardly. "That was a little rough, don't you think?"

Death worked his jaw in an odd, animal-like way. *"Hungry."*

"Same," I said. Laughing uneasily, I cast another desperate look around us to find one of the reapers. But all I found was a wall of shadows surrounding the roof. "I could really go for some chicken nuggets right now. Or a Big Mac. Anything but disgusting flesh like mine . . . "

Death freed a low hiss through his fangs, darkness pulsing from his wings. I felt rooted to my spot.

"I don't want to hurt you," I said, my teeth slightly chattering from both fear and the cold. "And you don't want to hurt me either. I think. But if I have to, I will hurt you, so snap out of it."

Death's full form prowled toward me in a slow stride. His sinful power saturated the space between us with menace, hunger, and undeniable seduction.

"Death, it's me," I said, finding it difficult to form a sentence. I could feel his hold on me even as I motioned for him to stay back with my raised hand. "It's Faith. You can fight this."

Death homed in on my raised hand and cocked his head, cold eyes fixated on my fingertips as if he were waiting for something to happen. Realizing this was my moment to scare him off, I focused to try to get a light beam going. I even started snapping a few times. The snapping thing ended up way too jazzy.

Needless to say, Light Beam wasn't cooperating. Now we both knew it.

Death's eyes slid to mine like two cynical slits. Doom settled. He grinned, sharp white fangs filling his gruesomely still-beautiful face.

"Give yourself to me, mortal," Death hissed, completing the cinematic visual. His voice: monstrous and grating. His talons: large and menacing. His hand: outstretched toward me. *"Give me your soul!"*

Death bared those outrageously terrifying fangs, and I launched the light at his face. Death's head turned at the last second, and he watched the light burn a wicked hole into the oak tree behind him before fizzling out.

Shadows snaked from Death like little beasts and pinned my wrist to the roof. When Death turned back around from his inspection of the damage I'd caused to the tree, his mouth had quirked up into a slight smirk.

"D-minus." He worked his jaw again, and his fangs retracted a little into his gums. Darkness shrunk back into his pupils, leaving behind two mismatched rings of green for his irises. "That's being very, *very* generous."

I looked up at him, completely dumbstruck.

"I didn't work you all day for weeks," Death continued, "for you to wear that doe-eyed look the moment an enemy is about to kill you. Had I truly not been in control, you would have been chunks of meat stuck between my teeth by now. Use your brain next time and not your weird quirks to dissuade monsters."

As Death continued to roast me into another life, my fury took over as I ripped free from his shadows like a madwoman. "You were *testing me*? I almost had a heart attack!"

"A heart attack?" His eyes flicked to my breastplate with interest. "Stimulating."

I launched to my feet. "I could *kill* you—"

"Shh." He clutched my wrist and pulled me toward him as he retreated smoothly behind the thick branches of the overgrown oak. A creature flew past us overhead, and I huddled closer to him. "I saw you fall to your knees. You looked like you were hurt, and then your mind barriers slammed shut. With the ravens circling you, I took matters into my own hands and brought you up. You had a vision, didn't you?"

I pictured the wrath I'd seen in Ahrimad's gaze, the way he'd looked like a parasite was eating him from the inside out . . . A shiver raked through me at the image. "Ahrimad is weakened. He looked sick, thin. He almost resembled a—"

"Skeleton?" Death offered. He didn't seem surprised by this information. "Yes, I suspect even with my scythe, Ahrimad can't properly feed. My scythe serves as an anchor for his soul to remain, for a short amount of time, in this world. His soul might be immortal, but it needs mortals to survive, and he has no power here without my scythe. Not as a soul. He'll need to become permanently corporeal to survive."

I touched my belt, where unbeknownst to any of the creatures I'd encountered that night, the book was tucked away, safe and sound.

"He'll need a dark spell for that," Death added gravely. "He'll also need a new body to possess. Someone who can handle his eternal soul."

An awful feeling settled in my gut that he would take Death. And I had no intention of watching Ahrimad overtake Death's corpse. I couldn't bear it. Lifting my chin, I met his gaze fiercely. "I won't let him get to you."

Death stepped into my personal space. "Faith," he growled in a deep, commanding voice that I imagined petrified his subordinates to the point of soiling themselves. "Do *not* start. You made a promise to me—"

"Don't get myself killed. I know. But guess what? No matter how much power you have, there are some things in this life that you will never fully control. One of those things is me."

We stared at each other, waging a silent war.

For once, he backed down. "You have so much trouble with authority that you can't even listen to me to save your own life."

"You *are* my life," I said, unable to hold back, "and we can't seem to stop fighting long enough to figure out what that means for both of us. I mean, seriously, Death. I can never tell if you like me or if you're prepping for your future favorite meal of the century!"

"You're the loudest, most stubborn, most annoying little vermin

I have ever met," he growled. "*Annoying* is too soft a word, really. Nothing I say or threaten you with stops you from doing what you want to do. It drives me fucking nuts. Of course, I don't *like* you—"

"Let me stop you there," I interjected, raising my hand. "This stressful battle from hell is enough torment for the day. I don't need you to roast me in the midst of it on top of—"

Death grabbed my hand and brought our faces close. "I wasn't finished, cupcake. Of course, I don't like you. Hell only knows, that would be much less agonizing. You are the genesis of a madness I can't escape."

My mouth parted in a small gasp, so he kissed me, stealing away the rest of my breath A touch of pure, unrelenting fire that melted me to the core. He lifted me off the ground, and I hiked my legs up around his waist, capturing his mouth again. His hands were rough weapons carefully cradling my waist. His fingers climbed underneath the tight fabric of my armor to clutch the bare skin of my lower back. The sweet and minty taste of his tongue. The masculine scent of him, his darkness flying all around us, unpredictable and merciless like the man who wielded it.

Suddenly, Death dropped me to my feet with a strangled noise. He went down on his knees, writhing in agony. The sharp prickles of claws penetrating my brain overcame me, and I went down with him.

"Well, that was rather easy," proclaimed a raspy voice. Through the blurring, debilitating agony, I saw Malphas Cruscellio with his hands clasped behind his back. "Awkward timing, though, I will admit. Perhaps there will be blessed water inside to douse my eyes with?"

"You *sonofabitch*—" Death tried to lunge for his father, and I watched the veins in his face and neck engorge as he went down on all fours. Panic slammed into me, but I couldn't move.

"Do not bother, Alexandru," Malphas said coldly. "You are severely out of practice against me, but I remember your mind inside and out." The raven demigod stretched a pale hand toward me. "Faith. I'm to escort you into the mausoleum. Shall we?"

His power let up on my mind, my whole body shaking from the aftermath. I thought fast, my mind whirling as I leapt into action. I fired my light quickly from my free palm. Malphas cursed as it burned through his pant leg, and that was when I unhooked a pair of cuffs from my belt and slammed one onto Malphas's right wrist.

"What the—?" Malphas's arm went limp at his side. He glared accusingly up at me, blackness webbing from his eyes. Pain exploded in my skull. I could feel his power trying to stab its way into my mind, but I kept shoving back in an internal battle of tug-of-war. His jaw set. Right when I thought he might win, I lunged forward with everything I had and shackled his other hand to the cuffs, binding his hands together.

"We shall not," I growled.

Freed from Malphas, Death leapt up from the ground in a blur. "I'm going to rip you in fucking half—"

"*Stop!*" I screamed, throwing myself between them. "He's subdued, Death. Look." I passed Death the leash attached to Malphas's cuffs—the same ones I'd subdued Duncan with. "We can use him as bait."

Death froze, his eyes still wild with anger as he processed the idea.

Malphas sighed. "This is a severe waste of your time—"

"Shut up," Death snarled. Then he handed me Malphas's leash. "You want to walk the dog, or should I?"

XXXVI

The mausoleum was trashed. Condom wrappers, crack pipes, and other paraphernalia littered the ground. Between that garbage, rot and decay filled the cracks of once elaborate tiles. Graffiti symbols arched wildly across the marble walls like scars.

Mausoleums were notorious for their meticulously clean appearance. The fact that this place was so ruined made me feel sad. I imagined the thousands of bodies crammed like sardines throughout this castle-like structure and became furious that this was what had become of the dead's sanctuary.

Malphas walked ahead of us, the line of his leash coiled tightly around my hand. He moved with a swagger, like he didn't have a care in the world, whereas Death was practically foaming at the mouth. *Nothing says family reunion quite like an estranged homicidal demigod father and his hybrid monster son coming together.*

"So," I began, attempting to break the incredibly uncomfortable silence. "This probably isn't the time, but I've always wondered . . . Do you guys ever pee?"

Neither of them responded.

I wouldn't let this go. "Because I haven't seen a single immortal drink a whole glass of water."

Death slowly inhaled through his nose, as if he wanted to duct tape my mouth shut and bind my hands together before tossing me helplessly into the ocean. Either that or he'd gotten bored with being undead and had taken a random mortal-like breath.

I shuffled a little faster to walk beside Malphas. It wasn't like he could do much to hurt me.

"Dehydration is a silent killer, you know."

Malphas gave me a strong "go away" side-eye. "We don't need water to nourish our bodies," he replied, surprisingly answering my first question. "If we consume water or mortal food, then yes, we'd have to use the restroom afterward."

"Interesting," I said, tapping my chin. "Very interesting. Even number two?"

Death hooked a finger into the pocket of my pants and yanked me back to walk beside him. Malphas's steps faltered a little as his line cut short.

Cut it out, Death mouthed, his eyes beseeching me to stop.

Then Malphas held up a hand, and we did stop. He turned his head over his shoulder and nodded to Death.

Frowning at what appeared to be a signal, Death stalked forward and shifted into predator mode. He slowly slid two swords out from the sheaths at his back. Powerful muscles tensed as he slunk past us to glide into the shadows. He pressed up against the wall beside an archway, his brilliant mismatched green eyes the only indication that he was there. He closed them and blended perfectly into the dark like an assassin.

Two vampires in armor rounded the hallway. Malphas moved to stand in front of me.

Death's skilled hands were already twisting each blade around his fingers in a mirrored motion, his arms coming down fast and hard to flawlessly sever each vampire's neck.

Another vampire launched out from behind him, but Death spun one blade backward in his palm and brought his arm up, stabbing the vampire through the throat. Death turned toward the creature and ripped the blade through the rest of the tendons of the newborn's neck, its head dropping amongst the growing pile.

"Adequate," Malphas commented.

Death's lip lifted in a snarl. *"Adequate?"*

Shadows collected from the darkest corners of the room, crawling toward Death like creatures on all fours. They curled up his frame and formed a menacing aura around his silhouette.

Death dropped his swords and pivoted, sprinting toward the entryway and launching himself at four more vampires that had reached the scene. His talons lashed out, slicing through an enemy's torso. When his fist drove through the chest of another, he walked forward with the vampire in his clutches and stalked somewhere out of view. Screams were heard. A chunk of flesh or an organ flew across the hall and smacked a vampire right in the face.

The vampires came sprinting in a panic through the archway toward Malphas and me like the T-Rex chase scene from *Jurassic Park*. Their clothes were mangled and covered in blood, and they clutched at their injured body parts. Death gripped the archway behind them and swung back into the hallway, landing on both vampires before they could reach us, his fangs bared. He crushed the backs of their skulls into the ground with his bare hands.

Awesome. And disgusting.

Death collected his fallen swords and rose to his full height, tossing a strand of black hair from his forehead. He stared icily at his father.

Malphas hummed and then picked at a piece of imaginary lint on his shirt. Looked like Death had successfully vanquished his father's criticism.

Moments later, the three of us stood in a passageway that opened onto a wider space with high ceilings. Pentagrams and hexagrams with symbols and languages I didn't understand covered almost every surface. The air was thicker in here, electric. Like rubbing a balloon vigorously against your skin and creating static. An eerie sensation clung to me from all directions, almost as if the walls had eyes.

"This room is giving me the heebie-jeebies," I said. "Is it hard to breathe, or is it just me?"

"Just you, cupcake," Death said.

Malphas lowered to the ground, his hand hovering outside the intricate lines of the pentagram design in front of him. His pale fingers tensed, the blackness along his fingertips crawling down the back of his hands. Smoke levitated from the lines engraved into the marble floor, and when Malphas looked over his shoulder, black branches webbed from his eyes and extended across his pale features like poisoned veins.

"The Seal of Solomon," Malphas said. "Ahrimad must have summoned this from the Underworld. I imagine a summoning spell like this would severely weaken him in his current state."

"You seem surprised," Death spat.

"As I've told your little girlfriend, I haven't been kept in the loop."

"You're Ahrimad's second-in-command. The reason I lost my goddamn scythe. You're telling me you haven't been kept in his loop?"

"That's exactly what I'm telling you. For the record, you lost your scythe because you were too busy doting on a temporary mortal. Old habits die hard, I suppose."

Death lunged for his father and knocked him hard to the ground. Malphas's leash went flying out of my hand as he nearly pulled me down with him.

"Hey!" I cried.

"What game are you playing at?" Death snarled, his hand wrapped in his father's shirt. "I'll give you five fucking seconds, and then I'm tearing your head off."

Malphas said nothing. Revealed nothing. The raven demigod's face flattened to an unnerving blank slate, but his jaw was clenched so tight that I could have sworn I heard molars grinding.

"Death." I gripped Death's arm, his flesh scorching to the touch. "He's not worth it, and he's our bait." I pointed at the pentagram, desperate to get him to calm down. "Why don't you tell me what a Seal of Solomon is?"

"It's a way to summon powerful demons," Death answered gruffly. He released Malphas's collar with a shove and stalked around the room. At every pentagram, he methodically checked it by tracing the design with his fingertips.

"You said Ahrimad was weakened," Death snarled at Malphas.

"Because he *is*," the raven demigod said. "He's not corporeal like you or me. It's why he must hold the blade so often."

Death and Malphas exchanged a long look, as if they had carried their conversation into a mental argument.

"Can someone explain to me what the hell is going on?" I asked. "High-energy demon sounds a little concerning."

"There are fifteen different pentagrams in here," Death said. "We've only entered one room. Corporeal or not, Ahrimad is anything but weak. Consider the graveyard a smokescreen."

Malphas nodded once. "You'll need more men."

Why did it suddenly seem like Malphas was aiding us?

Death stalked away toward another doorway, but Malphas slunk into his path. "You're hardly prepared for what this room alone forebodes. The vast knowledge and capabilities of Ahrimad's soul are unfathomable."

"I know," Death snarled. "He's the first and only pureblood of his kind."

"Which would make him a Prime," Malphas continued. "The apex predator of his own species." Malphas glanced at me in an odd manner, as if to try to gain my support, before returning his attention to Death. "You're weak. Weaker than you've ever been. Your control over your other half is dwindling. Tonight is your last opportunity to get back to your full power. You need to keep it together, control your feelings, and request more men."

"Get out of my head," Death grated.

"I'm not in your head. I can sense this in other ways."

"Why the hell are you giving me advice?"

"Because I'm your father."

"You are *not* a father," Death hissed. "You don't give a shit about me, and you never have."

Thunder crashed above us, the stained glass ceiling flashing with light. The sigil beneath Malphas and Death glowed red, plumes of smoke spiraling in the air around them. Both of their heads snapped back, their eyes matching the inflamed bloodred color of the sigil.

"Ohhhhh no," I said, holding my palms up to protect my face from the heat of the sigil as it burst outward with a hiss. *"Ohnonononono!"*

"None of this would have happened if you hadn't cast my soul into Limbo!" Death suddenly exploded. "You turned on your own family again, like the psychopath that you are!"

This was bad. This was really, really bad. As their anger rose, wind swirled around the space. I gripped a marble structure, my mind frantically racing to find a way to free them from whatever spell they were under.

"If you hadn't been so hell-bent on defying me as a child," Malphas roared in a fiery rage, "with your obsession with befriending the very mortals that *ostracize* our kind, you would never have encountered Ahrimad to begin with!"

"I went into those woods in the first place to *get away from you!*" Death roared, and the sigil flickered angrily around the edges. "So I could cling to the sliver of normalcy that you left me as a child. The *only* thing that kept me alive after what you did to my family was the damned immortality Ahrimad gave me."

Malphas flinched at this, the red glow to his eyes faltering briefly with emotion. "You have no idea the sacrifices I made for you, Alexandru. I was trapped in the Underworld for *two thousand years*, while you've paraded around with Lucifer like a king."

The two charged at each other, the sigil walls distorting their forms into shadows as the flames rose higher and surged outward again. I reeled back before I got burned. They would fight to the death like this if I couldn't snap them out of it. However, I was worried that my light would absorb into the sigil like a sponge or make things worse.

Crawling on the ground, I found a fallen vase amongst the rubble on the floor. I wrapped a fist around the base and managed to climb up to my feet, the wind hurling my braid to the side as I chucked the vase at the sigil. Energy surged from my hand to the vase as it pitched from my palm, forming a grenade of sorts. It shattered into a million pieces on impact and exploded against the sigil. I shielded my eyes as a burst of energy ricocheted back at me, slamming me into the wall.

I blinked away black splotches, the storm calming. Malphas came into focus at the center of the sigil. He stood in a wide stance, staggering, his black eyes wide and crazed. A brutal slice from a talon marred his pale cheek. Oily black blood dripped down his neck to the floor as he looked down at his bare wrists. He no longer wore the cuffs that had bound his power.

And Death was nowhere to be seen.

"Where is he?" I demanded. "Where's Death?"

Malphas's coal-black eyes darted around the room, as if he'd woken from a dream.

"Damn it!" He crossed the sigil in a quick stride and dragged his dress shoe across the marking, smearing the lines. His lifted his palms out in front of him and commanded, *"Revelare!"*

My eyes widened at the sight of a feminine creature with bat-like wings who appeared from nothing at the center of the room. White hair framed a small face half covered by a silky scarf, drawing attention to her lustful gaze. Her small, ballerina-like figure was clothed in elaborate gold material that covered only her private parts.

"Oh," I said, uncomfortable with her lack of clothing, "hello."

"Don't talk to it," Malphas hissed, his livid gaze unwavering against the demon's.

"Goodbye," I said quickly.

"Goodbye, blue-eyed bimbo," the creature purred in a thick accent.

Malphas stalked toward me. "Give me your sword. *Now.*"

I touched the hilt of my blade protectively. The weapon I realized I hadn't reached for once that night. "Why? So you can make me disappear too? Where the hell is Death?"

"We will deal with that *after* this," Malphas said, his gaze locked on the creature. "This is a high-level empath demon. Death and I were fevered by her power. He must have shifted elsewhere in the mausoleum. I assume he is taking longer to shake off the effects because he's weakened. He could be delusional. More reason to *give me your sword—*"

The beautiful creature lunged forward and hissed something in a language that sounded quite rude. The fabric over her face shifted around as she screamed, and I started to get the sick feeling in my stomach that the scarf was hiding something I did *not* want to see.

Three more she-demons crawled down the side of the room like spiders, their long fingers stabbing into the marble like it was made of papier-mâché, anchoring them to the wall. Malphas grabbed the back of my hood and yanked me behind him as the demons flipped upright onto the floor beside us, bloodred eyes flickering like flames. The one in the middle appeared the most confident, the leader.

"Malphas," the golden demon drawled, her accent matching the other, more deranged demon. "*Magna praeses inferos.* Do my eyes deceive me? The last time I saw you, you left me in an empty bed and never called."

"Layla," Malphas replied with a nod.

"Yikes," I said. "Ex-girlfriend?"

"*Silence,*" Layla snarled, her voice vibrating the magic in the air. "Stupid blue-eyed bimbo!"

The nameless demon with the cloth over her mouth laughed.

I fisted my hands, heat centering in my palm. I had no idea what these creatures were capable of, but apparently, Malphas did. He stood in a protective stance in front of me. Or maybe, I thought, as I slid my hand possessively over the harness at my side, he was just protecting the book.

Layla strutted closer to Malphas, her hips rocking side to side seductively as she walked. The fabric over her groin barely covered what it was supposed to—if it was even supposed to.

"Yes, I remember that handsome face in the Underworld," she purred. "So much sadness behind that cold, stoic face. Everyone wondered if you had been summoned to Earth or if you had escaped. How did you do it?"

"I'm a walking enigma," Malphas said dryly.

"I am enslaved to my new master, Ahrimad," Layla said. "He ordered me to destroy whoever crosses into this room. It's nothing personal." She put her hands on her narrow waist. "I promise to make your demise as painless as possible, for an old friend. If you tell me what you offered Hades to free yourself."

"As much as I appreciate such a kind offer"—one of Malphas's hands, which was clasped with the other behind his back, reached blindly behind him and gripped the hilt of the sword at my hip—"I'm going to have to decline. And, as the mortals say, 'Go fuck yourself.'"

One of the demons sprang forward with her blade drawn. Malphas's nails ripped my sword and its scabbard straight from my belt. The sword turned over in his hand in a whirl of motion before his other hand joined on the hilt. His whole body moved with the violent action as he evaded the empath's attack and arced the blade upward, slicing through her heart. Another swift movement of his hands and her head was severed clean, smacking against the ground with a wet thud.

"Sister!" Layla screamed. The crippling grief on her face vanished, traded instantly for vengeance. Her hands spread out, and she chanted quickly.

My vision swam as the air thickened with magic. Multiple sigils on the floor glowed red. Air heaved like a mighty hurricane as it had before, and I planted my feet wide to stay balanced. "Can't we ever catch a break?"

"She's cocooned herself in magic to summon the rest of her sisters!" Malphas shouted over the looming chaos. He tilted his head down to me. "Go! Find Death!"

I couldn't help but think that I was leaving Malphas to die. I also couldn't help but think that he had a greater part in all of this. If I never saw Malphas again, I needed to know if my gut feeling held any truth at all.

"Is it true?" I demanded. "Did you kill his family?"

The frantic darkness in Malphas's eyes seemed to settle, like black stone lying at the bottom of a river. In a heart-stopping moment, he handed me back my bloody sword. "I have done unspeakable things in this world that have left me entrenched in sin, but my greatest offence is my most painful secret. A secret that I will take to the grave. You must discover these answers on your own."

My breath caught in my throat. The same answer as the one he'd given me in the projection with the willow tree, verbatim. Like a broken record.

I was struck by the eerie possibility that he *couldn't* answer my question.

The raven demigod stepped into Layla's chaos, a blurred figure amidst a whirlwind of red mist. She released a shrill shriek from her magical freaky butterfly cocoon, and the marble crumbled. Pieces from the ceiling came loose and hit the ground in an explosion of debris. I pivoted and committed to my escape from the sigil room, sprinting down another hallway. When I looked over my shoulder, the archway behind me had crumbled, blocked by debris. The sigil room had buckled in on itself.

I turned and kicked into a run, tears blurring my vision. Where was Death? When I turned another corner, I crashed into somebody, and Master Vampire Duncan slammed into sharp focus.

He held some sort of weapon. I saw the flash of Ace's cane in his fist as he punched it hard into my gut. It knocked the wind right out of me, the momentum sending me flying backward until I landed on the marble floor.

"Going somewhere, bitch?"

Adrenaline fired as Duncan kept coming at me. I struggled to catch my breath as I clutched my stomach and crawled backward. His hand gripped me around the throat, faster than the newborns in the graveyard, and plucked me straight up off the ground. With no ability to cry out, I stayed silent as Duncan slammed me against the wall. I pictured all his newborns we'd destroyed as his nails dug into my throat. I tried to writhe out of his grasp, blood dripping down my neck.

"I see you managed to get past the summoning room," he breathed into my face. "Ahrimad wanted you alive, but I don't care what that old bag of bones wants anymore. I'd rather dump your dismantled body right in front of the Prince of Darkness—"

Duncan's whole body tensed, a strangled gasp escaping his mouth. Realizing he was immobilized, I pried his hands off me and ripped free. Duncan remained locked in a rigid position, his silvery eyes wide with shock. Tendrils of color surrounded his body like chains.

"Warlock," Duncan hissed.

I lifted my gaze down the hallway, and my heart plunged at the sight of Ace. He stood with his free hand casually outstretched toward Duncan. The elegant, Victorian-style outfit he'd been wearing earlier at his library was torn, exposing bite marks and cuts all over his body. His once beautiful shoulder-length hair had been shaved down to the white roots, and blood, vivid red against his pallid skin, dripped down his forehead from an open gash.

"Ace!"

"Look at you, you crippled fuck," Duncan laughed, blood seeping out the corners of his mouth as he remained unable to move. "My newborns really did you in. And your poor little pixie pet. I heard she was ripped apart in seconds."

My heart plunged. Trixie. She was dead.

Ace's face trembled with rage, his violet eyes glowing neon and crackling with electricity.

"Kill me now, and your pledge of passivity is over," Duncan said, grinning wider. "You'll no longer be a neutral force. The title you've worked centuries for—"

Ace crushed his hand into a fist, and the indentation of his fingers engraved Duncan's neck. *"Morior!"*

Duncan released a horrific scream. Veins swelled in his face, and a wheeze emptied his lungs as blood vessels exploded beneath his skin. His eyes bulged out of his head. I turned my head away; the sound of Duncan's eyeballs exploding made an involuntary noise of shock escape my mouth. Still, I peered back—I had to. Duncan's skin melted off his body like wax sliding down a burning candle. His corpse collapsed in a pile of sludge and bones.

I looked up at Ace in quiet horror. I'd seen plenty of gruesome deaths that night, but that one took the cake. He didn't look proud of what he'd done, but he didn't look regretful either.

Ace limped to the pile of gore on the floor and picked up his cane.

"Have you seen Death?" I asked.

"I believe I have," Ace replied. "He wasn't himself, though."

"We were supposed to meet the reapers and Death's Fallen in a different part of the mausoleum. Death and I entered another way. We were using Malphas as bait, but then—"

"Malphas?" Ace's full attention snapped to me. "Malphas Cruscellio?"

"Do you know anybody else on the planet with that name?" I joked. "I know you can't talk about your vision anymore, but I can't shake this feeling that Malphas has a bigger part in all of this. Especially with the riddle he keeps repeating—"

Ace seized my arm in an iron grip. *"What* riddle?"

My attention clung to Ace's fingers around my wrist. He'd touched only a sliver of my skin, and cold speared through me like frostbite. My heart rocketed into overdrive.

I wrenched my arm free and stepped back. "You're not Ace."

Ace appeared puzzled a moment longer.

Then he straightened, his entire affect changing in an instant.

"Your power is stronger, Chosen," the impostor said, taking a confident step toward me as I took another backward. "Ace put up an honorable fight against me. But after he watched the consequence of refusing me, his lover brutally torn apart, well . . . " His slow smirk brought chills down my spine. "He ultimately succumbed to my will."

I could hear the tremor in my voice as I whispered, "Ahrimad."

Ace's violet eyes clung to the torn part of my belt. "You're just in time for the show." His hand rose toward me. *"Somnus."*

The command shot out like gunfire, a gust of magic blasting out and knocking me from consciousness.

XXXVII

Dim light from a filthy lightbulb filtered through the metal bars and lit the confined space. With barely enough room to stand, I felt as if I were sitting in large coffin with jail bars for walls. Beside my claustrophobic cell was another.

Pure dread speared through me as I noticed another person behind the barrier of metal bars. Edging closer confirmed my assumption—it was Ace. He was so still, lying face down with his head angled away from me. I crawled across the space, my body aching with every movement I made.

"Ace?" I whispered. I fought not to burst into tears. I pictured his wounds, his tattered clothing, and my heart clenched. The thought crossed my mind that Ahrimad might have continued to possess his body, so I reached out and shook his arm. No sensation of coldness. "Ace? Ace, wake up. Please, wake up."

He inhaled a horrible, wheezed breath and coughed, blowing dust all over the tiny space.

"Oh, thank God—"

"No!" Ace's chest heaved faster and faster into hyperventilation, his nails raking against the dirty marble beneath us.

"Ace it's me, it's me," I said quietly, clutching his hand. "Everything's okay. It's Faith."

"Ma chérie," he croaked in a parched voice. "Where are we?"

"I don't know," I whispered. "I think we're underground. Maybe underneath the mausoleum?"

Ace heaved a few times. "I'm going to . . . sick." He crawled to the furthest corner of his tiny prison to vomit.

"What can I do to help?"

He slumped against the wall in exhaustion with his arm sprawled over his stomach. "I could really use a power nap, and maybe an ice cream sundae."

"Ace . . . " I trailed off. "Ahrimad, he possessed your body—"

"Oh, I know. He's gone now. Hence the retching and the unbearable headache."

We stared at each other for a moment.

"It happened so fast," Ace began in a quiet, tired voice. "We were disagreeing, Trixie and I. Shouting at each other like an old married couple over something stupid." He shut his eyes. "They breached the ward at the Crossroads and ambushed us . . . tortured us. I told them that if they let Trixie live, I would concede and serve Ahrimad." His hand tightened around mine as a tear trailed down his bloody cheek. "They tore her apart in seconds anyway. Because of me . . . "

"It's not your fault, Ace," I said softly, feeling the heaviness of his sorrow was if it were my own. "I'm so sorry this happened."

"Me too, *ma chérie*. Me too." Ace took a moment to collect himself. "We need an escape plan."

"Agreed." I moved toward the bars and peered out into the

shadowy space in front of our cells. Angling my head to the left revealed a long hallway with another dim lightbulb hanging from the ceiling at the end. "Without Death, or his reapers, or Malphas, I don't know how far we could get, but it's worth a try."

Ace's gaze snapped to me in the dark as if something had been slow to register. "Did you say *Malphas*? Malphas Cruscellio?"

"Why does everybody have that same reaction whenever I say Malphas?"

"Why would Malphas help us escape?" Ace inquired.

"We entered the mausoleum together," I said. "Me, Death, and Malphas. I managed to get these magical cuffs on Malphas's wrists and contained his power. We were going to use him as bait, but then we were in a room of sigils, and Death and Malphas were fevered by empath demons."

"Empath demons. You weren't affected by their power?"

"Only Death and Malphas, who were standing within this huge sigil. When the sigil's energy died down, Death was gone. Which left Malphas and me to defend ourselves. He no longer had the cuffs on, but he didn't try to hurt me. Instead, he told me to go look for Death and gave me back my sword . . . "

I sat back on my heels and froze. In the sigil room, Malphas's hand behind his back hadn't just rested on the hilt of my sword. It'd rested on the sheath that concealed the *Book of the Dead* . . .

"Oh my God."

Panic clicked into place as I rapidly felt around my belt, patting down my armor. The full reality of what this meant was too overwhelming, and blood whooshed in my ears.

Malphas had the *Book of the Dead*.

My mind whirled.

"We are so screwed," I said. "I almost trusted Malphas. I almost trusted him when nobody else did. How could I be so stupid?"

"This is not your fault, *ma chérie*. He's a formidable demigod of manipulation."

But the projection, I thought to myself. *Was that really all a lie?*

I remembered Ahrimad's surprised reaction when I'd mentioned Malphas was in the mausoleum. Ahrimad's slight smile when he'd glanced down at my waist, where my broken belt remained.

Was it still possible Malphas was working against Ahrimad? Would he use the *Book of the Dead* for his own gain?

I'd asked Malphas point-blank if he'd killed Death's family, and he'd gotten that weird, dead look in his eyes. It had been like he was incapable of answering. I'd thought it was possible he was bound to some sort of deal or spell.

Now I knew the truth. Malphas was evil to the core.

"My main concern lies with the Fates and the consequences of how I've interfered already," Ace said. "This was not supposed to happen to me, Faith. Or to Trixie."

"We can't sit here in this shitty cage and wait to be used again. Then Trixie's death will have been for nothing."

Ace ran his hand over his short hair. "I'm too depleted of energy from Ahrimad to get us out of here. I'll need my staff to channel anything significant. You, on the other hand, might be able to quietly—"

I gripped two of the cage bars in front of me, and some sort of magic electrified my hand. It twisted around my fingers like thorns, but I only gripped the bars harder.

Break! I punched my hands forward, my fingers igniting the entire metal frame as the bars of my cage blew off. The frame clattered against the wall and floor in fragments. Heaving in air, I crawled out of the small space.

I held out my hand toward Ace's bars. "Back up."

Ace pressed against the corner of his cell. Light blasted from my hand, destroying a portion of the cell.

The warlock exited his cell with a proud smile. "Incredible, *ma chérie*. But perhaps it would be best to practice subtlety next time?"

"I can't help it," I said, my fingertips still sparking at my sides. "I'm furious. And I'm done running from destiny. It's time to face it head-on."

Ace and I edged down another long, dim passageway and reached a crossroad where we had to decide left or right. Ace leaned against the wall to give his leg a break.

"I'm so sick of this leg," Ace grumbled. The sweat on his brow and his pale complexion concerned me.

"Maybe you find a place to hide and rest," I suggested, even though the thought of being left alone in this place was the most frightening thing I could imagine at the moment. "Let me go ahead."

The air visibly rippled around us.

"Did you see that?" Ace asked, turning to face me.

"Yes. The same thing happened earlier when we first entered the mausoleum."

"Ahrimad must have opened a portal. A large one."

"Big enough for an army," I whispered.

The trepidation of arriving at that portal without Death made me sick to my stomach. Where was he?

As if reading my thoughts, Ace smoothed down the back of my braid with his hand. "You've made it this far. You must stay strong. For all of us."

We were walking together down another hallway when a trap-door beneath us blew open, and we fell into a chamber, hitting a slope that slid us down into the dusty depths of an even lower level. We sprawled across the floor. Ace processed what was happening faster and grabbed my bicep. He rose with me quickly as a group of monstrous creatures encircled us. Faceless creatures with reflective skin like mirrors and wiry, distorted frames.

My mind harkened back to the projection with Malphas and the creature that had almost killed me, fear overtaking my senses. "What the hell are these things? Demons?"

"Worse," Ace whispered with dread. "They're Forsaken."

One of the creatures leaned into me with a low noise rattling its throat. I trembled violently as its frightening, reflective face hovered beside mine.

"What do we do?"

"You give up," said a female voice.

Layla. The empath demon from the sigil room.

The Forsaken backed away from us.

Layla flipped her hair over her bare shoulder and posed with her hand on her hip. "Hello, hello," she greeted, her stare lingering on Ace as she studied him with interest before darting her red gaze to me. "Night not going as planned?"

The mocking tone in her voice set me off. Ace fired a warning look in my direction and clutched my wrist.

She hooked her talon-like nails into Ace's shirt and kissed him hard on the mouth.

"Ace!" I screamed.

The Forsaken howled. Red plumes expelled from Layla's pores and seeped into Ace's skin like a poison. His violet eyes widened, his palms trying to push her away as the kiss continued. A dreamy look overrode his features. The plumes of smoke tainted his irises from the inside, turning them a bright red. She pulled back.

"He tastes like grief," she purred. "It's a shame I can't torture him like I tortured the Grim Reaper."

"*What?*" I could feel the power within me start to rise to the surface, the thought of Death suffering under the hand of this crazy bitch too much. "Fix him," I demanded, jabbing a finger toward Ace. "Fix him right now, Layla, or I'll—I'll fry you to ash!"

I really needed to work on my intimidating phrases.

"Now, now, Faith," Layla purred, pressing herself against Ace. In his delirium, his mouth was plastered with a big, goofy, lovestruck grin, and his hands eagerly gripped her body. All he needed was heart-shaped pupils to complete the visual. "You have to play along to attend the party. Kill me and the emotion incantation will never wear off for your friend. Both the warlock and Death are fine, as long as *you* don't act up."

Heat tingled in my fingertips at the thought of ending this bitch once and for all. But if she was telling the truth, killing her wouldn't be worth it. I breathed deeply, trying to calm myself down. I had to keep it together. I had to keep moving forward.

"Take me to Ahrimad," I said.

Layla's mouth curved. She led me and high-as-a-kite Ace further into the catacomb. Torches lit polished marble on the walls and the floors, a reflection of what the upper part of the mausoleum used to look like before it was shit on. The further we traveled, the more I became aware of a buzzing vibrating through me like the ground had a pulse. Finally, we stopped in front of a metal door.

"Get in," Layla commanded, Ace's bicep still imprisoned by her sharp talons. I couldn't leave him like this. "*Now.* Or I'll slit his throat."

"Do what she says," Ace said in an exhausted voice. "I'll be fine."

Anger fueled my courage as I stormed inside. The door shut behind me with a resounding thud, sealing me inside the capacious polished-marble room.

Oh my God.

Six of the reapers were tied in a circle on the floor. Their backs faced one another, and they had been stripped of weapons. Their heads lolled to the side, drawing my attention to the dreamy, far-off look in their red-tinted eyes, showing that they were under the empath demon's spell.

Romeo stood flat against a marble wall, shirtless and covered in . . . hickeys?

"What are you doing here?" Romeo whispered.

"Layla stuck me in here for the, er"—I glanced around at the empty room—"party?"

Romeo glanced to the side toward a staircase leading deeper into the catacomb. "Could you maybe hide behind that pillar and not breathe or excrete any smells for, like, five seconds?"

"What's going on?"

"Layla's lovely sister didn't know that charming me wouldn't work like it worked on my brothers," Romeo explained. "I tried to explain it to her. Turns out, she never learned English in the Underworld. Which is unbelievably hot . . . "

"Romeo, get to the damn point," I hissed, gesturing to the six tied-up reapers.

"Long story short, they think I'm charmed. I'm a little rusty with the empath demon language. Whatever I said to the sister made her uncuff me and want to bed me. But don't worry, I'm a professional. I politely declined the one-on-one action. Now she's bringing her other sister to—"

"Now is *not* the time for a gang bang, you idiot—"

"If you would let me *finish*, cheeky," Romeo said, "the *other* sister has the keys to our chains. And she will rid me of these ones, so I can move my hands and kill them." My gaze turned to the cuffs around his wrists, and I realized they were similar to the special handcuffs that I'd used to debilitate Duncan and Malphas.

"Ah."

"Yeah, ah." Romeo's attention snapped to the side again, as if he'd heard a noise. He waved me off and mouthed, *Hide*.

I ducked quickly behind the pillar, but not without peering around the corner. Sure enough, two empath demons rounded a marble wall and prowled around the tied-up reapers with seductive murmurs before heading toward Romeo. Talons outstretched, red eyes flickering, one of them spread her fingers through Romeo's pink Mohawk while the other fondled his belt.

Romeo smirked and seemed to be forgetting about the *plan*. One of the demons managed to unzip his pants. His eyebrows shot up, and he pursed his lips in consideration.

Unable to see any more of this, I pointed a finger gun at a wall light by Romeo's head and closed one eye to aim. The empath twins broke away, startled, as the light fixture exploded. Looking at Romeo, I jabbed a finger at the empath twins and made a punching motion, communicating my impatience, then I pulled back quickly behind the pillar again.

"Ha ha, sparks are literally *flying* with us!" Romeo said loudly.

By the time I peered back around the pillar, the girls were back to climbing Romeo like a tree. He wiggled his pelvis out of one empath's grasp while battling an aggressive French kiss from the other sister.

While Romeo had the twins distracted, I searched every corner of the room for an exit, but we were surrounded by walls with no doors. Even the way I'd come in had disappeared.

When I turned back to Romeo, his hands were free of the cuffs. One of the sisters lay gasping for air on the ground, her bronze skin a horrifying gray. Mid-kiss with the second sister's skull clenched between his two palms, Romeo came up for air and crushed her head with a horrifying crunch.

I gawked at the whole ordeal, open-mouthed.

Romeo snarled; his normally playful pink eyes seethed around the edges with a ring of fire. Black markings similar to Death's shifted over his left pectoral. He glanced down at himself and cursed, zipping up his pants. And just like that, his affect snapped back to normal.

"Oops!" Romeo chuckled. "Almost lost my grip and ate your face off there." He held up a ring of keys and jangled them. "I'll get to work freeing my brothers. You keep lookout, yeah?"

"Sure," I said, uneasy over the way Romeo had crushed that girl's head like an eggshell. "Try to hurry up."

Romeo freed each of his brothers one by one, pressing his finger into their hearts. Each time, the empath's venom expelled from their bodies in plumes of red smoke, and they awoke in a state of confusion.

"What happened?" Denim asked.

"When we entered the mausoleum, we were attacked and enchanted by empaths," Romeo explained, glancing at the mutilated corpses of Layla's sisters.

Wolf cupped a hand over his mouth. "Yo! They are dead as shit!"

"Do any of you remember seeing Death?" I asked.

"I thought he was with you?" Leo walked closer as he worked out a knot in the back of his neck.

"Death was enchanted. Like you guys. I don't know where he is, but I know that Ahrimad needs a body, and Death was in a vulnerable state. So we need to find a way out of here fast."

For some reason, Layla had led us into this room, and now we all had to figure a way out.

"Well, it looks like Ahrimad is going to have to come to us," Wolf said. "This room is sealed tight with a ward. Anyone see my weapon?"

"Up your pretty arse and around the corner," Blade replied, bending down to pick up a knife wedged into a secret compartment in his boot with a snicker. "They took our weapons."

Wolf jabbed a finger at Blade. "Not for nothing, but I distinctly remember *you* getting us into this mess."

"Those twins sucked up all his pent-up anger like leeches and strangled the rest of us with their power," Gunner said to me. "We wouldn't have been enraptured had he not gone rogue and attacked them before the rest of us were ready."

Blade scowled at Gunner. "Don't be a wee narky hole because I'm better at fighting. Always whining like a little babe when you're ravening."

"He has a point, Blade," Leo said, taking charge. "Your wrath is spiraling faster than the rest of us. Focus on your patience. We all need to stay in control of our sins tonight."

The ground trembled beneath our feet. Our heads turned in unison as a segment of the wall beside us vanished like a mirage, and an archway that hadn't been there began to appear, revealing another room with a mirror-like object in it.

My heart pounded.

"The portal," I whispered.

"Nothing gets past you," commented a familiar raspy voice. Malphas appeared in the portal room, rounding the narrow archway and standing in the middle of it, bracing his arms on either side. "But apparently, many things get past me . . ." He looked down at the dead empath twins and grimaced. "Ouch."

The sight of him made my whole body shake uncontrollably. "You bastard!"

Malphas's onyx eyes flicked to mine, amusement dancing within their endless depths. "Is that any way to talk to family, Faith? I'm practically your father-in-law."

I stormed toward him, but Leo's hand gripped my upper arm and stopped me.

"You stole the *Book of the Dead*," I growled.

The Seven moved in behind me.

"We killing the bird or what?" Blade demanded.

"*Bird?*" A muscle in Malphas's face twitched. He sauntered into the room. "Ever seen a moron with his dick attached to his forehead like a unicorn?" He paused. "Would you like to be the first?"

Blade snarled a little.

"Here's how this is going to go," Malphas continued, his dark gaze sweeping over the Seven. "Surrender to Ahrimad. All of you. Or don't."

The sly smile that tilted one side of his mouth communicated he'd very much rather they didn't.

My fingers rolled into fists. "So, this is what rock bottom looks like for a demigod. You're just Ahrimad's bitch."

"Excuse me, holy dove," Malphas said, holding up a finger for me to be quiet. "I am talking to the Seven Deadly Shits."

Suddenly, Denim and Wolf lunged forward on either side of Malphas. They both cried out in agony and dropped to their knees, their bodies arching back as their faces locked in twisted distress. Darkness had webbed out of Malphas's eyes, spreading outward across his pale skin. Blade lunged forward to strike the raven demigod, but he too was crippled by pain and dropped to his knees.

Chills raked through my body at the awareness that I couldn't move either. He'd affected me without me even knowing it. Every part of me was locked into obedience.

The reapers were paralyzed on the ground, their screams of raw torment unbearable. They clawed at their skin and thrashed their heads like they were trapped in a nightmare with their eyes wide open.

Malphas stood motionless in the middle of this violent torment, his expression void of any emotion.

"Don't do this!" I screamed at him, the muscles in my neck so tight with his power I could barely breathe. "Please, Malphas. You're going against your own flesh and blood!"

Malphas's onyx eyes slithered to mine. "Maybe next time he'll make sure I stay dead."

The sensation of talons scraped the inside of my brain.

My knees locked as the floor moved beneath my feet. The reapers' screams were muffled as I was thrust across a threshold into another room. I hit the floor and landed on all fours, still unable move any of my limbs on my own. I stared down at my hands and tried to move my fingers, but my brain betrayed me. The ringing grew louder, my head tilting up to gaze at the massive mirror across the way. The portal.

Malphas's power wore off as I inhaled a sharp breath and regained the ability to move. I lurched up onto my feet. The archway through which I'd entered closed, leaving behind a marble wall. I banged my fists against it, begging my power to unleash as I imagined the horrible things that psychopath was doing to the reapers on the other side. But my body was drained, fatigued, and nothing sparked from my hands. I pressed my back against cool marble and desperately tried to keep from panicking, but my emotions were spiraling out of control.

Coldness washed down my spine.

I turned my head to the side and froze.

Death.

Hanging limply from the ceiling by chains.

XXXVIII

I rushed to him, my hands lunging for the cuffs around his wrists, but when my fingers touched the chain, some sort of magic fired back at me. A surge of electricity rushed through me, and I fell to my knees, my teeth gnashing together.

"Cupcake."

My head jerked upward. Death looked down at me through half-open lids, his irises pinkish red with Layla's charm. "Hey," I said gently. "Hey, you're okay. I'm going to get you out of here. I'm going to figure this out."

"Pretty." His eyes clung to my lips with a less intense version of Ace's goofy, lovestruck grin plastered on his fanged mouth.

My mouth tightened. "You've got to be kidding me." Glancing over my shoulder, I started brainstorming. How could I break Layla's spell on him?

Death tilted his head all the way down until his head flopped, blatantly staring down at my chest. "Yummy."

I grabbed his chin with my gloved hand and lifted his head up. "Death," I said extra sweetly as his tongue darted out to try to lick my thumb. "I know you're riding an empath demon fever, but I need you to focus and tell me how to get you free. Because that shock I got earlier? Yeah, that sucked."

"Yes," Death said.

"Yes?"

"Suck."

"That's it. You're freaking me the hell out." I pointed a finger gun at him like I had with Romeo and the empath twins and shut my eyes. *"Lo siento!"* I managed a tiny zap of light, which exploded on Death's pectoral.

Death snarled at the impact, his bare skin sizzling as his whole body spasmed. Plumes of red evaporated, swirling away from his eyes as his familiar mismatched green returned.

"Fuck!" His roar thundered around the room, and the lights flickered. He groaned in discomfort, catlike pupils tightening under the light above. "Faith? *Ow!*" He spasmed a little and tilted his head down to his chest. "You fried my nipple—" Realizing his hands were shackled, his features turned livid. He writhed in the restraints and yanked hard, his muscles bulging as he ground his fangs together.

"Death, stop. You have to calm down."

"Calm down? I'm chained to a *ceiling!*" He heaved himself up the chains with his upper body strength and yanked as hard as possible before dropping back down. Pure fright crossed his face, something I'd never seen in him. "I have to get out. I have to get out right now—"

"Death, you're okay. Everything is going to be okay. Focus on me."

His nostrils flared. He blinked hard, his chest pumping fast.

"How did I get here?" he demanded. "We were in the sigil room. We were in the sigil room, and now I'm here."

"You were enchanted by empath demons."

"Empath demons." His breathing eventually slowed until I could barely see his chest moving. "I remember that. Malphas was there. . . ." He analyzed my face as he spoke, reading me. "What happened? Tell me what happened."

"Malphas stole the *Book of the Dead*," I said in a hollow voice. "I thought there was a chance—*like an idiot*, I thought there was a chance he was . . . on our side somehow. But I was so wrong, and now he's in the other room with the reapers doing God knows what to them, and you're tied up, and I don't know what to do. I don't know what to do, Death! Everything is going wrong, and the universe is against us! Just please, *please* tell me what to do! You *always* know what to do!"

I expected some sort of explosive response. Death didn't seem at all surprised. He looked . . . cold, so cold.

"Death?" I whispered.

"I should never have brought you into this. Now I'm running out of time, and when I leave, you'll be stuck in this mess."

"You're not going to run out of time. I'm going to figure this out—"

"It's over," he said in a rough voice. "All my life. All my life, he's had it out for me. I was never good enough. No matter how hard I tried, I knew I wasn't the son he wanted." The deeply pained look in his eyes made me want to hold him close and never let go. "But I didn't think he'd actually . . . honestly . . . "

"Want you dead," I finished, feeling like my heart was breaking. "Death, you have to know, none of this is your fault."

"But it is. All the wrong choices I've made have led me to this."

"But they also led you to me," I said, and his eyes flicked to mine and held on for a significant moment. "I'm getting you out of here. One way or another."

"Look at me, Faith," Death said. He looked exhausted. Defeated. It hurt. It hurt too much to see the truth, and I fought back tears. "I'm strung up like an animal to be butchered. This isn't easy for me either."

"You're not going to be butchered. You're giving up. You said you wouldn't give up."

"I'm not giving up." It sounded like he didn't even believe himself. "I'm being realistic—what are you doing? *Wait!*"

I closed one eye as I aimed, tongue poking out as I fired a finger gun. A small beam of light bulleted forward and struck the manacle around Death's wrist. The light bounced off the metal and fired down at my foot. I jumped out of the way at the last second, nearly falling over in the process.

"Damn it!" I stomped my foot in frustration.

"Is this your new approach? *Finger gunning* your power?" His mouth lifted in a small grin. "And stomping your foot like a child?"

I wiped my sleeve over my eyes as I nodded. A foolish part of me had thought Death would have an answer for all of this.

His grin slowly fell. "Don't cry."

"This whole night, all I've wanted to do was help, but I haven't managed to do anything right without someone else's help."

"You can start by pulling the knife out of my back."

"Now is not the time to get figurative, Death."

"I'm being literal. There's a blade wedged in my lower back. I haven't been able to move my legs."

I rushed around to look at his back, gasped, and pointed a finger. "Holy cheese!"

"Holy *cheese*?"

"Why didn't you say something sooner?"

"Because I'm not a little bitch." He managed a laugh, despite the situation. "And I kinda like the pain."

"Of course, you do." I reached forward to solve the problem at hand, then pulled my fingers back at the last second. "Can we please give Faith some instruction here? Faith didn't learn this in Death's boot camp."

"I'll make sure to add 'third person panic attack' to the lesson board," Death growled. "First, take a deep breath."

I did.

"Rub your hands together nice and fast, so they're not too cold."

I rubbed my gloves together so vigorously it was like I was trying to start a campfire.

"Perfect," he said. "Now grip the hilt with both hands, firm but not too firm, and just . . . stroke it out, cupcake."

I flipped him off, and he burst into strident laughter.

I marched in place, anxious again. "All right, here we go. Here we go, I got this!"

"You're screaming."

"I got this," I whispered.

"Just pull the damn thing out of my spine."

"At least it's kind of cool-looking. It's got these weird designs on the hilt."

"Don't touch the blade!" Death suddenly roared.

I jumped back and clutched my chest, startled.

Death craned to look over his shoulder, trying to get a glimpse of the blade. "It's my scythe. It can turn into a normal dagger. If you had touched it, you would have burned to ash. In a heartbeat."

"Shit," I said, pushing sweaty baby hairs away from my forehead with my hand.

"This was all a game to Ahrimad," Death said. "Leaving us both in this room, paralyzing me with the very weapon I was looking for all along."

Suddenly, I sensed we weren't alone. Fear shimmied down my

spine as I slowly turned to investigate the room. The little hairs at the back of my neck rose at the sight of the six massive demons. They manifested with fanged mouths and snarled in unison from across the room. Burly frames, massive horns, giant fangs, and bat-like wings with translucent black membranes.

These must have been the high-level demons that were summoned by Ahrimad.

"Shit," Death muttered.

Layla came skipping barefoot through the wall, melting through it like a phantom.

Behind them, Malphas stormed in with Ace in his clutches. Death's chains rattled, his features sharpening into something *else* as his gaze laser-focused on his father.

Malphas had his hand wrapped around Ace's upper arm. He steered the warlock toward the front of the room. Ace's limp from his bad leg was more prominent than usual, and he was so delirious that Malphas practically had to carry him.

Layla climbed onto the edge of a raised platform beside the portal and balanced on her knees on the edge. I thought she was reaching seductively toward Ace, but I realized it was toward Malphas as he came over to deposit the warlock into her care. Malphas shrugged Layla's advances off and jabbed a finger at Ace. Rolling her eyes, Layla turned her affections to Ace. She ran her hands all over his short white hair, smooshing his bruised and cut-up face with kisses.

Malphas pivoted sharply toward me and Death, his determined strides, paired with the chilling blackness webbing out from his onyx eyes, making my pulse spike. I took a protective backward step toward Death, and Malphas came to a sharp halt. He stood in a wide stance with his hands clasped behind his back, reminding me of a general.

"Faith Williams," announced a voice that made my blood curdle. At the head of the room, beside the portal, stood Ahrimad. "Welcome to my humble abode."

Ahrimad looked even worse than he had in my vision, but he was powerful. I could feel it on my skin as he crossed the room toward me, like a high-voltage power line looming closer. His eyes were a vibrant amber, blazing so brightly they seemed to flare like stars bursting in the dark.

"I feel congratulations are in order," Ahrimad continued, while I tried to maintain my cool under his frightening, piercing stare. "After making it through all those vampires and the twists and curves of this building, you also managed to break free of your confinements and free the warlock. I must say, I'm impressed. Especially because you're a woman."

Misogynist dick.

"It's hard kicking ass in between reapplying my lip gloss and changing my tampons, but I do my best."

Ahrimad's brows bowed inward. "I'm afraid you have referenced a word I do not understand in your language." He turned his head to the side, drawing my attention again to Death's father standing dutifully behind him. "What is *tampons*?"

"Cotton devices females use for menstruation, my liege," Malphas answered.

My liege? I stared at Malphas in in puzzlement. Eyes arrowed straight ahead, he did not flinch or exhibit any signs of life. Like a robot.

"I am delighted all my guests are here," Ahrimad continued, drawing my attention back to him. He reached out and placed a hand on my shoulder, and my whole body went rigid. "There is much we have to discuss."

I didn't have to see Death's face to know he was seething with rage throughout this entire exchange. A low growl unfurled from his throat like a warning. "Do not. Touch her."

"Or what?" Ahrimad asked, gently amused.

"Or I'll shred you to pieces with my teeth."

"You can try all you want to pull in the reins of your darkness," Ahrimad said. "But I know the truth. You never really had it under control. You never tapped into your full potential. Now it's closing in on you like a black hole. Soon your monster will take over. You'll be a creature of pure, animalistic instinct, and your power? It will be mine. Along with your soul."

Death's lips pulled back from his teeth as Ahrimad let go of me and moved closer to him.

"Are you frightened, Alexandru? You will be." Ahrimad reached behind Death and yanked the dagger from his spine. Death tensed and tightened his lips together.

The moment Ahrimad held the blade again, his soul became more solid in appearance. His complexion gained color, and his golden eyes flared to life.

Ahrimad pointed his hand at the brackets connecting Death's chains to the ceiling, snapping them off. Death dropped to the ground, landing perfectly balanced on the balls of his feet. Two menacing high-level demons caught the ends of his chains and kept him restrained.

Darkness nearly consumed Death's furious features, expelling off his shoulders in tendrils.

"You once used the mortals for their true purpose, Alexandru," Ahrimad began. "As your sustenance. Oh yes, I saw glimpses of the havoc you wreaked from the Underworld. But you've become too entrenched in the mortal world. It seems you're right back where you began. Back to that sad, pitiful, naïve little boy who wanted to be loved." Ahrimad gestured vaguely in the air toward himself. "Bring the girl to me, Layla."

"Sure thing, honey bunny." Layla clutched my braid in a tight fist and hauled me to the front of the room.

As we walked, my gaze clung to the enormous portal, its mirror-like surface swaying back and forth like waves. We passed what appeared to be a broken marble structure at the center of the room that was a few feet tall and shaped like a circle. Something compelled me to peer over the rim of the marble wall as we went, and my stomach churned at the sight of blood filling the container to the brim.

Layla shoved me so that I smacked right into one of the terrifying demons holding Death's chains. The gruesomely ugly creature had skin made of scales. Orange heat glowed along the cracks of the scales like lava. As the demon glared down at me with its freaky, fiery eyes, I felt a little faint. Balanced between its lips like a cigarette was a chewed-off finger.

I shrunk back so that I stood flat against Death's chest. "At least we have a great view of your giant pool thing filled with more blood," I said, nodding toward it. "Ties in perfectly with the whole 'teaming up with vampires' theme. Solid evil lair vibes all around. Although— and this is just my opinion—a hot tub would have been a much more welcoming piece of furniture."

"Because bubbles and jets of hot water firing up my ass is exactly what I need right now," Death seethed.

"I apologize that my lair does not reach your expectations, Faith Williams," Ahrimad said, linking arms with Layla as he came to stand before us. "I've had very little time to redecorate."

"Hiding in another realm like a coward must be quite time-consuming," Death hissed, his voice dripping with disdain. "You didn't even have time for a sandwich."

Ahrimad glanced down at his withering form. "It's nice you're finding humor in this, Alexandru, even as you're chained like a sacrificial lamb."

Death grinned, displaying a mouthful of fangs. "You seem bitter. Is it because you're so short?"

The massive demons on either side of Death boomed with laughter, and suddenly the whole room was laughing.

"Weaken him, Malphas," Ahrimad snarled. "*Now.* He's far too coherent."

All eyes were on Malphas. He'd betrayed us by stealing the *Book of the Dead*, and my heart sank at the notion that he'd also possibly killed the reapers.

Malphas's gaze flicked to Death, the haunting, blank look within its cold depths unsettling. He stepped toward Death like a summoned doom. Blackness webbed out from his onyx eyes as his sharp black nails reached toward his son, and Death's face shuddered. His fangs gnashed together as he held back a scream, his eyes flashing between mismatched green and black as his shoulders crumpled inward.

I looked between Malphas and Death, breathing raggedly, adrenaline pulsing through me. I didn't even know my power had triggered until I felt a spark of heat against my thigh and realized my fingertips were sparking.

Fearing for Death's safety, I started to raise my hand toward Malphas when Ahrimad appeared in front of me in a blur and grasped me around the throat in a vise grip. In my peripheral view, I saw Ace move to try to help me, but Layla stopped him with her razor-sharp claws aimed at his throat.

Blackness splotched around the edges of my vision. As I gasped for air, a sensation that I could only describe as wilting spread through my limbs. The light from my fingers flickered out as Ahrimad's fingers constricted around my throat.

"If I see even a *flicker* of that light again," he seethed, "I'll rip Death's heart out and make you watch."

Somehow, Death's heart being ripped out sounded less painful than whatever Malphas was doing to him. The tormented noises that tore from his throat communicated an agony unlike any other, like he was being eaten alive from the inside out.

"You *need* me," I grated, turning toward Ahrimad. "You need me or else you can't touch the *Book of the Dead*. If you kill him, I will do *nothing* for you!"

"I do believe this conversation is taking an interesting turn," Ahrimad said with a sadistic smile. "I'm going to have to be persuaded more than that."

Death dropped to his knees under his father's torment, his eyes rolling back into his head.

"I'll give you anything you want! I'll make a deal!"

The words had sputtered out in a frantic effort to save Death.

Ahrimad's burning golden eyes snapped to mine.

Malphas finally let up on his son. Death inhaled a large gasp of air. Like he'd been drowning, like it was instinctive to breathe, even when he didn't need to. Death bowed against the ground, silently quaking.

"A deal, you say?" Ahrimad tapped his chin. "What an attractive notion. I suppose I can weave something else fun into tonight's plans. In order to use the *Book of the Dead* to restore my soul into a proper vessel, I will need a corpse strong enough to contain my power for a long length of time. The warlock has ways to extend his lifespan, but at the end of the day, his blood runs red. He is therefore disposable to me."

"Lovely," Ace muttered.

"You need a corpse that can maintain your soul," I elucidated. My heart flipped. Death was one of those possibilities.

"Death's curse is already deteriorating his mind," Ahrimad said with an unsettling madness in his own grin. "He's entering a weakened state, which makes him susceptible to me. And though he is an abomination, we do share similar abilities. Why, he'd be the *easy* option tonight. At least for a few centuries, until his young corpse deteriorates. But, in all honesty, Faith, I'd prefer to keep my old vessel. That body has, unfortunately, long deteriorated, but I can bring it back. I'll need some assistance from forbidden spells to do so. Spells found only in the *Book of the Dead*.

"Another pressing issue is my tether to the mortal world," Ahrimad continued, looking down at the supernatural dagger in his hand. Death's scythe. "I'm bound to the blade, just like Death. This is no ordinary weapon, you see. It's a blade created by Hades, god of the Underworld. And to finally release my soul from it, I will need a second spell. One to revitalize my corpse and make it strong enough to maintain my soul. Another spell to lift my curse from this blade. That is all that I require of you."

"Spells of that magnitude could end in utter devastation," Ace chimed in, flinching away from Layla as she unbuttoned his torn shirt and glided her hand over his smooth chest. "Surely a creature of innate impartiality wouldn't want to upset the balance between good and evil?"

"My only ties to this world are the mortals from which I feed," Ahrimad answered coldly. "Without my curse, I won't need the mortals anymore. I can wander anywhere I please without my infinite hunger driving me back to this decrepit realm." He turned to me. "I will strike a deal with you, Faith Williams. If you retrieve the spells I require from the *Book of the Dead*, I will leave this realm, and you will never see or hear from me again. I will give Death back the blade, thus recovering his strength, and all will be well again."

Death released a frightening growl as he regained consciousness. I hardly recognized his face it was so otherworldly. The man that I'd fallen for had waned away and left behind the irredeemable monster again. I feared he would be lost forever at any moment.

Ahrimad walked a slow path around me and stood at my back. "You can feel what he's becoming," he whispered at my ear. "Would you be able to live with yourself if you let him succumb to his monster?"

My chest tightened. The portal crackled behind Ace and Layla, and I could feel it on my skin like electric pulses through the air. This was my decision and mine alone.

"If I do this, you'll let Ace go too," I said tightly. "And once that portal closes, you'll be on the other side."

"Deal." Ahrimad braced his hands against the vat of blood before him. "Layla, my dear, come here."

Layla abandoned her games with Ace and slid seductively across the floor. Her eyes playfully slid toward Malphas as she passed him.

Layla cuddled up against Ahrimad's cloak with a small smile. "Yes, Master?"

"You are a true loyal servant, Layla." Ahrimad's long fingers drifted down the curve of her cheek, and she leaned into his touch. "I'm afraid a traditional blood sacrifice of a high-level demon is imperative for the dark spells I seek."

Layla's eyes widened. "I—*what?*"

Malphas suddenly came up behind Layla and snatched her by the back of the neck, securing her in place.

"No, no, *no!*" Layla's screams were horrifying, the anticipation of what was about to happen rattling my bones. "*Malphas!* Malphas!" She tore her head toward Ahrimad. "You lying bastard, you promised to free me!"

"You will be free," Ahrimad said with a chilling smile.

Malphas grabbed Layla's exposed throat and *tore*. Tore her throat straight out. An involuntary scream escaped my mouth. Layla gurgled out a choked sob. She fought, writhed, her hand reaching back and her talon-like nails clipping Malphas in the cheek, but it was no use. Malphas restrained her arm behind her back, her blood spilling like a river along the floor.

"Dump her," Ahrimad said once the empath's body stilled.

Malphas lifted Layla's limp body and carried her to the marble vat at the center of the room. He lowered her into it until her body disappeared. The blackness webbing out across his features withered back into his eyes as he looked down into the marble container. I'd almost missed the flicker of emotion that danced across his face. Disgust. Malphas wasn't proud of what he'd done.

I couldn't shake this feeling. My intuition told me I'd missed something. Malphas still had a greater part in all of this. And yet, here he was, obedient to Ahrimad. Doing his dirty work. Why? What had Ahrimad guaranteed him? What was he holding over his head?

Malphas's black eyes swept up and caught mine in what felt like a surreptitious moment before the blank void slid back over his pale features, and he returned to his station with his hands clasped behind his back.

"I have done unspeakable things in this world that have left me entrenched in sin, but my greatest offence is my most painful secret. A secret that I will take to the grave. You must discover these answers on your own."

A cold chill of fear slipped down my spine, and suddenly it all made a little more sense.

"I know how you did it," I announced to Ahrimad's retreating frame.

Ahrimad faced me, cocking his head. "Dear child, I haven't the faintest clue what you are talking about."

"Malphas was the one who freed you from the Underworld. But he didn't do it to spite Death, did he? No . . . " I straightened my back, conviction strengthening my voice. "He's been your slave this entire time. You *made* Malphas free you that night. You keep making him do your dirty work because you have something over him. I bet . . . it's a secret he must take to the grave."

A slow grin tilted Ahrimad's lips. "You *clever*, clever girl. From the moment Malphas was freed from the Underworld, he was in contact with me, where my soul was trapped. He offered to bring me back too. In order for him to free me, I needed the purest of sacrifices, and Malphas needed to throw Death a little . . . off-kilter. Distract him. And what better than a disastrous family reunion?"

"You're the reason Malphas went after me," I speculated.

"That's not possible," Death hissed, seemingly alert. The demons gripped his chains tighter, as if anticipating him lashing out.

Ahrimad ran his finger over the edge of his dagger, laughing like there was some joke we'd all missed. "You know, I really should thank you, Faith Williams. I hadn't a clue Malphas had arrived here until I ran into you in the hallway in Ace's corpse and you mentioned that he had entered the mausoleum with you. Malphas was supposed to be in another realm, establishing my army of Forsaken like a good pet. Now I know to keep him on a much shorter leash."

"You said your scythe was created by Hades," I said, trying to piece this all together. "He punished you, didn't he? That's why you were imprisoned in the otherworld."

"I was born with an endless hunger for mortals," Ahrimad explained. "Let's say it got a little . . . out of hand. Hades tried to control my violence so I wouldn't tarnish his neutrality. I would reap the souls of the living for his kingdom and skim off their souls for sustenance. I was young and naïve. Naturally, I rebelled, and when Hades confined me to my prison in that mirror, I doubt he planned on freeing me."

Death's catlike eyes radiated. "Sounds like you're the son he never wanted."

"Oh, yes," Ahrimad said. "Hades *is* my father, after all. *Our* father." His sudden pause left an unnerving feeling in the air. "Isn't that right, Malphas?"

"Ho-ly shit," Ace blurted, beating me to it.

"You're brothers," Death said in a flat, detached voice.

"*Half*," Ahrimad corrected, clasping his hands behind his back. "Malphas's mother was a different mortal whore. Speaking of mortal whores, Malphas and I would never even have crossed paths had it not been for his wife. Phoebe, wasn't it?" He sighed, gazing out into oblivion as if reminiscing over a beautiful memory. "I suppose it would be a shame for us all to part ways without absolving the feeble innocents in this room. Do you want to tell this lovely story, Malphas, or shall I?"

Malphas's features were so warped with stifled rage that he looked almost unrecognizable. "You do love the sound of your own voice."

"Once upon a time," Ahrimad began with a dramatic turn toward his audience, "Malphas Cruscellio died on the battlefield with our father's DNA in his mortal body. He would have been reborn into a demigod and come back to life once his corpse was buried. However, Phoebe, his young bride, didn't know that. Neither did Malphas, who knew nothing of his biological father.

"Phoebe tried every spell she could find to bring Malphas back to life. She even merged his heart with a raven's. Running out of time, she turned down a dark path. She went to the woods and prayed. Prayed to every god, prayed to anyone that would listen to her desperate, pathetic little sobs. Now, here's the hilarious part." Ahrimad held Malphas's eyes for a prolonged moment. "*I* answered her prayer. *I* helped her resurrect Malphas. When he rose, Phoebe realized he was different. Of course, he was. When I brought Malphas back to life, I stole his soul. Oops.

"Bringing Malphas back to life came at a price," Ahrimad said, a coy smile playing on his lips now. "One life taken for another returned. Now, being the decent brother-in-law that I am, all Phoebe had to do was never use black magic again, and the life taken would not be *hers*. However, if she did use the magic, she would succumb to a madness unlike any other. And if Malphas wanted his soul back, all he had to do . . . was free me. Free me from the otherworld in which I was trapped throughout all of this. But he didn't, did you, Malphas? You kept me imprisoned in that mirror under the willow tree. Now, the details of what happened next are a little fuzzy . . . "

"We'll all turn to ash and bones by the time this little fable of yours is finished," Death hissed.

"Ah, I remember now," Ahrimad continued, relishing in the spotlight. "Throughout all of this, Phoebe had been pregnant with their little half-mortal atrocity of a son. Once he aged, I drew the boy into the woods to free me. Because of *you*, Malphas. Because you were afraid of me. Afraid of what else I would do to your family if you released me. But you found out exactly what I was capable of, didn't you? Now your son had a bleak future for freeing me, and you were as soulless and cruel as ever.

"Poor Alexandru had a difficult boyhood." Ahrimad walked a slow circle around Death and the high-level demons on either side of him. "One day, he couldn't take the pressure anymore. He killed himself. How sad. And to think, his own mother had to discover the horrifying scene. The deal was done. One life taken, for another returned."

I was sick to my stomach.

"You can finish the rest, Malphas," Ahrimad said, sounding bored. "I'm sure Death is dying to know how the lovely story ends."

Malphas refused at first, defiance in his onyx eyes and visible restraint in his jaw and neck. But he ultimately succumbed to Ahrimad's command. "I was away, traveling, and your mother used black magic to resurrect you on her own."

"When I said to tell him the rest," Ahrimad snarled at Malphas, his voice slipping into something monstrous as he bared his fangs in a malicious smirk, "you know what I meant."

Malphas's hands clenched at his sides. "I won't."

"And why is that, I wonder?" Ahrimad asked, feigning sympathy.

Malphas grated his teeth. "Because it will destroy him."

Death yanked at his chains with a hiss. "The fuck it will, old man. I already know what you did next. I was there."

"No, you don't," Malphas said. "You remember what I wanted you to remember."

Death stared back at his father, motionless.

"Your mother wouldn't let you die," Malphas said after a long stretch of silence. "She used the blackest of magic, and this time, it worked. But the consequences were instantaneous. She became seriously ill. Bedridden for weeks, though we hid the true reason from you. In those weeks, I saw glimpses of rage, violence, hate in a woman who had embodied selflessness and love. I thought we were losing her. Then, one day, she was fine. It was a miracle. The dark side to her had vanished entirely.

"You fell in love with the mortal Annona," Malphas continued, and Death visibly flinched. "When your mother found out about Annona's pregnancy, she tried to convince me to bring her into our home. She was so excited about having a grandchild. She loved babies. But I was so furious with you. You'd disobeyed me by being with a mortal, you'd risked our exposure to outsiders. So I renounced you and your unborn child. Your mother and I fought for weeks. It drove you and her out of our home.

"For months, I lived in solitude. I wanted to mend things with you both, but my pride kept getting in the way. One night, I had this . . . terrible feeling in my gut. It was nightfall, and I rushed to your home on horseback. As soon as I entered the front door, I heard screaming. Annona shouting for help. Ahrimad's power had gained full possession of your mother, and she was in a . . . rage. She killed Annona, ripped into her womb . . . You were crying, horrified, confused. I could only imagine what you'd witnessed. Your mother saw you like that, and she fought with everything she had. A glimpse of her came through, and she begged me to save her from herself. She begged me to kill her before she hurt anyone else. When I hesitated, the madness controlled her again. Then she lunged for *you*, and I . . . "

Malphas bowed his head, his eyes tightly closed.

"I did what I had to do," he said with finality. "I couldn't stomach the idea of you remembering your mother in those final moments. She was never the monster in your life. I was. I thought if you knew the truth, if you knew that your mother resurrecting you had triggered Ahrimad's deal, you'd hurt yourself again. Blaming me for their deaths meant you'd live. Live to seek vengeance. Your mind was fragile—you were in shock—and I changed your memory. I made you believe it me who killed all three of them."

"And then your son went and killed you and died in the arena with me to become an eternal god of death," Ahrimad interrupted chirpily. "Wow. Your parenting skills are unmatched, Malphas."

"No," Death said, his voice breaking. "No, *no*. I was there. I saw you kill all three of them. You're lying. You're lying because that's what you fucking do. That's all you know!"

"Show him, Malphas," Ahrimad commanded.

Blackness spread from Malphas's cold eyes, but the raw emotion staining his features remained. "Yes, my liege."

Malphas made a small motion with his hand, and Death's head snapped back.

Death swayed on his feet like he might fall, his eyes wandering all around the room. He dropped to one knee, and then the other. His head hung forward, his arms restrained by the high-level demons. My heart clenched at the sorrow glistening his eyes as he looked up at Malphas. "How could you?"

"I wanted to tell you," Malphas said. "I *tried* to tell you, I—"

"Two thousand years," Death whispered in a rough, hollow voice. "Two thousand years!"

Suddenly, the mirror-like surface of the portal oscillated and swelled with a loud crack. A new ripple shimmied across its surface. Ace, who stood closest to it, backed away, whereas Ahrimad gazed curiously at it. His amber eyes snapped to mine.

"Time to find me those spells." His hand wrapped around mine, and I grew taut with fear.

Ahrimad dragged me to the front of the room. One of the high-level demons now guarded Ace. He looked over at me and gave me a small nod as we passed, which I didn't quite understand. Ahrimad led me up a few steps onto a small stage. Death watched me like a hawk, his mismatched green eyes dark and cold.

"You promised," he said so softly I had to read his lips. I knew he was talking about putting me before him.

"I lied," I whispered.

Ahrimad stopped at the top of the stairs, and I realized that was as close as he could stand to what lay on the podium. My heart beat like a battle drum and my scalp prickled as I saw the full-size *Book of the Dead* on the marble stand.

"H-how will I know what to look for?"

"The *Book of the Dead* knows what we seek," Ahrimad said.

The rippling portal beside the stage seemed to ring louder, and I shut my eyes the moment my fingers touched the leathery cover. Then something I'd never expected happened. Nothing. My stomach churned at the immediate thought that this wasn't the *Book of the Dead*. With trembling fingers, I brushed the sides of the thick manuscript, a unique fold in the page catching my attention. I held the fold and opened to that page slowly.

Noise stilled as I read the handwritten note inside. The only words on the entire page.

Let there be light.

A frown creased my eyebrows.

"What did you see?" Ahrimad roared, startling me. He moved to stand behind me like one of Death's shadows, and my whole body locked up. I slid my palm carefully over the page and collected the note. "Do not waste my precious time!"

"I-I saw a glimpse of what you desire most," I said, cowering away from him. "But there's—there's some sort of block."

"A block?" Ahrimad's eyes narrowed. "I see. Perhaps you need some motivation, then? Malphas, I'm bored. Torture your son."

It happened so fast. Blackness webbed out from the raven demigod's entire face, his pale features devoid of emotion. Death's whole body locked up again. Obsidian curls sprawled over his forehead as he tilted his head up, jaw clenched, glaring defiantly back at Malphas. *"Don't do it, Faith!"* Death bellowed. "Don't let him win!"

"Better hurry," Ahrimad taunted. "Death's looking a little feral, isn't he?"

"You said you wouldn't kill him!" I cried.

"Technically, he's already dead." Ahrimad flashed his fangs. "Semantics are a funny thing, Ms. Williams. Better hurry."

There had to be a way out of this. But I couldn't *focus*.

"I said, *continue*, Malphas!" Ahrimad barked.

"His mind barriers are wide open," Malphas said. "If I continue, he will be unconscious in seconds."

"It appears your son has given up. Quite the strong warrior you bred."

Malphas's face tightened. "Hades banished you to that mirror because you were an obligation."

Ahrimad stared at Malphas with a frighteningly calm rage. He descended from the stage. "What did you say to me?"

"I said, you're a *nuisance* to Hades. He said it to me himself when I met him in the Underworld. P.S., that's dad code for he wishes he wore a condom."

My vision strobed in and out as Ahrimad disappeared and reappeared before Malphas. He clutched Malphas by the throat, and Death lurched forward in his chains. "Soulless fucking bird! I'm going to crush your heart in my bare hand!"

"Wait!" I exclaimed. "I need more time!"

Ahrimad's head snapped over his shoulder, darkness consuming his amber irises. "Dear girl, the last thing we all have tonight is time."

Ahrimad grabbed Malphas by the throat. Panic overworked my lungs as I breathed in and out faster and faster, my whole body shaking uncontrollably. I glanced over at the rippling portal, and it hit me.

"Hey, *Nuisance*!"

Ahrimad turned sharply away from Malphas and faced me, massive fangs filling a mouth that belonged to a distorted, evil creature of death.

"Lights out, bitch."

Power surged up my forearm like liquid fire, white light seeping through my knuckles and consuming my entire hand. I hurled my fist toward the portal, a scream tearing free from my throat as I fired everything I had into the rippling surface. The portal trembled violently against my chaos, glowing a blinding white until it finally detonated with a sonic boom, cracking the mirror with a mighty force.

The portal spewed out energy in violent gusts. A windstorm unlike any other hurled around the room, nearly knocking me off the stage as its vortex of fury swept across the mausoleum.

"Your *Book of the Dead* isn't salvageable!" Malphas shouted as his braids tossed to the side from the wind. "While you were busy with your obsession with destroying my son, I hid your precious tome and replaced it with a red herring. Do what you want with my soul. Without that book, you're done. There is no corpse in this room or anywhere else in the universe that will withstand your vexatious soul."

Ahrimad's expression hardened, his head trembling with rage, and a cruel smile turned up the corners of his bloodied mouth. His arm rose, his fingers flexing as the scythe appeared in his hand. Designs appeared along the staff, rippling symbols, as Ahrimad's otherworldly eyes pulsed with light. "You are all sentenced to death."

Death's chest heaved fast; his eyes went wide. Shadows pulsed from his frame and slid over the ground, consuming his space. His whole body shuddered uncontrollably as he visibly tried to keep something at bay.

And he lost.

Shadow expelled from Death's skin like inky tendrils in the air, blotting out the light in shapeless terrors. They coiled around the high-level demons beside him like vipers. The demons' screams suffocated as the darkness crawled down their throats. Death yanked one of his chained arms inward, pulling the demon toward him, ripping its throat out with his fangs and slicing the rest of its thick neck away with a vicious swipe of his talons. His feet kicked up off the ground as he punted the headless corpse away. He launched back into the air in a blur, his chain wrapping around the other demon's neck as he took him down and strangled him to death.

Wind hurled around Ahrimad like a twister, cocooning the original Grim Reaper, imprisoning him in thick magic. Ace moved fast and threw out his hand, and the hurling energy spiraled out of control in blacks and reds. Ahrimad was imprisoned in a blustery mass of pure chaos that Ace kept together with his two hands.

"How long will that hold?" Malphas demanded.

The warlock's back foot slid across the ground until he replanted himself. "Not long enough!"

The remaining high-level demons suddenly snapped into focus. Their snarls turned on us.

One of the demons materialized in front of Malphas. It lunged for him and took a swipe with its deadly paws, but Malphas evaporated like a mirage. The creature staggered back in confusion, gripping Malphas's shirt in its meaty hand.

Malphas rematerialized behind the monster, furious. "That was my favorite silk shirt." His hand shot out, blackness expelling from his eyes. The creature gripped its own skin with razor-sharp claws and began tearing at the scaly flesh covering its face, howls unleashing from its throat.

A monstrous howl thundered through the room. A grin lined Death's mouth, like a lunatic wanting in on the grisly war. His mismatched green eyes glowed against the dusky hue of his skin. His jaw flexed, veins engorging in his angular face. Fangs lengthened into knives, filling his mouth in a nightmarish image as his jaw unhinged and an animalistic roar ripped free from his throat.

"That can't be good," I muttered.

Ace had seized the opportunity in the chaos to attack the demon guarding him. Swirls of violet magic permeated the air as the creature burst into flame on Ace's command. Another creature gripped Ace by the throat and lifted him off the ground.

"I hate my liiiiiife!" I sprinted at full speed, pushing off the stage

as I leapt and slammed my fist forward into the monster's face, the force of my punch taking the creature down to the floor.

Quickly sitting up on top of the wriggling monster, I realized two things. One, my supercool outfit that Romeo had given me was definitely fire-retardant. And two, my fist was currently embedded in the monster's face, and I couldn't get my fingers out of his brain.

"Ew, ew, *ew*! Rewind, rewind!"

Two hands gripped my shoulders from behind and tore me and my hand away from the monster. Malphas. He brought his sword—my sword—down into the creature's skull, killing it. Another demon came at him, and he executed it in an effortless whirl of silver.

"The containment spell won't hold Ahrimad for much longer," Ace said, limping heavily to stand beside me. He turned his head to Malphas with an accusing look. "Where is the *Book of the Dead*?"

"I tossed the damned thing into the portal."

Ace's eyes widened. "You're *serious*? I don't buy for one moment that you would throw one of the most powerful artifacts in the world carelessly into a portal!"

"Believe it, wizard," Malphas grinned. "Want it for yourself, do you? By all means, go for a dive and fetch it in the Unknown."

Ace growled out something nasty in a foreign language and lifted his hand up to his ear with a readied command, magic uncurling into his palm, but I grabbed his forearm.

Suddenly, two more demons manifested around us. Malphas took on one by himself, and Ace and I took on the other. Light sparked from my fist as I connected with the demon's hand coming down, my other fist uppercutting as I slammed it into its gut. Ace finished it off with an incantation, and I pivoted around to face Malphas.

"What'd you do to the reapers?" I demanded.

"All you have to know is they're alive, and they'll recover."

"Great, that doesn't sound ominous or anything!"

Ace staggered to us, panting, and splattered with blood. "Let's all focus on the *current* issue at hand, shall we?" He jabbed a finger across the room to Death, who happened to be punting a demon head soccer-style into a wall.

"We'll need your help to get him to resurface," Malphas said to me. "He's still in there, Faith."

"And how do I do that? Kiss him on his big, fanged, covered-in-demon-gore mouth and snap him out of it?"

"Do what you did on the roof," Malphas said as he thrust his sword backward under his armpit and into a creature coming up behind him. He pulled the blade out and turned to slice off its head before pivoting back around without breaking a sweat. "Try not to get your face eaten off, though, yeah?"

Ace scoffed, his eyes glowing white as he shouted a command at another demon, bringing it to its knees. "Can we be serious right now?"

"Agreed," I said firmly. "We need to work together. I don't know if you've noticed, but we're kinda the Dream Team." I motioned to Ace and Malphas. "Or at least you two are, and I intermittently come in clutch." Then I stuck my hand out in the middle of the three of us for an epic huddle break. "On three: 'Get Death's pruner back!'"

Malphas looked at Ace. "What is wrong with her?"

"So many things," Ace said with a shake of his head. "I will work to keep Ahrimad contained with another cocoon of magic. Long enough for you, Weirdo, and the rest of the Scooby gang to euthanize Grandpa Time."

"That was funny," Malphas admitted with a stiff, soldier-like nod. "Funnier than what Weirdo said." He put his hand forward. "I'll break on that."

I unenthusiastically broke with them, realizing my new nickname had become "Weirdo."

"Wait, *ma chérie*," Ace said, clutching my hand. His eyes carefully searched mine, and I could see the hesitation as he chose his next words. "See you on the other side."

A small drop of dread landed in my stomach, as I didn't quite know what he meant by that.

Just then, a demon manifested behind Ace, hulking and seething. It threw out its massive arm and shoved Ace into the hard marble floor. With little time to react, I tried to punch my fist forward at the creature, as I'd been doing, but no light fired.

I shook out my hand, panic rising as the creature opened its jaws in a howl, putrid saliva dancing between its fangs. "Dude. Breath mint."

Darkness spread like an aura from behind the beast, and its whole body jerked. Death stood behind it with his fist gripping its bloody backbone.

What had seemed like Death saving me from certain death turned into a nightmare once he looked down at me with a feral, empty look in his eyes.

"Cupcake," I said, trembling.

Death dropped the spine in his hand with a low, predatory noise. I stumbled over my feet as he stalked toward me, his movements so fast they blurred in my vision.

Suddenly, a massive piece of marble hurled into Death's side, knocking him slightly off-balance. A roar unleashed from his mouth as Malphas manifested and drew his sword.

"Can't let you kill your girlfriend, son. She's goofy, but I rather like her."

"Liar!" Death hissed.

Death lunged for Malphas, swiping out his claws at a speed that Malphas barely evaded.

"I know there's a lot you're processing," Malphas said. "Don't give up because of me. Giving up means that Ahrimad wins."

Another swipe of deadly talons forced Malphas to fight back as he disappeared and reappeared behind Death. His sword sliced into the back of Death's legs, nearly bringing him to his knees. Faltering, but refusing to fall, Death released another thunderous roar.

"Remember who you are!" Malphas shouted. "You're in control!"

Death straightened to his full height, towering over Malphas. "Murderer . . . "

Shadows twisted down Malphas's blade and ripped the weapon straight out of his hand. Death moved his head sharply to the side, and the shadows punched into Malphas's torso, slamming him into the ground.

A shoe bounced off Death's head. Ace's shoe. Death's horned head snapped toward him, and he snarled. His feet launched into the air as he pounced off the ground, landing in front of the warlock like a monstrous cat. Ace crawled backward along the ground, clutching at his shoulder, which he'd landed on, his face tight with pain as he tried to pick himself up. Death plucked him up by the shirt like he weighed nothing, pinning him to the wall as his long, black fingers gripped Ace's jaw. The fast drum of my heart pounded my vision as I watched, frozen. Deadly fangs elongated—

"*Cowabunga!*" I leapt onto Death's massive back, grabbing two fistfuls of his hair and yanking his skull backward. Darkness flashed in front of me as Death abruptly transported, taking me with him. I choked on my breath as we reappeared elsewhere in the room.

Death landed on all fours. Shadows manifested in front of me like vipers trying to latch on to my limbs. My fingertips ignited with white light as I smacked them away like gnats. Death's clawed hand reached back to grab my thigh and rip me off his back. I shrieked, tugging at his hair again, and he had the same knee-jerk reaction. We vanished and reappeared forty feet away from our previous spot.

"Onward!" I bellowed, pointing toward a demon.

"What the . . . fuck?" Death growled. *"Faith—?"*

I yanked on his hair. We vanished, and he landed not so gracefully this time but caught himself. "*Stop* that."

"Looks like pulling your hair resurfaced you. You're back!"

"And with barely any of my luscious locks left," Death huffed.

From the side, a demon charged at us.

"Left!" I shrieked.

Death dodged out of the way, intercepting the blade-like nails of the demon. The demon lashed out again, but Death's hand was faster. Hard muscle tore as Death ripped into the creature's torso with his claws. Another hard swipe of his deadly hand and the creature's throat was cut clean through.

I laughed hysterically against his neck. "That was so *awesome*! And *sick*! I think I'm in shock!" I clicked my heels against his side. *"Yeehaw!"*

Four more demons manifested in front of us.

"Hold on tight, cupcake."

My stomach lurched as Death jumped to his feet and straightened his legs, launching his massive frame off the ground before they could grab him. He leapt onto the wall beside us, talons penetrating the marble wall as he anchored to it and climbed higher. The demons launched into the wall after us in a less graceful fashion, their terrifying roars reminding me of the dinosaurs from *Jurassic Park* as their clumsy climb upward ripped out pieces of marble; none of them could seem to hold themselves up. They backed away from the wall, snarling at Death.

"Admit it," I said, feeling dizzy as I looked down at the drop. "You wanted to show off."

Death turned his head over his shoulder and grinned. "You do have your legs around my waist."

A screech escaped my mouth as Death dove backward off the wall, the world arching upside down. He landed on all fours and reached back, grabbing onto the belt loop of my pants. He dropped me to the ground in one smooth motion before slinking up the length of me. "Stay," he whispered. His feet gripped the ground as he sprang somewhere over my head, the sound of a gory fight out of my line of sight.

When I tried to sit up, my limbs wouldn't work. I suddenly felt pinned, as though trapped in a sleep paralysis dream. *Stay . . .*

Ahrimad stood facing the portal, the surface undulating like waves in a violent sea. Something was terribly wrong: the portal whirled with chaos, but I wasn't afraid. I felt only rage, and so did he. Ahrimad turned toward me, silently roaring, his golden eyes flaring. The skin of his face pressed rapidly tighter against his skull, tautening with fury as his scythe swung out toward me, the portal slowly rippling closed behind him like an iris. Blood sprayed my vision. My blood. Pain exploded in my abdomen, cleaving through me—

The marble room was falling apart. The ceiling cracked above me as my chest heaved with adrenaline from the revelation of what I'd seen. What I'd felt.

Taloned hands yanked me out of the way before a piece of marble came crashing down onto me. Death pulled me to my feet, his frame enormous and sleek with blood and sweat.

Ace stood with his hands outstretched toward Ahrimad and the twisting wind that concealed him, visibly straining. Suddenly, a massive bolt of darkness sliced through the vortex of air. Ace stumbled back, collapsing to the ground in exhaustion as Ahrimad ripped free from the containment spell.

Ahrimad swung out his scythe, energy firing out from the movement and rippling the air in a crescent shape around him. Ace and Malphas were the closest to him and were hit hard, their bodies tossed back onto the stage and sent rolling. More chunks of marble fell away from the ceiling as bits and pieces of the room disintegrated from the damage done.

Ahrimad kept coming as he swung out his scythe. Time seemed to slow as his sharp features strobed back and forth between a humanoid face and something otherworldly and alien. His blade arced another crescent in the air with a cruel gleam of silver, and this time I was hit by his shadow. Darkness wrapped around my limbs and slammed me down to the floor, where I was pinned by shadow.

"Faith!" Death moved toward me, but a cobalt wall of fire erupted between us, forming a large circle around Death and Ahrimad. Death jumped back, clutching his hand as the seared scent of flesh permeated the air.

"Kneel." Ahrimad raised his scythe again but didn't swing it. Through the flames, I watched Death's muscles tighten, the tendons in his neck straining. "You don't have the strength to fight me."

Death fell to his knees in anguish, in defeat, in obedience. Ahrimad's long, bony fingers gripped Death by the skull. I felt my whole world come crashing down, and *I couldn't move.* The harder I fought to be free, the tighter the shadow coiled around me. Tears poured from my eyes, and I sobbed, forced to watch what played out before me.

Ahrimad's lips peeled back in a fiendish grin, and his scythe vanished from his side, refashioning itself as a dagger.

"They think what you seek is true death, Alexandru, but I know better. For only you and I know the truth." Ahrimad held the dagger out, and Death's entire affect changed, black markings lighting up white against his obsidian skin like ancient encryptions. Panic broadened his catlike eyes, and he tried to move away, but Ahrimad pierced his nails into Death's throat and held him still. "The blade from which you reap is the key to your demise too. Yet you've chosen life all this time. I do appreciate the pitiful irony."

Then he stabbed Death in the heart, the sickening crunch like a sharp pierce to my own.

"DEATH!"

Death's body lurched on impact, veins protruding in his face, his eyes wide. His hand shot out on instinct, talons ripping into Ahrimad's arm.

A cruel smile turned up Ahrimad's sinister mouth. "May you never see the light again, my nephew."

With final hard nudge of Ahrimad's powerful hand, the blade plunged home.

Breaking free from Ahrimad's hold on my limbs felt like knives cutting into all parts of me. Nothing else mattered. Nothing else mattered but getting free as white blinded my vision.

Shadows hissed and retreated from my light, and I could feel Ahrimad's hold on me weakening. A scream tore from my throat as I battled against the darkness until a part of it gave way from my hand, and I was able to fire the light at my legs. The shadows withered away, and I shoved the rest off me. I was free. I was free, and I was on my feet. Sprinting hard toward the blue firewall separating me from Death, I dropped to my knees and shielded my face, the flames burning away the sleeves of my fire-retardant clothes as I slid into the ring of fire.

My lungs tightened at the sight of Death writhing on the ground. Ahrimad yanked the dagger from Death's heart, but the ghost of the handle remained embedded in his chest, pulsing with shadows.

Ahrimad gazed up from Death to me in calm astonishment. "No mortal can move through the flames of the Underworld."

"You talk way too much," I seethed.

I punched the air toward Ahrimad, chucking my power at him like a spear. Ahrimad easily deflected it with his scythe, as though it were a fly. I watched the stream of my light hit the marble wall beside the portal and eat into it like acid.

Another idea came to me.

A moment too late, as Ahrimad manifested directly in front of me, smashing my hand with his before I could ignite again. Bone snapped as my whole hand crumpled. Black splotched my vision as he shoved me back the ground. I screamed in agony, crawling backward, the rippling waves of the portal growing louder behind Ahrimad.

Ahrimad laughed as he loomed over me, his black robes billowing out. "You have prevented me from creating a new vessel, but you have not stopped my army. My Forsaken are waiting in the Unknown. At my command, they will devour your little realm from the inside out. Too bad you will not be alive to witness the massacre."

Fire raced down my forearm. My left arm hurled out toward Ahrimad with a violence I had never known. Ahrimad held out a hand at the last second to shield himself, his eyes glowing bright as he reacted fast. Too fast. Too fast to focus on precision as he ricocheted the power of my light directly into the rippling portal beside him.

The portal soaked up my energy again, marble cracking on either side of it as a black void formed at the center like an impending doom. Ahrimad's eyes widened. The rippling portal broadened, vacillating, as if it were unable to contain itself. As if it would explode.

A piece of the ceiling came down beside me, the blue flames around us disintegrating. My eyes rapidly searched the ground for Death, but he was gone. He was gone, and I couldn't even process what could have happened to him. I leapt to my feet, forcing myself to turn and run. I ran as hard as I could, with the instinct to survive. A high-pitched whistle pierced the air, the sound carrying to me and painting a clear picture of the portal exploding, forcing a surge of energy back out.

I turned back, and a swarm of rippling air was hurtling toward me. I had little time react as the unforgiving force from the portal swept me away in its vicious wave. I went airborne, arcing high toward the ceiling. My arms swung helplessly in the air, gravity plunging me face down, the ground coming in fast. My arms shot forward at the last second to shield my head, bracing for a fatal impact that never came.

Ringing. My eardrums ringing. The thought crossed my mind that I had in fact died, but my breath was so loud, and my whole chest pulsated to the hard beat of my heart. Warm wetness dripped from my ears and down the tip of my nose. I slowly opened my eyes, watching my blood collecting into a puddle beneath my face. Strands of damp black hair that had escaped my braid aimed down at the floor. I realized I was suspended off the ground. Levitating. My fists were both healed, locked tight on either side of me and ignited with white electricity.

I dropped the short distance to the ground, catching myself on my hands. As I stood with wobbly legs, my vision swam. Everything still felt heavy, bruised, broken, but I was alive with adrenaline. Through the smoke and debris in the air, I stumbled over the rubble, my hands searching frantically.

The ringing in my ears grew louder as I followed a path not covered by debris and made my away around a fallen marble pillar. My eyes made a stronger effort to focus as I saw that rippling mirror again, its surface tunneling like an endless void.

"Death? Death!" My eyes swept over the ground, and I stepped over large pieces of debris. The ceiling of the room was almost completely destroyed, and I could see up into the floor above. When I gazed down, thick, black liquid coated the floor. Death's blood. My fingers curled into my palm, my whole body shaking with fury as my throat tightened.

"My destined night, gone. You . . . ruined . . . *everything*."

I turned slowly to find Ahrimad facing the portal.

"The night yields to no one," Ahrimad murmured bitterly. "The day breaks on, and death is unmoved. And yet, I have been thwarted by life . . . "

The portal swirled with chaos, but I wasn't afraid. I saw rage, and so did he. Ahrimad turned toward me, and the sight of his face made my blood curdle. The skin of his face was translucent, the skeleton of an otherworldly creature glaring back at me.

Ahrimad's eyes radiated a wrathful gold. *"You will pay for what you have done!"*

His arm swung out, the portal rippling closed behind him like an iris. I remembered my vision of my blood spraying, my abdomen splitting open as the scythe buried into me. Right before the blade could come down and seal the fate I'd foreseen, shadows piled in front of me like an armored wall as Death manifested between me and Ahrimad. His taloned hands shot out and gripped the staff of Ahrimad's scythe, their faces close as he met him in a deadlock.

"Over my dead body," Death seethed.

Death ripped the scythe straight from Ahrimad's grasp, kicking him back toward the portal. The markings along the staff kindled to life as the staff rotated over Death's head. Intricate groupings of lines developed over its massive silvery blade, matching the dark tattoos curling down Death's neck. His long fingers gripped the staff again as it turned over, and he carved the air in front of him. Ahrimad's eyes widened as he split completely in half. Another quick, clean movement of Death's blade and Ahrimad was decapitated. His translucent body evaporated into a dark essence before he even hit the ground and then evaporated altogether.

A heaviness expanded in my core as I stared at the spot where Ahrimad once stood, uncertain if he would return again. "Is he ...?"

"He's gone," Death said in a solemn voice.

"We did it. We really did it." I rubbed my hand over my forehead, a rush of emotions flooding over me. "We have to help the others. We have to—"

Death's scythe fell to the ground, the clatter snapping me into reality.

It wasn't over.

Death swayed on his feet, his body tipping. Adrenaline took over, and I hurried forward, wrapping my arms around his torso. But he was too heavy. He was a deadweight, and we both went down to the floor.

"Death? Death!"

Everything felt muted, frozen, pained, my palms resting on his chest as I hovered over him. The phantom of Ahrimad's dagger remained protruding from Death's heart. Shadows pulsed from the handle, the surrounding skin rapidly losing heat, leaving behind a growing coldness beneath my palms that I'd never known.

"No . . . *no*."

When I reached to pull the dagger out, my fingers went right through the handle. I tried again and again until a hand weakly clutched mine. A hand I didn't recognize. A man's hand. A normal hand, one without any markings.

Everything in me trembled as my eyes finally rose to his face. His face. I felt gutted. Death's features were thinning, sickly, just like Ahrimad's. I hardly recognized him, except for his mismatched green eyes. They were too large, too dim against his colorless complexion.

"You're going to be okay," I said, because it was all I could say. "I'm going to get you help. We're going to figure this out—"

But when I tried to get up, Death's hand tightened around mine. "Stay," he said weakly. "Just stay."

"I don't understand." Even when I knew the truth, even when I stared him right in the face, my mind didn't want to believe it. "I don't understand. We won. We *won*, and I was supposed to save you."

"It's not your job to save me."

"No," I choked out, tears welling in my eyes. "*No*, this isn't happening. How can this happen? You're *Death*. You're not allowed to die. I don't give you permission." I held on to his hand for dear life. "What will I do without you?"

Death's eyes were half open now, his smile sad. "You can write a book about how sexy I am."

I laughed, even as I cried.

"All this time," Death began, "I thought I wanted to die. You showed me I wanted to live." His eyes gleamed with tears. "I want to live."

In front of us, the portal sputtered to life, electric currents flying and charging the air. Death's whole body quaked beneath my hands, his throat convulsing. I gripped his head and tried to keep him still, but I felt so helpless. The seizing eventually stopped, his eyes opening tiredly.

"Eternal return," he said faintly. "I was afraid to let you in and then lose you. If you only knew . . . "

I held his limp hand tighter. "I'm here. You've always had me."

Black dripped from the corners of his mouth, pooling onto the marble floor. I watched, horrified, as the roots of Death's hair slowly began to turn blond beneath my fingertips.

"Forgive me. I love you, Faith."

A sudden blast detonated from the portal. It crashed into my body, and I rolled back onto the floor, my side slamming into a fallen mass of marble. The sensation of being pushed turned into a pull as my fingers clung to the marble beside me, and I held on for dear life. I turned to look back toward Death, but he was gone again. My mind scrambled to understand. A piece of fallen marble skidded across the floor, tossed into the deep void, and I knew what had happened. His body had been pulled into the threshold, into the

Unknown. By the time I figured it out, the portal's energy had waned until it was a mere sliver of rippling life in a normal mirror.

Everything pulsed around the edges, the world muting to nothing as I stood before the dying portal. Broken, enraged, robbed.

This couldn't be the end.

In the shattered reflective surface, my eyes flamed white as I slowly raised my hands on either side of me. I called upon every ounce of power I had left. It answered, releasing from my hands in the form of a chaos I'd yet to master. A chaos that nearly exhausted me, until I thought of him. Until I remembered what we'd senselessly lost. I willed the light to grip the thinning remains of the portal, anchoring the sides of the narrow gateway. The weight of the portal grew heavier, threatening to collapse and crush me alive.

"I need you to choose you over me," Death's voice replayed in my head.

I couldn't keep that promise.

Tears poured down my face, and a roar unleashed from my throat as white light exploded all around me. I pulled my hands wider apart, and the portal broadened, reopening halfway.

My arms fell.

I took off in a hard sprint, casting all fear aside as the rippling void narrowed fast.

I jumped through to the other side with the fading thought that *this* was my destiny.

ACKNOWLEDGMENTS

What a *ride* this journey has been since publishing *Death is My BFF*. Seeing my debut novel in real life in bookstores, holding my book in my hands, smelling its pages (this was a lot less weird sounding in my head, but if you know, you know), signing books, meeting my readers face to face . . . you just can't beat it. Now I get to experience these magical moments again, and I want to let you know just how grateful I am.

This novel would not have been written if not for all of the incredible people in my life. Mom, Dad, and Christina: Thank you for always being there when I need you, encouraging my passions in life, and pushing me to be the best that I can be. Thank you to my friends, as well, for always supporting me and laughing with me (and *at* me, since you know I love to entertain!). A special thank you to my boyfriend, Brandon, for being so supportive that you're willing to dress up as my character Death for events. I love you all so much!

Thank you to Elaine Spencer, my rockstar agent, for always having my back. Thank you to Fiona Simpson, my marvelous editor for *Death is My Ride or Die*. Your expertise, hard work, and organization with breaking up this giant book to edit helped shape this book into a final product that I feel *so* proud of. I also want to thank my first editor, as well, Deanna McFadden, for all her amazing work on book one, *Death is My BFF*. Thank you to Andrea Waters and Delaney Anderson, Rachel Wu and Maeve O'Regan, Monica Pacheco and

Kimberly Hacuman, and the rest of the incredible Wattpad Books team for making my dreams come true!

Finally, a *huge* thank you to the Cupcakes and Reapers. My readers are a force of nature and have gotten this series to where it is today. Your kind messages and positive feedback over the years have led to me finding my passion in writing and have encouraged me to keep creating stories. I am forever grateful for each and every one of you and appreciate your support. *Heart hands*

Until next time, cupcake!

All my love,
Kat

ABOUT THE AUTHOR

Katarina E. Tonks is an award-winning author who began her career on the Wattpad platform. Since then, she has amassed nearly half a million followers—or "cupcakes" and "reapers" as she calls them—whom she loves to interact with in forums where "Death" will sometimes jump in and respond himself. She has over 100 million reads collectively on the early drafts of her Death Chronicles and the Vendetta series, and she is considered one of Wattpad's most influential writers.

Kat has been creating stories since she was old enough to hold a crayon. Never one to color between the lines, her books are often dark romance with morally gray love interests. She graduated from Fairleigh Dickinson University with a bachelor's degree in creative writing and is pursuing her master's degree in clinical mental health counseling. Kat is a Jersey Girl and lives with her family and many pets.

Get updates on Kat on her social media!

f Katarina E. Tonks

📷 @katrocks247

♪ @katrocks247

LOOK OUT FOR BOOK THREE
OF **THE DEATH CHRONICLES**

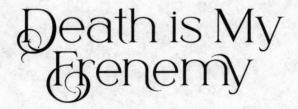

COMING SOON FROM WATTPAD BOOKS!